OVER MY DEAD BODY

Praise for Dave Warner's previous novels

♦ Australian crime writing at its apex–a seemingly simple case that becomes ever more convoluted, widening to encompass protection rackets, early pornographic films, racism, and country-club politics. That it takes place against the backdrop of a burgeoning 1960s counterculture is refreshing as a sea breeze. *Australian Book Review* ♦ Captures the heyday and spirit of the surf music scene perfectly … a pitch-perfect crime thriller of epic twists and turns. *Jim Skiathitis, The Atlantics* ♦ Part *Goodfellas*, part love letter to Australian coastal towns, this wonderfully imagined crime novel is like riding the perfect wave. *Michael Robotham* ♦ A densely written book, redolent with sun, sand and surf, informed about music and full of engaging, well-drawn characters and local activities that form a disarming background to a classically convoluted murder investigation. *Adelaide Advertiser* ♦ Warner builds the suspense with an even hand, his stock in trade a deft turn of phrase that would do Chandler or Hammett proud … his ear for dialogue and the period is faultless, his characters well-drawn and entirely believable. *Courier Mail* ♦ Warner keeps things moving at a lickety-split, while allowing the likeable female characters … room to negotiate their own trajectory through the reprehensible gender politics of the era. *Sydney Morning Herald* ♦ As Australian as a Tim Tam, this is fine descriptive writing that conveys both the searing heat and vast distances of the Outback. *Adelaide Advertiser* ♦ Laid-back and laconic, but with sentences as snappy as a nutcracker. *Books+Publishing* ♦ Gripping. *Herald Sun* ♦ An extremely likeable main character, a fast-paced plot and writing that is dense with colourful vernacular and Aussie humour. *Sun-Herald* ♦ Sophisticated crime fiction with a WA flavour. *Sunday Times* ♦ Lively, funny, with enough plot for three novels. *Sun-Herald* ♦ Consistently hits the target, skilfully creating a parallel world where crooks, their victims and pursuers breathe a different fetid air … full of surprises and contradictions, wit and suspense. *The Weekend Australian* ♦ Alive with the flavours, rhythms, cadences, corporate buccaneering and political adventurism of that era … so good one wonder[s] what Warner could possibly do for an encore. *Australian Book Review* ♦ The plot is impressively complex, with clues scattered like land mines, and the suspense enough to keep you riveted to this thriller. *Courier Times* ♦

Dave Warner is an author, musician and screenwriter. His first novel, *City of Light*, won the Western Australian Premier's Book Award for Fiction, and *Before it Breaks* (2015) the Ned Kelly Award for best Australian crime fiction. *Clear to the Horizon* features the lead characters from both these books, and his most recent crime novel is *River of Salt*. He first came to national prominence in 1978 with his gold album *Mug's Game* and his band, Dave Warner's from the Suburbs. In 2017 he released his tenth album, *When*. He has been named a Western Australian State Living Treasure and has been inducted into the WAMi Rock'n'Roll of Renown.

www.davewarner.com.au
@suburbanwarner

DAVE WARNER

OVER MY DEAD BODY

 FREMANTLE PRESS

Every writer needs a partner in crime.
Thank you Tony Durant, for adventures past and to come.

SWITZERLAND 1891

He had begun to accept the background noise of the falls was no natural phenomenon but rather the thundering tears of gods. His own tears he had stalled, as ridiculous hope sprang in his breast that survival was not impossible, even from that terrific height. Long after the sun had collapsed he had insisted they continue the search downstream by lantern-light. It was too dark for a boat to be used with safety, though he would have risked it if his eyesight had been keen enough. They confined themselves to the banks but were not rewarded with anything but chilled bones. When the others had finally left for the comfort of the inn, he had refused their entreaties to join them, paying the boy to stay with him just in case, for if he was able to manage some rescue, the boy would have to ride for help. Around midnight, the innkeeper returned on horseback with some bread, cheese and a small flask of brandy. This sustained him for a few more hours but he had less glow about him than the lanterns, no appetite, his eating purely mechanical. He'd allowed the lad an hour of rest and, finally alone, had sobbed with a volume of tears he would not have thought his body capable of producing. As soon as light had peeped above the mountains he roused the lad again.

The boy pulled evenly on the oars in a slow circle as instructed. They were able to use the rowboat for this more passive part of the gorge. His jacket felt damp, whether because of the giant shroud of mist or his own lacrimation he could not have said. The sun was too thin yet for warmth. At one point he fancied he heard the strains of a violin from somewhere beyond the towering cliffs, and again he fell prey to that lascivious strumpet, hope. Stupid dumb hope that it was his dear friend playing a trick, pipe in mouth, testing him for the sake of it, another one of his endless experiments on the human personality.

And of course, I'd forgive him, he thought. So long as he were alive. But the scientist in him told him this was not possible. He plunged his hand into the water, freezing. A heart would stop beating instantly even if the impact –

'Over there!' he heard himself shout, and pointed so that the boy, who had little English, was given the direction. The boy guided the boat quickly. There was definitely something, a small dark shape in the water.

'To the left!' he yelled louder, gesticulating. He reached over the side of the boat and snared it, though his fingers felt petrified from the contact with the chill lake.

Now as he held the soggy item in his trembling hands he was at once weighed down with an iron melancholy.

There was no mistaking that deerstalker.

1. CATSKILLS NEW YORK 2000

WATSON

Icing on a giant wedding cake. White. As far as the eye could see. On the edge of the frozen lake, trees, their branches frosted, huddled like guests outside the church waiting to congratulate the bride and groom.

'It's absolutely beautiful.' Her mom squeezed her dad's arm. This was the highlight of her mom's year, out of Flushing and traffic and away from a flightpath for two glorious weeks. Her dad switched off the engine and the heater died with it. You could feel the cold outside beating on the glass to get in.

'Are we here?' Earphones in, Simone yelled. She had been bopping away the whole trip. There was nothing more annoying than a twelve year old little sister, unless it was a twelve year old little sister singing Destiny's Child songs out of tune. Georgette pulled out Simone's earphones.

'Stop shouting.'

Her mom chimed in. 'I've told you, Simone. Don't have the music up so loud. You'll go deaf.'

'It's nowhere near as loud as a gun. Is it, Dad?'

'Simone ...'

Their dad's tone was a warning to desist but the cat was out of the bag. Their mom didn't think guns had any place near families. She tolerated a gun in the hand of a sensible cop like their father but that was it.

'You took her to the range?'

Simone had been pestering him relentlessly.

'Only so she knew how a gun worked.'

Georgette found her sister's gaze and shook her head: Did you have to?

It was the only time of the year her parents got a break together. Teachers and cops in New York City had no downtime on the job.

'How many times?' Her mom knew how to wind up the pressure.

'Just the once.'

Which Georgette knew was a lie.

'And you?'

Georgette found herself suddenly in her Mom's crosshairs.

'Of course not.' Georgette preferred to read, science biographies especially. Madame Curie was her hero.

'You made her wear earmuffs, right? At the range.'

'Of course, sweetheart.' Her dad said, 'We can have lunch here.'

Simone thrust open the car door. The cold rushed in, smash-and-grab style.

'Hey, girls, careful on that ice,' her father cautioned. Simone was already ripping her skates from her bag and lashing them on.

Her mother opened her door and went to swing out. 'Darn.'

Georgette saw the bright red spot of blood on the snow. Her father handed his wife a tissue to dab her nose.

'When we get back, you see Bernie.'

'It's just the sudden cold. Georgette, where's your sister?'

Like that idiot was her responsibility. Simone had vanished around a big heap of snow. But she didn't want her mother to worry, so Georgette ran out, her father's words at her heel.

'Tell her to be careful.'

Georgette trudged around the big white hill. Simone was already below, a dark raisin rolling in a big circle.

'Simone!' Georgette shouted but her sister didn't even look up. 'Screw this,' she muttered and slid on her backside down the icy slope to the edge of the frozen lake. She started across it angrily.

'Didn't you hear Dad?'

Now Simone seemed to notice her. She pulled out her earphones.

'What's your problem?'

'Dad said to wait. It's dangerous.'

'You're only two years older than me, stop acting like you're the principal.'

Georgette strode towards her. 'It would serve you right if you –'

There was no warning. Just a soft snap. Simone screamed.

But it wasn't her that plunged through the ice.

Georgette understood, in that fraction of a second, the icy grasping arms of the lake dragging her warm blood to its bosom, that before she could even finish this thought she would be d–

When he heard the scream, Harry Watson grabbed the rusted gaff hook from the roof of the car, the hook he had never used but kept just in case, and began running. He had chased car thieves down back alleys, he had raced for help when two of his colleagues had been shot in a bungled bodega robbery, but he had never run this fast. Simone was standing on the ice, wailing. He could see the tear in its surface from here. And no Georgette. Simone took a step towards the dark hole.

'Stay there!' He skidded down the slope. He knew he shouldn't run, did anyway. He reached the spot and looked down. Nothing. He jammed the pole down. Nothing. As far as it could go. Nothing.

He got down on his knees and used it like a giant swizzle stick and felt it snag. He pulled it with all his strength, across and up. The blue Gore-Tex jacket became visible.

Below he saw fanning hair. He hauled higher, got an arm across Georgette's chest and yanked her out, her body leaving the water's gullet with an audible suck. He began dragging her backwards across the ice, turned and saw Helen on the bank.

'The foil blanket, hurry!'

A quick glance. Simone sobbing but for once doing as she was told, staying put. Georgette's face as blue as her jacket. Memory flash: as a young patrolman a few years back, boat smash in the East River. He'd dived in, pulled out two teenage girls, the second one, a child Georgette's age, blue. Too late.

He'd learned CPR as a result. Drummed it in: unresponsive, check airways, clear mouth, feel abdomen for rise and fall. Did it now. Like touching a marble slab. Nothing. No more time, ripped open the jacket, two breaths, thirty compressions. Helen slid down with the foil blanket. Must be four minutes gone easy.

Nothing. Breathe, compress. Nothing. Breathe, compress ...

Nothing.

2. NEW YORK 2020

'So, you were dead for probably twelve minutes?'

'At least. More like fifteen.'

Georgette had been through this kind of interview many times. It was second nature to her but even so, here, in front of peers and students in the setting of the lecture hall, she felt unusually nervous.

'Do you remember anything?'

'The cold as I hit the water. My heart must have stopped instantly. Next thing I remember was my father's face, surrounded by bright blue sky.'

Professor Anita Mirabella might have been a world-renowned neurologist but she was also a very skilled interviewer. She angled herself on her scalloped chair.

'And tell us, what we all want to know ...' A very deliberate pause. '... do you still talk to your sister?'

This brought hearty laughter from the audience. Two hundred and eighty was the capacity and through the curtain of lights, Georgette could see hardly a spare seat.

'We are still friends.'

'Did she feel guilty?'

'My sister never feels guilty for anything but she did make a small concession: no more Destiny's Child.'

This, Georgette was pleased to hear, brought a chuckle.

'So she didn't go into medicine or nursing then?'

'No; something the world needs far more of ... acting.'

This time there was a communal guffaw. That would serve Simone right for not coming.

'Some of our audience may have seen the article on you in the *Times* a couple of weeks ago. You sometimes consult for the NYPD?'

Georgette was sure she blushed. She'd hoped the article, prompted by Mirabella working her media contacts, would have focused on her research but it wound up being nothing more than a human-interest story about a girl who once died, coming back to life and ultimately working alongside her cop father. It made her sound like one of those TV pathologists who solved crime.

'Occasionally. If they need help on time of death or if there is some element of a body having been frozen. My dad has been a cop for thirty-eight years; it's not as weird as it sounds.'

'You work cases together?'

'They tend to use me for Homicide and he's not Homicide. He's a lieutenant at the one-fourteen in Queens, so not so far.'

'Is he here tonight?'

'I believe so.'

'Could Georgette's father please stand?'

Harry would be lapping this up. The lights found him. There he was, off to the left about six rows up in his favorite blazer. The crowd applauded and Harry politely waved. Highly embarrassing but sweet too.

'Thanks, Harry,' said Mirabella and the lights swung back to the stage and her father was once more swallowed by black.

'So the course of your life continues to be intimately related to death, your own included.'

'Absolutely. I became fascinated with cryogenics and the possibility of life after what we tend to think of as death.'

'Resurrection.'

More appreciative laughter for Mirabella, the in-house kind.

'You could call it that.'

'Okay, so this is the fun part of the evening. You guys...' the audience she was meaning, keeping it casual, '... have seen, on stage here when we started this event, and in videos shot earlier, where Doctor Watson snap-froze her hamsters. You don't like people saying you "killed" them, right?'

Georgette agreed she did not. That was the way media liked to represent it.

'They aren't any more dead than I was; just inert, showing no vital signs.'

Professor Mirabella gestured to the wings, and three honor students who had been designated as stagehands for the night strode onto the stage wheeling what looked like three incubators with various gas cylinders attached. Inside each was a recumbent hamster.

'Okay, Georgette, talk us through this.'

Georgette stood now, her lapel mike crackling slightly.

'Here we have Amelia. You all saw her placed into limbo – that's my term, not a scientific one – twenty-one minutes ago, by a mixture of extremely low temperature gases. These students have been monitoring to make sure there has been no replacement, right?'

The students, two young women and a young man, nodded.

'Next to Amelia is Benjy. He has been under for ...' she checked her watch, '... exactly one week. And this here is Columbus, boldly going where no hamster has ever gone before. He has been clinically "dead" for four weeks and three days. This is the longest I have ever had a subject in limbo.'

And now she was nervous, because what if it didn't work this time? Georgette moved to the incubators and placed her hands on a switch.

'As you can see on these monitors, there is absolutely no sign of life at present.'

Here goes. She flicked the switch. There was a low hiss as the neutralizing gas was pumped into the cages.

'I have flicked the switch.'

Bing. Right on cue Amelia's monitor panel lit up. Interest from the audience but restrained – Hey, you could hear them thinking, it's only twenty-two minutes.

Bing. Benjy's monitors started beeping and blinking. There was audible movement in the audience now, people craning to get a view and a few gasps from those close enough to see Benjy stir.

'Seven days dead and brought back to life,' Mirabella was a ringmaster, and genuine applause followed. But that sputtered to a halt because as yet there was nothing happening with Columbus. Georgette tried to reassure herself. Some of the others had been sluggish, no cause for real concern.

The monitors remained blank. Amelia was already up sniffing around her incubator but nobody was paying the slightest attention.

'Is this concerning?' asked Mirabella finally.

'It is.' Georgette could hear the tension in her own voice.

'Can you "up the dose" as it were?'

'No. It's a very precise formula. Either it works or ...'

'Or you kill a helpless animal,' someone shouted from the audience.

Tonight was always going to offer potential for disaster but if she were to convince the doubters to give further funding, she needed a home run. Georgette felt she had to respond to the heckler.

'I love my research animals but the implications for treatment of humans is ...'

She didn't know how to finish. It all sounded like self-serving crap. I've been arrogant, too arrogant. I should have tried this in private first, she thought.

Bing.

The monitors began flashing, beeping. Columbus blinked awake, an eye opened. And then he managed a huge yawn. The audience laughed and applauded.

Georgette didn't laugh, she was still scolding herself.

'You cut it fine, kiddo. Was Columbus like the tightrope walker who pretends to fall?'

Harry had made something of an effort. His blue blazer was a trifle small but you could forgive that because it matched his eyes. Since his hair had silvered up a year or so back, they seemed even bluer. Simone and Harry were in the corridor behind the stage, nobody else in earshot.

'It's not a circus.' Although on reflection, that's exactly what it was. 'No. It was stupid of me. I should have –'

'Could have, should have. It was great. I'm proud of you. Your mom would have been too. No Simone?'

'She called. She had a rehearsal.'

'Always the rehearsal. That girl will be rehearsing her own funeral. You hungry? You want to get something?'

She heard the need in his voice, would have succumbed even though she was emotionally exhausted but she caught a glimpse of Mirabella breaking off from a small group, ready to leave.

'I need to speak to Mirabella.'

Harry didn't press. 'Don't forget, Tuesday, your cousin, the Scotsman.'

'I'll be there. Thanks for coming.'

He squeezed her in a big hug. 'Wouldn't miss it for the world. Go on.' He jerked his head in the direction of the exit that Mirabella had just taken.

Georgette found the professor on the sidewalk waiting for her car to pluck her from the cool October air. Car lights cruised by, krill in an ever-flowing dark ocean.

'I'm sorry, I wanted to thank you.'

'That's okay. I didn't want to interrupt you and your dad. He enjoy it?'

'He did.' Georgette couldn't help herself. 'I don't suppose you've heard anything about my request?'

Mirabella gave a half-smile. 'I'm guessing you've been waiting most of the night to ask me that.'

Georgette shrugged, busted. Like many other scientists exploring cutting-edge research she was dependent on grants. The university grant not only gave her a salary, it triggered matched funding from Rasmussen, a large bio-tech firm that provided her with a fully-equipped and serviced laboratory in their nearby facility and a rental supplement for an apartment otherwise beyond her means. She had applied for further funding but the next stage she had proposed would be contentious.

Mirabella said, 'I'm not actually on the committee.'

'No, but you know a lot more people on it that I do.'

'Your work is impressive, Georgi, really impressive, but I'm not going to lie. University boards and committees are by their nature conservative.'

'The *Times* article didn't help?'

'They are a lot more worried by the cons than they are excited by the pros. Trying your process on a human being ...'

'You and I both know that I can't go much further with hamsters. There was a teenage boy in Buffalo last month who drowned. I might have been able to save him.'

'I know that.'

She went to interject. Mirabella showed 'stop'.

'I also know that you have worked out a portable system whereby the body can be transferred to your lab; the chemistry was beyond me but one of my colleagues talked me through it. Even so ...'

She didn't need to finish, Georgette could have done it for her: even so, a human is a whole other situation – if they are "dead". The limousine was pulling into the curb. Mirabella reached for her door.

'They meet next Thursday. You'll be the first to know. Just ... be realistic, okay?'

The door closed, the car merged with traffic, leaving Georgette like a shipwrecked sailor watching a clipper on the horizon disappear from view.

3

She was naked from the waist down, a pair of silken running shorts absurdly electric blue against the grey October sky lay beside feet still encased in expensive, almost-new sneakers. The blood had zigzagged over her chest before beginning to crust. Her hair was brown, about Georgette's length and her freckles were cute and far too friendly for the monster who must have looked down upon her before discarding her in the crumbling ruins. It could have been a film set, gothic horror, a pretty victim in a tuft of tall grass where chunks of old masonry and bricks fought for territory with angry bracken. But this was no movie, it was all too real, the location just a few hundred yards from Manhattan's east flank.

They were in the ruins of the old smallpox hospital on Roosevelt Island jammed between Queens, where Georgette had been born, and Manhattan where she was still trying to grow up. And looking at a dead young woman who would never get the chance to grow one day older than this. Maybe twenty-five, younger than me, thought Georgette. The current in the East River rushing downtown like office workers who'd caught a signal delay seemed a weird juxtaposition against stony death. Fifty yards away, beyond the iron picket fence that surrounded the tourist attraction, a crowd was growing behind the crime tape. Murder played well in any theatre.

'Gina Scaroldi. A local. Cornell Tech student ID on her.'

Garry Benson was the lead detective. He probably used Georgette more than any of the other Homicide cops. The wind played havoc with his fine fair hair. Scandinavian genes back there somewhere. Georgette noted most guys of that ilk were bald by fifty. Benson still had a good decade to enjoy mussed hair.

Georgette checked her thermometer, felt the chill breeze across her own face, judging its strength and smelling the faint tang of diesel on the back of its hand. Whenever you were estimating a time of death on a body left outdoors, you wanted to use every sense you had. A body left a long time would be far better off with an insect specialist. Drownings or near fresh corpses, that was Georgette's arena.

'Three and a half hours, somewhere around there.'

It was just on 9.15 now.

'So about five forty-five this morning,' said Greta Lipinski, Benson's partner, as if she knew him well enough to realize math wasn't a strong point.

'What I've always said, jogging is a dangerous sport.'

It was one of the crime scene guys. Georgette had been around cops all her life. She didn't take offense even if their comments seemed heartless. It was just a way to cope. But she noticed the photographer react. She didn't recognize him. He was new. He'd get used to it. Or go into aerial or marine photography to escape the memories.

'Twenty-four hour surveillance,' said Georgette, who had noted the sign on arrival.

Benson said, 'Looks like he picked the lock on the gate, made sure it was open, ready. I don't think this is the sort of guy gives us a look at anything useful.'

The gate faced Queens. The path was narrow at this point. There was bracken closer to the river where the killer could hide without having to pick a lock, but it would have been ucomfortable there, and the bracken could have clawed right through his clothes and ripped out DNA. If he had any brains at all he would avoid that.

'It would have been dark,' said Lipinski. ' He'd be invisible.'

Georgette couldn't help running in her head the kind of nature film that shocks you as a kid. The crouching lion, the stray impala. Benson put himself in the shoes of the killer.

'If he was hiding back in here, he'd be able to hear her feet slapping the paving, and even if she's cautious, she's not thinking any threat is coming from here because it's fenced off. He dashes out, hits her on the side of the head, see that mark? Drags her in here, rapes her, cuts her throat, or vice versa.'

As Georgette went to stand, she noticed a wound on the inner thigh of the dead girl. 'Wound' was not exactly the right word. It was like a cube of flesh had been excised the way you cut shapes out of dough with a cookie-cutter. It was only about an inch square but deep, almost to the bone:

'You get photos of this mark here?'
'Yeah, Kelvin got plenty. Sorry, Kelvin – Doctor Georgette Watson.'
They each nodded. She wondered if he would puke.
'What do you think it is?' asked Benson.
She said she thought it looked like a hat, side on.
'Like there's the thin brim and here's the crown.'
'That's what Greta thought.'
'But see here...' Benson leaned down and pointed with a pen to the 'brim', '... the ends seem angled in.'
Georgette scrutinized. He was right. She took Benson's pen off him and copied the shape onto her arm. Turned it around. It looked like an inverted house with most of the pointy roof chopped off. That was as close as she could get.
'Got me beat. Maybe it's a symbol.'
Benson scuffed the dirt. 'Whatever it is, I don't like it. They start doing this shit, it means more might be in store.'

The worst part of the NYPD job – besides the inevitable corpse – was having to write up her report. Though she was able to record her observations on the spot, they still had to be transcribed into a hard-copy document, so she hauled herself back to the Homicide squad room, that on this occasion meant the Queens North command at Forest Hills. Benson and Lipinski had stayed at the scene to interview potential witnesses. If the victim was a regular, chances were somebody would recognize her.

Was it her imagination or had Garry Benson been flirting with her when he told her how the *Times* photograph made her look like a film star? No, she was going to shut that thought down. As well as whether Mirabella might have had any success in talking the board around. That question had been ransacking her brain every spare minute.

A shadow fell across her desk. The new guy. He was standing there with a coffee in each fist.

'I got you a long black, or one with cream.'

The only time she grabbed coffee here was when the heat was down and her hands needed warming. Her guess was East River water might taste similar. But Kevin – no, Kelvin – had gone to the trouble so she took the one with cream.

'Thanks, Kelvin.'

When he hung there, she added, 'Is there something?'

He lowered his voice, looked around, warily. 'Is it always that ... bad?'

'Often a lot worse.' There was no point sugar-coating it.

'You get used to it, right?'

'You can tolerate it better, that's all.' She didn't say that the majority of those in his job would go onto something else after two or three years. He didn't comment, just nodded and headed over to the elevators. That was the thing with murder: you could ignore it, but it never left you. She did this job for one reason only, money. She needed the money to make her dream a reality. That dream was to bring people thought dead back to life. But if the board wasn't going to ...

There she went again. Full circle.

By the time Georgette arrived home, she'd resisted at least a half-dozen times the urge to call Mirabella. Tonight she was going to meet her cousin – or, more correctly, Harry's cousin. Maybe bagpipes and haggis could take her mind off her research. She stood at the door of her apartment building looking for her keys. Not them too. She couldn't have lost them, could she? But maybe she had. She always kept them in the inside pocket of her handbag but they were not there. A disaster script had already been written in her brain – buzzing her neighbors to get inside this door, then calling Simone to get the spare pair to her apartment – when her frantic search revealed them underneath her hairbrush. That's right. After she'd discarded the crime-scene suit she'd re-brushed her hair and for some reason she must have grabbed her keys. Well, she had been distracted. Garry Benson. He may not be that attractive but he was single ...

She stopped herself: No, don't even think about it, girl.

An hour later, she was on the sidewalk out front, freshly showered and dressed. Where the hell was Simone? Surely her band rehearsal had finished by now. Probably having hot sex with the drummer – Presley, was that his name? Or was that the bass player who preceded him? A deep rumble gave away her sister's imminent arrival. The old Silverado cut across a lane of traffic and skidded to a halt to the eruption of angry horns. Simone's finger extended out of the window and pointed to the dark sky.

She yelled, 'New York's Finest, assholes!' Which, like most of what came out of her sister's mouth, was a lie or at best distortion. From Simone's point of view, having a dad and sister on the department transferred all benefits to her.

Georgette got in. 'You're late.'

'Not anymore.' Simone tramped it out of there, more angry horns in her wake. Georgette always missed her sister until they were actually together again. She shuddered at the mess: used take-out containers, a hairbrush, scripts for TV commercials and some aspiring-director's no-budget short film.

'How did your talk go?' Simone asked, looking in the rear-view, admiring her curls. 'I would have been there but ... well, you tell me your news.'

Georgette couldn't fathom how Simone was not involved in accidents, figured her modus operandi hadn't changed; she caused them but skated by unscathed.

'Pretty good. For a minute I thought Columbus wasn't going to make it. I was worried. But he came through. You got a mention.'

Simone smiled, pleased. 'You tell them I have an audition for *Cabaret* starring as Sally Bowles?'

'Get out!'

This was great news. The last time she'd seen her sister on stage she had been playing rat-excrement in some play 'developed' by the members of Simone's co-op. Homeland Security could have used it as the ultimate threat on suspected terrorists.

'What venue?'

'St Christopher's.'

'The all-boys school?'

'Yeah. The boys are doing their own production. They wanted the real thing for Sally so they advertized. That's where I was last night, casting.'

Georgette knew her sister well enough to figure the audition story was in part a deliberate distraction to cover up her being late again.

'You were late because you were having sex with the drummer, am I right?'

Simone crunched a gear. 'That's over.'

Aha, exactly as Georgette had predicted when they last met.

Simone turned narrow eyes on her. 'Yeah, come on, give me the gloat.'

Georgette said, 'I'm not gloating.'

'You are. You're glowing in gloat. Like you swallowed kryptonite or something.'

More or less true. She said, 'I feel vindicated, that's all. I told you, dating at work is a bad idea.'

'I didn't date him, I just slept with him. And anyway, a drummer is stuck up the back, you don't have to look at him.' She changed the subject again with the same speed and lack of warning that she changed lanes.

'Dad told you anything about our cousin?'

Harry Watson had long since ceased trying to coordinate with his younger daughter. He figured it was much simpler to pile that responsibility on Georgette while he studied the ponies or had relaxing drinks with his pals, most of whom were retired cops.

'Other than he's Scottish and a university professor, nothing.'

'What's that on your arm, some jailhouse tattoo?'

Georgette told her about how her day started with a murdered girl on Roosevelt Island.

'Benson called me a little while ago to say they now think she was strangled first, then raped and stabbed.'

Simone made the kind of small bitter sound you do when it's too horrible to find words. Then she said, 'He's sweet on you.'

'Benson?'

'Yeah. I can tell. You have no radar with sex. Actually, I think his partner likes you more.'

'She's not gay.'

'She's on the precinct softball team, come on.'

Maybe Lipinski was gay. Georgette wondered if that made life simpler for her. Doubted it. There was nothing easy about finding partners, or people wouldn't spend so much time worrying about it. Simone of course didn't worry, she just kept sampling. True, Benson was attractive but then Vance had been undeniably handsome and look where that had got her.

'It's a ship,' Simone said matter-of-factly, nodding at the image on her arm.

And now Georgette looked at it again she saw what she meant, like a container ship or one of those fancy cruise ships that housed a thousand people, in a big apartment building–style structure.

'You could be right, you know.'

'Of course I'm right. Call Benson. Or I will.'

'I'm not giving you his phone number.'

'See, I knew you were hot for him.'

Georgette's turn to change the subject. 'He's cooking,' she said.

'Dad, not our cousin?'

'Yeah.'

'Pity.'

It would be steak and salad. It was always steak and salad.

Harry Watson stood outside in the cool, still air and flicked the steak over on the grill. You went to a restaurant these days and ordered a steak, it practically bleated. He liked his steak approaching black but you asked for that, they looked at you like you had been found with a young woman chained up in your cellar, or worse, claimed you didn't believe in global warming. Personally, he was a climate-change believer. His bones ached a lot more now than thirty years ago. He glanced through the window into the kitchen, saw his two girls preparing the salad and getting the cutlery, chatting. It made him feel warm inside. He recalled the same scene twenty years earlier when they were just girls who played with dolls and read pony stories. Helen would have been so pleased. Mind you, she'd be fretting – neither one married yet, not even close. He'd got a little excited earlier in the year when Georgette let that publisher guy move in. But now the publisher was pulped. Not that Harry actually liked the guy, but Georgette had, and he'd forced himself to listen to the wisdom of Helen who was always whispering into his ear, 'Harry, stop being a cop, give the man a chance.'

Simone was at the other extreme. Four guys a month, most losers or druggies.

Georgette poked her head out. 'We're pretty much ready.'

'He texted to say he's on his way. So, Benson called you in?'

They had talked briefly earlier.

'Twenty-four year old female student jogging on Roosevelt Island, raped, throat cut, around six this morning.'

Harry never heard about a homicide of a young woman without thinking of his daughters. He had trained both girls relentlessly to be careful, to be aware of human predators, but with Simone there was always that dark fear crouching in a corner that he'd turn up one day and discover his own daughter was the victim. You could only play with so many loaded weapons before one went off. And the way she dressed! Tonight was no exception, and this was a family gathering.

He needled her: 'Ah, there's that postage stamp I was looking for – disguised as a skirt on your butt.'

'Ha, ha. You should go into comedy work.'

'No, I should go into dressmaking. That skirt works out about thirty bucks a thread.'

'In contrast to that shirt. You obviously clothed yourself for zero from a dumpster.'

'Not zero, there was the cost of the bleach to get out the bloodstains.'

Harry enjoyed the banter with his daughters. If a jibe had been a jab they both could have fought welter-weight.

Georgette said, 'I like the shirt. It's the one Mom bought you, right?'

She never missed a thing.

'Yes, it is.'

He loved them. They were all he cared about in the whole world. Woe betide anybody who did them wrong.

The bell rang. His guest was here.

Ian Watson was somewhere in his late fifties, sandy-haired, warm of nature. Whether that was his natural disposition or enhanced by the consumption of whisky from the bottle he'd brought for her father, Georgette couldn't decide. They were around the table in the modest dining room where she had grown up. The Scotsman had described his family and life in Edinburgh with a deal of vivacity, a natural storyteller.

'Your father tells me your field is cryogenics?'

'She is the leading expert in the US,' Harry said.

'Cryonics,' corrected Georgette.

Simone tag-teamed with a Scots accent. 'It's troo. She revived this hamster had been did fer a month.' She winked. 'How's my accent, dope hey? I played Lady Macbeth off-off-off Broadway.'

'Impressive, Simone but … reviving a dead hamster?' Ian Watson shook his head at the magnitude of that and sipped his whisky. 'If that's not proof of genetics, I don't know what is.' He appeared to realize they had no idea what he was talking about. 'You've not heard of your great-great-grandfather, John Watson?'

Georgette found Scottish people hard to understand but enjoyed the rising lilt. She shook her head.

'You?' he turned to Harry but he was equally lost.

'Well, then …' Ian Watson leaned forward. Georgette could see he was relishing having a tale up his sleeve. 'I think your progenitor, old

John Watson, was into what in those days, the eighteen nineties, was a verboten area, the dark sciences, necromancy even.'

Simone slugged her brew. 'Do tell. I love a skeleton in the family closet.'

Ian Watson poured himself a nip more whisky and elaborated. Some years ago, when his father died, he had inherited trunks full of old family memorabilia. His father, an engineer, had never troubled himself to investigate these old family treasures but Ian, on long-service leave and laid up for a month after a hip operation, had slowly waded through them, and eventually came across the diary of John Watson.

'Eighteen ninety-two were the earliest entries. Tragically, flooding and mould had gotten to it and much of it was destroyed but I gathered our forebear was a medico living in London. The really fascinating entries however, indicated that he was experimenting with cryogenics.'

'No!' Georgette was not one given to exclaiming and she noticed both her father and sister raised eyebrows at her outburst.

'I am afraid so. There is no doubt that our relative met with James Dewar in London in eighteen ninety-two ...'

Georgette explained for Harry and Simone's benefit. 'Some consider him the father of cryogenics.'

'He made a good whisky, didn't he?' Harry's eyes twinkled as he poured himself a shot. Simone chuckled. Georgette could have slapped them: this was actually interesting.

'Anyway, it seemed their meetings were somewhat secretive but I couldn't make head nor tail of it until, right at the bottom of the trunk, I found a few surviving part-pages from the diary that had obviously fallen out.'

These were dated 1891 and, according to Ian Watson, shed new light on the mystery.

'I'm not saying everything became clear but what I gathered was that at some point, around early ninety-one, one of John Watson's great friends had perished in a lake in Europe ... Switzerland, I later worked out. John had evidently retrieved the body from the freezing lake and was keeping it frozen somewhere in the hope that one day there would be a technology capable of reviving his friend. It was all very hush hush of course because in those days it would have been considered akin to witchcraft.'

Georgette was flabbergasted.

'Well before Walt Disney,' cracked Simone.

'It sounds like one of his stories,' said Harry, reaching for a refill.

'I assure you, this is genuine. I've seen plenty of old documents and these were the real deal.'

'I gather he didn't succeed?' Georgette forked an olive.

'Not from what I read. It was quite touching actually. There is a section written much later, after World War One. John Watson laments not achieving his goal, says he's too old now. I'll send you the diary when I get back. I would have brought it if I realized.'

'That's very kind of you.'

'No trouble. A toast to our erstwhile relative, John Watson.'

They all drank, Georgette only with water. What a terrible thing, she reflected, your whole life dedicated to a project you never achieved. Then she shuddered and thought, I hope that's not a curse that runs in the family.

Even from the distance behind the crime-tape he had recognized the Watson girl. He'd zoomed in with his camera too, got a good look at her face. Strong resemblance to her father. Ironic she was trying to raise the dead while he himself was intent on increasing their number. They were like Greek gods lined up on opposite sides. He wasn't quite sure yet what he wanted to do with her. Oh, he knew how she was going to end up, but for full satisfaction you wanted the sequence of things just so. Still, it was tempting. Groundwork had been laid. And it would be ultimately so satisfying. People had to be punished for the wrongs they had done, and the punishment needed to be exquisite, not just pain but the worst kind of pain – 'If only I had done this and not this, if only I had seen what was staring me in the face ...'

Too few people read the Bible these days. They talked of Yin and Yang and all that trendy shit but they mocked those truths that anybody with any experience in life came to realize were inescapable. Life is pain. Escape from pain was possible, but not without correct planning, and adherence to that plan.

He dropped his car into gear and cruised away from the modest Queens house.

Soon, he told himself.

For now there were other matters that needed his attention.

4

There was nothing she didn't love about this life: investment banker, Manhattan, Upper East Side apartment, Jaguar. It was like a list. In fact, it was a list, one that she had doodled on her notepad way back in the prehistoric days of her Midwest high school. With her grades, she could have gone into whatever profession she wanted: medicine, law, media, you name it. But if you wanted the really big money and the playtime after work, there really was only one game in town, the one she was in, finance, Manhattan.

She zipped up her skirt, leather, you just couldn't beat it, especially not an Armani, still the sexiest beast and hopefully it might allow her to tame one tonight, although that would just be a bonus. She was really looking forward to trying the Brazilian place in Chelsea, celebrating Didi's birthday, and then maybe later to Valhalla. See if he was there again tonight. She had a feeling he would be but if he wasn't, no problems, she wasn't going to chase him, no way, that was a lesson she'd learned in elementary school. She examined herself in the entrance hall mirror. You look hot, Carmen. And she wasn't sure if she had thought it or said it but whatever, it was true. She did, especially with the natural red of her hair highlighted. She grabbed her jacket and slipped it on. The bag fitted neatly in her hand, smooth and sleek as a small bird. It had enough room for a credit card, lipstick, phone and condom. She scooped up her keys with the chunky silver keyring Brad had said was a genuine antique.

She could have taken a cab but what was the point of having a super-sexy car if you didn't use it? She took the elevator down to the resident's garage. One of her only gripes about her building was that her car space was at the back but hey, at least she had a car space in the building and didn't have to use a public parking garage.

She stepped out of the elevator. The basement seemed darker than usual. Some of the lights weren't working. Something she'd never got out of her small-city system was the threat you always felt in these underground garages. It was ridiculous, she knew. A building like this was very secure, and the crime stats on New York were way down. Even so, she was not comfortable in the dark. She started on the route to her space, the light from the elevator area fading like a dying patient's heartbeat. She thought about getting her phone from her purse, using it for light, but she was almost there. If she remembered, she'd drop an email to the super about lights being out.

What was that?

She stopped. It had seemed like a footfall, somewhere close by. Or was it just the echo of her Jimmy Choo heels? She cocked an ear. Nope, imagination. She turned around the concrete hump that sectioned her area. There was her car, its silver gleam dulled to the color of the concrete by the closest globe a good twenty feet away.

'You look hot, Carmen.'

This time the voice was not in her head. She swung around. A face appeared in front of her, a white blur. Before she could scream, something smashed into her forehead. She was dazed, felt herself dragged down, a hand reach up under the leather skirt, seize her underwear and rip it down. She prepared to loose a scream, then was struck again and her last conscious thought rushed out and impaled itself on the sharp spike of imminent death.

5

'They thought your research was extremely promising but at this stage not sufficiently advanced to justify them supporting a human subject.'

Anita Mirabella twirled the stem of her wine glass. It was clear she was hoping the chardonnay in this uber-trendy, chocolate-brick wine-bar two blocks from campus would dull any sense of defeat or rejection in her companion.

It didn't. Georgette felt both of those no less keenly than if she were drinking vinegar.

'I'm sorry,' added Mirabella, as if she knew that sentiment was absolutely useless to her. Which of course it was. It had always been a long shot but Georgette had refused to be a glass half-empty gal. Now the whole bottle was suddenly looking bone dry.

'What do they expect me to do, use a chimpanzee?'

Mirabella shrugged. There was never an answer that solved your problem, just more questions.

'I mean, it's just … stupid.' Georgette was acutely aware that her vocabulary was pathetic and blunt. She should have left it there but the burn was spreading and the wine had loosened her tongue. 'If I revive a hamster after six months, or six years, what does it matter? In the real world who revives a hamster? It's meaningless. And I don't imagine too many chimpanzees fall through the ice or get buried by an avalanche, so rule out primates.' She sighed, rested her forehead on her palm. She hadn't expected a different outcome but she had hoped.

Mirabella, who probably delivered this type of bad tidings five times a week wasn't fussed. Her elegant nails smoothed the tablecloth.

'You could look at private funding.'

'Without the university's rubber stamp?'

'I didn't say it would be easy. Okay, your research isn't applicable to mass-marketing like a cure for acne but there's always a company looking for a prestige project, like a studio making an art movie to win an Oscar. Your research is news. That's a positive.'

Georgette was worried about losing control of her research. The university was nurturing but a commercial company would put their interests first. Mirabella read her.

'Sometimes we have to give up something to move forward and get what we dream of.'

'They'd what, get me subjects by paying families for the bodies of their loved ones?'

'I suppose.'

'A bit like Burke and Hare isn't it?'

'Except if you manage to revive their loved one it's win-win: they get them back, you get the Nobel prize.'

Georgette swallowed her wine. There is that, she admitted.

By the time she got back to her apartment building, she was warming to the idea of working with the devil. It was that or move back in with Harry. She did not want to lose this place. No doorman but it was roomy, two-bedroom, in a nice neighborhood, with an elevator.

It sucked.

On the one hand, they stymied you from the research you had to do, on the other they cut off your money because your research wasn't going to some bold new level. More consulting with the NYPD would supplement her income but that wasn't her preferred option.

She entered the small lobby of her apartment building. It was gloomy now and cold. As if tendrils of ice had pushed through crevices in the walls. Funny that you could be in the heart of one of the world's biggest cities and still find a minute where you were as lonely as if you'd been laid in a grave. In her mailbox she found a brown-paper package which mystified her until she turned it over. Despite the fading light she could see it was from Ian Watson, Edinburgh. The diary.

The elevator rattled and swayed but it was clean and didn't smell. Most of the dives in her student days were walk-up, and the couple that did have an elevator made you feel you should climb into your biohazard suit before entering. She really didn't want to move from here. And Harry, well ... she enjoyed her dad's company but moving back was an admission of defeat. Her mind flicked back a few months, Vance next to her, the smell of his cologne and the take-out they'd share on the sofa. But naturally he turned out to be an asshole. She unlocked her door and entered the apartment, dropped the package on the reception table. Time she vacuumed again. Sure she had a cleaner in once a week but that was more a safety net. Georgette had vacuumed yesterday because she'd been anxious and it took her mind off things. Today she would do it because, okay, Simone was right, she was a neat freak. Everything in its place, everything dusted, washed and ready, that was how she liked her place to be, like a lab except with a sofa and bookcase.

Her phone buzzed. The Harry Potter theme. She wished she could go to Hogwarts right now and have toasted marshmallows with Hermione, Ron and Harry. Juvenile? Yes, but sometimes you needed that when your world was, as Mirabella had pointed out in their interview, beholden to death. A thought flashed through her brain: had Gina Scaroldi read Harry Potter too? And there it was again: death.

From the display she could see it was her father.

'Hi, Dad.'

'How did it go?'

'They're not going to allow me to test on human subjects.'

'How the hell can you prove that it works then?'

'Yeah, welcome to my world.'

'Chin up. We'll have pizza tomorrow.'

Tonight was his poker night so that was out.

'Go get 'em tonight, old man.'

'I plan to. Mirsch has been on a streak like you wouldn't believe.'

No sooner had she ended that call than her phone rang again. Garry Benson. Maybe Simone was right? Perhaps he'd be inviting her to coffee or ... something.

'Hi Garry.'

'Looks like we have a serial killer. Woman strangled, throat cut in her apartment garage sometime last night. Carmen Cavanagh, mid-twenties, investment banker, Upper East Side. The precinct cops were switched on, recognized the same mark on her arm as we found on Gina Scaroldi's thigh. I called but you didn't pick up and I didn't have time to leave a message so Verstigian did it.'

Tom Verstigian was one of the coroner's people. He wasn't a time of death specialist like she was but he was thorough and experienced.

'Tom's good. Anything on the DNA from the semen on the first girl?'

'The semen matched Gina Scaroldi's boyfriend. They had sex before she went jogging. When she was being strangled, he was in a cab on the way to work. We're sure she was raped by the killer but we got no other DNA at all. He's careful, maybe suited up.'

Thanks to crime shows on TV every psycho had learned how to avoid leaving DNA. Somebody called to Benson and he yelled, 'Coming,' then returned to her. 'I gotta go. I'll call you when I'm free. Thought you'd like to know.'

'Appreciate it.'

After Benson rang off, she sat slumped on her sofa, inert as a stain. Time crawled. She didn't even have the energy for TV. It was getting colder but even that couldn't get her up to turn on the heat. She churned over the idea of private financing, continued to balk at being beholden to a corporation.

Summoning all her willpower, she forced herself up, was about to get the vacuum cleaner when she caught sight of the parcel from Ian Watson and, venting her frustration, ripped it open without any of the caution she would normally have employed. Revealed was a very old diary, bigger than the current sort people use, if people use one at all. This was more like an old ledger, heavy. The binding was falling apart. Ian Watson, she presumed, had placed loose pages back in the diary at appropriate points. A long, ancient, iron key hung on a piece of rotting string looped around the back cover. As he had warned, some of the pages had rotted away or were stained so as to be unreadable but remarkably much of it was quite legible, written in a stately hand. She turned on the heat and, flopping back on the sofa, started reading. She imagined the scratch of the quill under a low gas globe in a cosy sitting room, velvet chairs, a wind-up clock on the mantlepiece, antimacassars, perhaps a tabby cat curled by an open fire and outside the window the lonely clip-clop of hansom cabs, drunken voices, policeman belting iron lamps to warn of their presence in thick fog.

The first entry that bore easy reading was dated May, 1891.

> *Perhaps what I have done is utter foolishness but I would damn my soul to hell if I did not try every option no matter how fanciful it may seem. I conjecture that his fall into the deep lake, so chilling cold at this time of the year, may have frozen him instantly. Only eleven hours had passed since his fall to recovery, and the body itself has not been moved from the frigid waters but dragged behind the boat into the secret cavern. Old Johann says the cavern*

was used as far back as the peasant war of the seventeenth century but only he and a handful of ancient villagers know of it. He is sworn to secrecy and refused remuneration, such is his esteem for our mutual friend. Remarkably, there was no physical trauma to the body, no broken bones. He is renowned for his ability to place himself into a deep trance and perhaps he managed this so that upon impact his body bore no more rigidity than a suitcoat. As the body can remain here in its secret tomb indefinitely I see no gain in attempting to move it.

The next entry she flicked to was dated July 7, 1891.

The desolation that I feel is indescribable, not just for my own self but for every man, woman and child in the civilized world. Without him to defend us, barbarism draws strength and confidence. I must find a way to turn my scientific conjecture into a reality.

Georgette could not help but speculate who this friend might be: a statesman, scientist or soldier from the sounds of it. Throughout August and September there was barely an intact page but piece by piece she was able to understand that John Watson was engaged in secret meetings with scientists.

L assures me that the theory is sound and a body stored quickly enough at a cold enough temperature may suffer no organic decomposition. With D we are working feverishly on a combination of gases that might revive our friend.

A later entry noted:

... can drive a turbine keeping the subject at the required sub-freezing temperature, season after season, year after year. We have time to make this succeed.

The ensuing months were followed by calculations, equations, chemical symbols, shorthand.

She was lying on her sofa now, her legs drawn up, unwilling to lay the book down for a minute. She had clicked on a lamp but the rest of the apartment remained in darkness. Her great-great-grandfather and his anonymous cohorts, she realized with amazement, had been using a very similar method to her, an almost identical mixture of gases, just the ratios different, with less capability than she had to insulate the subject and monitor levels.

But progress, it seemed, had been uneven. Encouraging successes were often followed by a fallow period. On December 25, 1891, there was an entry that brought her almost to tears:

> *Christmas without you, my dearest friend, is one of unbearable pain. I pray to the Lord for help in this enterprise that, if it were publicly known, would see me condemned as a devil-worshipper. I refute this. I believe in the goodness of the Supreme Being and in His help for our quest.*

And then in January of 1892 came an entry that had her riveted.

> *I can hardly believe it myself. The rabbit, frozen at minus 90 degrees F and having shown no signs of life for four minutes, revived absolutely. We are on the threshold of success.*

But then three months later in April came the admission:

> *Once again, our attempts were futile. What has time and again proved efficacious on a rabbit does not succeed on our subject. L says he can spare no further time on this. D will continue to help me. I pray for success.*

There were then long tracts of blank spaces with occasional notes about certain changes in formula, all finishing with *FAILED*. After that a great chunk of the diary was missing. But she did find a note marked *July 1, 1914.*

> *The incident in Sarajevo has I am afraid put paid to any immediate resumption of our experiment. The sabre rattling can be heard in the butcher shops, grocers and school halls of every little hamlet in this nation, and no doubt is as bad or worse on the continent. I fear gravely for the peace we have been blessed with. Had he been alive, I have no doubt that much of this could have been avoided, almost certainly the assassination, and thereby the pit into which this world has fallen since his absence.*

So absorbed had Georgette become in her activity, making herself coffees on automatic pilot, pages of the diary still in her hand as she poured and sipped, that she was shocked to glance at her phone and see the time was well after two in the morning. The diary was almost at an end and she resolved to press on.

It was a quarter to three when she reached the final heartbreaking entry.

> *… my optimism, alas, was misplaced. After labouring nearly thirty years without success, I am forced to acknowledge defeat. At the age of sixty-seven, in less than robust health, I find I must devote*

what remaining time I have to my family. I am so sorry to have failed you my dear friend. I leave these notes to be read in the hope that some later generation of men and women of science may succeed where I have not. It may take fifty or a hundred years but I still believe with all my heart, weakened as it now is, that the quest is possible – and if achieved the world shall be inestimably the richer for it. Your servant, John Watson.

There followed a biblical quote:

Rejoice not against me, O mine enemy: when I fall, I shall arise; when I sit in darkness, the Lord shall be a light unto me.

As Georgette closed the heavy covers of the book, the frustration and the futility contained therein seemed to be absorbed up through her fingertips. The curse of the Watsons, she thought to herself as she took herself to bed.

Wham! She sat upright like a schlock vampire who had just smelled blood, checked her phone: 3.48. She'd been asleep for only three-quarters of an hour but it felt like a week. Her brain was buzzing. One big idea: WHAT IF HE WAS STILL THERE? What if the unnamed friend, this statesman, as she had come to think of him, was still lying frozen somewhere in Switzerland? For it had to be Switzerland, as Ian Watson had surmised: the lake, the name Johann, other mentions she had found of Alpine weather, the peasant war of which she had vaguely heard. John Watson had desired somebody to carry on his work, as he said, fifty or a hundred years hence. He had provided a key, literally. Somewhere, surely he must have provided the location where it was to be used.

She bounded out of bed in the long pajamas she had found in Anchorage on one of her research trips. She had never let Vance see them but had kept them in her drawer tucked under her sexy underwear, near the unused vibrator that Simone had thought was an hysterically funny gift to give her for her thirtieth birthday, and that Georgette had been too scared to dispose of less she be caught in the act. The pajamas saved on heating. Scientists needed every cent and, heck, if you could keep a little fossil fuel from being burned, all the better. Perhaps the location of the body had been mentioned in the diary and she had missed it as she had skimmed over it. Of course, it might have become part of a rat's nest but for now she was staying positive. She made herself a massive mug of hot chocolate and started scrutinizing the diary page by page. Halfway through her mug she found it:

February 11, 1918. It becomes increasingly unlikely I shall be able to return to finish my mission. But the mission must not end. Brothers and sisters in Science I implore you make your way to

To WHERE? There should have been a destination but the rest of the page was blank. No, no, no, no, NO!

She checked ensuing pages but there was no further reference to the location. Laboriously she read right to the end of the diary but found no elaboration. Either he had slipped in a separate piece of paper which had since been lost or destroyed, or else, more likely, he had simply thought better of it, worried the diary may fall into the wrong hands.

She felt frustrated, angry and spent. So close. It had seemed the hand of Fate had been guiding her whole life to this point, that she who had died and been revived was destined to finish the work of her great-great-grandfather. But it had turned out to be yet another of life's practical jokes.

She slammed the book down and went back to bed.

'I can't believe it. Ten-thirty and you're still in bed.'

Simone was rustling through her wardrobe. Georgette's brain was Swiss cheese.

'I didn't get to sleep till five.'

'What were you doing?'

'As it turned out, wasting my time. I was going through our great-great-grandfather's diary looking for something. It wasn't there.'

Simone likely hadn't heard a word. She turned, held a summer dress, strawberries on white, against her body.

'What do you think?'

'Tell me again what you are doing here?'

She had better get her spare key back from Simone who'd had it since she house-sat during the Alaska interlude. Sooner or later there would be a problem.

'I told you. They're not doing *Cabaret* now, somebody complained it glorified Nazis, so now it's *Rocky Horror*.'

Tired as she was, Georgette was not so fatigued she did not instantly suspect her sister's hand in the change.

'You were the one who complained, weren't you? Anonymously, I guess. Because you already know most of the songs from *Rocky Horror*.'

A stab in the dark really but she could see from Simone's expression she'd drawn blood.

OVER MY DEAD BODY

'Hey, they'll have more fun. Men love dressing up in fishnets. And I'll be playing Janet, so I need something more ...'

'Demure.'

'... frumpy. And your wardrobe is just the place to find it.'

'Thanks.'

'Come on, I'll make you coffee. Maybe I can help.'

'With what?'

'The diary. I was listening, okay? I can multi-task.'

They sat on the sofa. The coffee had helped. It was a waste of time going through it all with Simone but she wouldn't let up so eventually Georgette had caved and shown her the diary, explaining the dilemma.

'See, blank. I think he decided not to write it down.'

'So why at the end of the book does he go on about people picking up on his research? And why leave a key?'

'Maybe he slipped it in on a separate piece of paper.'

Simone got up and rummaged in the ceramic bowl on the kitchen bench.

'You got a lemon?'

'It's too early for tequila, even for you.'

'Hey, please, a little faith.'

Simone found what she was after, took a sharp knife from the block and sliced. She walked back, bent over the diary and squeezed the lemon.

'What the hell are you doing? This book is over a hundred years old.'

'And hopefully, this is still going to work, but it's a long shot.'

'What's going to ...' No! Symbols had started to appear on the page.

Simone said knowingly, 'Like you said, he was scared of being caught. Invisible ink.'

'You're a genius.'

'I did the same thing with all my own diaries because you would have snooped.'

'Would not.'

'Would. What does that mean?'

What had appeared was the following string of numbers and letters.

24 12 h 7 g 17 f 24 e 22 29 12 d 13 18 8 c 11 b 18

Georgette took a photo in case they faded again.

'I'm guessing it's a code.'

She copied it onto a notepad she always kept at hand. Simone was tickled pink.

'Oh, I love codes. I finished that book, all of it.'

'About them breaking the German code in the war?'

'No. Jesus and Mary Magdalene and those mad monks, the Da Vinci thing.'

Georgette hadn't the faintest idea what she was talking about. She was already trying to crack the code.

'The most common letter is e. 24 and 18 each appear twice. I'm going to start with that.'

'But there's an e there too?'

'Probably a smokescreen.'

An hour later she still hadn't cracked it.

Simone said, 'I have to go. I have pilates. I'm sure one of the kids from St Christopher's has some app that can bust this in like five seconds.'

'I'll text you a copy. I'm going to keep working on it.'

Georgette felt alive again. She placed herself in her great-great-grandfather's shoes. He wouldn't make a code so difficult that somebody trying to follow his research would likely fail. It had to be relatively simple. Think how John Watson might have. If e is the most common letter, and he would have known this, then perhaps he would disguise it? What if all the letters shown were simply code for e? That's what she would do in his place.

She tried it. Now she had:

24 12 e 7 e 24 e 22 29 12 e 13 18 8 e 11 e 18.

Not enough to crack it but she wasn't discarding the idea just yet. There were only twenty-six letters in the alphabet but in the code was the number 29, so perhaps he simply took a letter value, A=1, B=2 and so on, and added another number, like A = 1+5? So if you subtracted values from the numbers, it stood to reason you would eventually find the letter.

She started by subtracting 3 from the numbers and using the new number as indicative of the letter. Nothing. But when she subtracted 4, the first three symbols became 'the'. She was sure she had hit the jackpot. She quickly substituted the letters. Decoded, Watson's message read:

The Cemetery Heindegen.

Her fingers danced over the keyboard. It took her some time to locate it. The town was tiny, near Meirengen in Switzerland. In fact, there appeared to be nothing there now but a cemetery. She checked ticket prices: doable. If she found the body, then she could use the body-transportation pods she had specifically designed. Getting the body here might present a difficulty. Hmm, she would lie, a white lie, say it was the remains of a relative who had been interred in Switzerland. Say it was John Watson himself. Mere administrative details. Her brain was gushing and bubbling now. The cemetery had some three hundred odd plots by the looks of it. How would she know which one? Watson must have left a clue on the headstone. Yes, that would be it … she hoped. She rang and booked, leaving in forty-eight hours. Her passport was in order. Simone could house-sit. She shuddered at the thought but it was only fair. She rang.

'Haven't had a chance yet to get it to my guys.' Simone was panting hard.

'Pilates still going?'

'Uh uh.'

Of course. What else would she be doing in the middle of the day but having sex.

'Pilates instructor?'

'You got it.'

Maybe house-sitting wasn't such a great idea.

'I cracked the code.'

The apartment door gave with a soft click and he eased his way in, then quietly closed it behind him. He felt a flow of satisfaction through his body. The key fit perfectly. The only light came from the glow of various electronic devices. He had taken the stairs so as to avoid any elevator cameras but he couldn't be sure there were none in the apartment. A cop's daughter, you just never knew. His fingers reached into his right pocket and he was reassured by the touch of the cord there. After allowing his eyes to adjust to the dark he edged forward towards the bedroom, just stopping himself in time from tripping over women's shoes that had been scattered on the carpet. On the table was the outline of three beer bottles and there was a faint smell of pizza. Nothing should surprise you in life, he thought, but one person he would have put down as neat and houseproud was her. He was almost at the threshold to the bedroom now and her shallow breathing was audible through the open door. This time he moved right to the doorway and peered in. She was lying on her back, head to the side, hair fanning, a naked breast was exposed. But the hair was too long. It wasn't her.

6

Pale blue sky streaked with white clouds atop towering mountains of lush green pasture, a temperature which here, in the middle of the day, required no more than a sweater; it was indeed a beautiful and quiet resting place. The cemetery of Heindegen, she had learned, was used extremely infrequently these days for burials, most of the gravestones going back centuries and barely a handful since the 1950s. The cemetery, surrounded by pastures, was perched on a sloping hillsidé some fifty yards above the surface of the lake whose waters lapped the base of the cliff on which it was located. It was three miles west of the two adjoining shops that constituted the village and was, Georgette had discovered, a pleasant bicycle ride. At the suggestion of her bus driver she had picked up a bicycle in Meirengen, a further three kilometres north. Whatever traffic there was appeared to be heading to and from some scenic falls and the narrow, potholed road she took south was quite deserted. Fortunately the ride had been gently downhill. Apart from a youth on a moped who had stopped to take pictures of the scenery, she had the place to herself. The cemetery consisted primarily of normal graves and headstones but there was also a cluster of mausoleums. When she had first laid eyes on them, pedalling along the dirt track that skirted the cemetery, her heart had skipped a beat. Surely it was here, in one of these, that her great-great-grandfather had placed his anonymous dear friend?

Having entered the cemetery by the main path, she rested her bicycle against a rotting fence post and walked purposefully to the vaults. There were about fifteen of them altogether, most grouped but a few outliers, and it was here that she ultimately found a vault bearing no name but rather a century-old depiction of two of the apostles arriving at Christ's tomb to find the stone which had blocked the entrance rolled back, and an angel waiting. The resurrection.

It had to be this one.

She slipped off her backpack. She had tried to prepare for all contingencies. The vault itself was some nine feet high and like most of the others, constructed of marble with a recessed, very weathered wooden door, rusted iron hinges and lock.

She pulled the heavy iron key from her pack and stood there, weighing the moment, then with her stomach swirling, slowly pushed the big old key in the lock. It slid in easily. But would it turn after what might be more than one hundred years?

No. It wouldn't budge. She fought the temptation to twist as hard as she could, the last thing she wanted was to snap it. Withdrawing the key, she pulled from her bag an aerosol can, fitted its slim plastic flexible nozzle into the lock, and depressed the spray button. She waited three minutes, counting the seconds, and tried the key again. It began to turn but not quite far enough. Again she sprayed it, then tried turning it, with no better result. This was literally the point of no return. Did she dare force it?

From her pack she pulled a pair of pliers, used their nose to grip the back of the key and levered, hard as she could. The key turned, the lock clicked open. She heard the moped putter away in the distance.

She was totally alone. The big, heavy door resisted her push. Over the years it had probably dropped. She threw her shoulder into the door and felt it give a fraction, shouldered it again and this time it swung inwards with a creak. Still she waited on the threshold, the smell of air trapped a century rushing out to meet her. She pulled out a flashlight, switched it on, and stepped inside.

The vault was empty. Confronting her was a semi-circular stone wall, bare except for a small ledge where candles or lamps may have rested with a vase. From the doorway to midpoint of the curved wall ahead of her, she estimated as being about five steps. Across, the tomb was wider, say seven to eight steps. No casket, no raised area. Now she focused on the floor, big smooth flagstones. A rectangular slab sitting perfectly flush with the floor in which it was embedded had engraved upon it:

> *Frohlocke nicht wider mich oh Du mein Feind: wenn ich falle, so werde ich mich erheben. Wenn ich in der Dunkelheit sitze, wird der Herr ein Licht sein.*

She had excelled at German at school and could translate this in her head.

Rejoice not against me, O mine enemy: when I fall, I shall arise; when I sit in darkness, the Lord shall be a light unto me.

The same quote John Watson had used to conclude his diary. Now she knew what they meant by saying people were giddy with success – that's exactly how she felt, light-headed. She pushed the door snug, plunging herself into darkness except for the beam of her flashlight. It went through her head that there must be limited air supply in here and she had to quell a rising fear of entombing herself. She knelt, felt around the rectangular border of the slab with her fingertips but could get no purchase, so perfectly did it fit. She pressed upon the letters as hard as she could but it wouldn't budge. Now the prickly sensation of panic rose behind her neck. There must be a way, a trick. She stood on the slab, jumped with all her weight. Nothing. She directed the beam up. Embedded in the ceiling was a brass crucifix about ten inches long. She reached up and felt it. It was not quite flush into the ceiling, like it was suspended by a nail or screw. Curious. She twisted it anti-clockwise and it gave. She continued to turn it until it unscrewed completely, revealing a narrow cavity. She reached up into this and touched metal and, using her fingers like a scoop, brought out a chain about six inches long affixed to something up in the cavity. She yanked.

There was a metallic clunk somewhere in the walls and then a deeper whirring, followed by a loud clang. The slab beneath her feet began to slide back. Quickly she jumped from it and watched it retract. It stopped with another loud clunk. Taking deep breaths, she moved to the edge of the space that had been revealed and shone her flashlight down, illuminating steep, narrow stone steps. They looked ancient. There were no cobwebs, she supposed the area too well sealed for spiders, but there was a smell of damp air, surprisingly not mouldy, rather fresh, and this reassured her. Still, she had to force herself to lock the door from the inside. She checked her backpack to make sure she had apples, water, and spare batteries for her flashlight and, with her heart in her mouth, descended into the abyss.

Step by step, Georgette found herself deeper in the vast empty belly of some natural cave. By the light of her flashlight she noted the roof and walls surrounding her were surprisingly smooth. And she could hear something, just faintly but there, a low hum. And another noise, a hiss.

There was no railing by which she might steady herself, so her movements were very deliberate. As she descended, the hum became louder. It was very cool now and her beam picked up moisture on the walls, and then something else below, a small wooden platform off to the side of the steps. In the wall above this platform, as she drew close, she made out a large iron lever, beside which, chalked clear as day, was the word LIGHT. She felt a rush: this was in all likelihood the writing of her own great-great-grandfather. A big cable was fixed along the wall heading down somewhere. Surely the contraption could not work after all this time?

She pulled the lever down. There was a buzz, then a flickering, and electric lamps sputtered on, revealing a cavity below so dark the lights could not penetrate. This was much deeper, she realized, than the base of the cliff could have been. The laboratory must be below the level of the lake? Carefully she continued down.

Soon came the sound of lapping water but at this depth the lamplight was weak. Presently it was swallowed altogether by black so that she was once more reliant on her flashlight. Finally, its beam found the end of the stairs upon a concrete apron. The hissing sound was nearby, regular and loud. The lapping she could confirm was water against the concrete 'pier' on which she now stood. She shone her flashlight first over the pier. This was the lab, had to be. She swung the flashlight the other way now, and its beam stretched out over the water and revealed something like anchor chains descending. It was bitterly cold. With trepidation she advanced towards the laboratory area and saw in the wall a lever like the previous one. Another light?

She pulled it down.

There was a sparking sound and then a crown of dim lights, previously invisible, slowly began to illuminate. They were fixed in the wall of the cavern but none of them threw more light than an old gas lantern. There was a creaking as of iron girders and grinding mechanical teeth. As the lights grew stronger, they revealed a mechanism built into the wall, iron wheels turning and some kind of crane being set in motion. It reminded her of an old fairground. The rattle of chains dragged her gaze to the water. The chains were moving, being wrapped around a capstan up high hauling something up.

And then it broke the surface, some kind of crate with a rubber hose, perished but intact, extending from each side. These, she realized now, were fastened somewhere below the surface. The crate ascended about four feet above the water and then was slowly swung towards her by the crane. And now, as the crate swung fully side-on, she saw it was actually a large glass container, like a display case, but she couldn't see inside yet because of condensation on the sides. The case began to lower as it swung towards the concrete apron. The top was glass too, but clear. She peered down into it.

She did not breathe, blink, move an eyelash.

Completely enclosed on all sides by ice, like a fossil in amber, looking up at her, his hands folded neatly across his Victorian waistcoat, was the frosted but completely intact body of a man.

'He's handsome.' Simone popped some nuts into her mouth as she peered into the special environment-controlled perspex case.

Trust her to reduce this amazing scientific breakthrough to *The Bachelorette*, thought Georgette and then felt immediately guilty. After all, Simone barely had two dimes to rub together yet had brought her a potted plant to brighten up the lab.

'What is this plant?'

'I'm not sure, ginkgo biloba grafted with deadly nightshade or something. This Haitian girl I do pilates with says it stimulates blood flow to the brain.'

'Deadly nightshade is an hallucinogen that can kill you!'

'Uh-uh. Not this stuff.'

'You don't know that.'

'I do, I smoked some. It cleared up my pimples.'

'I don't believe you.' The trouble was, she actually did.

Georgette finally found a place for the miniature plant. Simone was right about the subject Georgette had denoted as X. As Georgette could apply a mix of sub-freezing gases there was no need to pack him in ice, and if you actually did look at him as a person and not an exhibit, she supposed he was quite attractive, about forty, with his own hair.

Simone waved to X and put on a cockney accent.

'Cor blimey! Wot 'ave we 'ere?'

Whenever Simone was in the lab it gave Georgette the heebie-jeebies but she had been busting to confide in somebody and didn't dare enlighten any colleagues. Not yet. Harry would have been first choice but he was off on his annual Catskill vacation with a bunch of old pals.

'Who is he?'

'I don't know. A diplomat of some sort I think, going by the diary.'

'Must be at least six foot, distinguished. I think we should call him Percy.'

'Why?'

'It fits. He looks like a Percy. So, Percy was like, frozen?'

It annoyed Georgette that her sister had already appropriated X by giving him a name. She'd done the same with every pet they'd ever had.

'Yes, more or less. One hundred and twenty-nine years ago he fell into the freezing lake. His heart would have stopped instantly. Our GGF got him into the secret chamber via an underground stream and then into a glass case where the cold temperature kept him pristine. A turbine driven by the waterfall delivered all the energy they needed for their lab. Working with what they knew at the time, it was ingenious, absolutely no skin damage.'

'How did you get him here?'

'Transportable pod.'

'No, I mean, legally, how did you bring him in?'

Georgette gave her best blank look. It did her no good.

'Shut up! You smuggled him in?'

'I said he was our American great-great-grandfather who had been working in the Italian ambulance corps during the First World War.'

'That's straight out of *For Whom the Bell Tolls*!'

'*A Farewell to Arms*.'

'Whatever.' Simone winked. 'They fell for it?'

'I had convincing paperwork.'

Simone wiggled her finger at Georgette the way an aunt might pretend to scold a favorite nephew who had tried to slip a little white lie past her.

'That guy from the embassy party you were flirting with – am I right?'

'Patrick. He was the one doing the flirting. He cut some red tape.'

'I'll bet he did. Why don't you date him? He's a bit of a dweeb but you'd be suited. Much more than Vance.'

Georgette had managed to temporarily blank Vance from her mind. Simone answered her own question.

'I suppose opposites attract.' And now she was peering in very closely at X as if imagining herself riding with him on a pair of matched thoroughbreds. 'So what now?'

'Now I have to revive him.'

'Shut up. How long has he been here?'

'Nearly three weeks. Everything is prepped. I thought you might want to watch the big moment with me.'

'You filming?'

'Of course.'

'You should have told me. I would have worn something sexy.'

'We won't be on camera.'

'You're kidding. You're missing the human angle.'

'Time for that later. You ready?'

'Hit it, sis.'

Georgette switched on the cameras and spoke into a small microphone. 'This is Doctor Georgette Watson, Wednesday November eleven, two thousand and twenty. I am attempting to revive an unknown male believed to have been frozen since eighteen-ninety-one. It is three-eleven p.m., New York time. Present are myself and my sister, Miss Simone Watson.' Simone stuck her face in front of the long-shot camera. 'I will now administer the revival gases.'

Georgette depressed the button. Indicators told her the delicate concoction of gases was now being pumped into the chamber.

Please.

'How long will it take?'

'I don't know. My best calculations suggest that if it's going to work, given the body mass, about two minutes, fifty-three seconds.'

Simone got in close. 'I haven't been this tense since *Silence of the Lambs*.'

Georgette checked the clock: thirty-eight seconds.

'I think I need to pee, Georgi.'

'You can't leave yet. We're in a controlled situation.'

'What about this beaker?'

'No!'

There was a clang and clatter. Presumably Simone fumbling the beaker back.

'Sorry.'

Definitely a mistake, should have done it by herself. One minute, twenty-six. Halfway. Georgette couldn't prevent her gaze straying to the monitors that would show the faintest trace of life: body temperature, heartbeat.

Simone said, quietly for once, 'You're amazing, you know that.'

Georgette looked up and saw her sister smiling at her, felt guilty for all the bad thoughts.

'I'm really touched you're letting me watch this with you. Especially after ... I'm sorry about, you know ... you falling through the ice and all.'

It was the first time Simone had ever said that, and Georgette didn't know how to respond, hadn't had a chance to think it through.

'Took you long enough,' she said.

Simone laughed. 'One day you'll thank me.'

That day might be now. Two-minutes, fifty-two.

Fifty-three.

Georgette studied the bank of monitors.

Silent.

Fifty-four, five, six ...

Three minutes.

She watched the clock tick around to sixteen minutes. Not a blip.

Simone said, 'He's been on ice a long time, I guess.'

For the next hour and a bit that was the only time either of them spoke. Or maybe Simone did speak and Georgette didn't hear her. It was like everything whited out while she was trapped in a blizzard of self-doubt. Couldn't feel her heart, sense herself breathing, smelling. Her thoughts were a tumult of endless calculations of what she might have done wrong.

Simone had said something.

'Sorry, what?'

'I've got a rehearsal.' Simone leaned in and kissed her. 'I'm sure it's just going to take him a while to heat up.'

Georgette appreciated the thought but it was like putting a drip of water on third-degree burns.

'Thanks for coming.'

'Thanks for inviting me. If Percy ...'

'You'll be the first to know.'

Only she had a terrible sinking feeling that nothing would be happening now.

Nearly twelve hours later what had been a sinking feeling was well and truly on the ocean floor. Percy – she bristled at the fact she was calling him that now – was like a big wax doll. Inert. Motionless.

If it was going to work, it would have done so by now. Georgette felt utterly dispirited. She had tried not to get her hopes up, pushed them down at every opportunity like you do with a puppy you're trying to train, told herself that just because it worked with a hamster didn't mean it would with a human, and certainly not one inert for that length of time, no matter how well preserved. She felt this big gaping hollow. It had been stupid to be optimistic. It was one hundred and twenty-nine years for heaven's sake. And who knew what contamination had happened, especially in those very early hours? The material of the clothes he'd been wearing was flawless and that had maybe made her more confident than she should have been. Maybe there had been contamination early on during the transference from water to the glass case. The war had probably been lost in the first assault, so to speak. Percy was still of great scientific interest but destined to be no more than a specimen, a relic for the historians and archeologists.

She yawned. It was 2.40 in the morning. In the lab she maintained a small room like a sea-captain's quarters with a simple bed, dresser and a small en-suite bathroom, where she slept when she was working experiments that needed her constant attention. Normally she would have crawled into bed there but it had been three straight days since she'd been outside, her freshest clothes were two days old and the bedsheets needed replacing. She figured she might as well head to her apartment, change and grab fresh sheets, then return to sleep. Nothing was happening here.

He couldn't stem the relief that rushed though him when the cab dropped her outside her apartment building. The very next day after his previous visit, he had called her lab on some pretext and asked for her. They had told him she was on a short overseas trip. Not wanting to arouse suspicion by asking how short 'short' was, he had given it a week and then started checking out both the apartment building and the lab. This was his second visit since. Yesterday he had called the lab and had been told that she had only just returned. Last night he had loitered for a couple of hours but had not caught sight of her. Tonight he had contemplated abandoning the vigil but decided to hang in until three. Ten minutes before his self-imposed deadline, a car stopped and she climbed out. They were hard workers, scientists, you had to give them that. It had crossed his mind that their encounter should take place in the lab. The apartment building was small and relied on cameras for security. Any halfwit could avoid them. The lab, on the other hand, had a security guard and teemed with cameras but sometimes such measures could provide a false sense of security. A lazy security guard was less dangerous than a nosy neighbor. He had already found a copy of the lab's plans and there was access through an alley to a security door. But then, if one thought laterally, there was an easy way to bypass all that. He looked up at the building in front of him. She'd possibly be showering this very second, ready to slip into the sheets. It was tempting. The sister – he had quickly established she was the young woman in the apartment whom he had previously spied on – had moved back to her own place, so now it was just her and him. It had grown chilly but that was good, the generic muffler a simple disguise. Winter was coming and it would bring snow, ice and death. He checked his watch, wondered how long before she would be asleep. Soon. Sleep is coming for you, Georgette, long and deep and, at least for him ... satisfying.

7

An even, regular rhythmic swish for a soundtrack. Cold on her face but not her body, which was active, pumping blood, muscles straining. She was skating, looking up at a sky crisp as a bright blue tablecloth.

Crack! Like a rifle shot. Terror, instant, complete through every cell of her body for that shard of a second that preceded the inevitable plunge. Nothing you can do to stop it. Freezing water, over your head in a blink, lumps of ice scraping your ears, chin, nose. She tried to reverse it, fight gravity, push up, telling herself don't panic, just make the surface, the weight of her skates an anchor. She wanted to scream but it was all water, rushing into her mouth and lungs, deadening her cries.

Hands seized her, pawing at her, not to help, she realized as they encircled her throat. This WASN'T A DREAM!

And there was his face up close ... a dead man, a dead man in Victorian clothing, his hands choking her so she couldn't ... couldn't ...

Georgette thrust up from the sofa gasping. What a ghastly nightmare. A panic attack, that's what it ...

She became aware of the deep burring sound of a cell phone on vibrate. She checked the time. Four-twelve. She'd grabbed her clothes and new sheets and sat down on the sofa for like a minute. She must have dropped off to sleep. The number showing on her phone was familiar but she was too groggy to place it yet.

'Yes?'

'Doctor Watson? It's Jason Cormack, the security guard at the labs. Sorry to disturb you at this hour ...'

'That's okay, Jason.' Jason's smooth dark skin and clear eyes had initially led her to believe he was in early thirties. Later she learned he was mid-forties with two tween daughters. Often, she and Jason were the only two hanging around the complex in the early hours. 'What's up?'

'I was doing my rounds down your wing when I heard a noise in your lab. I opened up. One of the hamsters was running around in there. I tried to get it but it ducked under some crates. I thought I better call you before I went poking around.'

Sleep seemed all the more alluring now that it had been shattered.

'You did the right thing.' Thank God he hadn't walked in on Percy. She forced herself to her feet. 'I was on my way back anyway.'

She picked up the sheets and bag of clothes. How the hell did a hamster get out?

The answer came without much effort: Simone. Fiddling with that beaker, probably accidentally unlocked the cage. Not hard to do, they were on a spring so Georgette could depress them with an elbow while her hands were full with a hamster in limbo. No time to waste, a maverick hamster could severely damage her settings, chew through equipment, make Percy unsalvageable even as a curio.

She grabbed her keys from the hall side table, stopped. On the table was a snow globe which she was sure she had never seen before. It showed Bow Bridge, the quaint bridge spanning the lake in Central Park. She hadn't noticed it until now but then the mood she was in she wouldn't have noticed King Kong. Once again, the solution announced itself: Simone. Likely when Georgette was away and Simone had been staying here she had brought it with her for some reason and left it under a bed or table. Jemima the cleaner must have found it and put it there.

The car had her at the labs in less than fifteen minutes. Jason was waiting behind the security door and let her in.

'Really sorry if I woke you.'

She'd not even had time to brush her hair.

'I'm glad you did.'

Assuring Jason she didn't need his help, she sped down the corridors and unlocked her lab. It was dark inside except for the life-support panel to which her glance was inevitably dragged: the lights were no more animated than when she'd left and she tasted anew the bitterness of failure. She reached for the main light switch, felt something touch her foot and jumped. But as her eyes adjusted she saw it was the escaped hamster.

'Columbus, that you?' She picked him up, tickled him. 'Rascal.'

On the way to his open cage she saw that the hungry hamster had shredded Simone's gift plant.

'Are you tripping, man?'

Columbus looked up with soft eyes. She kissed him on his head and replaced him in his cage. The other hamsters were up and about, their water and food adequate. Percy, though, might have been carved of soap.

'Sorry I couldn't do the same for you,' she said.

Picking up her bag of clothes, she shuffled to her captain's cabin and was about to cross the threshold when she heard a beep. She froze mid-stride, not daring to turn. Was it her imagination? Two more beeps followed, and then a whole salvo. She swung towards the monitors suddenly ablaze with dancing lights.

The incubator was illuminated by a dim blue glow. This showed the activation of sophisticated low-illumination lamps triggered by the sound of a beating human heart. These she'd installed to protect Percy's long dormant eyes from sudden, potentially damaging light. For an age she stood there, summoning courage. She made herself look into the incubator. Percy seemed as before, eyes still closed, but there was one big difference: the slow rise and fall of his chest.

He was breathing.

'Oh my God, his eyes are open!' Simone's excited shout reached her from the captain's cabin where Georgette had moved Percy once his vital signs were stable and he was breathing normally at room temperature.

'Hi there, gorgeous.' Simone did a flirtatious little wave.

Trust Simone to be the one to be there when his eyes opened the first time! Two whole days Georgette had spent cramped in an armchair, waiting for this moment, the culmination of her life's work. Heart thumping like a jazz drummer she forced her sister aside. Simone was right, cloudy grey eyes were blinking awake.

'Hi. I'm Georgette, Doctor ...'

That was as far as she got. His eyes closed again. Simone gasped.

'Dope-a-funkendelic. He must be what? One hundred and seventy ...'

Georgette put a finger to her lips to silence her. It was extremely important that Percy didn't get overwhelmed.

Without giving away the reason for her interest, she had consulted with neurologists and psychologists who had dealt with people regaining consciousness after a long coma. All of these specialists had stressed the need for a period of gradual acclimatization before the patient was given the real facts of their situation. Premature disclosure might be literally, mind-blowing.

First things first, make sure they were breathing, eating and drinking. Georgette checked the drips that were supplying the body with nourishment and removing waste. Everything was good. She gestured for Simone to join her in the lab proper. Simone bent to kiss Percy on the forehead.

Georgette hissed, 'No! I told you.' Who knew what bugs he might be susceptible to? Simone sulked and followed her into the lab. Georgette quietly closed the door.

'You just want him all to yourself,' Simone said.

'He has to be looked after.'

'Then why isn't he in a proper hospital?'

'Because he'd have to be signed in with a name and address.'

'Just say he's some homeless guy.'

'He's my responsibility. And he needs to understand his situation in a way that can't be overwhelming.'

'How long can you keep him here?'

Truth was she'd been asking herself that same question. The fact that she hadn't planned better made her consider that she'd never truly believed she would be able to revive him.

'Once he has strength, can walk, talk. Probably two or three weeks.'

That meant the only way that she might be able to leave the lab herself would be if she had somebody absolutely reliable and discrete to babysit. Unfortunately, she had no colleagues who had been on this journey with her and Harry was still on his annual vacation. Simone had already been entrusted with far more information than was prudent but to date had kept the secret. To give her any actual role however was an invitation to disaster. At any rate, while it was hardly convenient, being closeted in here wasn't the worst thing. Georgette had stocked up on food, she had the Internet, a Netflix subscription and enough clothes to keep her going for a while. If those scientists at the South Pole could handle it, she was sure she could.

Simone said, 'I have to get off to rehearsal. Call me if he starts talking. You are a fucking genius.'

Georgette reminded her she could not breathe a word to anybody.

'Hey, it's in the vault. It is funny though, it's just like *Rocky Horror* isn't it?'

Which was not exactly the comparison Georgette would have chosen. Her mind was running more to Curie, Fleming or Pasteur.

Displaying no sense of the occasion nor any flair for originality the very first word Percy spoke was 'water'. It was late the next day. He had been waking more frequently and staying conscious for longer, the cloudiness gone from his eyes, now alive, intelligent. Georgette was attending his nails, smiling at him.

'It's alright, I'm just trimming them.'

She had not been expecting a reply.

'Water,' he whispered, so surprising her that she fumbled for the filled cup she kept ready and spilled some of it. She had to refill it. He gripped her arm with surprising strength, was able to raise himself and sip quickly. A coughing spasm followed.

'Don't be alarmed, coughing is quite normal in cases like yours,' she said trying to reassure him.

He slumped back. His eyes tried to take in the room which she had kept deliberately bare and free of modern devices.

'You must have many questions.'

He nodded.

'You need first to get your strength up. You have been unconscious for some time.'

'American,' he managed. It was only one word, but he sounded English.

'Yes, I am American. There is water here, and fruit. The bathroom is through there but you may not yet be strong enough to use it by yourself.'

'What ... happened?'

'You had a fall. Do you recall anything about that?'

He slowly shook his head.

'Your name? Do you know your name?'

His eyes rolled back as if he were calculating some difficult formula. Then once more he shook his head.

'Never mind. It's been quite an ordeal you've been through.'

He closed his eyes again and she left him but her whole body felt electrified.

She had done it.

Over the next forty-eight hours he continued to progress, taking solid foods – cereal, fruit and a little rice – but he remained confused and still did not recall his name. Simone had visited in the afternoon on the way back from her rehearsal but was disappointed to find the patient sleeping.

'Wake him up. Please.'

'No.'

'I could just bounce a ball near him or something.'

'He needs rest.'

Her father had left one message to say he was having a great time fishing and playing poker and may never come back to work. She could have done with him now. She would have to tell Percy something soon. After he was aware of his situation she could think about going public, doing it in a tasteful way, not too sensational. Although exactly how you did that when you have revived a person thought dead for one hundred and twenty-nine years she wasn't sure, but perhaps one of the public news channels or maybe through the university. She was tired. It had all caught up with her. She closed her eyes.

She couldn't say what had woken her but she was alert in a second. The lab was in darkness but the clock told her it was near five in the morning. She felt uneasy, knew she hadn't woken for no reason and was worried something had happened to Percy. Maybe he had called out? She got up off the foam mat on which she'd been sleeping – now that her patient was conscious she wanted to give him his privacy so she slept in the lab on the floor – and listened.

Something wasn't as it normally was. Too late, she sensed a presence behind her and opened her mouth to scream. A powerful hand clamped it, and something sharp pressed into her jugular.

'No sudden movements, no screams.' An English accent. 'I gain no pleasure threatening women and I shall unhand you forthwith, but I warn against any attempt to raise an alarm.'

His hand was removed. She breathed evenly.

'Now tell me. Who is your master?'

She was spun around. Before her, in the murk, stood Percy, wearing his old clothes, one of her sharp scalpels in his hand. She couldn't contain her stifled cry. He allowed a lopsided grin.

'Yes, a lot fitter than I pretended. I have been able to walk for the last two days, exercising while you slept. From an examination of my surroundings I conclude that this is a scientific laboratory. Now, miss, you must tell me, whose laboratory and where precisely I find myself situated.'

The scalpel could slice the skin from her bone, kill her with the flick of a wrist. She wanted to reassure him.

'You are in Manhattan. The laboratory is mine.'

He leaned back, the scalpel dropping to his side but remaining in his hand.

'Yours?' The word was smeared with disbelief.

'Yes, well part of the Manhattan complex of Rasmussen Biotech. There are over thirty labs in here and this one is mine. You have been through a lot. You should not exert yourself.'

'I could not feel more well-rested than if I'd slept a hundred years, thank you. Your accent adds credence to your assertion that we are in New York, however, that could simply be a clever ruse, the brainchild of You-Know-Who.'

'Who are you talking about?'

'The professor.'

'The professor has nothing to do with this. This is all my work.'

He was taller than her by a good five inches and he looked down a longish nose at her as if examining a specimen under a microscope.

'What are you? Mormon? A mason? To what arcane purpose have you kidnapped me?'

'I did not kidnap you, I revived you.'

'Revived?'

His eyes were piercing, demanding. Perhaps he had been a lawyer.

'Yes. You were in ...' she was about to say 'inert', caught herself. '... Switzerland.'

'Switzerland?'

He said it with an inflection of curious wonder. She could see him trying to think that through.

He shook his head. 'Unfortunately my recent history is a fog. Perhaps induced by some opiate. I wonder might you be deceiving me, Miss ...'

Waiting for her to supply her name.

'Doctor. Doctor Watson.'

He chuckled, waved the scalpel at her in the way one might wag a finger.

'Oh, indeed, you are playing with me. My senses are not so distended that they cannot tell the difference between my dear colleague and an imposter – albeit an attractive one – of the opposite sex.'

'Sir, this is very difficult to explain ...'

'Of course it is. You must attempt to conceal your nefarious intent from the one to whom no secret is secure.'

She was having trouble following his Victorian-era phrasing. 'Who is that?'

'Me, of course.'

'You have me at a disadvantage, sir. I know only that you are a man of some repute who is ... was ... a very dear friend to ...'

'*Some* repute? Miss, I am not one who needs to wallow in public admiration but I will speak plainly and truly and in this spirit I tell you, that I am without peer in my chosen profession.'

'Diplomacy?' Georgette suggested hopefully.

'Detection. And I detect right now that you, with your pretty face and innocent wide eyes, dissemble, and that I may be in some little danger. I seem to remember being in Chen's den at Shoreditch pretending to chase the dragon while I followed the American sailor Ernest Evans who was in London to assassinate ...' he stopped and offered a knowing chuckle. 'But then again, that may be your game, might it not? To find out what I know. Such information would be like gold to Professor Moriarty.'

The last two words slithered from his lips. 'I am certain his hand will be revealed somewhere behind the curtain pulling the lever.'

Finally, the veil was yanked from Georgette's brain. 'Moriarty ... that's the professor you were ...' She stared at him, seeing him truly for the first time: well over six foot, wiry, a longish nose though not as long as one might have been given to believe.

'You can't be real,' she said, wondering if she might still be dreaming.

'I assure you I am. Despite many finding my methods astonishing, I am quite as human as my good, but somewhat more mundane friend and colleague whom you purport to be.'

Her breath caught. Her great-great-grandfather was John Watson, living in London in the eighteen-nineties. Of course. It seemed so obvious now but how? It was a fiction. Or perhaps not. Like a child following a rolling ball she let its path drag her onwards.

'You reside at Baker Street,' she said, as if she were certain, when it was no more than more speculative fat tossed on a hot fire.

'Still claim not to know me?' There was a twinkle in his eye.

Oh my God.

'You are ...'

'Sherlock Holmes.' He bowed slightly. 'And now, miss, for I fear the snare could be tightening, I must bid you ... adieu.'

With that he leapt for the exit door, pushing down on the handles and vanishing through as the alarm sounded.

'No, wait!' she cried and tried to follow but slammed into one of the hamster cages. She regained her feet and ran outside into the alley and cold morning air just in time to see a shape leap from the top of the adjoining wall to the other side.

'Please, stop!' she shouted but knew it was hopeless.

It could not possibly be, and yet it was.

She had revived not simply a one-hundred and twenty-nine year old corpse but the greatest detective of all time.

8

The biggest challenge playing in a musical with schoolboys, Simone had decided, was getting up in the morning. The boys all had sporting commitments right after school, and were basically on a nine p.m. curfew anyway, which for rehearsal left only lunch hour or the mornings before classes started. Lunch hour was out because it clashed with her pilates. That left early morning but she'd got too used to the night-owl lifestyle to give that up so had taken to coming straight from clubbing to the school. So here she was at nine in the morning removing her make-up after the rehearsal and feeling not even close to alive.

The whole cast of the show except for Frank N. Furter, a very precious and bitchy gay kid, no doubt from some ultra-rich family, was gathered round picking up her pearls of wisdom. Somebody had asked her what her favorite role had been.

'I luvvvved the Spark-Fix commercial. I had to play this hot cheerleader who was stuck in traffic because I hadn't used Spark-Fix.'

'You get any lines?'

It was Ambrose the director, the kind of nerdy kid who was just so sweet you wanted to mix him with vodka.

'No, Ambrose, I did not but the catering was amazing: mini-hot dogs, mini-burgers, even donuts. Once on *Most Wanted* I played a dead prostitute.'

'That shouldn't have been much of a stretch.'

It was Frank N. Furter taking off his lipstick.

She narrowed her eyes, was about to use a barrage of four-letter words but remembered she'd signed an agreement with the school and needed the money, so restrained herself.

'Actually it was very challenging. My body was found crammed into a laundromat's dryer.'

Frank quipped, 'Don't tell me, your clothes shrank and you were nauseous for days.'

A number of the boys laughed. The little shit was undermining her. Fortunately, Ambrose came to her rescue. He proffered a red rose.

'Thank you for allowing me to share the stage with you, Simone.'

Ambrose also played Brad to her Janet.

'That's so sweet, Ambrose. Okay guys, I have to fly. See you tomorrow.'

She sashayed out of there showing Frank N. Furter how to strut. She could grab three hours shut-eye and still make pilates. As she approached her car – the school let her park in the bursar's spot – she was blown away to see Georgette standing there. She looked upset.

'He's escaped.'

Georgette's brain had been scrambled. She'd spent hours wandering the streets of the Upper West Side near the lab, looking for Holmes the way you might look for an escaped red setter. Now she was scanning the area around Central Park while Simone drove and talked infuriating nonsense.

'This is dumb crazy. You revived Sherlock Holmes.'

'Yes. It all makes sense now. There were waterfalls upstream of the cemetery in Switzerland. The legend was that Sherlock Holmes and Professor Moriarty plunged to their death after wrestling above the Reichenbach Falls. Readers were distraught and demanded Holmes be brought back.'

'Sherlock-fucking-'Olmes.' That horrible cockney accent of hers again. 'And we're related to his sidekick?'

'Yes, John Watson's our great-great-grandfather.'

It was hopeless around here, so many people, dense traffic. In a crowd on the sidewalk, she saw a tweed jacket and her heart reared until she caught a better look of the man wearing it. Younger with dark curly hair. She was still trying to come to grips with it all herself.

'I mean, apparently Holmes and Watson were real people.'

'Of course they were. That guy Conan ...' Simone rummaged through the dumpster that was her brain for the name that Georgette guessed her sister had seen somewhere on a film credit, '... the Barbarian ... he wrote books about them.'

'Conan Doyle. Yes, but everyone thought they were fictional.'

Simone turned towards her, sceptical. 'Really?'

'Simone!!!' she screamed.

Simone turned back to the road, jammed on the brakes, stopped an inch in front of a man with a white cane.

'They shouldn't be on the streets.'

'He had the light.'

Simone rolled her shoulders, like that didn't count, returned to where she had left off. 'I always thought they were real.' She let out the clutch, started up again.

'They *are* real.'

'You just said they ...'

'Nobody, apart from you apparently, believed them to be real.'

'And now you've lost him,' said Simone sounding affronted. 'How could you do that?'

'I wasn't expecting him to threaten me and then escape.'

'Exactly. I always said you should do improv. Makes you think on your feet. We have to find him. You could win the Nobel Prize. And I could win an Oscar playing you winning the Nobel Prize.'

Georgette was despairing. By now he could be anywhere.

Simone said suddenly with authority, 'We're wasting our time. We don't need to find him. He's the world's most famous detective. He'll find you.'

She did a U-turn to a crescendo of angry horns and not for the first time Georgette found herself stunned by the genius of her insouciant sister.

When Georgette and Simone entered the foyer of the Rasmussen Biotech Medical Regeneration Department where her lab was housed, the daytime security guard hailed them before they had made it to the security gate.

'Doctor Watson.'

'Yes, Steven.'

The guard walked forward, a small folded note in his hand. 'Doctor Cherry said some homeless guy stopped her on her way in and asked this be delivered to you. He said a gentleman had engaged him to deliver it.'

'Thank you, Steven.'

Her fingers were trembling as she flipped it open and read.

'Two blocks north, the small park. H.'

Simone squeezed her head in for a look, whispered, 'Is it him?'

'Has to be.'

It took them under ten minutes to reach the park. The day was fine but only grudgingly, the wind razor sharp. She realized she'd been cooped up in the lab long enough to miss all but autumn's tail. A mother with one child in a stroller and another young child bravely feeding pigeons were the only occupants apart from a bum huddled in the far corner, an empty bottle by his side. Georgette couldn't stifle a cry of frustration. He must have been and gone.

Simone tried to reassure her. 'He'll be back. We can wait.'

'What if he has some episode? Fits, collapses ... his muscles haven't been used in over one hundred years. As for his brain ...'

'Evening, ladies.'

The bum was advancing towards them. Georgette was in no mood for him and was ready to tongue-lash him when his hunched shoulders and dragging gait vanished before her eyes. Standing before them was Holmes, looking match fit.

Thrilled and relieved she said, 'This is my ...'

'Sister,' said Holmes, bowing.

'Simone,' said Simone. 'I'm a huge fan. I was the first person you saw when you regained consciousness.'

'I am appalled the memory is not burned into my brain. Delighted to meet you, Simone. As for your sister,' his eyes drilled into Georgette, 'I believe an apology is in order. Please accept mine. I was quite discombobulated. You really are, as you say, Doctor Watson.'

Georgette felt herself flush. 'And what would be my profession?' asked Simone, twirling.

'Your skin is white, I smell a faint trace of vodka consumed several hours ago, and that attire ... yes, I would say without doubt, a lady of the night ...,' he offered the hint of a smile before adding, '... an actress.'

Simone put her hands together and brought the fingers to her mouth in a show of astonishment and gasped, 'How -'

'There is a trace of theatrical makeup by the right-side of your temple, you project your voice seemingly without effort and you clearly love attention.'

Simone beamed and said, 'He's amazing!'

Georgette could have brained her. She began, 'Do you understand -'

'It is November seventeenth in the year two thousand and twenty? Yes. Within minutes of my decamping from your laboratory it was apparent that either I was in the afterlife or in some world future to the one I remembered. The ubiquitous screens, some giant ones on top of buildings, others miniature, have not escaped me. I take it they can somehow show events happening at this exact moment in other parts of the world. New York has changed more than a little from when I was last here. I deduce that, apart from in Central Park, horses have been replaced by motor vehicles and people travel vast distances through vehicles of the air, called airplanes, that telephony has become an everyday facet of life through devices that can fit in the palm of a hand and, most impressive of all, milk is now sold in a paper carton. So, that leaves the most obvious question. Where might I find Wells?'

'Wells Fargo?' asked Simone. 'I think there's a branch about two blocks south.'

'H.G. Wells. It is evident that he has managed to get his time machine to work. That is how I arrived here, is it not?'

Georgette looked to Simone who looked back to Georgette.

She said, 'I think we should go to my apartment.'

For the last forty odd minutes, Holmes had been reading Watson's old diary while he sat on Georgette's sofa. The world of instant electricity and gas heating appeared to have no strangeness to him. Like an adopted pet he had readily accepted his new reality, though to Georgette's surprise he had barely nibbled at the blueberry muffins, the only food she'd had at the ready. He finished reading with a sigh, slapping the book together with the finality of a full stop.

'Bless his soul. My dear, dear friend.' He sipped his tea, grimaced. Simone had insisted on making it, saying she was an expert on the basis of having spent a week playing Miss Marple in an amateur production.

Holmes recovered, said to Georgette, 'So you went into cryogenics as a result of finding this diary?'

Simone jumped in. 'No, she went into it on account of falling into a frozen lake when she was a kid. She was dead for twenty minutes.'

'A little over thirteen,' said Georgette. 'And, more correctly, cryonics.'

Holmes said, 'Remarkable. It is not unreasonable that three or four generations on, one finds the same kind of trade or profession: cobblers, solicitors, sea-captains ... but that your interest came from plunging through ice, well, your predecessor, my dear colleague, would certainly ascribe it to divine intervention and for once I may find that a difficult argument to parry. It is as if you were meant to be the one who completed his work.'

Georgette, who was more atheist than agnostic but who detested the idea of coincidence, could not escape the fact that he had parroted her own thoughts. 'It is quite remarkable,' she said.

'Like you two are soul mates,' added Simone, for whom everything could be reduced to a social media grabline.

Georgette squirmed, said, 'You must be starving.' She indicated the muffins, was sure her anxiety would be obvious. 'I'm sorry, they were all I had in the fridge but I could order something in?'

'I have already eaten.'

She wondered if he had found money in her lab. Not that she would have minded.

'You conjecture how I was able to pay for it? There was a chap playing the violin, not badly but not well either, with the case open for gratuities. We came to an arrangement whereby I would play and we would each take half of any proceeds. It was soon apparent that the key to pecuniary success was playing to the most sympathetic audience so we relocated to an Italian area where my recital included a number of tunes that I recalled from my travels there. We were handsomely rewarded and I furnished myself with a delightful meal. The napkin I retained as I was using it to make notes with one of those marvellous nib-less pens my companion loaned me. I highly recommend the place.'

With a flourish he produced a McDonald's napkin with his scrawl across it. Simone turned on her smugly.

'Told you there was nothing wrong with a little fast food.'

Holmes swung back to Georgette. 'You do not approve?'

'The meals are high in sodium and fat.'

'Just what the cold weather calls for, and believe me substantially tastier than boiled yak. Watson and I once found ourselves trekking across ...' He suddenly stopped and pointed to a print on the wall, van Gogh's *Irises*.

'You have one of the Dutchman's paintings!'

'Vincent van Gogh.'

'I only knew him as the Dutchman. I liked his way with colors. I'm pleased to see he finally sold something. I always told Watson he would succeed. Your great-great-grandfather would have none of it: "Don't look like any flowers I've ever seen."'

Holmes employed what to Georgette's ear sounded like a Scottish accent but not as broad as her cousin Ian's.

Predictably, Simone gushed. 'You're amazing. Please, you have to help me with my Brit accents.'

'He may have more urgent priorities,' said Georgette with an edge even Simone couldn't miss. She explained that van Gogh died impoverished but was now considered one of the world's greatest artists.

This seemed to prick Holmes' high spirits. 'Ah, time can be cruel,' he said, and instantly turned inward seemingly overwhelmed by some deep reflection.

Georgette gave him a moment before probing gently. 'So, you have no memory of the events in Switzerland?'

'None at all. My last clear memory is about two months before – February, eighteen ninety-one. It was bitterly cold. Most days I was disguised, walking the streets of East London trying to pick up clues on Jack the Ripper. Did they ever apprehend him?'

'No, his identity remains a mystery.'

'I had my suspicions.'

This time it was her turn to jump in before Simone sidetracked him by asking what those were.

'Forgive me if I seem impertinent,' she was getting the hang of his speech now, 'but you have always been considered a work of fiction, created by Sir Arthur Conan Doyle.'

Holmes stretched, then folded his arms. 'Conan Doyle was a close friend of your great-great-grandfather. When he saw Watson's notes on our case that he ultimately titled *A Study In Scarlet*, he convinced Watson that they should be made public and offered to write them, assuring us that nobody would believe them real. Amazingly, by publishing the story in a Christmas annual, he achieved that.'

'But you kept your real names?'

'Conan Doyle said that Watson was a common enough name that nobody except people from his club might recognize him. "Sherlock Holmes," he said, and I quote, "is such a lurid name that nobody of sound mind will believe it belongs to a real person." The police detectives, who were, I am afraid, as dim as he made out, did have their names altered, as too did the various protagonists and antagonists.'

'Except for Moriarty?'

Holmes looked shocked. 'He wrote about Moriarty?'

'Yes. In a story about ... your demise.'

Holmes stood, began pacing. 'He must have felt that as I was dead, it mattered not. I had forbidden him to write about that evil fellow, lest it inspire more followers. The diary makes no mention of how I came to be on that ledge above the falls. I suppose that shall remain another mystery until my memory returns.'

Simone was about to open her mouth but Georgette's look stayed her.

Georgette felt she should tread carefully here. 'Actually, according to the books, you wrestled Moriarty and tumbled from the ledge together. Neither of you survived. Well, not originally.'

His look told her to proceed.

'There was such an outcry from your legions of fans that Conan Doyle ... brought you back.'

'Brought me back?'

'Yes, you turned up alive after all.'

Holmes made a small dismissive kind of grunt.

Georgette said, 'Perhaps John Watson needed the money to fund his mission to revive you.'

Holmes nodded thoughtfully. 'He would not have taken the money for himself and Conan Doyle could not have continued without his support.'

Georgette said she would pick up a copy of the newer stories. Holmes thanked her.

'And of Moriarty?'

'You were the only body stored in that mausoleum.'

Holmes was deadly serious. 'We must thank the heavens for that.'

Simone, who had begun sneaking pieces of muffin at an ever-increasing rate said, 'So even back then, people didn't think you were real?'

'It is a strange quality of human beings that many who have no reason to imagine you real, still do, while those who have evidence in front of their eyes that you are flesh and blood refute it. One sensible thing Conan Doyle did was to provide an incorrect address. I never had rooms at Baker Street but around the corner in York Street. The Baker Street address was deluged with letters and these provided one or two interesting cases. The police and those who had used my services continued to recommend cases to me but the location was York street.

'Now, I don't wish to seem ungrateful but I would like to acquaint myself with something of the last one-hundred and twenty-nine years, so if you might point me in the direction of a public library ...'

Georgette scooped up her laptop. 'I think you will find everything you need right here.'

She demonstrated the capacity of a computer and the Internet, leaving Holmes thunderstruck. 'You can google most anything,' she explained, leaving empty the search box the way an angler dangles a lure. Holmes' finger started diffidently on the keyboard. Georgette realized even typewriters had probably been quite new to him. But like a bird pecking on some foreign seed who discovers a pleasant taste, once Holmes had typed a few characters he increased his pace. She wondered what he had decided to google and craned her head to see the words 'Sherlock Holmes'. Talk about vanity!

'Now hit enter.' She pointed and he did as commanded. His eyes lit up as an array of movie titles and books filled the screen. Simone materialized at his shoulder.

'See, you're famous. I can show you lots of cool movie sites.'

'Thank you, Simone, that is most kind but I am more comfortable with solo study, divining how the machinery works and improving through trial and error.'

Georgette told him she would make him up a room.

'There's a spare television in there too.' She pointed at the flat screen to show him what she meant.

'Splendid. I don't suppose you would have a pipe and some smoking tobacco?'

'Nobody smokes nowadays, except actors and gamblers. It creates disease and shortens lives.'

'Well I'm one-hundred and sixty-six and it hasn't done me any harm.'

Like a celebrity playing to his fans he directed his smile and quip to Simone who lapped it up.

'You're a pistol, Sherlock.'

Georgette resented feeling like a third wheel in her own apartment. 'There's a tobacco store ten blocks south. We can buy some later but no smoking inside. It's strictly forbidden by the residents committee.'

'Then they should get a new chairman.'

'I am the chairperson.'

Holmes looked down that long nose and said without blinking, 'Of course you are. Fear not, Watson, I shall follow your instructions to the letter.'

She nodded at his outfit. 'And we had better find you some new clothes.'

Simone said, 'I got a whole wardrobe from my last ex. He's about your size.'

Holmes thanked them. 'If you do not think me rude then, I might avail myself of a warm bath.'

Georgette showed him the bathroom and found him a fresh towel, toothbrush and razor. Vance had left a can of shaving cream, which delighted Holmes enormously. He was chuckling, squirting frothy piles on his palms.

Georgette said, 'Anything else you need, I'll be here.'

'Thank you both,' he replied with a charming smile and shut the door.

As soon as they were alone a big grin spread across Simone's face. She whispered, 'He is so hot. "Avail myself" – don't you just love the way he talks?'

'Please. He is older than this building.'

'Given the guys I've dated, I could do with some maturity.'

'You're not going to be dating him. Don't even think about it.'

'So you're interested?'

'Don't be ridiculous.'

'I guess it would be unethical, like a doctor dating a patient.'

She was *soooo* trying.

'He's not a patient.'

'Okay, like an undertaker dating a corpse.'

One thing about Simone, she had a way with words.

'I'll check in later,' she added.

'I'd prefer you gave him a day or two to settle in.'

'You're banning me?'

'Of course not, but he needs to take it slow.'

'Don't worry, I've got an audition tonight for a collective. You've got thirty-six hours Simone-free. After that, may the best butt win.'

Simone was opening the door when Georgette remembered the snow globe.

'You must have left it here.'

Simone examined it. 'Cute. Never seen it before. You don't want it?'

'No.'

Simone pecked her on the cheek and left with her booty.

It was only then when she stood alone in the room, Holmes' humming of 'Rule, Britannia!' seeping from the bathroom, that Georgette allowed herself to savor for the first time just what she had achieved. A man thought dead for well over a century was alive and well, happily humming while bathing. Simone was right: she would win a Nobel prize for this. Her legs felt suddenly weak and she took herself over to the armchair and sat down. She would have to begin writing a press release. Probably the media would do their own photos but she might need to think about what she was wearing. Right now, she resembled a bag lady who'd crawled out of a dumpster. She looked around the room, taking in its simplicity: the family photos, the small treasures she had acquired over the years from second-hand shops.

She knew her life would never be the same again.

8

One of the few good things about being a head taller than most everybody else around was you got to see if there were any blockages up ahead on a sidewalk. Everything else was pretty much downside. The seats on the subway were too cramped, and if you stood, you had better have your hair down. You wear a high pony in a subway car, you were asking for trouble. And airplanes, forget it, torture. Unless maybe you were in first class, which she definitely could not afford, although one day she planned to get there. It was easier for tall men – people looked up to them, not just literally, ha ha. Tall women, you were a freak, and it didn't matter if you were black like she was, or white, it was just as hard. Sometimes at a function she would be standing there and look across the room and her eyes would meet those of a tall white girl, maybe not as tall as her but close, and they would share that moment – you're like me, sucks, right?

And people would always say things like 'you'd make a great model', except you knew you wouldn't because you had big chunky thighs. At high school they'd made her play basketball but she wasn't competitive and didn't have the coordination you needed. She was just tall. And that was why it was kind of ridiculous that what she was really good at was working with minute pieces of things. Although, she supposed, having those long bony fingers helped. She loved her job at the museum, loved putting together the puzzle of an ancient tunic from tiny fragments, or a wall-hanging or, on one occasion, a shattered tank turret.

That had given her the shivers but she had not complained and was happy to help out her colleagues. Tanks had been a horrible memory, one she had wanted to erase forever, but you can never erase, you must simply learn to be able to live with the past. She had been nine years old when her family fled to the United States where they had been accepted as refugees fleeing persecution. 'Persecution' was a nice name for what her family and fellow Christians had experienced at the hands of the Sudanese army; murder, rape and torture were more appropriate words. She had been lucky, young enough not to be collecting water with her older sister and two cousins the day they had vanished. One girl, who was behind the others and managed to hide, said they had all been carried off by soldiers. Their bodies were never found. As terrible as their circumstances were liable to be, she prayed they were still alive. She felt no resentment toward her fellow Americans but they really had no idea how fortunate they were. All those schoolgirls taken in Nigeria, and there was barely a ripple in the pond. But she did not have the luxury of turning a blind eye. She knew from what terrors she had been spared and every day she thanked God and prayed for her sister and cousins.

She left the busy stream of people and, as was her daily routine on the way home from work, turned into St Thomas'. It was quiet this time of night, the lights set dim. It was a large church, long, not so wide. In summer during the day, the stained glass near the altar threw beautiful fractured colors but it was night and near winter, and shadows triumphed.

Like I'm in a Rembrandt painting, she thought idly as she walked down towards the front of the church, turned into a pew on her right and kneeled down. There was only one other person in the church, a woman, small and solid, who got up and blessed herself before leaving. She looked Latina. Most of the faces she saw at mass were like that. She didn't bother now with formal prayers, just let herself drift, bringing to her mind her sister's face as she last remembered it when she was thirteen. If she was still alive, she would be thirty, likely with children but not allowed to pray to her God, or celebrate her family, all of that long buried. But she would have her children and would love them, that would be something.

She wondered if her sister thought of her every day too. Hoped she did, and knew she was loved and missed and not forgotten.

She heard the soft scuff of leather soles somewhere behind her. Please let Ivy be well and happy, she prayed. If she has children, let them be beautiful, if she has a husband, let him be kind. If she is dead may she be experiencing the joy of eternal –

Bang!

Something hard hit her from behind and immediately her brain slowed, even before the throb. She tried to cry out but there was no air, steel hands on her throat. She threw her arms out, tried to turn around, leveraged herself up somehow, lashed back with an elbow rotating her body, striking something, but the strength was rushing from her quickly and she was dizzy, everything darker like she had been swallowed by the beast and was disappearing into its maw.

10

They were strolling back towards her apartment, the brisk air numbing her cheeks, or maybe that was the reaction to what she'd had to pay to outfit Holmes tip-to-toe. She wouldn't have been surprised if her card had been rejected for lack of funds. She had to say though, he looked impressive in his three-piece suit – Holmes had insisted on a waistcoat and been taken by a homburg but in the end had settled for a woolen cap. Cell-phones, tablets and video screens he took in his stride but on hearing the price of his clothes he almost gagged. When she handed over a credit card to pay, it rattled him to the core.

In a kind of awed wonder he had said, 'A piece of plastic I can carry in my pocket and use in any country in the world. My Lord, what criminals would do with this.'

She told him exactly what they did: gave it to their customers for free and charged them twenty-seven percent interest.

The one item that did look rather odd was the watch with the Hulk on the dial that Holmes sported on his wrist. They'd bought it from a discount store where she'd picked up a bunch of old Sherlock Holmes DVDs. It was the cheapest one in the store. Holmes said he did not mind so long as it kept time, and was delighted that it did not even need to be wound. Earlier they had taken the subway downtown to the Mysterious Bookshop and bought a Sherlock Holmes complete collection. This was now being rapidly perused by Holmes who appeared immune to the ever-present wail of vehicle sirens. The subway's spidery station map he had comprehended within minutes.

'What he's done,' Holmes said, stabbing the book with his finger, 'is to include many of my earlier cases and pass them off as post-Reichenbach.

And look at this fellow ...' he was brandishing the DVD case featuring Basil Rathbone, '... this is supposed to be my likeness? You could play billiards with that nose.'

Walking beside him now, Georgette thought there was a likeness. True, Holmes' nose wasn't quite so long and after more nourishment he probably would gain weight, but Rathbone was in the ball-park. As they passed a female patrol cop, Holmes openly stared and she returned the favor.

'Women police?'

'Women lawyers, judges, dentists, truck drivers, soldiers. You disapprove?'

'I merely observe. In my experience women have always been the cleverest and most resourceful adversaries. Properly trained, a female, even in physical conflict, can match a male of the same or greater mass and I have known markswomen of astonishing accuracy.'

Her phone buzzed. She guessed it would be her father, still on vacation and feeling guilty now it was in its second week. He'd called twice during the shopping expedition but fearing it too precarious to let Holmes shop by himself she had ignored the calls. She checked her phone. Yep, Harry alright, he'd persist until she answered. She'd call when she was back in the apartment where she could isolate Holmes. Holmes considered her thoughtfully.

'I hope you are not ignoring that on my account.'

'Not at all. It's just somebody trying to sell me floor coverings or something.'

Holmes gave no indication whether or not he believed her. Carrying the paper bag containing his old clothes, his eyes drank in his environment.

'This Hitler was what your great-great-grandfather would have called a "rum fellow". And yet, despite those terrible wars and seemingly ceaseless conflicts, the world here continues to prosper: man's innate goodness overwhelms his desire for evil. Although I see ...' his eyes had fixed on a point up ahead where a crowd was emerging from the subway, '... it is not a victory can be assumed won. Some games remain the same: the dip and the runner.'

Without warning, he took two quick giant strides and then his long arm shot out and he seized a passing youth.

The kid snapped, 'Hey, what do you think you're doing?'

Exactly what Georgette was thinking. The kid tried to pull away but Holmes' grip was iron.

Holmes said, 'Hand me the wallet now or I break this arm.'

Something about his manner brooked no resistance. The kid, not more than eighteen, reached into his pocket with his free hand. But what he brought out was not a wallet but a knife. Like a sinkhole had opened in front of them, the swarm of passers-by began to divert.

'Oh, dear,' said Holmes, the way a guest might react if told their hotel room had been double-booked. Then, as the kid lunged, Holmes calmly stepped aside, and twisted forward the arm he had not released, forcing his attacker into a somersault. The youth landed on his back on the sidewalk and cried in pain, dropping the knife, which Holmes snared, retracted and pocketed, before reaching into the boy's jacket and removing a wallet. Nodding at a tall man in a bomber jacket who had stopped to witness the affray, he handed it to Georgette and said, 'That gentleman's I believe.'

Feeling like the Boy Wonder to Holmes' Batman, Georgette held out the wallet.

'Sir, is this yours?'

The man checked his pockets, amazed. Those in the crowd who had witnessed the whole thing began applauding. For a moment Georgette thought Holmes looked as if he was about to take a bow but he made do with a wave. Taking advantage of the distraction, the would-be thief scrambled to his feet and dashed away across the street to the accompaniment of honking horns.

Georgette was still lecturing Holmes when they entered the apartment.

'You need to be careful. These days most criminals are armed. They'll blow you away soon as spit on you.'

Holmes nodded sombrely. 'I forgot myself, pontificating on man's innate goodness.' He made a derisive sound. 'Men are as men have always been: some very good, a few very bad, most in between, cutting their cloth to whatever they might get away with; in a monastery a piece of extra bread, on Victoria Station a wallet, on the battlefield a scalp. And weapons – my God, I have never seen so many weapons: airplanes and submarines that can obliterate a city in the time it takes a man to drink his tea. Don't worry, I have seen the moving pictures. I tell you, Watson, when it is easier to purchase a gun than a pipe, a society is in trouble. The death of schoolchildren at the hands of fellow students is madness. And what is worse, predictable.'

There being no logical way to explain why nothing changed, Georgette did not even try.

'It must have been safer in your day,' she observed.

'Coal dust and disease carried off a lot more children than bullets. Man fixes one malaise only to disseminate another. Our stupidity never ceases to amaze.'

Holmes went to the gas heater and clicked it on. He'd learned that quickly, observed Georgette. It was around nine now and she was hungry.

'How about I order in some Chinese food?'

'You can do that?'

'Yes.'

'Perhaps for yourself. You have been more than generous. But I promise I shall repay you at the earliest opportunity.'

'Thank you for your offer but believe me, when we sell our story we'll have more than enough cash.'

'What do you mean?'

Georgette explained that the story of his return from the dead was going to be huge.

'The media will pay a lot of money. It'll fund my research, pay off my debts ... and my sister's debts. And you'll be able to do whatever you want to do. I thought we could go fifty-fifty on the initial piece, everything else from then on, lecture tours, TV appearances, is yours.'

'You understand none of that is possible.'

'Oh yes, it is. This is the biggest story since man walked on the moon.'

'We did? I must have missed that, I was skimming, I'm afraid. The point is, Watson, we simply can't go public, I will be treated like a freak. That's even if they believe you.'

'I have the evidence. Everything has been recorded.'

'What if I deny it? Or simply disappear? Where is your evidence then?'

'My research could save thousands of people who were thought dead.'

'It still can. Just without me.'

'There is no story without you.'

'No story but a truth. As a scientist, which is the more important?'

The Harry Potter theme cut in. Garry Benson was calling.

'Garry?'

'I heard you were back,' he said.

'Yes, sorry. I've been working on something.'

'Well, I don't know if you're free right now ...' Typical timing. She was about to beg off when he said, '... but our serial killer has struck again.'

'Oh no. Is this victim number three?'

Like a beagle that has picked up a scent, Holmes' body straightened.

'That we know of,' said Benson. 'If you have a chance to give me a second opinion on time of death, I would appreciate it.'

There was never anything good about a murder crime scene but they were all memorable. Seeing the outline of Sherlock Holmes waiting patiently in the umbra beyond the techs' lights made it especially so. She had told Benson she had a friend, a detective, visiting from England and hoped he might join her at the scene. Benson had said sure, so long as he wore the crime suit and took no photos. Georgette had thought Benson had given Holmes the once over when they had met just inside the church.

'You with the Yard?' he had asked.

'Private. I have consulted with them on occasion.'

'Well, sorry we're not meeting under better circumstances. If you could wait here for now, Percy?'

'Of course.'

Lipinski, Georgette had seen, was down the church aisle where the lights were set up. Benson walked Georgette down.

'The second victim, Carmen Cavanagh, was killed identical to the first: knocked out, raped, throat cut in that order. Her body was found in her apartment garage Upper East Side. That was three weeks ago. No wits, no prints, no DNA. Now this.'

The techs had begun processing the scene but had stepped aside for her to give a second opinion on time of death. The body of the female victim had been found folded into a confessional whose door was now propped open. One look said it was the same killer.

Georgette and Lipinski shared a short greeting and then she squatted down to get to work, the smell of blood familiar and repulsive. While most of the girl's blood had pooled in the confessional doorway, there was still plenty around the body. Georgette thought the dead girl striking, verging on beautiful. She was black with high cheekbones and a very slender neck with a deep, dark, slash. Her tights and underwear were bunched around her ankles.

Georgette remembered the new photographer from the first murder.

'Sorry, Kelvin, can we dim these for now?'

The heat from the intense lights from the camera and from those positioned around the body could make judging time of death difficult but Georgette knew how to allow for that. The lights dimmed, Georgette gave it a moment, then carefully felt the body. After checking her thermometer, she consulted the charts stored on her phone that gave insight into idiosyncrasies of buildings in the area, a mountain of data she had begun accumulating in her undergrad days. She carefully lowered the girl's arm, noting a matching wound to that on Gina Scaroldi's thigh.

'Best guess, six forty-nine.'

Greta Lipinski said, 'Tom put it between six forty-five and seven ten.'

Good. It was rare Georgette had a disagreement with the medical examiner, and never so far with Tom, but occasionally there were elements they hadn't quite considered – the insulation of various clothes for example. Lipinski, who had obviously been briefed by the first responders, continued for Benson's benefit.

'She was discovered just before seven-thirty. One of the helpers came in to make sure all was in order before lock-up. Midtown South recognized the similarity to our cases right away and called us in.'

Georgette guessed that the Midtown South Homicide detectives had allowed Benson to take over the case. This being the third homicide though, it was likely help would be drafted from all the affected homicide command posts.

'Please tell me there's a security camera,' Benson said.

'There is but it hasn't worked for three months.'

'No joy from the Roosevelt Island camera then?' guessed Georgette.

'A shape, nothing more. May not have even been the killer. We cross-checked all the social media contacts of both victims and got squat.'

Benson asked Kelvin if he'd downloaded his photo files from the scene. The young man, with a subtle correction, confirmed he had 'uploaded' everything already. Georgette could tell Benson was ready to head back to the central command.

Georgette said, 'Might Percy take a look?'

'Sure.'

Georgette signalled for Holmes to join them. Clad in his crime suit, Holmes made his way down the aisle. Holmes had approved heartily when Georgette had explained the crime suit was to avoid contamination of evidence.

'We don't have long,' said Benson, 'the techs are still going and will want to get back to her.'

Holmes squatted down and examined the girl without touching her. He also sniffed all around her like a bloodhound.

Benson said, 'Her name is Lucy Bassey. Looks the same as the others, except they were white. Killer is careful, no DNA on the previous victims.'

Georgette saw Holmes was mystified by the arcane words. 'DN ...'

'A,' she added.

'Right,' he said, meeting her gaze. The lights had not yet been turned back up so Georgette shone her flashlight for him.

She asked if Holmes noticed anything unusual.

'She's extremely tall,' he muttered and Georgette realized it was probably foolish to expect Holmes to have some blinding insight. 'And there is a faint odor of ... turpentine.'

'Her ID says she works at the museum,' said Benson.

'That wound pattern on her arm is the same as the others had,' said Georgette.

'May I?' asked Holmes, gesturing he wanted to touch the body. Benson nodded.

On the way over, Georgette had explained about the flesh taken from the victims. Now Holmes examined the wound.

'Would anybody have a magnifying glass on them?'

'Man after my own heart,' said Greta Lipinski, handing one over. 'I don't care what they say about using a camera. I love this little sucker.'

Holmes scrutinized the wound. He sighed, handed the glass back with a thank you and stood.

'You think that mark is a ship?' Georgette was unable to contain herself.

'I'm not sure what it is. I am afraid I need more information.'

Benson had been accommodating. Georgette had expected him to refuse her suggestion Holmes view the crime scene photos of the first two murders, but though he looked sorely tempted to deny her, he did not. In the car on the way to the command centre, Georgette quietly alerted Holmes to the fact that these days, homicides were pictorially documented with both stills and video but he'd already deduced as much, watching Kelvin work.

'What's DNA?' he whispered.

She thought about how best to explain. 'The cell matter that is unique to each of us. Think of it as a genetic fingerprint. It can be passed from the killer to the victim by blood, skin, saliva.'

Holmes' face took on a kind of rapture. 'For years I yearned for such a weapon of detection.'

'It only helps if the DNA is on file or we can match it to a suspect. But thanks to a whole lot of TV shows and crime novels, somebody who plans to kill in advance knows to wear a suit just like we did and leave no trace.'

Holmes stroked his chin with his long fingers. 'There must have been much blood and yet nobody seems to have witnessed anybody leaving these scenes covered in blood. Yes, he plans.' He pressed his face to the window. Outside, Manhattan blurred like a flying bird photographed by a cheap camera.

Because of the expanding geography of the crimes and the number of victims, there was a likelihood that the command post would be moved. For now though, it was still in the squad room of the 112 in Queens. Leaving the arduous doorknocking and canvassing of potential witnesses with Midtown South detectives and patrol officers, Lipinski and Benson were gathering all background information on Lucy Bassey, preparing to head out to interview family and colleagues of the dead woman, pretty much ignoring Georgette and Holmes. Having mastered the idea of a touchscreen, Holmes was zooming in and out deftly as he minutely examined the photos of the three crime scenes.

'My Lord, Watson, if I'd have had these aids in my day of investigation, there'd not have been a criminal free in the whole of Queen Victoria's empire.'

He was looking at photos of Carmen Cavanagh's car in its garage when he suddenly let out a small cry and furiously flicked back through the gallery of crime photos.

The exclamation he'd made had drawn the interest of Benson and he came to peer at the screen.

'What is this?' Holmes was pointing at a close-up of the sneakers on the feet of the first victim, Gina.

'You don't have Puma in England?' Benson was surprised.

'A brand logo,' whispered Georgette to Holmes.

'The manufacturer's stamp?' said Holmes. His face was impassive but Georgette sensed his mind churning.

Georgette nodded, aware that Benson was growing more suspicious by the minute. Holmes flicked back to the garage shot and pointed at the car's bonnet.

'And this?'

'A Jaguar,' said Georgette.

'I know you got those in England.'

She picked up an edge in the detective's tone, like Holmes was acting the fool. She tried to smooth things.

'It's Percy's process.' Georgette had mixed with enough detectives to know that to some degree they all followed some obscure, largely personal 'process'. The word covered a multitude of indulgences and failings and could provide Holmes a smokescreen.

Holmes might as well have been in a silent chamber. He paid them no attention at all but rather began smiling, flexing his feet, lifting himself up as he balanced on his toes before dropping down on his heels and repeating the ritual.

'What did you observe about our third girl?' he asked Georgette.

'That she'd died around six forty-nine.'

'But what was the most obvious thing?'

Georgette had no idea what he was driving at. He turned his gaze.

'Benson?'

'That she was dead.'

The detective's answers were growing more terse. She would have to tell Holmes not to use people's surnames.

'Was that the most obvious thing? She might have been sleeping if we didn't already know.' Holmes turned back to her now. 'At the time you asked me if I'd noticed anything, do you recall?'

'You said that she was tall.'

'Not just tall, very tall. A giraffe.'

Benson's mouth opened. He was about to say something but Holmes stole the words away.

'A puma, a jaguar and a giraffe. I know what this is.'

He spun the screen to a close-up of the killer's mark.

'We think it's a ship,' Georgette said.

'Almost.' Holmes took an actor's beat before delivering. 'It's an ark.'

11

Holmes patiently clicked through all the photos Benson's team had assembled on the case. Not just the actual crime scenes but the homes of Gina Scaroldi and Carmen Cavanagh. Gina Scaroldi, a small studio apartment, neat, bare walls bar for a couple of photos, inexpensive furniture, typical of a student. Carmen Cavanagh: opulent investment-banker apartment, spacious, modern art, widescreen.

Lipinski was talking, 'We've checked everything we could think of – pest exterminators, medical records, you name it. We couldn't find any link between our first two vics, no Facebook pals, no Instagram followers, nothing.'

Holmes looked up from his labor and Georgette mouthed a silent 'Later.'

Holmes returned his gaze to the photos. 'He hunts them but only, I think, in his mind, to rescue them.' Now he swung around, wriggling this way and that trying to make the office chair more comfortable.

Greta Lipinski turned a pen over as she pondered. 'Rescue them from what?'

'The end of the world, if I were to hazard a guess. Or a godless world, which might to him be the same thing.'

'You a profiler?' Benson wasn't being a smartass. It was a genuine question.

Holmes, she saw, had no idea what Benson meant. 'I think Percy is more a follow-the-evidence kind of guy. At least he was in the past.' She hit that with special emphasis, hoping Holmes got her drift. 'I don't think he lays claims to knowing what is in a criminal's mind.'

'No, that is true,' said Holmes. She sensed he would normally have waved his pipe around but without one was at a loss what to do with his hands. 'Nonetheless, we can generally deduce, can we not, whether a criminal may be acting for financial gain, out of revenge, because of love, or in this case, what seems likely, because of a perverse line of logic and reasoning? Clearly there would appear to be no financial gain here. Love seems highly unlikely, and there's no indication yet of revenge, although that may play some role in his selection, it's too early to say.'

Benson said, 'Well, that's what we've figured all along, that we're dealing with a sexual psycho. But are you saying he thinks he's doing them a favor?'

'It's an interpretation. It may not be the right one. Dr Watson is correct, I am no expert on the human mind but prefer to follow the objective nature of physical evidence. Nonetheless one cannot help but conjecture on the significance of the ark.'

'You think the killer is religious?' asked Georgette.

'I don't think we can speculate on anything more than he is familiar with the story of Noah's ark, although the slitting of the throat is a typical Old Testament manner of offering sacrifice.'

'The techs tell us it is a curved blade, as traditionally was used for slaughter. You think he's targeting these women in particular?'

Holmes stood, becoming more animated by the minute. 'The first young woman may have been a type. He is Noah looking for a gazelle – or in this case a puma. Where will he find a puma? On a running track. He may not have selected this particular young woman until he was on the spot, able to see she matched his metaphor.'

'Or,' said Georgette, 'he might have seen her in her Puma gear in a gym or at her apartment and marked her out. It would have been dark that time of morning.'

'Absolutely true, Watson. The second young woman, Carmen Cavanagh...' Holmes pointed at her headshot, '... he may have known more intimately. There is no public access to the murder location. One surmises he lives there himself, works there or was already with her when she arrived.'

Benson said, 'We figured the same. Manhattan North canvassed the area. No witnesses, no CCTV, no murder weapon. We checked out every resident we could find in the apartment and got no flags.'

Greta Lipinski added, 'But of course, somebody may have had a friend or guest staying they never told us about.'

Benson explained that vision of Carmen driving into the building's garage that evening after work showed only her in the vehicle but he had a gut feeling the killer may have secreted himself inside Carmen's car when it was parked elsewhere. Holmes' head was bobbing up and down, showing he approved of this theory.

Lipinski said, 'We've checked out the CCTV of the parking garage she used near Battery Park, all the vehicles that arrived within forty-five minutes of Carmen leaving work for the day and climbing into her car. Theory being ...'

Holmes jumped in. 'That the killer may have arrived in his own vehicle, parked, hidden in her vehicle and waited for his moment to strike.'

'Exactly,' said Benson. Georgette felt like she was watching a tennis match. Lipinski ran on.

'Unfortunately there's no vision of where Carmen's vehicle was parked, only of her leaving alone. No red flags on the drivers of any of the vehicles that arrived at the garage that day, or the staff. However, we did have one vehicle, a car stolen from the Bronx two hours earlier. It drives in forty minutes before Carmen left work.'

Benson embellished. 'We got footage of the driver,' Benson said, 'cap, glasses, gloves – could be male or female. No fingerprints. We're running DNA tests just in case.'

Georgette got their theory, Holmes enunciated it.

'You think he knew where she worked and parked. That the killer stole a vehicle to gain entry without identifying himself. Yes, that makes sense. And it would seem to indicate he had been in her apartment garage as well at some time, and knew he could strike unobserved. He may simply have got lucky with the relative isolation of the murder scene, although I fear otherwise. Miss Bassey, on the other hand, could easily have caught his eye on the night. She would be a head taller than most people, hard to miss. Or he could have noticed her some previous time, realized she used that church.'

Benson said, 'But Noah's not keeping them in captivity. He kills them and has sex with them, mutilates them and abandons them.'

'"Noah": we have our moniker.' Lipinski nodded approvingly. While Georgette wasn't overly fond of these handles, such shorthand was probably inevitable. Holmes was not to be distracted.

'His saving them, I am afraid, is only metaphorical. What he is really interested in would appear to be a symbolic continuation of the species, or at the very least his own line, by having intercourse with these women. He then discards them. Perhaps he wants to have children but cannot.

Then again, it may simply be ...'

'An excuse to get his perverted fucking rocks off.'

Lipinski sat back and flipped the pen she'd been fiddling with.

'Aptly put, Detective.'

Holmes stifled a yawn. I need to be careful, thought Georgette. Who knows what his stamina is like.

'We should actually be heading off,' said Georgette. 'Percy has had a long journey.'

Benson said, 'We'll need to visit Lucy's relatives. Midtown is checking CCTV images near the church, hopefully we get lucky. Thanks for your help, Percy.'

'You realize,' said a sombre Holmes, 'that if I'm right about the ark, there will be more victims.'

The two detectives shared a look.

'Yeah, we'd already considered that. Also, that these might not be the first. We'll put out requests for any homicide-sexual assaults that might have any connection with an animal theme. You'll be asleep long before us.'

As the cab brought them home, they sat once more in silence, the electric lights of the city bathing them in the same jaundiced river. She thought Holmes looked drawn, and was worried she had allowed him to do too much and said so.

'No, not at all Watson. I admit my demeanor is perhaps not quite the top pickle but that's because I have this idea in my head that I should know more about this case than I do.'

'You've had a fairly lengthy sabbatical.'

'Indeed. What is Facebook?'

She gave a cursory explanation of the nature of social media.

'The twenty-first century's equivalent of the first-class dining car,' he mused and then, pursing his lips, recommenced brooding. When they were a dozen blocks from her apartment he suddenly sat up and pointed out the window.

'There!'

He'd spied the tobacco store she had mentioned. She asked the driver to pull over. It was only a twenty-minute walk from here and the night though cool, was fine and clear. While she paid the fare, Holmes scampered inside.

She found him perusing a variety of pipes. The shop assistant, a man who if you met him on the street you might guess was a German butcher, asked what he was in the market for.

'Full bent.'

'Briar or meerschaum?'

Georgette said, 'Whatever is under thirty bucks.' The cold threat of austerity had made itself at home in Georgette's bosom ever since Holmes had kicked up about the media deal.

Holmes and the salesman shared the kind of look that Georgette might have given somebody who said a Kandinsky looked like a kindergarten painting.

'Best I can do is this one, thirty-four ninety-five.' The salesman whisked a pipe from under the counter. They all looked the same to Georgette.

She said, 'Okay, but for that you can throw in some tobacco.'

The guy turned her way as if he wished he had his cleaver handy.

When they emerged from the shop, pipe and tobacco snugly in his coat pocket, Holmes said, 'I must say, Watson, you are rather adroit when it comes to negotiation.'

'I'm not adroit, I'm near destitute, and will be completely if you don't change your mind about publicity.'

'Come, Watson, not so gloomy. Once we solve this case, we can devote our attention to these other trifles.'

A Nobel prize, and he called it a trifle?

'What do you mean, "we" solve the case?'

'Let Benson make his enquiries and we shall make ours.'

She was about to tell him that would not be happening when they passed a twenty-four hour pharmacy and more mundane matters like toothpaste elbowed their way into her thoughts.

'Need some supplies,' she said and entered. Holmes followed. She grabbed the cheapest toothpaste and some razors.'

'You have no brother do you, Watson?'

'No.' She turned to find Holmes weighing a can of the same brand of shaving cream as Vance's.

'It crossed my mind as to whom the can in your lodgings belongs. Clearly it is not yours, as it was covered in a film of dust, yet was almost full. The absence of a wedding ring suggests you are not currently married and the absence of photos and the use of your father's surname testify you are no widow. Divorce is possible but given your age and studies, unlikely.'

Like she wanted this discussion in a public place.

'That's correct.'

Holmes pursed his lips. 'So you find yourself a spinster?'

Several women in the shop looked around. She felt like tearing a razor from its packaging and using it on him.

'Yes.' She moved on quickly.

'The gentleman was a ... lodger?'

'If you have a very loose interpretation of the word ... gentleman.' She realized she was clamping her jaw. Vance had informed her he was breaking up from her by Snapchat, embellished with an image of a broken heart. Two weeks later he'd moved in with a twenty-two year old Brazilian graphic designer. 'I'd rather not talk about this in public.'

'Of course, my apologies.'

Holmes bowed and took himself off. Now she would have to explain to him about Vance and sex before marriage and ... her attention shifted. Fifty percent off Nina Ricci perfume? She had always been a sucker for Nina. On the other hand, there was twenty percent off a cleanser and she knew she'd have a lot more use for that. But could she really afford either?

A raised voice stopped her in her tracks.

'Call yourself a pharmacist, and you don't stock cocaine?'

She charged around the aisle to find Holmes wagging his finger at the young man behind the counter.

'Please, Percy. They may not get your sense of English humour here. After all ...' laying it on, '... cocaine is *illegal*.'

He was aghast. 'Not possible. Freud's treated half the parliamentarians in Europe with it. They would never ban it.'

She uttered a stagey laugh. 'That's very convincing.' She turned to the pharmacist. 'For his new role his acting coach told him to live every minute as if he's a Victorian English gentleman.'

The pharmacist was probably normally bored out of his skull through these hours because he instantly perked up.

'Who are you supposed to be?'

'Sherlock Holmes,' Holmes said.

The pharmacist eyed him carefully then shook his head. 'No, too short. And you need the funny little hat.'

'"Funny little hat."' Holmes tossed his cap onto the sofa, still rankled despite the exertion of walking back. Georgette was busy sorting through a large garbage bag of men's clothes that had been left inside the door:

Simone, true to her word. It was all pretty much jeans and tee-shirts, bar a pair of short pajamas and an old overcoat. Georgette was pleasantly surprised to find they had been freshly washed. She handed them to Holmes. He sorted through them the way an English master might a pile of badly spelt essays.

'The fashion of gentlemen these days, if I may say so, is bereft of style. With the exception of the fellow in the poster above the tobacco store.'

Georgette rifled her memory. 'James Bond. He's a fictional spy.'

'Definitely fictional from what I have seen in the manner of gentlemen's attire. Thank Simone. I shall make use of these.' He held up a pair of jeans, and a half-dozen tee-shirts bearing the name of death-metal or thrash-metal bands or whatever they were; scrap-metal as far as Georgette was concerned. He also scooped up the short pajamas and a pair of complimentary airline slippers. After hanging the clothes in his wardrobe, he re-emerged, entered the kitchen and began clattering in the fridge.

'I must say, Watson, this idea of the cold meat safe is extremely functional but does not appear to be being put to any use.'

'I'll shop tomorrow. I've been a fraction busy bringing you back to life.'

He closed the fridge, wiped his face with his palm.

'My apologies. It's frustration. This case is tolling a bell but I am deaf to its ring. Had I been able to purchase some cocaine, the cloth covering my ears may have been ripped away. Every investigator could do with the assistance of that wonder drug.'

'I'll be sure to suggest that to my father.'

'No matter how impressive the scientific tools at one's disposal, if one has not an agile brain to wield them, they are but skittles without a ball.'

'Perhaps you'll be sharper in the morning after a good night's sleep.'

'Indeed. Thank you for everything, Watson. I mean that most sincerely. Your great-great-grandfather would be justifiably proud. If you would allow me to excuse myself?'

'Of course.'

Holmes entered his bedroom and closed the door. The weird thing was, this was starting to feel normal. Georgette checked her messages and saw three from Simone. For more privacy she headed to her own bedroom before calling her sister.

'How's Sherlock doing?' asked Simone.

'Please, call him Percy. He thanks you for the clothes.'

Georgette ran through all that had happened. She expected a

sympathetic ear from Simone on the question of publicity but was surprised.

'You can't blame him. He's right. He'll be treated like a freak.'

'Not handled the right way. This is one of the great scientific discoveries. I can't keep quiet about it. Lives could be saved.'

'Maybe he'll save lives in another way. Like with this investigation.'

'It's not the same. He could still do that.'

'No, I'm sorry, Georgi, but you want this to be about you. Hey, I get you're pissed you can't tell anybody. But you know what? You still did it. So what if those nerds don't know about it. Play their game. Find some frozen monkeys – or a woolly mammoth, right? Get some mammoth buried in an avalanche a thousand years ago and revive that. I'll catch you tomorrow. I really want to see our friend again.'

The call ended with Georgette miffed. Worse, part of what Simone had said was eating away. Maybe she did just want this to be about her?

Something woke Georgette, a sound, close by. She blinked awake, listened. Yes, somebody was moving around in the apartment.

'Holmes, is that you?'

The instant she called out, she regretted it. What if it wasn't him? She'd just alerted an intruder. Footsteps moved to her door. She tensed, cast about for a weapon, grabbed the book off her nightstand. A paperback. Hopeless.

'My apologies if I disturbed you.'

Holmes' voice was muffled by the closed door. She looked at her phone, saw it was 2.45.

'Are you okay?'

She clicked on her light, got out of bed, threw on her robe and opened her door. Holmes stood there in short pajamas wearing a Slayer tee-shirt and holding a glass of water.

'I was working on something and got thirsty.'

'You were working on something at three in the morning?'

'I commenced an hour ago. I suddenly woke and realized what I should have done the instant I saw those victims.'

'What was that?'

'It has happened before: in Rome in eighteen eighty-eight.'

Ten minutes later they were side by side on the sofa hunched over her computer. Holmes was talking.

'I was contacted by an Italian detective, a friend of the mayor of Rome but I was fully involved with the Ripper case at that time and could offer no assistance.'

'Are you sure it wasn't the Ripper?'

'There were many differences. The Roman killer strangled and used a knife to cut the throat, no genital mutilation. At each body the killer left a picture of an animal cut from a children's book.'

Georgette tapped away on the computer, searching for hits with keywords Rome, Murder, 1888. Nothing remotely echoing Holmes' story showed up. She tried different keywords. Still nothing that sang. She couldn't help wondering if he might have imagined it, hated herself for doing so.

'There's no mention here.'

'The murders were never made public but I committed to memory the sequence: puma, jaguar, giraffe. There may have been more after that but I would have been dead by then. If I may?'

She watched as Holmes typed in a query in Italian and hit Enter. Only one hit was thrown up. He translated.

'This mentions the murder of a young woman whose body was found by the Spanish Steps in September of eighteen eighty-eight. A cut-out of a drawing of a giraffe was left by her body. The case was never solved.'

'There's no mention of other murders?'

'They were attempting to suppress information so as not to cause panic but I suspect the Spanish Steps was such a public location that the murder became known.' He reflected a moment and then typed in the words 'Pasquale Ometti'.

'He was the Italian who contacted me,' he explained.

Apart from a few Facebook pages for contemporary Pasquale Omettis there was only one entry, and it was in English. Georgette couldn't help herself, she swung the computer back her way.

On the screen appeared: *Crimini d'Italia*, Pasquale Ometti. First edition 1904. Summer Catalog 2020, Edwards Rare Books.

Holmes uttered a cry of affirmation. 'It seems Ometti finally wrote about the case.'

'Do you think it was solved?'

'Given the lack of entries here, I doubt it. The police love to trumpet a success.'

A webpage link followed. Georgette hit Enter and up flashed a page showing a website for Edwards Rare Books. On Contacts she found a phone number with an address for Greenwich Village.

'This place is local,' she said in case Holmes hadn't followed but his eyes were those of a hawk's on prey. Next, she searched within the site, typing in the title and author's name. Up came the listing with the word 'Sold'.

'Logically,' said Holmes, 'whoever the killer is had knowledge of these earlier murders, and as the only reference would appear to be Signor Ometti's book ...'

'It must be somebody with access to the book.'

'Precisely. We need to find out to whom the book was sold, who supplied the book in the first place, and who may have handled it between those times.'

Georgette felt obliged to point out that they would not have much say in the matter.

'We need to make Benson aware of this information.'

Holmes seemed about to object but all he said was, 'Quite so. The scent of a crime almost makes me forget that I am many thousands of miles and more than a century from my usual jurisdiction.'

With that he wished her goodnight and returned to his room. Georgette could not help but empathize. You didn't have to be a century out of step to feel you didn't know your place in the world.

Tonight, when she let herself into the apartment, it felt different. Oh, the furniture was the same as she'd left it, the bamboo dresser, the rattan chairs with the colorful cushions that she was still pinching herself about – thirty dollars, you just never saw them anymore, anywhere. She had preceded that whole tiki-bar, Tahitian vibe by ... how many years ago did she buy them? At least seven. One day she would make it there. Maybe with him. It was a long time since she had allowed herself to think like that. She looked at the photos of her and her girlfriends that she had slung under the mantlepiece on a piece of string. All of them in leis. That had been a fun night, and who would have thought Sirena could make cocktails like that?

She had invited him to dinner and he had accepted. That was why tonight felt different, the promise of something shared, the idea that this room, much as she loved it, wouldn't just always be for her alone. She wondered what his place would be like? He dressed well, and the picture of his apartment building and the street looked nice. It was a good area, like here, a nice normal place. She slipped her shoes off and walked in bare feet. It had been chilly without pantyhose but anything to make her legs slimmer ... and her taller. In the best of all possible worlds, men didn't care how tall you were. She had a good bust. No, make that a great bust, but what she liked about him was that, unlike the last couple of times she dated a guy, his eyes stayed on her face.

Maybe she would have a splash of rum and Coke? Celebrate. It had taken a long time to feel like she could have a future, like she actually might deserve one. You can carry your past like a saddlebag. But we all make mistakes and though she didn't go to church that often anymore she still remembered that bit about forgiveness. Finally, she was beginning to forgive herself. She fumbled in the freezer for a handful of cubes, pulled out the sliced lemon, sat it on the rim and poured. She could do this for him, not just for herself. He didn't drink much, virtually not at all, and that was a good thing. Of course, she had been nervous and felt like quaffing the cocktail fast but she had sipped slowly, made it last. Didn't want him thinking she was some lush. She sat down in the rattan chair and sipped. It tasted so good. She'd thought of dating sites, all the girls were on them. Sirena swore by them. But she'd always been wary of them and it seemed she had been proven right because they'd met in her local bar with just a casual word or two that time, and then nothing for two weeks and she had sort of given up as you do until tonight, there he was again and it was a kind of play it by ear for both of them, just strolling around, chatting. He bought an inexpensive meal for them and then walked her home and when she'd invited him for a home-cooked meal next time he seemed genuinely delighted. He said he had been hoping she would be in the bar tonight because he had been thinking about her but hadn't told anybody about their meeting, he didn't want to jinx them. She felt the same, although of course she would have to let Sirena and Rosemary know that there might be somebody. Or maybe she wouldn't say anything because it might all come to nothing, but she didn't think so. She had a good feeling about things.

12

At eight a.m. sharp, her head still fuzzy from lack of sleep, Georgette tried to contact Benson but got only his voicemail. Not wishing to leave a confusing message about her potential lead, she simply asked him to call her as soon as possible. Holmes, who had been listening in, twirled his razor.

'Each storm brings a silver lining, Watson. Now we can investigate.'

'We can't do that.'

'Why on earth not?'

'It's a murder investigation,' was all she managed.

'It is *our* investigation. Time is of the essence, Watson. We have no idea when Noah may strike again. I place no expectation on you accompanying me but I may need some stipend. And by the way, these razors are a marvellous invention.'

Until the resurrection of Holmes, Georgette's recent life had been unremittingly dull. Well, apart from the horror of murder. She knew Simone would have seized upon Holmes' suggestion, and asked herself now why her sister should have all the fun. Even as her desire for potential excitement was balanced by the unnerving, inevitable consequences, she found herself saying, 'Okay, I'm coming. Where?'

'Yes?' Though it was a single, small, unprepossessing word, it strode through the tinny security-door speaker with its nose well and truly pointed up in the cool morning air.

Holmes, changed into his new suit, had prepped Georgette on the way downtown in the cab. She was starving. There had been no time for breakfast with Holmes insisting on coming here immediately. He nodded to her and she leaned in to the speaker.

'Doctor Watson and Mr Percy Turner. We saw your summer catalog.'

'Please, come on up,' said a male voice that conjured heavy silver cutlery, cravats and meticulous gardening. 'Third floor. Ring the bell when you arrive.'

The door clicked and they pushed in.

'Could have done with one of these at my lodgings,' observed Holmes. 'It was a devil of a thing running up and down those stairs.'

'I thought you had a housekeeper?'

'We did, of sorts. Conan Doyle improved her somewhat. She was usually under the weather by the stroke of midday and I feared for her safety tackling the stairs.'

It had been raining in the early hours and the morning sky had remained the color of a battleship. Only the most adventurous rays of light snuck into the narrow vestibule from the single grimy window above the door. It was a walk-up. Georgette started to climb the very steep wooden staircase so narrow they had to ascend single file. On the second-floor landing they passed a frosted glass door that bore no name and gave no indication as to what kind of business might be conducted therein. Edwards Rare Books on the other hand presented a large clear panel of glass and the business name in gold lettering. There was no handle to the door. When Holmes pressed the bell, Georgette realized he was sporting the Hulk.

'You need to get rid of that, now!'

Holmes had just enough time to slip the watch off his wrist and into his pocket when on the other side of the door's window a gentleman appeared, immaculately dressed in three-piece suit and bow tie. Georgette put his age at about fifty. The door swung back.

'Morgan Edwards, please come in.'

He ushered them into a beautifully furnished large room, like the drawing room of an old-fashioned gentleman's club. The carpet was thick blue-grey, the walls bare of books, but there were two large paintings in a Miró style on the wall ahead and on the wall to the left. Potted plants sectioned the room and made it feel homely. Edwards, clearly security conscious, locked the door behind them. Georgette wondered if anybody had ever tried to hold up the place: 'Give us your first editions!' was something she couldn't quite imagine.

In the middle of the room was a large rectangular wooden reading table around which sat four bentwood chairs. There was also a leather sofa and two additional stations of armchairs. At the wall opposite the door through which they had entered was a simple but expensive-looking, highly polished desk. Behind that, a closed door.

'Now, how may I help?' enquired Morgan Edwards, not yet offering them a seat.

'My friend Mr Turner only just flew in from London and he browsed your catalog on the plane.' Georgette was pleased at remembering her lines.

'I am a collector of late-nineteenth-century works, criminology and related subjects,' said Holmes, injecting his voice with the anxiety of an aroused collector. It changed his personality so drastically and quickly that Georgette was forced to remind herself not to react. He also exhibited the kind of twitch a collector might get when on the scent of a sought-after piece. 'In your July catalog you had for sale a book, *Crimini d'Italia*. Is it still available?'

'I am afraid not. It was snapped up rather quickly.'

'Oh,' Holmes' whole body seemed to puncture and deflate. 'I've looked for that for years.'

'Would you be able to let us know who purchased the book?' asked Georgette innocently.

A hand gesture that was so reverent and restrained it may have been in the armory of a funeral-director, suggested that would be impossible.

'I'm very sorry but I pride myself on my discretion. However, I do have some other very interesting books on criminology, and other topics that may be of interest from the late Victorian era: palmistry, psychology.'

'I had my heart set on that one but I can always be tempted,' said the new Holmes.

'Please, take a seat.' Edwards gestured to the sofa. They sat themselves down. He crossed to his desk, picked up an iPad and began flicking across the screen.

'Here,' he said, handing over the iPad.

Seeing Holmes at a loss, Georgette took charge. Holmes got in close as she showed him the various titles Edwards had for sale. Each book was represented by a small photo and very brief description. Holmes made impressed noises. As soon as he spied the cover for *Crimini d'Italia* he gave another plaintive sigh. Georgette expanded the photo.

'Ah, there it is.' He sounded like he was pining for a well-loved pet long deceased. 'Who took the photo if I may ask?'

'I did,' said Edwards. 'I do all my own photos, write all the blurbs. These days, books are a dwindling passion and my survival depends on keeping costs down.'

'You speak Italian?'

'And French, and German. I just skim so I can have a handle on what is in it. If my memory serves me, that one went before I'd even finished the summary. I always publish a photo of new acquisitions, cover and title page. Often that's all collectors need.'

'But you still published the summary.'

'Most of the work had been done. And you never know if another one may crop up and then everything is ready. Mind you, that's the one and only time I have ever come across that book.'

'I believe it.' Holmes nodded vigorously. 'I looked everywhere. Where did you find it?'

'Deceased estate sale, Park Avenue. There were a dozen books in a box, all first editions. The seller was not interested in haggling.'

'So you were the only one who actually handled the book?' Holmes sounded incredulous.

'Yes, well as I said, one needs to keep costs down but also to be brutally frank, these are valuable items and you simply can't trust just anybody to handle them correctly.'

Holmes nodded at the wisdom of this. Georgette meanwhile surreptitiously checked for security cameras, spied two, one over the entry door and one above the internal door. Edwards got down to the business at hand.

'So, anything that takes your fancy?'

'As a matter of fact: H.G. Wells, *The First Men in the Moon*. I should be most interested to see how it turned out.'

Edwards looked at him oddly.

Holmes said, 'I saw some early drafts. He was toying with the idea a decade earlier.'

'I've never heard of those.' Edwards sounded intrigued.

'I can assure you. Do you have a copy I might peruse?'

'I'll just be a moment.'

This, Georgette knew, was her cue. As soon as Edwards disappeared through the inner sanctum door he had opened via a keypad, she began searching the iPad for accounts information. There was no guarantee Edwards would keep this information on it but within seconds she had found spreadsheets including books, bought and sold. But then she actually started to think about what she was doing and her fingers turned to hooves.

'Shit!' Three times she made an error.

'Haste makes waste, Watson,' whispered Holmes.

She forced herself to calm. July: Got it! She scanned down the list. How long had Edwards been? She was breaking the law ... there! *Crimini* ... She managed to click on the title. The purchase and sale information were clearly displayed by date but there were no dollar amounts entered, simply whether it had sold and to whom.

'I'll get a photo of it,' she said.

But the door was already beginning to open.

'Here,' Holmes swung the screen towards him and stared at it intently. Then as Edwards was almost upon them he rose and blocked his vision, reaching for the book Edwards had brought with him and gasping, 'Oh my ...'

Edwards pulled the book away and handed him a pair of cotton gloves. 'Precautions.'

'Of course.' Holmes said. 'I take it you do your own bookbinding and restoration?'

Edwards looked surprised. 'I do. My father started the business and that was his craft. He learned there was more to be made in selling books than restoring them. I did no work on this book though, it was in pristine condition, as were the others. Usually I can do whatever work is needed. Occasionally some very special restoration might be required but that was not the case here.'

'So you have no staff?'

'No, as I said, I am afraid there is not enough money in books these days for that. It is the era of the Philistine.'

Apart from key moments in her research, Georgette had rarely been quite as excited or anxious as when searching through Edwards' iPad. To say she was relieved to be out of there was an understatement.

Holmes had spent a good twenty minutes thumbing through a book he'd never intended to buy. Edwards hadn't displayed overt disappointment at failing to clinch a nine-hundred and ninety-dollar sale. Perhaps Holmes indicating he might be back in touch had left hope burning within. Or perhaps he really didn't need the sale. The phone had only rung once while they were there and the enquiry had been perfunctory.

Just as they were preparing to leave, Holmes had turned to Edwards.

'You know, I really can't get the idea out of my head that a copy of *Crimini d'Italia* actually lurks. I wonder if you would mind contacting the buyer and asking him to contact me, in case he would agree to sell it?'

Edwards hesitated.

Holmes added, 'Naturally you would earn a middle-man commission. Ten percent?'

When Edwards asked how the buyer might contact Holmes, Georgette gave her card.

'For the time being you can reach Mr Turner through me.'

Edwards said he would see what he could do.

There was little or no improvement in the weather. Autumn was grinding to an end in a manner reminiscent of most of the romantic relationships Georgette had known. You wished for a return to earlier, unspoiled times, but accepted you would be better off in a bracing winter with the comfort of a heat pack. Holmes signalled a passing cab. When it stopped, he opened the door for her and gave the driver a Park Avenue address.

'Four hundred and fifty-eight Park Avenue,' Holmes told the driver.

'What's there?' asked Georgette, sliding across the seat.

'Who, not what: the seller, Miss Margaret Dutton.'

'You got that off the iPad?'

'Of course. And the buyer, one Professor Avery Scheer, but I should like to think about our approach to him a mite longer and see if he makes contact of his own accord.'

It staggered her that Holmes had managed to read both in such a quick time. Her brain had been like pizza spilled on the sidewalk as she had sought to quit the accounts file. Speaking of pizza, she could do with one now. A very large one.

'How did you know Edwards restored his own books?'

'His hands showed some wear, especially around the inside of the fingers, and yet he did not appear to be a man who had a history of manual labor, ergo he was in the habit of some type of hobby or work where he employed his hands.'

'Do you think he could be ...' she hesitated. 'Murderer' wasn't the kind of word one bandied about in the back of a cab. '... our man?'

'He had access to the book; by his own admission he can read Italian. He said he'd skimmed but of course he could be lying.'

'But if it were him, wouldn't he suggest others might have read the book?'

Holmes presented a smile which could have been interpreted equally as condescending or benign.

'Noah,' said Holmes, 'is not one who wants to pass credit to another. He alone will be the savior. I am afraid that Mr Edwards has not yet cleared himself.'

His gaze strayed through the window at the steady stream of cars and the constant sidewalk crush.

'So many people,' he mused. 'And each one a locked box. If we could read their minds Watson, it would take several lifetimes. Even if we included lifetimes as long as mine.'

With that he sat back in silence, his expression blank, just one more locked box in the mighty city.

13

Either Margaret Dutton or one of her progenitors had made some serious money to be able to afford to live in this apartment building. Unable to help comparing her own place, Georgette felt like a finger painter standing in front of a Goya.

'Mr Percy Turner and Doctor Georgette Watson. We wish to speak to Miss Margaret Dutton,' said Holmes to the doorman, a man of about sixty, broad of shoulder and chest.

'Is she expecting you, sir?'

'I doubt it. I am a consultant detective and I hope she might speak to me about a book she until recently owned.'

The doorman went to the intercom. Georgette had been thinking that Margaret Dutton might have been at work but on reflection realized that anybody who could afford to live here was unlikely to work. The doorman spoke into the intercom and then returned.

'Might I see some identification, sir?'

Georgette stepped in and showed him her university card. It seemed to satisfy the doorman, who admitted them and told them, 'Apartment 404.'

'You were in the navy?' asked Holmes of the bemused doorman.

'As a matter of fact. Have I met you before, sir?'

Holmes smiled.

'No, but in my town of London you could guarantee that a man of your age in this position with your bearing had a military background; courteous to the tenants, yet able to deal with a bothersome intruder. And I note that the knots securing the blind here are reminiscent of those to be found on rigging.'

Impressed, the doorman pushed the elevator button for them and ushered them inside.

After a brief ride they found themselves in a well-lit hallway on golden carpet. There was an art-deco mirror down the hallway: from the looks, original. It occurred to Georgette that was a style that came after Holmes' demise. To him this was all modern. Holmes pressed the bell. The door opened, revealing a small-boned woman with brown hair and keen eyes. Georgette put her in her fifties. Her dress was two-toned, blue and black in some sheeny silk-like material, clearly expensive, and she wore it with the air of a woman for whom the expression 'casual wear' would be heresy. Holmes introduced himself under his alias and Georgette introduced herself.

'Our doorman said you were a detective?'

'Yes. I wish to speak to you about a book you sold to Edwards Rare Books.'

Dutton lifted her eyebrows and showed them past the reception hallway to a sitting room where a Siamese cat draped itself upon a cushion by the main window. The room was immaculate and devoid of the ordinary odors of domestic life – cooking, slightly ripened fruit, dust toasting on a warm television. It gave the room a sense of this being little more than a set.

'The books were my late mother's, actually my late father's, but my mother never got rid of them. All first editions. They'd been in the family for at least forty years so there can be no doubt as to their provenance since then.'

'I'm really only interested in one book at this stage,' said Holmes. '*Crimini d'Italia*.'

Dutton waved a dismissive hand. 'I couldn't even tell you the names of the books. Is there some issue?'

'On the contrary, I have been hired by a client who collects rare books. They were particularly interested in that book and wondered where it came from so to speak, in case that might lead him to more copies.'

'I can't help you, I'm afraid. My father would from time to time come across a book he liked for whatever reason and buy it. I think there were about a dozen books in the box I sold to the book dealer. There are no others.'

'How long would they have been in that box?'

'My father died twelve years ago, so at least that long. My mother never read them but she refused to sell up my father's things. I'm not sure if that is sad or pathetic.'

'And where were they stored?'

'Here. I moved in when my father died and now, there's just me. And Sierra.'

'Your daughter?' asked Georgette.

'No, her.'

Dutton pointed at the Siamese, and now Georgette noticed there was no wedding band on Miss Dutton's hand.

Holmes said, 'Just to be clear, these books you had were from different sources, stored here for at least ten years and not read by yourself or anybody else?'

'That is correct. I am afraid I am no help to your client at all.'

Georgette, who had been around her father enough to know his various tricks-of-the-trade, asked if she might use the bathroom. Margaret Dutton looked as if she wished to refuse but politeness got the better of her and she swept her hand in the direction of the corridor.

The bathroom was palatial in comparison to her own, fresh flowers and barely used scented soap bars. Georgette did a quick once-over of the cabinet and sink area: one toothbrush, no sign of male usage. She took only a few minutes, flushed the toilet and returned. On approach she heard Holmes holding forth.

'... found myself in Staffordshire investigating a matter of extreme delicacy.'

Georgette re-entered the room and Holmes, who had been pointing to a plate on the wall, politely stood. Georgette realized Dutton was enjoying every minute of this gentlemanly extravagance.

'I was just boring Miss Dutton with a story about the Wedgewoods.'

'Not boring me in the least, Mr Turner.'

Holmes bowed. 'Most kind of you to say so, Miss Dutton, but I fear we have taken up enough of your time.'

'Not at all. I wish I could have been of more assistance.'

'Well, perhaps if I think of anything more pertinent I shall call on you again.'

'Please do.'

Margaret Dutton had her hands pressed together in rapture. It would not have surprised Georgette if she had curtsied as Holmes left.

'She was putty in your hands.' Georgette didn't know why the wizened Dutton still rankled but she did. Probably the fact that she'd never had to work for anything and yet still owned a large apartment in Park Avenue. Her own chance to ever attain that had run aground on the reef sitting opposite. That also rankled. 'I'm surprised she didn't ask you to stay for lunch.'

'I'm glad she didn't. I would not have wished to be denied these superb comestibles.'

They were eating in Chinatown. The restaurant had been a regular for her and Vance. They had laughed at the constant background of clanging aluminium and the loud bickering in some Chinese dialect that inevitably followed. Back home they would open a bottle of white wine and then ... no, she definitely didn't want to go there. Perhaps the Victorians were right in discouraging sex before marriage. Who actually benefitted from it?

Not her that was for sure. It was the first time she had been back here since the relationship blew up. Part of her was terrified of the possibility Vance might show up, part of her would have welcomed it. Holmes was, she could admit it to herself now, not as good-looking in that typical way that Vance was – all even teeth and gym-toned upper body – but he was something Vance would never be: substantial. And polite. Vance's sensibility was that if he gave her an orgasm he'd fulfilled all obligations. He didn't smoke though, that was one thing he had over Holmes, but he did get jealous, so if he saw her here with Holmes that would bug the shit out of him.

'Did I miss something?'

She realized Holmes was looking at her over his wonton soup. 'What?'

'I asked, did you find anything of interest in Dutton's bathroom?'

It was disappointing she had been so transparent. 'How did you know?'

'I could say that it was because neither during our cab ride nor at any time previous were you anxiously casting about for a bathroom, yet while that might be true, it would not be wholly so. This morning while you were dressing, I spent a short time watching a television drama in which the detective used the same ploy.'

Georgette was surprised. She said she thought it may have been one of his own tricks of the trade.

'Watson, in my day the bathroom was likely no more than an outhouse or a tub in front of the fireplace.'

She told him there was nothing to indicate any other person lived in the apartment.

'Hmm, I think we can safely assume that Miss Dutton is, as she appears, a spinster.'

Like me, Georgette thought.

Holmes continued, 'I am inclined to believe what she told us: the books were boxed for years, and consequently it is most unlikely the Ometti book was read by anyone for a number of years prior to its sale to Edwards.'

'So you think Noah is somebody who has only recently discovered the book?'

'I do. Edwards purchased the book in late May and sold it on the eighteenth of June. So far as we know, only Edwards read the book before he onsold it. So now we must focus squarely on the purchaser, Professor Avery Scheer.'

'He does not appear to be on Facebook, however, he is on LinkedIn.'

That brought Holmes up.

'I checked it up while you were outside smoking your pipe.' She felt pleased with herself for getting in that detail. 'Scheer is forty-three years old, American, and has a doctorate in psychology. He appears to have lectured at several large universities and his curriculum vitae indicates he had also been involved in private practice and worked as a consultant for various psychiatric facilities. His current employment is with Endymion University not far from here. I don't know a lot about it.' Her cursory reading indicated it was a small, private university with high fees offering several courses which Georgette considered 'soft.' No engineering or microbiology but courses like psychology, film studies, anthropology and creative writing. There was one mathematics course. 'Essentially, it seems to be a college for rich parents to send their indulged children to so they wind up with some kind of degree before crashing their Porsche … an expensive car. I can ask around, try and find out if any colleagues can tell me about Scheer.'

Holmes wagged a finger. 'No, Watson, that you shan't do. It was most foolish of me to involve you in this enterprise. Noah is a killer. He targets women of your age … perhaps a touch younger.'

That stung. Holmes continued, ignorant of his slight.

'Who knows what triggers him? You could become his next target. It was wrong of me to take you to Edwards. I shan't repeat the mistake.'

'I am thirty-three years old and I think and act for myself. This is not eighteen ninety-one. Women, in case you haven't noticed, have made a few advances.'

'And some men have not changed one jot. They are still murderous animals who will use the city as their hunting fields. I stood this close and looked at the gutted victims of Jack the Ripper. Please, Watson, do not make the mistake of being the lion tamer who sticks her head in the wrong mouth.'

She felt her hackles rise. 'Would you have banned my great-great-grandfather?'

Holmes straightened his very straight back and inhaled. 'Likely not.'

'So why him and not me?'

'Your great-great-grandfather had been in a war. And he knew his way around a weapon. Can you shoot a pistol?'

'Not really.'

'What does that mean?'

'I've never tried.'

'So we'll take that as a no. Have you ever been instructed in martial arts?'

'I've seen a few Jackie Chan movies.'

'This is no matter for levity.'

'I agree. Like John Watson, I have seen terrible things. In case you forget, I saw Gina Scaroldi close up. And she's not the first person I have seen who has been slaughtered and discarded like unwanted trash.'

'I apologize if I seem ...'

'Chauvinistic?'

'Over-protective.'

They sat for a moment in silence.

She felt impelled to add, 'You wouldn't be here if it weren't for my great-great. And me.'

'True but hardly relevant.'

'It is very relevant. He never abandoned you. It grieved him, to think he had failed.'

'John Watson was the most loyal ... stubborn man I have had the pleasure of knowing. You appear to exhibit at least one of those traits.'

'He loved you.'

Holmes nodded slowly. 'Dearer than a brother.'

'And would you have done the same for him?'

Seemingly asking himself that, Holmes looked out the window. 'Almost certainly not. Had he been robbed, murdered, wronged, I should have left no stone unturned to find the perpetrator but in all honesty ... no, I would have left him in that cold limbo, got on with life.

I am a pragmatist. John was a dreamer. My brain may have been sharper but his will was stronger. I am not a good person, Watson. I don't claim to be. John summed me up in an instant, my good qualities, and my poor.'

Her phone rang, a number she did not recognize.

'Georgette Watson,' she said.

'Doctor Watson, my name is Avery Scheer. I believe a friend of yours is interested in a book of mine.'

14

Avery Scheer was almost exactly the same build as Holmes, tall and lean, but his mop of light brown hair and his clothes – slacks, dark casual shirt, no tie, loafers – made him seem younger. Of course, she told herself, he was, by some one hundred and twenty-odd years.

Scheer stood in the frame of his impressive doorway and extended his hand.

'Avery Scheer.'

If he is Noah, she thought, he may well suspect why we are here. The long, soft hand of an academic hung there like bunting. It could be the same hand that wielded the knife to slash the throats of three women. Burying that fear she took Scheer's hand and did the introductions.

'Georgette Watson, Percy Turner.'

'Come in.' Scheer stepped back to allow them in to a large, den-like room before closing the thick oak door behind them as if sealing them in to a vault, an impression accentuated by deep carpet and light adjusted low. Endymion University was housed in a refurbished factory on Lafayette only a short distance from where they had lunched. The entrance area had been given the usual makeover that emphasized space, light and functional furnishing but Scheer's office was in stark contrast. Holmes, she figured, should fit right in with the Victorian furniture, the heavily carved fireplace and the large dark painting above it that made you feel you were in the British Museum. It was impossible to tell what view Scheer had from his window, for heavy velvet drapes were drawn. It was almost too warm for an overcoat. Scheer addressed Holmes.

'Doctor Watson told you that it is highly unlikely I would sell *Crimini d'Italia*?'

'As you agreed to see me, I must presume to hope.'

'I must confess a small deception.' Scheer flashed a charming smile at Georgette. 'I wanted to attend your lecture but regrettably had a prior engagement. I find the idea of triumph over death fascinating. Most of my work, I'm afraid, is at the other end of the spectrum: dealing with the dark spaces of the human mind. I'm a psychologist, specialising in criminal behavior.'

He gestured they sit in two large leather armchairs positioned in front of a very long and comprehensive bookshelf. Scheer grabbed his more modern office chair from behind his desk, on which sat a marble bust, she was pretty sure, of Freud. Scheer rolled across to a point equidistant between his visitors.

'When I realized fate seemed to have brought you to me, so to speak, I simply could not resist the opportunity to meet you in person. Forgive me, Mr Turner, but I am only human. I would not however wish to raise false hopes about my parting with the book.'

'Please, call me Percy. The opera has an aria or two to run yet,' said Holmes, 'and sometimes its outcome is not what we may have predicted.'

'Well said. You never know, you may compel me yet. Doctor Watson mentioned you're a criminologist?'

'For many years I have made a study of criminal cases. My particular interest is of the nature of evidence: soil samples, bloodstains ...'

'Ah, you're a chemist?'

'Of sorts.'

'Forensics, I suppose I should have said. The other end of the spectrum to where I place myself: the mind. And how did you two come to meet? Were you at college together?'

The question, addressed to her, dragged Georgette back. She had been studying the painting, the sort she'd seen loads of during summer vacation of her freshman year when she bummed around Europe and used the clean bathrooms of the Louvre, Prado and Uffizi. The gloomy oil on canvas depicted two bearded men in robes in a life and death struggle over an ax.

'We met in Switzerland actually,' she said. Then, 'That painting would seem to set a certain tone for the room.'

Scheer, who had his back to it, held one knee and swivelled to look.

'Yes, I found it in a flea market in Boston. *Cain and Abel*, a poor man's attempt at a Titian. But, I liked it, and well, it *was* allegedly the first murder. A subject close your heart?'

He turned back to Holmes with a mock-playfulness. It might have been simply the tone he used with his students, or it might indicate that he was well and truly alert to their intentions, a cat playing with mice. Whichever, Georgette was certain he was studying them as closely as they were him.

'Yes, it is. I have been searching for years without success for a copy of *Crimini d'Italia*.'

'I confess I had never seen anything about the book until I viewed that catalog. How did you know of it?' He leaned forward now, the playfulness gone.

'Somebody mentioned a story of the detectives involved in the Jack the Ripper case being made aware of a serial killer in Italy operating at the same time. And then somewhere or other, I saw mention of the book and it seemed that very case may be discussed in it. I confess I had drawn a blank finding any other information on it.'

'You've made me even more reluctant to part with it.' Scheer got to his feet and walked to his desk. He selected a key and unlocked a drawer. 'You read Italian?'

'I do. You?'

He made the universal wobbly hand gesture.

'But with the translation apps you can get these days, it's simple. You literally scan it and it spits it out in English. Very handy when you are setting tasks for students.'

'You've had your students read this book?' Georgette said.

'A small discussion group which I run monthly. It was my August selection.'

'Is that popular?' Holmes threw it away as neither here nor there.

'Only my two masters students, and two others.'

Georgette wondered if Holmes, like her, had just breathed a sigh of relief. A pool of only four additional suspects was a bonus.

Scheer was continuing. 'A contemporary case might draw up to thirty but it's always lower for historical gems. And by the way, we did not discuss the whole book, just the case you refer to, Percy, and one other that involved,' he pointed up at the painting, 'a younger brother killing the older brother.'

He was now displaying the book as a model might, resting it upright on a lower palm, his other hand across the top. The book was not more than seven inches high and not thick. Its cover was a faded green.

'May I?' Holmes reached for the book.

'I might normally ask you to sign something regarding damages but I'm sure Doctor Watson would not be friends with a vandal.'

He passed the book across and Holmes eagerly began skimming.

'Do you mind if I read?' Holmes asked, his gaze not even on the psychologist.

'Not at all. I have about fifteen minutes free.'

Georgette tried to smile the way she had smiled to Vance when they had first been introduced at a Canal Street gallery, the smile that says 'I find everything about you fascinating'. She was long out of practice.

'Your CV says you are a criminal psychologist. I looked you up.' He seemed to like that. 'Are you a profiler?'

'That is a small part of it. I am not a profiler as such but I am fascinated by the background of killers: what drives them, what brings them into contact with their victims. It's very sexy to focus on the serial killers, like for example the Picture Book killer in the case there, but most murders are domestic, and boring: somebody is tired of their husband or wife, or wants money. That's why I gave the group the two cases to look at.'

'So, you gave them the stories and asked them ... what?'

'I gave them the stories and asked them what they thought drove the killer in each case. I withheld the last few pages as if there were a solution provided. As you will see, no suspect was ever identified in the Picture Book murders but in the second it seemed obvious that the younger brother murdered the older brother because it was the only way he would inherit the farm. But it actually wasn't that at all. The younger brother was what we would now recognize as schizophrenic. He heard God commanding him to do it.'

'All very biblical,' said Georgette and saw Holmes' eyes slide her way to show he was listening.

'These days the voice the killer heard would most likely be Kanye West,' quipped Scheer, and rocked back in his chair. Georgette wondered if this worked with his students; she made a show of laughing at his wit.

'And you, Doctor –'

'Georgette, please.'

'I can't help but be fascinated by your personal backstory. You were dead for what, ten minutes or so? And you have been able to bring hamsters back from as long as a month. Is that right?'

She confirmed it, becoming aware as she blabbed on about her experiments that she had covered her earlier fear with barely a leaf. The man sitting across from her might be a serial killer looking for his next victim.

Thankfully Holmes returned to the fray.

'Has anybody but yourself had access to this book since you purchased it? Your students for example?'

'No. Why do you ask?'

'There is a mark here,' he flashed the book. Georgette thought she detected a smudge but wasn't sure. 'If my finances allow it, I would be prepared to double the price you paid for it but would be reassured to know it is in the same condition now as when purchased.'

'As I told you up front, even for twice what I paid – I'm not convinced I want to sell it but I can assure you that it hasn't been out of this room. I even scanned the pages here. I treat books as sacred objects.'

Sacred. Georgette was reminded of the curved blade and old testament sacrifice, and suppressed a shudder. Scheer smiled at Holmes. 'So, are you hooked?'

'I am, but I need consider my finances. I don't wish to waste either of our time. Are you prepared to tell me how much you paid?'

'Seven hundred dollars.'

Georgette wondered if that were true.

'So, fourteen hundred dollars. That is at the top of my range. I need to think on it.'

'Me too,' said Scheer. 'Where do you work exactly, Percy, if I may ask?'

'Private consultancy mostly, sometimes with the police but generally on matters such as authenticating wills. Or blackmail.'

'Yes, that's become so much more prevalent. There's always a camera snapping somebody doing something they'd rather not be seen doing and of course it is so much easier to hide money with bitcoin and Pay Pal and international transfers.'

Holmes stood to indicate he was ready to go. 'If I may take a day or two to think on it?'

'Of course. I need time to reflect too. I'm quite fond of that little book now. And Georgette, if you ever have time for a lunch I would love to hear more about your work. Percy, of course you would be more than welcome too. There is a very decent cafeteria here and a very nice Romanian restaurant a block away.'

If it weren't that he was possibly a serial killer, Georgette might have felt a tingle of triumph.

'Of course. You have my number now.'

As they moved to the door Holmes said, 'What were your own conclusions about the Picture Book Killer?'

Without so much as a glance at Holmes, she knew that his focus on Scheer was intense, as when you take a magnifying glass and concentrate the sun's rays onto a dry leaf to make it smoulder. Perhaps Scheer was a consummate actor. He betrayed no guilt, his demeanor millpond.

'I would say there is some plan to it that makes sense only in the killer's mind. Perhaps he sees the world as a human zoo with himself as the keeper.'

'You use the present tense,' observed Holmes.

'Well, yes, I think of the killers as if they were alive today. To me, the more interesting question is why did the killer cease? Or did he? Did the Italian police simply stop reporting the murders? As with Jack the Ripper, why such a spree and then nothing? Was he imprisoned, did he die, flee overseas or was he sated?'

There was a knock on the door.

'That will be Melissa, one of my masters students.'

Scheer opened the door.

The woman was an inch shy of Holmes and broader across the shoulders with a strong chin. Georgette was certain she was transgender.

'Melissa Harper, this is Mr Percy Turner and Doctor Georgette Watson.'

Harper looked like she was hemmed in by life, her shoulders slightly rounded, her smile stunted and her greeting no more than a mutter. Holmes expressed his delight at meeting her but Georgette sensed him weighing Harper like a butcher might assess a steer at the abattoir. Holmes swung back to Scheer.

'I shall call you,' he said, then added, 'Do you think it would be permissible to take a look around the building?'

'Of course. All the lecture theatres are on the first floor. Second floor is film and creative writing, this floor is staffrooms and postgraduate study rooms.'

They had walked a half-dozen steps along the corridor before Holmes spoke.

'Clearly Melissa Harper would be physically capable of killing any of our victims.'

He peered through the glass door panel into a study room. The whiteboard had math equations written on it. He continued along the corridor. 'So we have at least four more suspects,' he said.

Georgette felt obliged to give Holmes a rundown on the changing nature of how sexuality was treated nowadays.

'I dare say it's a good thing,' said Holmes, 'that Melissa and those like her need not hide in a cupboard, but it is nothing exactly new, Watson. I'll never forget the look on your great-great-grandfather's face when he burst into the room of the Earl of –' He stopped at the room on their left, peered in and smiled. 'This one I believe.'

He opened the door and walked in to what was a basically furnished room with two clear workstations, a whiteboard affixed to the wall, a sofa, coffee table with newspapers scattered over it, and a small kitchen area, consisting of a bench with a sink. A mini refrigerator was located under the bench, propped against which was a slim young man about twenty-five with thick dark curly hair, sipping a coffee while studying his phone. He looked up, surprised at the intrusion. Holmes had downplayed his eager-collector persona with Scheer but now he resurrected it.

'Sorry to disturb you. You would be Professor Scheer's masters student.'

'That's right.' Confusion struggled with sullen defense on the young man's finely featured face.

Georgette said, 'He invited us to look around. Please don't let us disturb you.'

'I am a criminologist ... Walter,' said Holmes, whose eyes had strayed to the folder on the desk with the name Walter Morris. 'I'd long been after the book *Crimini d'Italia*. You read it, I believe?'

Georgette admired Holmes' skill at putting Walter in a situation where he felt compelled to answer.

'Just some extracts.'

Walter's voice was neutral, no highs or lows but there was an unmistakable polish that suggested a schooling involving blazers and oars upon a glassy river.

'I am terribly rude; I am Percy Turner, and this is Doctor Georgette Watson.'

Holmes extended his hand and Walter took it without enthusiasm. Holmes cast about the room.

'Much better digs than where I studied,' he said. His eyes fell upon a metal sculpture about a foot high, sitting beside a computer on one of the workstations. It was constructed of copper and thin strips of steel and put Georgette in mind of a medieval knight. The figure appeared to have a broadsword placed directly into the ground, point first, and its hands rested on the pommel, though its face was unformed and blank. Coming from its back, folded down, were quite distinct wings. Georgette did not like it. Simone would have called it 'creepy'.

'That is impressive. Yours?' said Holmes.

Walter shrugged with self-deprecation. 'I do the odd piece when my time allows.'

Definitely used to spending summer in the Hamptons, thought Georgette.

'You did it yourself?' Holmes was effusive.

'It's nothing much.'

'Is it an angel?' asked Georgette.

'The avenging angel,' said Holmes, beaming.

'Yes.' The young man's eyes were carefully studying Holmes now, perhaps trying to fathom whether he was a threat, or a genuine eccentric.

'Bless the Lord, O you his angels, you mighty ones who do his word, obeying the voice of his word!' Holmes quoted with great enthusiasm. He picked up the angel and studied it.

Walter said, 'I'm not religious. It's just ... a hobby.'

'Professor Scheer mentioned a discussion paper about the Picture Book killer.'

Georgette watched Holmes assessing Walter Morris the way a cat waits for the first hint a mouse is going to move.

'Yes, that's right.'

'He said you might have a copy I could look at?'

A bald lie. Holmes' gaze did not waver and then Morris broke.

'Um, yes.' He reached for a folder and flicked through it, found the place he wanted.

'What was your take on it?' asked Holmes as he scanned the documents.

'They were all pictures of animals. I thought he viewed himself as a hunter.'

'And the others?'

'I don't remember what the randoms thought. Melissa, the other masters student, believed they might represent animosity to a mother who first read him stories from a picture book.'

'Well, keep up the good work. Doctor Watson here consults with NYPD Homicide. She may put in a testimonial on your behalf.'

Morris swung towards Georgette. 'You work homicides?'

'Sometimes. Time of death mainly.'

Holmes had some sort of coughing fit. He fumbled in his jacket for a tissue and held up his hand apologetically. 'Sorry. Well, thank you, Walter, I apologize if we disturbed you.' Holmes replaced the angel but in doing so knocked a pen off the bench into a work bag. 'Oh, no, there I go. I've been too excited.' He fumbled around for it.

'It's alright, don't worry about it.'

Holmes ignored Walter and ferreted till he emerged triumphant with the pen. He handed it to Walter and beamed, 'The pen is mightier than the sword ... although your angel may not agree.'

'What do you think the name of his thesis is?' Holmes said almost immediately after they had left.

'Hmmm, "The animals two-by-two"?'

'Not quite. "Victimology – the elements that attract the killer to a victim".'

'I'll check him out on social media. How did you know that was the room?'

'You saw the coat stand just inside the door?'

'Yes, but there was just a coat hanging.'

'Not "just a coat", Watson. A coat whose shade matched the shoes Melissa Harper was wearing. It was what I call a reasonable leap of probability, ergo, that it was the room in which she studied.'

Holmes had already produced his pipe. He noted her disapproval. 'I apologize, but I need to think. And then perhaps I could buy you supper.'

'You could if you had any money.'

'You loan it to me and I shall repay you with extra.'

'At least we have one thing in common,' she said.

'Which is?'

'My credit card.'

He forced a smile. They descended the staircase. Students scurried up late for lectures. The brightness of the day had slid away like a bored party guest, and gloom and cold were seeping into the building, defying the exposed bricks and bright plastic furniture that its architects had perhaps hoped would act as talismans.

They stepped through the automatic doorway. The chill of evening frisked their bodies. Holmes said, 'The fourth and final victim of the Picture Book killer had a picture of a zebra left beside her body.'

'You read the entire chapter while we were there?'

'I did. I presume we don't have the finances to buy the book?'

'It would be a struggle.'

'Well, it is not necessary. I am sure the police will confiscate it the moment they realize the futility of their current lead. No word from Benson?'

'Not yet.'

Looking up into the grey sky, Georgette found herself confronted with the twisted threatening faces of gargoyles, and this released a shudder that had been pent up from the first moment they had entered Scheer's office.

'So what is our next requirement, Watson?' Holmes asked, tamping tobacco into the bowl of his pipe.

'You shouldn't be doing that. You're already coughing your lungs out.'

'My apologies. Now, answer my question. Next step?'

'We need to find out who were the other two people who attended the discussion group.'

'Very true. I am hoping there might be an indication here.'

From his coat pocket he produced a sheet of typed paper that had clearly been ripped from a folder.

'When did you –?'

'When I told Walter Morris you worked homicides. As I predicted, it produced the necessary distraction.' His coughing had been a ruse. He'd not been fumbling for a tissue, she realized, but pocketing the goods. 'I already had the page open so I just …' He made a ripping gesture.

'So it seems I paid my way?'

'You did. In fact, there were moments I felt I was working with the original, Watson. I mean that as a compliment.'

She felt chuffed.

'However, our vigilance, yours in particular, must remain paramount. If one of those three is Noah …'

She really did not want to think about that. Saving the next girl, that's all that mattered. She nodded at the page.

'Any help?'

'It appears to be a letter to the discussion group.'

She could see now that it was an email that had been printed into a hard copy.

He sighed. 'Unfortunately there are no names here of the other participants.'

'No names but these email addresses are as good. We should be able to find out who attended.'

'You can discern that?'

'I can't but I know somebody who might know somebody who can.'

15

The rain, which had dropped as suddenly as a magician's cape, now seemed to have set in. Those on the street under umbrellas or with glistening coats hoisted over their heads danced like crows around roadkill. Simone's arrival was greeted with the inevitable fanfare of angry horns as she cut across lanes and hit the anchors, fanning up a spray. Georgette was already chiding herself for even suggesting her sister could help. Holmes opened the rear door for her – definitely not something Vance would have done. In fact, casting her mind back, she wasn't sure any man except a concierge had ever opened a door for her. Holmes took the front passenger seat.

Simone said, 'If there's one thing I place right at the top of the tree, it's good manners.'

She pulled straight out into the path of a vehicle, forcing the driver to jam on his brakes. Simone looked Holmes up and down and said, 'For somebody who is a hundred and sixty-six, you're looking good.' She winked, Holmes smiled. It was sickening.

'So, you need somebody who can chase up some email addresses?'

Georgette had given bare bones over the phone. She explained in more detail now.

Holmes said, 'You are acquainted with somebody who can do this?'

'Absolutely: sixteen year old boys at exclusive schools. They could crack the Kremlin. My buddy Ambrose says he can organise Valerian, the best hacker he knows, for us.'

'What's it costing?' Georgette was suspicious of the generosity of young schoolboys.

'I promised I'd teach Ambrose to drive. He'll look after Valerian. We're going to pick Ambrose up and he'll take us to him.'

Holmes said, 'Did he give any indication of the time it might take to get the identities?'

'Ambrose said for something simple like email addresses, they should have names by the morning.'

Travelling too fast, she was forced to slam on her brakes to avoid rear-ending a van. Some object flew along the dash towards Holmes and would have smashed into the passenger window but for his lightning reflexes.

'I was an unimpeachable first slip,' he said immodestly. Georgette had no idea what he was talking about. Now he examined the object and she saw it was the snow globe.

'A rather pretty ornament.'

'I meant to glue it down.'

'Where is this exactly?' Holmes was examining it, fake snow falling gaily.

'Central Park, I think. See the little bridge? It is Central Park, right?' Simone looked up into the rear-view for her support.

'There are two bridges in Central Park. That's Bow Bridge.'

'And this has significance for you?' Holmes asked Simone.

'It was Georgette's.'

'You think that's my taste?'

'It was in your apartment. It must have been Vance. A parting gift?'

Georgette hoped Holmes was too busy staring at the passing billboards to be following.

No such luck. Holmes twisted around. 'Vance?'

Georgette went all prickly.

'The lodger,' she said. Before Simone could blab, Georgette fessed up. 'We lived together. People tend to do that now before they ... marry.'

'Oh,' was all Holmes said.

Damn. Now she was worried she might have offended him, yet simultaneously annoyed that she was worried about it.

'Personally,' said Simone, 'I would have loved your era: courtship and balls and hansom cabs. And fog. Was it really foggy?'

'Yes, frequently.'

'That's very mysterious too. Footsteps in the fog, a piercing scream –'

'Don't even think about it,' warned Georgette, feeling hampered by being stuck in the back, but knowing Simone was about to let loose some horrific wail.

Her phone buzzed. It was Harry.

'Hey, Dad. How's it going?'

'I'm freezing my butt off and Mirsch's winning tear shows no sign of slowing.'

'Tell Dad not to forget my show.'

'Simone says don't forget her show tomorrow.'

'Are you in a car?'

'Yes.'

'Is she driving?'

'Affirmative.'

'Is she sober?'

'Hopefully.'

Simone yelled back, 'If he asked if I'm sober ask him if he's still a crusty old tightwad.'

Harry was in her ear again. 'Yes, I am. Not crusty but a tightwad, definitely. What's this I hear about you and some limey?'

'What? Who told you that?'

'Never you mind.'

But she had already narrowed the candidates to Simone or Benson.

'Who is he?'

She tried to lower her voice. 'A friend.'

'He's in the car with you?'

'Yes.'

'Where's he staying?'

'My place. In the spare room.'

'I look forward to meeting him. What's his name?'

'Percy.'

'Give Percy my regards. I gotta go and hide in the bathroom or they'll send me to haul in the firewood.'

Simone called out, 'Tell him not to be late and to dress properly.'

'What, no corduroy jeans? Don't worry, I won't disgrace her.'

'What time do you get back home?'

'All being well, lunchtime. Don't sweat it, I'll be there.'

'His ticket is at the door.' Simone pulled another sharp maneuvre.

'Your ticket's at the door.'

'Gotcha.'

'See you Dad.'

'Love you. And love to Simone.' He rang off.

Simone said, 'It wasn't me. Must have been Benson.'

'What I was thinking.'

'Is there a problem with your father?' asked Holmes.

'Yes,' they answered jointly. 'He's our father.'

'He brought up the two of you by himself?'

'Yes, he did,' said Georgette, regretting she hadn't spoken to Harry longer but already worrying about the complication of his return.

'Well,' said Holmes, 'your father is very different to any of my era.'

'In what way?' asked Georgette.

'We never spoke to our fathers. They spoke to us.'

'We'd better get our stories straight for Dad,' said Georgette. 'Percy is an old friend I met at the London conference and he is over here investigating ...'

'A spy ring,' put in Simone.

'No! Not a spy ring. Something simple.'

'An academic teaching post,' suggested Holmes. 'Like Avery Scheer's.'

That would do the trick. Harry would want to steer clear of any academic.

'So you think this professor guy is a psycho?' Simone was darting through traffic, fearless.

'I dare not yet speculate. What did you think, Watson?'

'I couldn't be sure if he was playing with us, or if that's his normal self.'

'Precisely, as though he were presenting an act. But was the act one of a killer, or simply a vain man? And we must not forget the others.'

Georgette said, 'Edwards seems less likely to me.'

'Perhaps he disguises his true self better. There is also the fact that he restores books. In the detective squad room on the wall was a board with the names of the victims and their occupations. Lucy Bassey worked in a museum as a restorer. It is quite possible her path crossed with that of Morgan Edwards. Remember, he said that from time to time he needed the help of an expert.'

It was true, Georgette recalled now.

'That's why you're the detective, I suppose,' said Simone.

Holmes took the compliment in his stride. 'And you, if I may say so, are a lively coachman!'

Simone preened.

Sickening. Georgette had been considering accompanying Simone and Holmes to meet Ambrose but duty demanded she check on her hamsters. Now she had no regrets. If this sycophancy was going to define the rest of the night she'd much rather be in her lab that now loomed ahead through the smeared windscreen. Simone pulled over, right out in front. Holmes made to jump out and open her door but Georgette beat him to it.

'Allow me to walk you to the door,' he said.

'No need. We have an armed security guard.'

'Then we shall wait to see you in. Be very careful, Watson. Do not underestimate our foe.'

The earnestness of his caution scared her.

'Good luck,' she called back and ran to the door more quickly than usual, not so much because of the rain but the shapeless fear that over a few short hours had become ubiquitous.

She punched in the code and entered the familiar gloom of her modern cave. With Noah at large, and outside a tempest starting to blow, she was comforted by the familiar outline of Jason, the security guard, but five strides in across the marble floor, that sense of well-being fled. It wasn't Jason standing there.

'Evening, ma'am.'

The man was about thirty, he looked fit, muscular.

'Jason's not on tonight?'

'No ma'am, he had an accident apparently. I'm his replacement.'

He had a badge across his pocket which proclaimed the name Sheffield.

'What kind of accident?'

'They didn't tell me. Nothing too serious, I don't think. I'm sorry, ma'am, but may I see your identification card?'

Georgette handed her card across. Sheffield studied it.

'Thank you, Doctor Watson. I'll remember you next time.'

He pressed the button and Georgette entered through the security gate and thanked him.

'Sheffield is your last name?'

'Yes, ma'am. First name is Dwayne.'

'Thank you, Dwayne.' She was going to ask him to try and find out more about Jason but then realized she'd be better served asking Steven next time she was here during the day.

Stepping back into her lab was an odd, dislocated feeling, like she'd been abroad for a long time and just returned home. It had been less than forty-eight hours. Theoretically the hamsters could survive for days in their cages. She had fed them fresh food two days ago and left them carrot pieces, seeds and so on. There was also a special self-serve trigger they could hit for nutritious pellets, and each cage was supplied with a similar mechanism that delivered fresh water. All the same, she did not like them being left continually in a small cage and so she would have special hours where they could enjoy themselves in a 'natural habitat' area she had created for them. Being nocturnal creatures, this recreation took place in the dark. Some breeds of hamsters were loners who would attack any other hamster they perceived as being on their territory but Georgette used a breed that were happy to socialize. All up, there had been fourteen hamsters in her program. The area of sand and grasses that she had created in a large perspex tub was not big enough for all fourteen at once so she would split them into two groups but tonight, having limited time, she decided they could all squeeze in together. She began transferring the animals from their cages. Zoe, her very first hamster, looked listless and had barely touched her food. That was a concern. Hamsters, from her experience, lived on average around two years. It had been fourteen months since she had revived Zoe after she had been 'dead' eleven minutes. That would make her less than eighteen months old.

'What's up, Zoe?' she asked, tenderly checking the small creature. Her phone rang. Simone.

'Sherlock wanted me to check you made it in safely.'

'I'm fine, you can assure him.'

'How's my plant doing?'

Shredded like a sail after a cannon blast. She'd have to ditch it.

'Thriving.' Something was definitely up with Zoe.

'I thought you, me and Sherlock might go clubbing after.'

'I'd rather swallow hot razor blades.' Georgette was reluctant to put Zoe with the other hamsters in case she had some disease.

'Anyway, I don't think you should be clubbing with some maniac on the loose in Manhattan.'

'There's always some maniac on the loose in Manhattan.'

Okay, she couldn't argue with that.

'Catch you later, then.'

When Simone rang off, Georgette once more felt very alone. Leaving Holmes in the hands of her sister would normally have given her a seizure but right now her concern was Zoe. Georgette adored these creatures. She spared a thought for her father. Imagine having a real daughter to worry about. She checked each of them over, made sure they had fresh water and feed. At nine-thirty, Simone rang again to say they had met Valerian the hacker and that he assured them he would have names within twelve hours. She had driven Ambrose home and left Holmes in Alphabet City. Instant alarm bells.

'What's he doing there?'

'He wouldn't say.'

'You just left him?'

'He's a grown man, what should I have done?'

Shackled him, maybe. Hit him over the head. First Zoe, and now Holmes on the loose, unsupervized. Simone was talking again.

'Hey, sooner or later you need to trust him. He made me promise to call you and tell you to go straight home. Said he would see you there. He's cute.'

'Let's not have this conversation again.'

'No, let's do. You've got him all to yourself. Don't waste this opportunity, over and out. And sis ...'

What now, a loan request? Georgette braced for it.

'... thanks for letting me be part of this. It means a lot you trust me. I won't screw up.'

She ended the call and Georgette felt chastened. Typical Simone, just when you thought you had her on toast, she flipped you over.

A little over an hour later, her Lyft dropped Georgette back to the apartment. The rain had eased slightly. She entered the lobby and remembered she had laundry to pick up from the basement. It had been wrong of her to leave her bedsheets in the dryer but Gwendoline, the elderly former schoolteacher, laundered every day and politely put whoever's laundry was left in a dryer into buckets for them. Unless Georgette got her laundry now, she'd feel like it needed washing again. She took the elevator to the basement. She never liked coming down here. The corridor was bare brick and ill lit and, even though the boilers were here, it was always cold.

Pure darkness greeted her when the doors opened. She quickly hit the round button on the wall and a creamy, blue glow was roused and reluctantly pointed the way down the corridor to the laundry room. Hustling down the short corridor, she reached the laundry, which was in total darkness. She pressed its light button. Overhead fluorescent lights kicked in but one wasn't working and another constantly flickered, so again she was left with light as miserable as charity and in the end had to use her phone. As she'd hoped, her sheets were in a bucket stacked on top of three others.

'Bless you, Gwendoline,' she whispered to herself and put the phone down on the narrow bench to pick up the washing, then froze at the loud bang of the staircase door. Nobody in here used the stairs. The light from her phone went out and she was back with just that flickering fluoro.

Why would anybody use the stairs?

With terrifying swiftness, she found an answer: to avoid the camera in the elevator. Footsteps slowly advanced down the corridor. She looked desperately for a weapon, anything, but it was a laundry, clear and bare and –

The steps reached the doorway and stopped. She grabbed for her phone but in her haste, knocked it straight off the bench. It clattered on the concrete floor.

Holmes stepped into the room.

She was flooded with a mix of relief and annoyance. 'For goodness sake, Holmes!'

'My apologies if I alarmed you. I had been waiting outside and then I saw you return.'

'What were you doing outside? Smoking?'

'And keeping watch. One can't be too careful.'

She wished he hadn't said that for it brought back that wave of terror that had drowned her just moments earlier.

A short time later they were seated in the apartment. Rain still fell, the lamps turning the street to a glistening seal-skin. Georgette stepped back from her window, her hands warmed by the mug of steaming tea. Holmes' effort was far more drinkable than Simone's, and he had made a large pot of pea-and-ham soup which was simmering on the stove. She could get used to this.

'I have to say, I had thought milk in cartons to be the most splendid advance since Queen Victoria but in truth, milk does taste better in glass. Teabags on the other hand are a superlative saver of time and space, though I pity the Enderbys.'

'Who are they?'

'Family that lived two along from us. He was a potter and glazier, specialty teapots.'

'What were you doing down the Lower East Side?'

'Nostalgia. The last time I was in Manhattan I found myself on a matter of some import that involved a sea captain with a twin brother.'

'I'd like to hear some of your tales.'

'Of course. I would be only too happy –'

His eyes had diverted to the gift she was offering, a spare phone she had kept in her bedroom drawer. 'I thought you might be able to make use of this,' she said.

He was like a child. 'I shall treasure this always, Watson.'

She showed him the basics. 'And remember to keep it charged.'

He pocketed the phone.

'So Valerian has taken the commission?'

'He was pleased to do so. He promises results forthwith.' He checked his watch. 'The soup should be ready but don't allow your expectations to get too high. I have never been much of a cook.' He nipped into the kitchen to check on progress. It only occurred to her now to ask where he had got the money for the ingredients.

'Were you street performing again?' She had to raise her voice above the clatter of aluminium.

'No, the money, you might say, came to me.' There was a terrible clang. She willed herself not to look. 'Just as I was concluding my sightseeing I was inveigled by a flimflam man to see if I could determine under which thimble I might locate the pea and thereby earn myself twenty dollars.'

'You can't win at those games. The pea is never even under the cup.'

'Of course not. Believe me, Watson, the game has been around longer than I and, as you know, that is a considerable time.' Holmes emerged with two steaming bowls of soup and placed them on the only table in the room, the small coffee table. He presented a spoon and folded napkin at its side, as a waiter might and with a hand signal bade her sit. Georgette did and Holmes sat opposite on the armchair.

'In fact I did not even have the stake to bet on the pea initially, merely two single dollar notes you had generously bestowed upon me, but it was child's play to spy the shill, a well-dressed young woman who naturally won. I congratulated her on her win and in doing so lifted her so called "winnings" back off her, using that as my stake.'

'Was that stealing?'

'Yes, however, stealing from a thief is a lower grade of theft in my opinion.'

'But you still lost.'

'Of course I lost but before I handed over my two ten-dollar notes, which was really their money, I made a great show of looking for the pea to see where it really was, and while the flimflam man was busy returning the pea – which of course had never been there – I switched a single dollar note for a ten. So, I handed over eleven dollars, leaving us with a profit of nine dollars and the means to buy the soup you have before you.'

Which, she was pleased to find, was tasty.

'Edible?'

'Excellent. Thank you.'

'I am not good at this, I know, but there was occasion when I had to prepare food for myself and so I restricted my ambitions to just two items: boiled eggs, and pea-and-ham soup. Your great-great-grandfather was, I'm afraid, far worse a cook than I, and could boast no fare at all.'

'Did my great-great also act as a kind of Medici benefactor to your art of detection?'

He chuckled. 'You know, as generous as he was, your progenitor did not have your turn of phrase. In answer to your question, yes, he did support me from time to time but he told me more than once that I enriched his life more than any novel or play and that he was grateful I was in it. We did manage a number of journeys abroad in which I was able through my work to provide for him.'

'The books make him seem ...'

'Stolid.'

'... yes, that is a good word for it.'

'By and large Conan Doyle rendered him accurately for one who was looking at our relationship from the outside but your great-great was not as conservative as he allowed himself to be portrayed. There was, not far beneath the surface, a rich vein of devilment which he preferred to mask. Understandable for one of his profession. He valued his status, his clubs, his regimental companions and so forth but he was his own man when it came to determining the morality of our actions. He would not defend a royal personage for example, simply on account of their royalty. His senses may have been dull in determining the nuances of peoples of different races and religions but he would tip over a prejudice as easily as a hurricane would capsize a dinghy. In the mind of Watson, a man's actions determined his character, not his upbringing or tittle-tattle.'

'Did you often clash?'

'Frequently. I would suggest one course of action, he another. We respected one another and acted as counterbalances. I doubt I ever once foisted my values upon him but I cannot recall a single occasion in which he ultimately refused to aid my enterprise.'

'A good friend.'

'The best, but as I say, for all his good points, and they were numerous, Watson was never one for the verbal joust.'

'Humorless?'

'Earnest to the border but not beyond. He saw humor in simple things where the joke completely escaped me: a man tripping over a cart, a singing dog and so forth.' He looked keenly at her, his spoon poised.

'Watson, I should feel privileged if you would at some point discourse with me on your research.'

Not only did this surprise her but his interest made her feel, for some reason, embarrassed. 'What would you like to know?'

'Everything. While the world at large would turn your efforts into a circus act, this does not negate the stupendous scientific leap you have made.'

'Thank you. Perhaps you would like to come back to my lab one day as a guest rather than a subject?'

'Most definitely.'

Her phone rang. It was Benson.

'Hi, Garry.'

'Sorry to take so long. It's been quite a day. We picked up a fingerprint in the church. Guy named Ricky Coleman with a sex assault history. CCTV shows him on the street a block away and very close to the time Lucy Bassey must have entered the church. We've been chasing him all day. I've only got five minutes as it is, we're heading to a KA of his upstate.'

It sounded like he was calling from the car.

'Percy and I came up with some information we thought might be important.'

'Shoot.'

She told him as quickly as she could about the book and how they had followed up to find out that four people had attended Scheer's discussion group. She heard him exhale the way annoyed people do, loud enough so you know they are annoyed.

'Georgi, I appreciate your efforts but please, leave the police work to us. That goes for your friend too. Especially for him.'

'Of course, but when Scheer called me, I couldn't ignore him.'

'I'll get onto it just as soon as. I don't want anything to happen to you. Your old man would skin me alive.'

She thought it best she say nothing about their hacking efforts.

'Soon as we grab Coleman, I'll follow it up. Maybe Coleman got a hold of the book somehow. Thanks.' She could tell he was about to sign off but he held up. 'And listen, when this is done, let's have a drink.'

She felt herself going prickly, Holmes eyeballing her. 'Of course.'

She ended the call, and gave a summary, omitting the final overture from Benson.

Holmes scowled. 'Over one hundred years and their competence does not increase.'

'It sounds like they have a strong lead.'

'Except that a murderer who is clever enough to cut somebody's throat without seemingly getting blood on themselves, and does not leave DNA or allow himself to be photographed, is bumbling enough to leave a fingerprint. That does not jibe, Watson, no most decidedly not.' Holmes twirled the spoon in his hand. 'We have little time. Once he takes the zebra, Noah is, to use a metaphor, in unchartered waters.'

The bottle of wine she had bought was not chilled yet, so she put it in the freezer to hurry it along. At fifteen dollars it was on the pricey side but she wanted to make a good impression. Ditto the waxing, painful, but her girlfriends said men expected it these days. Darn, she really wanted to take a sip of that wine herself, right now, to settle herself down. It had been a long time between drinks. She smiled at her pun. She had absolutely no concerns about her lasagna. Half her life she had been preparing that dish. It sat ready in the oven. And there would be plenty left over which she could freeze for lunch or dinner. Earlier she had been excited by the beautiful lace underwear which she had been able to get at a ridiculous sale price. Nobody could afford the list price, nobody *she* knew, but she'd been watching and knew they always discounted before Black Friday. She had been ready and waiting. There was no guarantee it would be on show tonight. Okay, she hoped it was, that it got to that stage, but he liked to take things slow, he'd said, and so it was no definite thing. And if it didn't get that far, it was still nice to be wearing classy underwear. You look back at your life, at the mistakes, especially Joey – 'mistake' hardly seemed adequate, but then again they were so young – but you looked back now, and you realized what it had cost you: classy underwear, a decent job and, most of all, peace of mind. She'd practically buried herself. Like in the old days they used to send you to a convent and girls would become nuns and never speak again. Well of course, she hadn't stopped speaking but she had definitely withdrawn behind walls, and they didn't have to be made out of stone.

She took herself back into the bedroom because that had the best mirror. Another quick once over with the brush wouldn't hurt. She thought she heard something, just a click. Was it him? Had he come a few minutes early? Her bell hadn't rung. Maybe he'd knocked though. Some people are so used to bells not working that they knock. She put the brush down and walked back along the short corridor towards the door. The light was dim and romantic, vintage lampshades over which she had draped a light sarong, just to take the edge off. The table had candles but she hadn't lit them yet. That could wait ...

She stopped mid-thought. That sounded like somebody's breath, right behind her. She only managed the first instance of the pivot before some terrible force was crushing her throat, cutting off air. Her arms flailed like those plastic men outside of car yards. She couldn't scream but lashed back with her elbow, felt her feet leave the carpet, the room spin, her hip smash into the floor but the pressure never subsided, and her heart was pounding and she could feel tears welling but no ... air. She remembered the bottle in the freezer, it would explode. Everything was growing dimmer, her lungs couldn't fill, she was terrified, peeing herself, that expensive underwear, couldn't help it, couldn't make a single word, not even a whimper.

In those last seconds she resigned herself to a fate that might have been hers long ago.

A tear froze in her eye and the light in it slowly faded.

16

Holmes sliced the top off her egg with a terrifying efficiency.

'Three-minutes forty-five. One thing that hasn't changed in a century, thank goodness, is the perfect duration to boil an egg.'

She thanked him. He was delighted with himself. He tucked the napkin into his shirt and sat opposite. She had woken to a text from Benson to say they had taken Coleman, the suspect, into custody. The message had been sent at four in the morning and it was now eight.

'No word from Simone?' asked Holmes.

'No. She normally doesn't rise before ten. I could call her, I suppose.'

He said there was no need. Valerian had indicated he would not have the email addresses before nine-thirty.

'He has swim squad, he told me. Did you sleep well?'

'Like a stone. You?'

'Two hours deep and dark as the Congo.'

'What were you doing when you weren't searching for Livingstone?'

'I met Stanley, you know. Wonderful fellow. I digress: in answer to your question I was cogitating and making a list which I took the liberty of printing. The machine I'm afraid took me some little time to decipher.' He hauled up a wad of paper. 'The first twenty or so I managed only one entry per page but then I mastered it.' He slapped the paper. 'Every business in this city I could find that had "zebra" in the title.'

'That's a very literal interpretation. Noah might simply choose a woman wearing black and white stripes.'

'That, I am afraid, is very true.'

'I need to visit my lab. One of my hamsters may be ill and I need to monitor her. You are more than welcome to join me.'

'Thank you but I wish to meet with Valerian. He was organising some surveillance for me on our four known suspects.'

'What?'

'Don't worry, it's only seven dollars per hour.'

The rate this was going, she'd be penniless by Thanksgiving.

'You need to consult with me.'

'There was no time. I promise I shall repay you, Watson.'

What the hell. She let it go. 'Don't forget you have a phone now.'

He raised his forearm to show where he had written his phone's number. 'I shall accompany you to the lab.'

She told him there was absolutely no need but he insisted and, as they would both be heading downtown, she accepted his offer.

The cold slapped her across the face. The rain had gone and with it any juice of life. It seemed her fingers might snap. Holmes' breath formed white clouds. Without any self-aggrandizement she found herself marvelling at what she had brought about. Nearly one-hundred and thirty years on, this man, who had been as inert as the pavement, was alive. Looking through the car window it was like they were touring an urban Disneyland. Pedestrians appeared inanimate, as if placed in position by a giant hand. The trees had become petrified. There appeared to be no life at all beyond the vehicle.

Snow was near.

Her phone buzzed. A text from Benson. He was back on deck and was about to continue his interview with Coleman but would call her as soon as he was out of there.

'I told you,' said Holmes snippily. 'Wasting their time. Wouldn't know how to find Noah if he were a homing pigeon.'

When the car reached the lab she stepped out and said, 'Please don't land us in hot water.'

'I shall do only what I deem necessary to apprehend Noah.'

A reply that fell well short of her scientist's desire for certainty. She was wearing gloves and a fake-fur hood but they were paper against a wolf's sharp claw and in the twenty yards to the door, the cold shredded her. What must it have been like back in Holmes' era? Unless they had fire-pits burning coal in the middle of the foyer, it would have been brutal in those big old buildings. Thankfully heating had come a long way and relief was instant as she entered. When she saw the friendly face of the security guard, Steven, she remembered to ask.

'What happened to Jason? Is he okay?'

'Getting better. He got hit by a motorcycle. It never even stopped. Fractured pelvis, some other stuff.'

'That's horrible.'

'Yeah, just goes to show. Can't take nothing for granted. How do you find the new guy?'

'Very formal.'

'Know what you mean. I tried to jaw with him a bit but he wasn't interested. They're saying snow tonight.'

She said she could believe it.

Not only had there been no improvement in Zoe's condition but Vernon, who had been the second of her revived hamsters, was looking listless, just how Zoe had the day before. It was possible they had both picked up some virus around the same time. And it was as she was reflecting on what might be responsible that she received a call from Anita Mirabella.

'What's going on, Georgette, I haven't heard from you?'

Georgette fudged, said she had taken some time off.

'That's a good idea. We can get too close. I haven't forgotten you and I'm getting a bit more positive reaction from the board now that they are seeing the news stories you got. Could you write me up a proposition, not too scientific, these people are lawyers and accountants. Email it to me and I'll reshape it.'

'That's very kind of you.'

'I want to see smart people advance,' said Mirabella. 'Let's do lunch soon.'

Georgette left it that and returned to the task at hand. She began carefully examining each of the hamsters, checking their temperatures and weight. So far, the rest of the hamsters were in good health but she was thinking she might need to segregate them from Zoe and Vernon, just in case. Her mind wandered to whether Harry had left himself enough time to get back for the show. It might well depend on whether he was still trying to end Mirsch's streak. Mostly though, she thought about Holmes, and what she thought about *thinking* about Holmes. Was there something icky about it? Like, Simone had suggested, Frankenstein falling for his monster. Holmes was intelligent, charming ... obstinate. But mostly he was extremely un-Vance, and that was the most compelling point in his favor. All the same ...

Her phone rang, and for a moment her system blipped, her thinking it was Holmes. But it was a number she did not immediately recognize though it seemed familiar.

'Georgette Watson.'

'Georgette, Avery Scheer. Have I caught you at a bad time?'

Holy crap! Think ... The silence was lengthening.

'I'm just in my lab,' she said and then kicked herself for divulging it.

'I probably sound like a schoolboy but I've not been able to think about much else since we met yesterday. I would love to hear more of your work and I thought you may be free for lunch.'

She looked at the clock and saw it was already past midday.

'Oh,' she said, surprised on all counts.

'I'm free for an hour or so. I could head your way. But, of course if it is inconvenient ...'

This was a chance to mine information, wasn't it? But then again, the man could be a psychopathic killer. Surely though, in a public restaurant in the middle of the day ... Stamping out the fuse a split second before the dynamite ignited, she said, 'That would be lovely.'

Rhumba was a medium-sized restaurant, crowded for lunch meetings. For the hundredth time she asked herself what the hell was she thinking accepting the invitation. Damn Holmes. She had tried him constantly but there had been no answer. She'd left three messages on Simone's phone, Harry was likely on the road, and Benson was still interviewing his suspect. Images flashed through her brain: Gina Scaroldi, throat slashed and dumped in ruins, Lucy Bassey squeezed into a bloody confessional box. And then there was no time for thought because Avery Scheer walked in through the door and headed straight towards her.

She forced herself to smile warmly and shook his extended hand.

'I'm so pleased you could make time for me,' he said smoothly.

'Your invitation was opportune. I needed a break.'

Silence inserted itself between them. It was removed by an attentive waiter asking what they would like to drink.

'I'm not sure about the lady but I would like a glass of merlot.'

Georgette opted for the same.

Scheer said, 'You know, at the risk of making myself unpopular with both you and Percy ... I meant to include him in the invitation, will he be joining us?'

She saw an opening. 'Quite likely.'

'Then I can tell him myself, but I wanted to declare up front that I've been thinking about the book and I really would prefer not to sell. Percy's offer is generous but now that I feel I know you, even just a little, it seems wrong to profit at your friend's expense. If that's why you're here, I am not offended but I hope we can still have a pleasant lunch.'

Georgette said, 'Oh no, that's not why I agreed. I'm famished and I thought, why not? A bit of intelligent discussion never harmed anyone.' Except perhaps your victims, she thought as she smiled. 'No, the book is between you and Percy and frankly I think he's better off saving his money.'

The waiter delivered their drinks. Scheer toasted her.

'Here's to happy accidents.'

She gave hers the merest sip. Scheer glanced at the menu.

'So please, tell me about your research?'

Georgette ran through the basics. Her breathing had levelled out and conversation was easier now.

'The next stage is to try human subjects but I am afraid the university is balking.'

Scheer shook his head. 'They really have no idea what we do at the coalface.'

The idea of Avery Scheer in a coalmine was absurd. He announced he was going to have the turkey salad. She opted for soup. After the waiter had taken their orders, Scheer sipped his wine and continued on the theme.

'I won't say my area is the same as yours, not at all, but I face the same kind of restrictions. I consult for a number of psychiatric institutions and the reality is they are compromised and don't see it. It is easier for them to keep a person tranquilized and confined than to rehabilitate them, let them free in the outside world.'

'In case they do something violent?'

'Primarily. So that's where we are the same, you and me. I can save people, mentally, but these institutions fear if something goes wrong, they will be sued, or worse, have their "brand" damaged. They would be terrified that if a person you revived subsequently displays any aberrant behavior, you – and by extension them – will be blamed.'

She hadn't thought of this before. What would the ramifications be if it were discovered Holmes was working on a serial murder case?

'You seem attracted to crime.' Scheer took another sip and looked deep into her eyes.

'Why do you say that?'

'Well, Percy for a start. He's a criminologist, right? And I'm sure I read that your father is a policeman.'

For the first time Georgette had the inkling that Scheer might be quizzing her under the guise of general conversation.

'Yes, he works out of Queens.'

Play it cool, straight up, she was telling herself. Scheer displayed no violent reaction.

'I'm sure your father is the exception but I've found the police to be ...' he searched carefully for the word he wanted, '... pedestrian.'

Her phone rang and with relief she recognized her old number.

'Percy,' she answered gaily.

'Afternoon, Watson. Are you at your lab?'

'No, I'm at Rhumba at lunch with Avery Scheer. Are you able to join us?'

'Lunch? My God, Watson.'

She rattled off the address from the menu. 'I do you hope can join us. Although don't get your hopes up, Avery says he does not want to sell.'

Holmes assured her he would get there as soon as he could. She relayed the message. Scheer made a show of welcoming the news.

'Returning to our discourse, it is interesting,' Scheer fingered the stem of his glass, 'that you do seem to be surrounded by those engaged in the understanding of the criminal mind.'

'I didn't have much say in my father's occupation.'

'No, but perhaps it has shaped you. Nobody has spent more hours than me trying to unravel the relative importance to criminal proclivity of genetic disposition as compared to environmental background. I still can't decide where I sit.' He suddenly changed tack. 'How did you meet Percy?'

'There was a conference in London on factors to be considered in determining time of death.' She was borrowing from the true facts. The conference had been real. 'I was there because of the significance to my research: I need to know as exactly as possible time of death in order to know the correct mix of gases. Percy was there for somewhat different reasons.'

Scheer said, 'I thought you mentioned Switzerland?'

Shit, she had too. Improvise!

'Actually, that is true. Our paths crossed there but we didn't know one other very well at all, just through a function we had both attended. The conference was where we got to know one other.'

Scheer seemed to take that at face value. 'What fascinates me are the moral questions. When is somebody responsible for their actions? Most people say: When they know what they are doing, but you can know what you're doing without being able to stop – just look at most golfers who keep two-putting.'

'You think it is a compulsion to kill?'

'Sometimes. But I have seen people kill because it's the right thing to do.'

'In their eyes, you mean?'

'Of course. Abraham was prepared to murder his own son because God had told him. Was he wrong? Was he mad?'

Again, the biblical reference did not escape her.

'It's hard to think killing your child could be right.'

'That's the whole point. Is somebody noble, or simply crazy? I treated a woman who killed her three children because she believed they were possessed. She was sure she had done the right thing. Many soldiers kill because they are told to by an unseen superior. We don't say they are mad. I'm sure for Abraham that God was just as real, maybe more real an entity than, say, the President is for a lot of his troops.'

The food arrived. Georgette said she supposed that was where his discipline posed a lot more questions than hers.

'Really? I would have thought bringing somebody back from the dead was the most morally contentious issue. Suppose you had a chance to bring back a despot, or simply a murderer. Would you do it?'

She found his intensity unsettling.

'I don't know if I have a choice.'

He pointed his fork at her. 'And that's exactly what many killers would tell you about their murders, that the average person just simply doesn't operate at the elite level they do whereby they can see the connection among all things: good–evil, life–death.'

'But those people are insane.'

His eyes twinkled. 'Isn't that exactly what so many people have said about you believing you can resurrect people long frozen? The truly insane thing is believing we don't have power over life and death. We do.'

'He said those exact words?' Holmes had arrived about ten minutes after Scheer had departed. Scheer had offered to give her a ride back to her lab. As if. Fortunately, she had been able to use waiting for Percy as an excuse.

'Yes, those exact words.'

Holmes had finally appeared, running down the street, arriving out of breath, and profusely apologetic, explaining his 'omnibus' had been at a standstill. He had then immediately quizzed her on the exchange between her and Scheer. They were still standing in bitter cold, out the front of Rhumba.

'Why didn't you answer your phone?' She heard herself, a worried parent scolding a child who might have injured himself.

'It appears I had the volume turned down.'

'Did your spies have anything of interest to report?'

'Both Melissa Harper and Walter Morris arrived home alone at ten-fifteen and ten-forty-one respectively, Scheer just before eleven, and Edwards did not leave the house.'

'Teenage boys: they could just be making it all up, too busy on their Xbox.'

'Whatever that may be. One works with what tools one has available. I don't need to tell you, Watson, that placing yourself in this kind of situation with Scheer is potentially dangerous, certainly inadvisable.'

While she might have agreed with him wholeheartedly, she was not about to give him the satisfaction.

'Almost any useful thing humankind has done has required an action that was inadvisable or dangerous or both. Look at your friend Livingstone.'

'Stanley,' he corrected. 'And he was not my friend but a friendly man.'

'What about Valerian?'

'A splendid young fellow. He explained it would be quite easy for him to have a "poke around" our suspects' computers. Said it was like looking through their trash cans – a method your antecedent and I employed to solve the case of the Nottingham Nobbler.'

'That's totally illegal.'

'Most effective crime-solution is. He delivered: not only the names of the other two attendees but he ran me through their Facebook profiles.'

The cold had got to her. She suggested they head back inside where he could tell her more over coffee.

'Capital idea,' he said.

The crowd had thinned, the warmth welcoming.

'Sara Ross and Hamilton de Souza,' announced Holmes. 'Neither with a police record, both postgraduate students from other states and both, so far as we could establish, in a different state at the time of the murders of both Carmen Cavanagh and Lucy Bassey. De Souza would also appear to have been in Japan when Gina Scaroldi was killed.'

'People can fake Facebook posts.'

'So Valerian warned me, but he was able to cross-correlate photographs of them with other Facebook users. He was also adept at finding his way into Department of Immigration records. I am confident neither Ross nor De Souza is Noah.'

'Which brings us back to our Endymion three.'

'Plus Edwards. Don't forget him. What do you make of Scheer, then?'

'If he's insane he hides it well.'

Holmes concurred, added, 'Many feel Napoleon was insane, and perhaps he was, and yet he could have explained all his actions quite soberly.'

She'd mentioned Scheer going on about Abraham.

Holmes nodded. 'He takes great pains to see things from the criminal's perspective: the woman who murdered her children and so forth. Whether that is empathy or whether he sees himself in the same light – pure egotism – I cannot decipher.'

In other words, the great detective hadn't a clue.

'Come on,' she ordered, taking two gulps of her coffee and leaving the rest. 'We need to get back and changed for the play.'

As they wound their way home, what was left of the day curled up and died, the sky dark as widows' weeds, the chill profound. Leached of color, cars scrambled about like beetles feasting on this decay. She would only have enough time to bathe and dress before having to head out again for Simone's play, which had an early start. Holmes went straight to the laptop on the living-room table.

Her hair annoyed her. Having it cut and styled after Vance left had made her feel good for all of four days. Then the reality had set in about how much money it was going to cost to maintain this new vision of herself, so now she was at that awkward in-between length. Sometimes she thought Holmes' intense stare into her eyes might have meant something more ... but no, that was preposterous. No word from Garry Benson. Maybe the suspect had confessed? When she stepped back into the living room in her towelling robe Holmes was still bent over the computer.

'Anything from Valerian?' she asked.

'I thought you considered yourself above our illegal ways.' He cocked an eye at her, leaning back on his chair and allowed himself a mischievous grin. 'Admit it, Watson, there is a criminal inside you waiting to break free.' Then, without waiting for an answer, he said, 'Valerian was as good as his word. He has sent me the contents of Scheer's computer. It will take some time to go through all this but I can find no communication from him with any of the victims. He has a number of case files with clients whose names are not revealed. They are simply given a number. There is one note I found under a file "students" you may find interesting.'

She was aware she was dripping on the carpet now but waited. Holmes savored the moment.

'He writes, "MH is sexually confused and I am not sure she is classic transgender. In our discussions she has confessed to sustained periods where she thinks of herself in her head as a male, while still viewing herself externally as a female, as if both genders could be simultaneously active within the one host body."' Holmes tented his fingers beneath his chin. 'There could be instances where the male takes charge of her thoughts and actions, however, the realm of the brain is best left to others than myself. Physical evidence, that is the Valhalla I seek.' His eyes fell on her and then darted away.

'I shall bathe,' he said and moved quickly to his room.

'Maybe Benson has a confession already?'

He stopped and turned, 'And maybe I shall go play hockey on Mars.'

'As a matter of fact ...'

'We've done that?' His face stretched the length of a football field.

'Gotcha,' she laughed and was pleased to see him smile.

17

Her agent, Vonny, had already taken the trouble of emailing a bunch of casting agents about the show, promising comps if they were keen, and one had said he might be attending. It wasn't one of the big timers but, Simone told herself, you have to begin on the lower rung and haul yourself step by step to the top. She wished she could tell the whole world about working with Sherlock Holmes. That would have her Snapchat and Instagram going through the roof. Ha, imagine the Kardashians trying to compete with that!

Not that she wasn't in their camp. Georgette had no time for any of this stuff, no time for any fun, period. If Holmes had been sharing an apartment with her instead of her sister, she would have buttered his crumpet.

Ambrose came up, jigging on the spot.

'Nervous?' she asked.

'Nah,' he said unconvincingly.

She looked up to see Frank N. Furter standing in front of her.

'Break a leg,' he said, in the way that their uncle used to offer them a piece of his pie, even though you knew he wanted it all to himself but felt it was still the right thing to do.

'You too,' she said. That was a good thing about theatre, you all sank or swam together.

To Georgette's surprise, Harry's attire featured not the blue blazer he'd worn to her lecture but a heavier tweed coat that fitted him better. No tie, but then you couldn't expect miracles. Holmes was in a line for complimentary wine. She'd prepped him relentlessly on the way over.

'Harry is a cop,' she'd said. 'He's not stupid.'

Holmes had assured her he knew his role but she was worried his mind was on Noah.

'I bought a new shirt,' declared Harry and spun for her. She could see he'd also had his hair freshly cut and was impressed. 'Where's the limey?'

'Lining up for wine.'

'Sort of thing I used to do for your mother. She said it evened out the time women spent waiting for the bathroom.' He nodded at the poster, which was extremely professionally done. 'I only ever saw the movie. I never saw the play. Your mom always wanted to.'

'She liked *Rocky Horror*?'

'Loved it. Loved musicals.'

'You see it together?'

'No. I hadn't met her yet. I was sixteen. *Grease*, we saw that together.'

Her father gazed into the middle distance, lost somewhere back in an era where video was a novelty. Holmes arrived with two red wines.

'Dad, this is my friend Percy.'

'Pleased to meet you, Percy.'

'You too, Harry.' Holmes was stranded with the wine glasses until Georgette took hers, and the men shook.

'Would you care for a wine?' asked Holmes, offering his.

'I'm more a beer guy. So, you're staying at Georgi's.'

'Yes, it was very kind of her to let me have her spare room.'

Good, he remembered that, even if did hit the "spare" a bit too obviously.

'You're an investigator?'

'Private.'

'You were a cop?'

'Mine is more a scientific background.'

'You ever work with the Yard?'

'Several times.'

'You come across Dougal Gray? He and I worked on some stuff.'

'I'm afraid I'm probably before his time.'

Harry chuckled. 'I see Georgi has briefed you to say all the right things.'

Fortunately, the bell rang.

'You guys can swap war stories later,' Georgette said, and prayed there was no chance of that.

She couldn't believe how good the play was. And Simone was outstanding. She played the uptight goody-two shoes Janet so convincingly. Harry was proud as Punch, she kept taking sly looks at him. On her other side,

Holmes was smiling, chuckling and more than once exclaiming, 'Oh, capital!'

It lifted her spirits, banished the darkness of the world in which she had lately found herself.

All the boys in the play were very good. Simone had relentlessly run down the kid playing Frank but Georgette thought he nailed it. At interval, Harry made for the bathroom while Holmes went to get the drinks again. She made a mental note to ask where this supply of money might be coming from. There was the inevitable long line for the ladies bathroom but Georgette's practiced eye had spied a disabled bathroom down a deserted corridor into which she'd blundered earlier while looking for Harry. She set off now for that, rounding the corner past the box-office area and then turning left again past the staircase. The bathroom showed vacant. She congratulated herself, entered, locked, slipped paper on the seat just in case and was quickly done. She opened the door, excited by the prospect of act two, and froze.

Morgan Edwards stood in her way. 'Doctor!' he exclaimed.

Later, thinking back over it, the reaction seemed overdone, staged.

'Hello.' She was ashamed to say that she stammered the greeting. He was holding a small backpack and she couldn't take her eyes from it. What she was thinking was that there were three hundred people just twenty yards away but he could cut her throat before anybody would locate where her screams came from. He made no move to shift away.

'You have a boy at the school here?' she asked, conjuring a carefree attitude from thin air. She was calculating if she could dart past him.

'No.' And the answer was like a slab sealing a tomb, until he suddenly smiled bashfully and said, 'Self-confessed *Rocky Horror* nut. See every production I can. Is Mr Turner here?'

'Yes, I should be getting back to him. It doesn't look like Professor Scheer wants to sell.'

'Oh well, if he does, it will be my pleasure to come and collect my wages of sin.'

Now her flesh was crawling. 'Well, nice to see you again,' she said and squirrelled past him. She found Holmes waiting with Harry but had to restrain herself from babbling about the encounter. The last thing she wanted was to alert Harry to her sleuthing. Holmes she could tell, sensed something was up and when the lights blinked and people shuffled back inside, she whispered what had happened.

'Morgan Edwards? Here?'

She relayed his explanation and then, as if trying to convince herself said, 'Perhaps it is pure coincidence.' Even as she said it, she was thinking, yes, it's possible that he just happened to be here but then he must have seen her in the crowd and followed her to the bathroom. Maybe he wanted to see if a sale had been made so he could claim his commission. But then she thought of the backpack and shuddered.

'Never fear, Watson,' said Holmes as the lights darkened. 'I shan't be letting you out of my sight.'

For the remainder of the performance, the encounter sat with Georgette like unpleasant foot odor. The play finished and all three of them were on their feet applauding heartily.

'Stay with your father,' whispered Holmes during the encore and bolted out. She saw Harry's head turn.

'The wine,' she lied. As they shuffled out she stuck like glue to Harry.

Holmes was waiting in the foyer when they emerged with the stragglers. He gave an almost imperceptible shake of the head to indicate he'd not spotted Edwards. By now she was feeling safer. A mini-supper was served back in the reception area. Georgette announced she was going to find Simone, and Holmes, of course, said he would come with her. Harry wanted to sample more mini-burgers.

Georgette and Holmes went back into the theatre and tracked towards the stage. Ambrose, whose 'Brad' had been very good, walked towards them on cloud nine, greeting Holmes with a prison-yard handshake.

'A most commendable performance,' said Holmes.

'You enjoyed it?'

'It was terrific.' Georgette meant it.

'You need to take a bow too,' said the schoolboy.

'What did I do?' asked Georgette.

'Simone modelled Janet completely on her sister,' said Holmes. 'Is that correct?'

'Exactly,' said Ambrose.

Georgette felt impelled to say there was a distinction between being a stuck-up anal-retentive and somebody who was simply tidy but, before she could, Ambrose asked to have a photo taken with her.

'Would you mind?' Ambrose handed his phone to Holmes.

'Delighted.'

'It's not every day I get my photo taken with a genius,' said Ambrose.

'Smile!'

The flash hit.

'What do you mean, genius?' asked Georgette, her eyes throbbing.

'Simone doesn't stop talking about you. Says one day you're going to win the Nobel Prize.'

'And I believe she is correct,' said Holmes handing back the phone, his eyes scanning the empty theatre, just in case. Ambrose shifted off to check the photo and Holmes said, 'I was pleased to see Alfred Nobel followed my notion to initiate prizes for those who worked unstintingly for the benefit of humankind – yes Watson, I am adopting your vernacular – however, I was disappointed that he chose to name the prizes after himself instead of my suggestion.'

'Which was?' She was fairly certain she knew the answer to that. After all he had googled himself first chance he had.

'The Watson prize.' And he smiled as if he had known exactly what she'd been thinking.

Ambrose returned. 'I'm texting the photo to you.' Conspiratorially he whispered, 'There's an agent with Simone. He loved it.'

Holmes caught a flash of somebody lurking by the far exit.

'Excuse me,' said Holmes. 'Would you mind Georgette for me?'

'Of course,' said Ambrose. Holmes bounded across to the other side of the theatre.

'Strange, dude,' commented Ambrose. 'Come on,' and then, with Georgette still craning to track Holmes, he ushered her down a back corridor. A middle-aged man with silver hair was just leaving Simone's dressing room.

'Call me and we'll set up a meeting. I've got some things could really suit,' he called back to where Simone waited in the doorway. Ambrose dug his elbow into Georgette's ribs: the agent. The man forced a tight smile as he passed and congratulated Ambrose.

Simone was beaming. 'He loved it. Says he has some film roles.'

'I loved it too,' Georgette kissed her sister.

Ambrose announced he had better be off to see his parents. Simone hugged him.

'Don't forget my driving lesson tomorrow,' he reminded her.

'I don't forget my co-stars.'

When Ambrose left, Georgette told her Harry was still scoffing his face in the foyer.

'But we're going to supper, aren't we?'

'I doubt that will affect his appetite. You know what he's like with anything free. Dad is so proud. You were sensational. You are an actress, you really are.'

'Don't sound so surprised.'

Georgette felt guilty. The truth was she never believed her sister would do more than dabble in anything.

Simone read it, said, 'I don't blame you. I've always been a mess-up. I never thought I could be anything either. Did Percy come?'

'I never saw him so happy. Well, for the first act.' Georgette explained about the encounter with Morgan Edwards but there was no time for further discussion because Holmes appeared.

'False alarm, sound technician.' Harry arrived next. Georgette watched Harry hugging Simone, saw the absolute love in his eyes and then looked at Holmes, lost for a moment, watching them. I'm so lucky, thought Georgette, I have sister, a dad, flesh and blood that I can hold and feel their heart pumping against mine. Holmes has only a long, empty corridor containing nothing but a wisp of memories.

Harry could not remember a night as good as this one in a very long time. He wished Helen could have been there but didn't go on about it for fear of seeming maudlin and spoiling the moment. Up until tonight he'd really wondered if Simone had it in her. I mean, playing rat excrement, he supposed, took a bit of moxy but it gave the audience no idea of the kid's potential. Tonight, she sang, danced, acted. After he'd congratulated Simone, they rejoined the rest of the cast for the best part of an hour where Simone and the boys relived their finest moments. Then the four of them walked to a Spanish restaurant a few blocks west. Snow was falling constantly. They ate, and after toasting the late Helen Watson, Harry regaled Percy with embarrassing stories about the girls. Had them squirming. Jeez, it was fun. When the girls had gone off to the bathroom, Harry did grow sentimental. He couldn't help it, the wine and the evening all bubbled up. He needed an ear to bend and Percy's was convenient. The guy was calm, had an air of ... gravitas, he was pretty sure was the word, so he figured what he wanted to say wouldn't be squandered.

'You know, Percy, when people hear about Georgette and what happened, they say "I know what it must have been like for you" but of course they don't. They have no idea. As a young cop on patrol, I was sometimes not only first on the scene, but then later had to break the news of a loved one's death. There were a couple of auto accidents, and a terrible boating tragedy where I had to swim in two injured girls.

One made it, the other ... I stood watching while the medics worked on her, and I felt absolutely useless.' Percy nodded, understanding. 'They couldn't revive her. And believe me I *thought* I knew, or had some inkling how the parents felt but when I pulled the lifeless body of my own little girl from that freezing lake and laid her dead upon the ice ... only then did I truly understand the utter desolation of a loved one dealing with the *fact*. Kneeling on that ice, it was like my body had been cleaved in two, and the universe was nothing but emptiness and pain. It was like you're naked, split open, in a winter that's never going to end, but is just ... eternal. And the horror of that emptiness, the reality that this is your life now, I can't ... no one can explain that. And yet I was blessed. I got her back and I swore to God I would never, ever forget that gift. And with Simone ... well, hell, I've had my heart in my mouth every day for thirty years but tonight, I felt just as blessed.'

He lifted his glass and the Englishman did the same. They shared a silent toast: to life, to the girls. He was pleased Percy hadn't tried to interrupt, like he'd known his role was to just listen, knew Harry could never say the same words to his daughters. Holmes stood as Simone and Georgette rejoined the table.

Harry said, 'Be careful, you do that here, you'll get a lecture on being a chauvinist.'

Georgette's phone buzzed.

'That'll be Spielberg,' quipped Harry.

Georgette read it, found Holmes' eyes on her. 'It's Benson. He can see us.'

'What on earth did you think you were doing?' Benson's hands were supplicant, as if he'd been lifted out of a Florentine painting. Lipinski leaned back on a bench, arms folded, unimpressed. Holmes thankfully remained silent. She'd just revealed she had been to lunch with Avery Scheer earlier in the day. 'This is what I was afraid of,' said Benson. They were up in the corner of the squad room where Benson was running the Noah task force. The minute Benson had appeared, Georgette could tell he'd got no confession from Coleman.

Georgette said, 'You were busy and we thought it too important to just ignore.'

'*We?*' Benson glared at Holmes.

Far from intimidated, Holmes said, 'You were fully occupied with your ... *suspect*.' Holmes dropped the word in the sentence the way a socialite drops a teabag into a trash can. Like it might splatter and get him dirty.

Georgette felt obliged to ease the tension.

'I'm sorry, Garry, but what *could* we do? Put yourself in our shoes: the book seemed a viable lead and then Avery Scheer called me and we thought ... there's no harm in meeting with him.'

'No harm? Noah slashes women's throats. And he could be Noah!'

Holmes needled, 'I suppose you are right. But we apologize for advancing the case while you were tied up. No doubt you would have got there eventually.'

Benson trained guns on the annoying British frigate. Georgette threw herself across the line of fire.

'If anybody is to blame, it's me. I suppose I shouldn't have accepted Scheer's invitation to lunch. Percy knew nothing about it.'

'Well, he should have. Who knows why Noah fixates on these particular women?'

Georgette kept it rolling. 'We found this in a bin in the study room of Walter Morris and Melissa Harper... it seems to be a group email for those attending the discussion group.'

He took it carefully and studied it. 'Only four people attended?'

'That's what Scheer told us and this would support that,' she said.

Benson pushed out a lip. 'Of course they could have talked – shown the discussion paper to somebody else. And then there's the book guy ...'

'Edwards,' said Holmes. 'Yes. You might want to look into him.'

Georgette explained his appearance at the play. Benson wrestled with an invisible demon, pointed his pen at her.

'See, this is what I'm talking about. If one of these people is Noah, you are in harm's way. Did you tell him you were going to the play?'

'No.'

'Anything on your Facebook?'

'Not yet but Simone would have posted.'

'So, if he knows you are sisters, it's pretty easy for him to guess you're going to turn up.'

'I suppose so.'

Benson rocked in his chair. 'And despite that, we can't say they are the only ones who have ever read this book, or parts of it.'

'It would seem extremely coincidental,' said Holmes, 'that if Noah had some other copy, he waited for Scheer's discussion group before beginning his activity.'

Lipinski glanced over to see if he would try to dispute Holmes but Benson seemed to concede the point. Georgette decided not to mention the others, De Souza and Ross. It would not take Benson long to find them and it avoided ... difficulties.

'One thing we can tell you, there was a sexual harassment claim filed against Melissa Harper at her previous college by a female student but that was withdrawn. Nothing on Scheer or Edwards. Morris wrote a pro S&M piece for a student paper but that's not illegal.'

'You found this out already?' Georgette was impressed.

'Soon as you told me about the book. Even though I don't believe that excludes Coleman.'

Holmes raised an eyebrow. He asked if Coleman seemed the type who would read a book more than one hundred years old.

'Frankly, I doubt he could read the *X-Men*. Judge for yourself.' Benson found a file on his computer of the interview with Ricky Coleman. Coleman was mid-to late twenties, Afro-American, wearing a shiny Knicks jacket. He appeared tired, perplexed.

'Why did you run, Ricky?' asked Benson.

'Cause you all were looking for me. Why you think? I know you got me in your sights for some shit. I ain't hanging around.'

'What were you doing in the church, Ricky?' Lipinski this time.

'What people usually do in church. Prayin'.'

'You're a changed man?'

'Yes, I am a changed man. I did my time and I have repented.'

They watched a few more minutes. Holmes indicated he had seen enough.

'You know the book is in Italian,' he said. 'Does Coleman speak Italian?'

'Says he doesn't. But he wouldn't have to. You know what happens, somebody tells some freak they read about this cool serial killing, and then that person tells somebody else.'

Lipinski joined in. 'Down the line it finally gets to the right freak and it all sings – in a bad way.' Clearly the two of them had kicked some theories around.

'You will investigate the phone calls of our suspects?' asked Holmes.

'Persons of interest,' corrected Benson. Georgette remembered a boy whom she sat next to in middle school pricking her with his compass. Benson's tone reminded her of it now. 'Naturally we'll check phone records, social media, anything we can that might give us some link to one of the victims.'

Holmes said, 'If he is following the book, Noah's next victim will be a zebra. I'm sure your resources, as you say, are superior to mine but this is a list of all things zebra I was able to find.'

He handed across his list. Benson regarded it as if it might be a trick but ultimately took it, and that, Georgette felt, seemed to suggest some form of truce.

'Okay. I'm not going to take this any further but I mean it when I say, we'll take it from here.'

Georgette asked if he was planning to question the – she stopped herself from repeating Holmes' mistake. '– persons of interest.'

'Not at this stage. I've already got surveillance on them, better to see if that takes us anywhere. We'll look into their phone records see if there is any interaction with the victims.'

'What's your impression of the four you've met?'

Georgette was flattered to have her opinion considered.

'Edwards seems ... devious. I don't trust him. You could imagine those women wouldn't give him a second glance. Harper is, well, physically athletic. We didn't interact with her much. Morris seemed relatively normal except for his sculpture: an avenging angel.' She called on Holmes to help her with the detail.

'And Scheer?'

'I'm not sure if there's a darkness in him or it is just his manner but he's intense and intellectually arrogant. He's the scariest.'

Benson said he would have them all watched around the clock.

'And we'll find out the other two people at that seminar.'

Georgette wanted to save them the time and trouble but didn't dare.

'Needless to say, you don't mention this to anyone.'

'Can we call you to check on progress?' she asked in her most deferential voice.

'I might be able to give you some very limited information.'

'We'd appreciate that.'

As they got up to leave, Benson called her back and said quietly, 'I don't want anything to happen to you. Hopefully we nail this case and you and I can enjoy some social time.'

She could feel the blood rising to the tips of her ears.

'Sure,' she said and walked to where a suspicious Holmes was waiting. 'What did he say?'

'He told me to be very careful and said we were to leave well alone.'

'After we've given him the best lead he has in his case. Typical.'

It was near one. Outside the car you couldn't see a face, just nylon hoods and knitted caps. How quickly the excitement of Simone's play had faded. When they reached the apartment, Holmes insisted on going in first. She was beginning to truly comprehend the reality of her new situation. Once cleared to enter, she made sure the heat was up and asked Holmes if he would like a coffee.

'First, we need to do something. Stand here.' With his hands about her waist he placed her by the table. It was the first time he had handled her firmly but gently like that and it felt ... well, good. In a smooth, stunningly quick movement, Holmes seized a spoon off the table and lunged at her, stopping the spoon handle an inch from her neck while his left hand strapped her in position better than any seatbelt. She'd not even had time to blink.

'When I seized you from behind in your laboratory, your lack of any adequate response revealed you would have scant chance of protecting yourself from one determined to harm you. You say you have no firearms expertise, and your reflexes leave much to be desired should you be subjected to a knife attack. It simply won't do, Watson. I'll not have your death on my conscience. Now, how do you think you would get out of this situation?'

'My best idea would be to leave anybody over one hundred frozen solid.'

'Ha, ha, droll, Watson. As I've mentioned, in wit you have the edge over your great-great-grandfather. In the question of self-defense, however, you are inferior.'

'He had the benefit of a war, so unless you are going to pack me off to the Middle East ...'

'No such extravagance is required. You are going to learn everything you need to know right here, in this room, tonight. Let us waste no more time. In a frontal attack like this, you block ...' he demonstrated, '... and then drive with the heel of your palm.'

He took her hand and demonstrated the action required against his chin. Her mind should have been on the necessity to defend her life but when their hands touched and she felt his stubble on her hand and looked into those eyes burning with intelligence and earnestness, there was nothing but the most pleasant tingling from her neck to her toes. And when he swung her round and pressed his arm across her chest and drew her to him, his warm breath on her, that very same stubble pricking her neck and sending a delicious shiver along her spine, she lost her breath. It shouldn't have been like this but it was. His manliness excited something deep and primal inside her. Perhaps because he feared injuring her, he suddenly relaxed. She felt his chest contract in the way a cry is stifled and he unhanded her and asked with great solicitude if he was being too rough.

'Not at all,' she answered.

'If you would rather we postpone –'

'No. I think it extremely important you school me to defend myself. Please, continue.'

'Very well,' he said and, looking about, settled on the umbrella stand in the doorway. He seized two umbrellas and tossed one at her, which she managed to catch.

'Hand to eye is good,' he said. 'I'd like to see you in slips.'

Had she misheard him? For the first time he seemed suddenly embarrassed.

'It is a cricket term, Watson.'

'Oh,' she said and wasn't certain whether she was disappointed or not.

'The beauty of bartitsu is that with so much as a stick, or an umbrella, we can even the odds against a physically stronger foe. Have you ever fenced?'

'Once, in the school play of *Romeo and Juliet*. I played Tybalt.' Simone of course had been Juliet. Even now it galled.

'You are a fast learner, Watson. I taught your great-great-grandfather and I have no doubt I can teach you.'

One could only hope. She watched him demonstrating pivots and thrusts, thought of how he had been holding back so as not to harm her, and such restraint and gentleness touched her and frightened her too, because she knew just how easy it would be to wish for more, and just how often our wishes go unrequited.

Each flake of snow was like manna from heaven. It was as if God were personally rewarding him for his diligence and months of hard work. How wonderful it had been earlier this evening to be that close to her you could smell her perfume. Would he smell her fear like he had with the other? There was no erotic satisfaction for him, he was simply the executioner charged with bringing about true justice, because sometimes justice slipped, missed the mark. He had known that of course for many years but what he'd not understood was that it was simply a challenge to rectify that, not a sentence that could never be overturned. Those who cared, it became their challenge, their burden; instead of self-destruction that did nobody any good, it was incumbent on them to enact justice.

Taking the other's life had been physically demanding, even with the element of surprise, and he wouldn't deny it, there had been, even at the height of the act, a voice urging him to let go, loosen up his grip, give her a chance. But of course, he couldn't, everything had been written before either of them had been born. Georgette would go the same way but with an ironic touch. That was most important. Perhaps it had been foolish of him to allow even the slightest chance that she might be saved but no, she wouldn't be saved, and then those little flourishes would be oh so much more bitter for the ones who remained. To think if only their eyes had been open and they had been more careful, they might have saved her. Which was the whole point. Negligence is no less blameful than a wilful act. Not in his mind. Turner was an obstacle forcing a change of his initial plans that had made him think outside the square. Now, not only had he found a way around that, it had made him realize he could double down. First you slash the Achilles, then you stab through the heart. He almost felt like calling for a drink.

Almost.

But no, he would not weaken, find himself down in the gutter where he had wallowed. It was a new him, unrecognizable. He chuckled at that. Well, that was enough gloating. It was time to move things along. He opened the freezer and stared down at her, that blue tint, like the snow outside. Sometimes life imitated art. Or in this case death. Oh, the irony was delicious.

18

She watched Holmes going through the boiled egg ritual but today it felt very different. Everything felt different, or to be more precise, didn't produce feelings at all, like she was a camera on the wall recording herself. That she'd barely slept was no doubt a contributing factor. Apart from anything else, the feelings she had experienced the previous evening were thoroughly unprofessional but she was honest enough to admit there'd barely been a single thorn of moral dilemma keeping her awake. No, it had all been about him. Whether he had felt anything like she had, whether what she'd felt with his breath on her neck, that thrill, was genuinely because she was attracted to him; or whether Simone had been bang on and she was merely Frankenstein falling in love with himself and his own cleverness by projecting that onto his creation.

But Holmes wasn't her creation. He was simply a man she had brought back from limbo. A very special man, but nonetheless a man. He had insisted they begin the day with a quick refresher bout of bartitsu. She would have preferred something more hand-to-hand.

'There you go, Watson, a reward for your excellent retention of last night's lesson.'

He delivered the egg with a flourish. Disappointingly there seemed to be not a trace of any reciprocal conflict within Holmes. Her spirit was returning from its wandering around the ceiling, slipping back into her body. She worried about her breath. Should she brush her teeth now? A bit silly as they were about to eat.

'I suppose you stayed up?' she said sinking her teeth into toast. The television was on but she had the sound turned down. You could predict the commentary anyway. The pictures showed snow had fallen, street sweepers. The streets were already pretty well cleared. An isolated fall, not a blizzard.

'Only for three or four hours.'

It was ten past eight now. He'd probably managed three hours sleep. The female anchor on the news had unbelievably thick and lustrous hair with a fresh knitted woolen cap perched on top. How could you extend credibility to anybody who looked like that? In comparison, she felt bald. The anchor also had long slim legs but that was one area where Georgette felt no inadequacy. Her legs were long and lean, her butt was firm, despite not having worked out since that post-Vance burst.

'Then you slept like the Congo?' she prompted.

'More like one of the octogenarians in the Lord's Long Room on a summer day when tiny gnats drone and young men take their womenfolk punting. Sorry, it all means nothing to you but sometimes I can almost make-believe that you are your great-great-grandfather sitting opposite me.'

She forced a grin. Felt like crowning him with the toaster. This was terrible. There was no reciprocation here. She'd turned hopefully down a street only to find it was one-way with a huge lorry steaming at her.

Her phone rang. Holmes was immediately alert.

'Benson?' he asked eagerly.

'Hi, Dad. I was going to call you later, fill you in on Benson.'

'I know what went down with Benson. He was just here.' Harry did not sound pleased. Shit. She had been going to ease him in on it today. Why did Benson have to stick his nose in?

'We just fished a dead woman out of the East River near Astoria Park. I've got the crime scenes until they work out who is free to run the case and I'm freezing my ass off. Benson came down to have a look but it's not one of his. He wouldn't say what was wrong about it.' It must have been missing Noah's mark. Benson was still keeping that in a closed fist. You let that out, the press would be onto it and everything would be ...

'You want to come down for TOD? Like I say, I got a free hand for now.'

'I'm there. Can Percy come?'

'Yeah, it'll make it easier to punch him in the face.'

'See you soon, then.'

She told Holmes.

'He knows what we've been doing and he is threatening violence.'

'He has every right,' said Holmes.

Now she wanted to punch him. 'Oh stop it! I'm thirty years old ...'

'Thirty-three.'

Boy, did she want to punch him.

'Pedant,' she snapped. 'There are young women dying and if I can make a difference, I am going to. And you are *not* my father.'

'No, I am considerably his senior.'

'Get ready. We're heading to the crime scene. If you want to risk it.'

Just under twenty minutes later, Harry met them at the perimeter of the crime tape. The skies were leaden, a greasy sleet descending like waste from a leaky sewage pipe, and Harry fit the scene in a thick overcoat with a longshoreman woolen cap on his head.

'I am definitely too old for this. First day back, I'm fishing out a body almost the same spot as twenty years ago. What goes around, comes around.' He directed that last remark right at Holmes. 'Georgi, why don't you go to the body? Percy and I need a chat.' She didn't budge. 'Go, on,' Harry pointed. Holmes nodded. She understood it might be more humiliating for him if she were to remain, so she moved over to the scene.

As it was a staging post, not the scene of the crime itself, she only needed to make sure she did not contaminate the body. Though he wasn't a homicide detective, Harry was the most senior cop in the precinct by years and it was his job to run the crime scene till the homicide detectives were assigned. She slipped into a crime suit, thought again about how easy it was to wrangle her non-descript hair and how difficult it would have been for the news anchor. And was still envious. Simone got the hair, she got the legs. But then Simone got the bust and curves as well and they were in fashion. Georgette stepped into the tent. Lights were on high. Kelvin was shooting the victim. The moment he saw Georgette, he called out, 'Could we have those lights off for a moment?'

Georgette nodded appreciatively.

The lights were doused. It was dark inside now. With the pale skin of an Irish ancestor, Harry's partner Zac Feeney was twenty years Harry's junior. Georgette greeted him, asked how Lara and the kids were doing. Zac replied they were all good. It was an odd discourse when you were looking at the body of a young woman. She clicked on her powerful penlight, played it over the corpse. One glance and you knew this wasn't Noah's work. No slashed throat, clothing intact but bruising already showing on the neck. Crime of passion maybe, boyfriend or husband.

'The ME has been?'

'Just missed her,' said Feeney. The medical examiner would have drawn her own quick conclusions before a full autopsy. Georgette wasn't here to determine cause of death, just TOD, but the eyes and the neck bruising told her it was likely strangulation, maybe drowning. She knelt down close. There was no saving this young woman, even though she'd been in icy water. Her skin was grey but there was no sign of decay. Recent.

Harry's voice came from somewhere behind. 'We got a call and the water guys were onto it quick.' She couldn't help looking around, saw Holmes standing at the back near the tent entrance. His nose didn't appear to be broken.

Harry started up again. 'By the look of her she wasn't in there that long. She had a business card on her, Rebecca Chaney, address in Jersey. All I need is your best guess time of death, then we get out of here.' It would be the junior patrolmen who would then have to freeze their butts off. Aware of his daughter's preferences, her father clicked on his more powerful flashlight and shone it over the body. Late thirties, early forties, she was thinking now. She held Rebecca's arm. As one would expect, it was like an ice block. Nails manicured, nice clothes, maybe her best, they looked hardly worn. No shoes. Georgette checked the nose, mouth, ears, then her chest and stomach. No bruising here. An expensive bra, her skin the same grey but her back was more purple. No sign that her underwear had been removed at any time.

'She'd been in the water about four hours before you pulled her out but she's been dead longer. My guess, kept in a freezer on her back.'

'How do you estimate that?' Feeney seemed genuinely impressed.

'Experience,' Georgette said. 'She was probably killed the night before last. She's had her nails done, and I'd be guessing, hair too. She's wearing three hundred bucks worth of new underwear. You're not wearing that to work, even for a lunch date. And she wasn't held captive for any length of time because her nails are perfect. She's in too good condition for it to have been any longer.'

'Okay, thanks for that,' said Harry. 'Feeney and me have to head to Brooklyn and secure the apartment for Crime Scene.'

'Brooklyn aren't doing that?'

'It's officially listed as Benson's case, hence Queens, till he assigns somebody else. We have to meet and greet Crime Scene and whichever Homicide Ds they send. My guess, it will wind up being Brooklyn, all ours are busy with the serial killer. Come on, Seamus,' said Harry to Feeney. With that he turned on his heel and left. She hurried past Holmes as if he were a spear carrier in a vast opera, back into the grey air, pulling free her latex gloves. Feeney had the good sense to hang back.

'Stop.' Her words flew back at her, carried on the lashing breeze.

Harry turned, faced her, grouchy.

'You can't blame Percy.'

'Why not? He's the one got you involved in chasing a serial killer.'

'I'm the one got me involved.'

'You wouldn't have had a clue about the book.'

'He didn't put a gun to my head.'

'No, but somebody else might have. You know what I went through when I thought you were dead?' Before she could answer, Harry jabbed a finger. 'And the worst thing is, I told him that. Last night, I told him what it was like to think you'd lost your child.'

'Percy wanted to keep me out of it, I refused.'

'So he just rolled over?'

'What was he going to do, slap me down? Look, everything we uncovered, we turned over to Benson.'

At least Harry was silent now. An improvement.

She pushed on. 'We tried Benson and he wasn't available. And neither were you.'

That was underhand, she knew, but she'd kept the dagger just in case. Now she went for her coup de grâce.

'You just said how terrible it was to think you'd lost me. The parents of three young women right now know exactly how you felt. We were trying to stop it being four. You're worried I might get hurt, great. How do you think Simone and I felt year after year when you went off to work?'

He went to speak, but thought better of it.

'Percy is a brilliant detective. Why don't you let him help?'

'With this? It's not up to me.'

'It is for now.'

She stared him down. He relented.

'After Crime Scene are done and until we know who's running the case.'

It was a nice apartment, Georgette thought, a kind of Hawaiian theme, bamboo, cane furniture, a vintage valve-radio. A corkboard in the kitchen area showed the dead woman in photo snaps with various groups of people. She knew Holmes' heart wasn't in it, knew he was still wrapped up in thoughts of Noah but she felt that if she could keep Holmes occupied on another case, the chances of him trespassing on Benson's turf would be so much less. He was gowned up, carefully studying the photos.

'Most of these are old,' he said pointing at the faded color. Rebecca Chaney looked younger in them but then, she hadn't been viewed in the most flattering of circumstances.

'These days people hardly ever get hard copies of photos done. Everything is stored in the cloud or on a USB.' As she said it, she had a pang, realising that the disappearance of all things familiar must be a constant for Holmes. There were three more recent snaps taken by the looks of it in the same session against the mantlepiece. They showed Rebecca Chaney and two girlfriends dressed up, ready for a night out.

'Those are polaroids. People take those for fun. They develop pretty well instantly.'

Holmes studied the images like he was straining their world through gauze. Crime scene techs were still processing the bedroom but had finished here. Holmes moved to the centre of the living room. Two empty wine glasses sat on a low cane and glass coffee table. So far Harry and Holmes had kept a wide berth, Harry knocking on neighbors' doors and scaring up the super. Holmes walked down to the bedroom, stood there a long moment, taking it in. Feeney drifted through.

'Rebecca Chaney, thirty-eight, divorced six years ago, no priors, works as a realtor. Looks like you were right about time of death. Just spoke to her boss. She never turned up for work yesterday, which was unusual. They rang her cell but nobody answered.'

'Of course she was right,' said Harry gruffly, from out in the hallway as he put on a crime suit. Eerie flashes of irregular light from the bedroom betrayed Kelvin's presence. 'My daughter is never wrong.' That with a lot of needle.

He finally entered the apartment and took a quick look around, not getting too invested.

'Carter and Gomez are on their way,' he told Feeney. Georgette knew them to be Homicide detectives from Queens. 'They're going take a look just in case then hand it over to Brooklyn.' Holmes re-joined them.

Feeney said, 'A bottle of wine had been left in the freezer and exploded.'

'She was expecting somebody.' Georgette caught a whiff of her own loneliness.

'How it looks,' said Feeney. 'Table set for two, candles, wine glasses.'

Harry and Holmes said nothing, more interested in one another.

'Had she cooked anything?' asked Georgette, looking in the fridge.

'Nothing in the oven,' said Feeney.

'Maybe they were having take-out,' speculated Harry as he checked the dishwasher, and found large mixing bowls freshly washed. 'No baking dish in here.'

Holmes broke his silence to ask what had been in the 'rubbish bin'.

'Garbage got collected yesterday morning,' Harry informed them.

Georgette was forming an image now. Rebecca Chaney had met somebody she wanted to impress. You couldn't be certain it was a man but chances were. She'd had her hair and nails done. If she did cook dinner, she'd cleared out the trash in the apartment and washed up prior to the arrival of her guest. Holmes checked the oven and then the drawers.

'There appears to be no baking dish anywhere,' he said.

'So they *were* having take-out?' Georgette was surprised. Something about this place, what she'd learned of Rebecca, suggested she would have been wanting to impress with a homemade meal. Harry was already ahead of her with Holmes.

'If she did cook, the perp took dinner with him, baking pan and all.'

'Charming. You kill the cook and then make off with the food,' said Feeney.

Nothing about human behavior surprised Harry anymore. The building super had said Rebecca Chaney was a nice young woman who lived alone.

'Social but not a party hound,' was how he had described her.

Georgette noted Holmes carefully studying the mantlepiece on which were a few nick-knacks picked up from pawn shops or perhaps kept from childhood; a figurine of a sprawled dog, a delicate ice skater, scented candles heavy enough to crack a skull. God, this could almost be her place. But that wasn't what he was looking at. What he was looking at was the first thing you noticed when you entered the apartment. Above the mantlepiece was a lovely old mirror. Scrawled across it in some kind of white marker were the words 'Save Me'.

'I don't like that, not one bit,' said Harry, coming to stand next to Holmes. 'Nothing worse than a psycho who murders and then wants you to save them. Like they're planning their defense before they are even caught.'

'You think she was killed here?' asked Holmes.

'I think so. Unless the killer came back later and wrote that.'

'Apart from the rug here,' Holmes indicated the rug where it was rumpled, 'there seems hardly any sign of a struggle.'

'You're right. Looks like the killer dragged her to the middle of the room and choked her there,' said Feeney.

'Security cameras?' asked Georgette.

'We wish.' Harry was rueful as a Red Sox fan recalling Bill Buckner's error of 1986.

'Why not leave her here?' asked Holmes as much to himself as either of them.

Feeney spoke. 'Maybe somebody knows he, or she, was going to meet Rebecca here and he or she wanted to make it look like she left of her own accord.'

'But then, why leave the message?' said Holmes, standing in front of the mirror and looking up at those words just above his forehead as if it might be a clue from God.

'Maybe it's the ex trying to make it seem like a psycho,' suggested Harry.

Georgette thought that made sense. Perhaps whoever it was who killed her wasn't whoever was supposed to be coming for dinner. Maybe the jealous ex killed her and the date turned up, thought he'd been stood up and left? She could imagine a jealous ex taking the dinner as his right.

'I'd speak to her hairdresser and manicurist,' said Georgette. 'This was a big deal for her. I doubt she would have sat on that. Even if she didn't tell her co-workers or best friend, she was sitting there for a long time. I think it had been a while between drinks.'

Holmes looked at her with a question rising to his lips.

'Experience,' she said, anticipating.

Harry said he would pass that observation on to Homicide.

'You have any amazing insights, Percy?' Harry's tone wasn't sarcastic but it wasn't quite genuine either.

'I am afraid not. The killer struck from behind, he used both hands and he was taller than her. But then she was a petite woman. He was careful. He almost certainly wore gloves. If he moved the body in a vehicle, which seems likely, then your best chance would appear to be him or his vehicle being identified as he disposed of the body, first here and then in the water.'

Harry's radio buzzed. It was one of the patrolmen stationed outside. He'd asked him to let him know the moment Carter and Gomez turned up and had warned Georgette and Holmes in advance.

'They're here,' came the distorted voice.

Holmes turned to Georgette and said, 'I think we should leave the professionals to it.'

In the cab on the way back, Holmes' mood was still of a dark hue. His facility to go from a human being to an automaton was disconcerting. You thought you were getting to know him, thought there was even something ... special, about your relationship, but it was in your mind. He was like a trout you saw every day in a stream. It gave you the illusion there was a connection but then it just swam off into parts unknown, down among weeds and cold currents and left you gazing at the water's unbroken skin with a wicker basket on your arm and too many sandwiches for one.

'You think Dad might be right? The message could be a deliberate distraction.'

Holmes came back from wherever his mind had wandered. 'Quite possibly. It is pointless speculating however, until their science has run its course. That is how you trap a killer, Watson. Noah on the other hand ...' he allowed silence to bury the end of the sentence while he studied the drifting snow.

Her phone rang, and this time it was Benson to tell her that they had traced the other two people at the discussion group and ruled them out.

'They weren't anywhere near New York,' he said. 'We asked them if they told anybody else about the Picture Book Killer, both said no, they hadn't even thought about it since. So far no indication that any of our persons of interest were in contact with any of the victims.'

She wanted to tackle him on why he spilled to her father but she supposed it was going to come up sooner or later. She hadn't asked him to keep it from Harry.

'I gotta go, catch you later,' said Benson and ended the call. She relayed the news, or absence of it to Holmes, who received it with a grunt.

'I should go to my lab,' she said. 'Do you want to join me?'

'Of course, Watson. A little scientific education can do no harm.'

Zoe's condition had deteriorated and Vernon's had not improved but the others seemed unchanged.

'I think it might be a virus,' she explained as she checked them. 'These two were in adjacent cages.'

Holmes was intrigued by the process of revival.

'The remarkable thing is that John Watson was absolutely on the right track with you. He simply didn't have the hardware to continually configure the gaseous mix.' As she was talking him through it, she was thinking that it would be best to test each of the hamsters individually to see if any of their cognitive or physical functions were showing deterioration. This involved creating a series of mazes or obstacles which the hamsters had been trained to negotiate in order to be rewarded with food. Holmes assisted her, raising no objection at being treated like a lab assistant. By the time they had tested all the remaining hamsters it was early evening. She began running a comparative analysis of each hamster against their previous performance. Esther and Jonas were showing signs of cognitive impairment too. Darn. They were in cages three and four and had been right next to Zoe and Vernon. And now she thought about it, closest to the air-conditioning ducts. Could there be some kind of bacterial infection spread via that? That would be potentially much more worrying.

She looked up to find Holmes studying her.

'What is it?'

'I am impressed by how solicitous you are, and how concerned for each of these animals. It is a fine quality.'

She felt self-conscious and looked for a diversion.

'You want something to eat?' she said. 'There's a dispenser up near the foyer. The soup is actually reasonable. Though I guess that's drinking not eating.' She was babbling now.

'That is kind of you,' Holmes said.

'Back in a minute,' she said and ducked out quickly. She was confused now. It wasn't supposed to be like this. She reached the tall dispenser in a back corner of the foyer and fed in her money. A buck for a cup of soup, you couldn't complain. The building was quiet now, most everybody would have left for the day. As the soup was filling, she smelled something rich and tantalising, and turned to find the security guard Dwayne there, a plastic bag dangling from his hand.

'Hi, Dwayne.'

'Doctor Watson. Sorry, I just came on.'

'Something smells good.'

'Homemade lasagna.' He lifted the bag. 'You want some, I've got plenty.'

She nodded at the soup. 'I'm good.'

Her phone rang. She answered eagerly.

'Hi, Garry, news?'

'I'm afraid so. Thought I'd keep you in the loop. We've got a fourth victim. A girl who tends bar at a club up in the Bronx. The Zebra Lounge.'

19

The squad room smelled, the heating on high seemed to bring out the worst odors that had impregnated the walls for forty years. Detectives were coming and going, uniforms filing reports. Greta Lipinski was busy typing and Benson was on the phone. They had come as soon as they received Benson's call that he could spare them twenty minutes. Holmes had spent almost the entire last two hours venting his spleen on police incompetence.

'We gave them the suspects on a plate, nothing changes.'

As soon as they were within spitting distance of Benson, Holmes, with more venom than Georgette had heard from him before said, 'You were supposed to be watching those suspects.'

Benson stared him down. 'We were.'

Holmes actually blinked. It was the first time she had seen his self-assurance punctured.

Benson gave him no chance to regain his balance. 'A team of four on each of them. My best people. At five-thirty, Melissa Harper was in with Scheer. We had two of ours in the hall posing as cleaners, and another six posted all around the building. Morris was at a café. We had eyes on him the whole time. Edwards was in transit from work and being watched. Noah isn't one of them, that's about the only thing we can be sure of.' Sending that shot across Holmes' bow before reloading. 'Ricky Coleman on the other hand was unaccounted for.'

'He's not in custody?' Georgette was shocked.

'We had to let him go. Seeing as we were applying for warrants on four alternate suspects we had no grounds to keep him. We had a surveillance team on him but he gave them the slip.'

Holmes made a mocking sound in his throat. 'So your team lost Coleman but you're certain they didn't lose any of the other four.'

'Coleman was on the lookout and had associates running interference. He would never have managed it if I had double the team on him – which I would have apart from needing eyes on your guys.'

Georgette couldn't believe Coleman, if he were Noah, would risk another murder knowing he was being watched, and said so.

'Maybe he gets off on the danger.'

Holmes, she saw, looked suddenly crumpled, the puff crushed out of him. 'Might we view photos?' he asked.

Lipinski pointed a remote at the large screen. An image of a dead girl, naked from the waist down, a crimson sash starting from her throat on the left side and running across her chest, was splashed across it. The young woman had been propped on a milk crate in a back alley but sagged, her long hair like seaweed frozen in a current. Benson gave the basics.

'Emily Cransberg, twenty-five. She arrived for work at four forty-five. They open at six. Her and the bar manager were the only ones there. She went out the back for a smoke around five-thirty. The bar manager noticed she was missing and went looking, found her like that.'

'CCTV?' asked Georgette.

'Not out the back. There is a camera over the bar but it captured nothing. Noah likely came over the wall from the adjacent property, a furniture shop, probably went back the same way. The techs are processing.'

'He needs to be athletic, then,' observed Georgette.

'Maybe. We can't rule out he was hiding in the actual club. The bar manager says they were really only setting up the bar.'

'Have you photos of the bar?' asked Holmes.

'Kelvin just downloaded them, I think.' He clicked around and found a bunch. 'These are taken from the bar.'

They showed a rectangular room with exposed brick painted in bold Lichtenstein-style murals. The furniture was trendy bohemian, milk crates, kitchen chairs, the odd bentwood. Benson pointed to the right-hand corner. 'The room is L-shaped. The short leg of the L runs off here and there are male and female bathrooms here too.' He found a photo of it, a few tables and chairs, a couple of vintage Space Invader tables. 'This area was in darkness. So, Noah could have got in earlier and been waiting.'

'But he would have had to leave over the wall?' asked Holmes.

'Again, we think that's likely but he's a cool customer. He might have snuck back through while the bar manager was occupied.'

'No bloodied footprints either way?'

'No. He suits up.'

'Noah's trademark?' asked Holmes. Benson hit the computer for the next image, a close-up of the ark on Cransberg's inner thigh.

Benson said, 'Noah's taking bigger risks.'

'Is it possible Noah could have an accomplice?' Georgette said.

'Our psych doesn't think so. He says this is all about Noah's own personal plan and power. The last thing he would do is share it. Our surveillance teams did witness two interesting events however.'

Georgette waited.

'Around three this afternoon, Avery Scheer entered a bodega, purchased candy and then used their pay phone to call. Only lasted about a minute, so nothing detailed. And nothing on the face of it that unusual ...'

'Except he's bound to have a cell phone or two on him,' said Georgette.

'Do you know who he called?' asked Holmes.

'Not who, not yet, but the call was to a Boston number listed as Sunrise House, the registered owners of which is a charity. We spoke to the CEO. Sunrise House is one of those halfway houses for alcoholics, addicts and people with mental conditions. We are assuming for now that it might be a patient of Scheer's.'

'A psycho?' speculated Georgette.

'We'll be asking him exactly what that call was about,' said Lipinski, gathering her things. They were going to be moving soon.

'So it could have been a prearranged call to an accomplice?' Georgette said.

'It's not impossible but our shrink really doesn't think so.'

'And the other incident,' said Holmes. 'You mentioned two.'

Now Benson was readying to go.

'Walter Morris, about three hours ago, not long after Emily was murdered, met with a guy in Bed-Stuy. Our team ran the plates and came up with a known drug dealer.'

Lipinski pulled on her holster. 'And where there's drugs, there's lowlifes.'

Benson said, 'We are on our way now to interview your four persons of interest. We've got warrants to seize computers and phones, see if they shared the discussion paper with anybody. There's no point holding off now.'

'You are going to inform the newspapers you have a serial killer?' asked Holmes.

'We have to clear it with command but I don't see them intervening. It made sense to keep it quiet while we thought we had the killer under surveillance but unless something pings when we interview them, we'll go public: TV, Twitter, Instagram, you name it. We'll hold back on the Noah line in case there are copycats or Noah decides he wants to contact us.'

Georgette understood they had hours of work still ahead of them. 'Thanks for keeping us in the loop,' she said.

Holmes rather stiffly also thanked them.

Benson said to Georgette, 'I don't have to remind you to take care until Noah is caught.' His gaze switched to Holmes, putting the onus on him.

'You have my word,' Holmes said.

Later Georgette and Holmes sat in a bar, the neon flashing outside making it seem like a cheap studio film set. Holmes nursed a brandy the way a longshoreman nurses a grudge. She took his silence to mean he was still brooding over failings in Benson's surveillance.

She said, 'I know these cops. They are not incompetent. They were watching the suspects. It can't be one of them.'

'You mistake my mood for petulance. It was very wrong of me to attack Benson. A young woman is dead because I missed something.' He dispatched his brandy in one gulp.

He cast about as if thinking of a second brandy but declined her offer. 'What I really need is the seven-percent solution.'

This she knew was a reference to his cocaine concoction that allegedly helped him in his dark and difficult moments.

'I have been reborn, Watson, but only in part, and I am afraid that in my diminished capacity I shall be worthless. We had a chance, a gilded clue that the next victim was to be a zebra, and yet still I could not prevent the murder of Emily Cransberg. Sherlock Holmes plunged off a cliff into that lake. Perhaps that should have been the end of him and this was not meant to be, this is some perversion, not some event ordained by God but quite the opposite, the joke of the serpent played upon those who would exalt themselves.'

He buried his head in his hands, then looked back up into her eyes and said, 'I have failed, Watson. That is the naked, awful truth.'

He studied his empty glass.

'My name is Ozymandias, king of kings:
Look on my works, ye Mighty, and despair!'
Nothing beside remains. Round the decay
Of that colossal wreck, boundless and bare,
The lone and level sands stretch far away.'

He placed his glass gently on the table. 'Shelley had a point: even the most powerful among us are blinded by our vanity. Time catches up with us all, Watson. It would certainly appear to have swallowed me.'

Serial Killer In NYC was all over Twitter. She had slept in and only been up about fifteen minutes. Holmes' door was still firmly closed. After they had returned to the apartment Holmes had retreated to his room with nothing more than a 'goodnight'. Not even a quick bout of bartitsu, the umbrellas forlorn in their stand like single women at a town-hall dance. She had been unable to sleep until something like four, and consequently overslept. She heard her phone ringing but couldn't locate it. Finally she found it under the *New York Times*. Holmes likely had been up after all, she realized. The phone clock said nine thirty-three. It was Benson.

'Morning,' she said as brightly as she could muster.

'A promise is a promise.'

Holmes bedroom door opened and she saw him standing there fully dressed.

'Have you slept?' she said into the phone.

'Enough.' She put the phone on speaker so Holmes could hear the cop continue. 'We've interviewed all four persons of interest. Every single one of them claimed to be shocked when we told them about the murders. Each of them has an alibi for at least one of the four murders, most of them for at least two. Both Avery Scheer and Edwards informed us the only contact they'd had about the book was with a certain Percy Turner and Doctor Georgette Watson. Walter Morris also remembered you and a weird dude with you, sniffing around. It's a good thing you can alibi your friend or he'd be our prime suspect.' Holmes flexed his shoulders, annoyed and looked about to speak but she held up a finger for him to be quiet. 'Scheer asked if you were part of the investigation, I declined to answer. Harper says she mentioned the case to a friend but only in general terms and certainly not the murder sequence. We checked out the friend and she's alibied too. Of course, any of them could be lying. But lying to protect who? Family would be logical but only Edwards is married. He has two daughters, no criminal records, one is in London, the other, Michigan. Scheer is divorced, no children, no relationship. Harper and Morris ditto. We've looked at siblings, parents. Nobody of interest.'

Studying Holmes' face, she was going to channel him and say, 'Well Noah most likely wouldn't seem to be of interest' but held her tongue.

Benson continued, 'We asked Scheer if he was certain nobody else had access to that book. He said he scanned and printed the discussion document himself and shredded any spares. The book was sitting on the shelf in his study with others but he says he never leaves people alone in his study, especially not students. The only other people who have a key to his office are the cleaners. We spoke to them, Koreans. Believe me they weren't kicking back reading an obscure Italian book. We can't rule out somebody made a copy of the key – either Scheer's or the cleaners', but if they went to that trouble why not take the book? I'll keep a team on each of them just in case but Walter Morris and Coleman might be our best connection.'

Holmes gestured a telephone call and she understood.

'What about that phone call Scheer made?' she asked.

'Scheer claimed he went to the store for candy, remembered he needed to remind a patient about medication but had left his cell at home so he asked to use the store's. He says he never got through to his patient at Sunrise House, they weren't in. We had some local Boston cops check and it stacks up. There's one phone in the hallway they all use.'

'What did Scheer say about the patient?'

'Didn't want to talk at first, gave us the doctor–client crap till we showed him the photos of the dead girls. Leonard Chester, twenty-four, alcohol and drugs. Scheer says he is non-violent. We checked. He was in a clinic being treated when Carmen Cavanagh was murdered. The Boston police found him sleeping rough around the time Emily Cransberg was having her throat cut up in the Bronx. It's not him, in fact, Scheer has not been consulting with patients for four months. He says he does six months on, six months off but keeps tabs on current patients by phone, so no consultations since he found the book. He said he would never give a person with violent tendencies inspiration by introducing talk of some crime case like that. Walter Morris's apartment reeked of pot and get this, the dealer he met with? He did jail time with a KA of guess who? Ricky Coleman. We've hauled Coleman back in and the dealer. I have to go. Don't forget, when Noah's down, we're having that drink.'

She regretted that last line being public. Speaker was always a bad idea. The connection ended. She looked up at Holmes.

'What do you think?'

'They were being watched by competent police, ergo none of them killed Emily. And though I am not a student of the diseased mind, I have practical experience of these matters and I agree with the police doctor: Noah would not delegate. This is his world view where he alone is the Messiah. I was wrong.'

'You think it really could be Coleman?'

'That some criminal osmosis from Walter Morris to Coleman has led to these deaths?' He shrugged. 'From what I saw of Coleman, I find it irreconcilable. But what do I know?'

There was no tone of self-pity, simply resignation.

'I'm going to my lab. You are more than welcome to join me.'

'I think not today, Watson. Although of course I shall accompany you.'

'There's no need. I'll use a chauffeur service. Have them ring me on arrival.'

He bowed. 'As you wish.'

With that he retreated to his room, pausing on the threshold to say, 'Your hamsters: rather than space, consider time.'

She would have asked him what he meant but he shut the door too quickly.

Recently he had restricted himself to a slow drive-by her residence. He couldn't be sure it wasn't being watched. He also took the precaution of alternating vehicles and taking a different route in case they checked street cameras, as later they undoubtedly would. The cars he'd purchased out of state and they were registered to an alias, so, good luck catching him off that. Mind you, he was resigned to the fact that he may not escape the subsequent investigation. Things could go wrong, mistakes could be made. When they figured out what he'd left for them, they would go looking for him. Nope, no sign of her. Turner was probably with her again, the bodyguard, he sniggered. Well, he'd be dealt with if it came to it but hopefully there would be no need. If she was not at her lab now, she would be sooner or later, and he'd figured his way around that problem easy enough. It was all coming together as it should. He smiled as he thought of the shell game he'd created: while you're looking there, the prize will be here. He began whistling softly. The snow had eased off but more was predicted. Good. The icier the better.

Zoe was clinging to life by a thread, Vernon was following the same trajectory and Esther and Jonas had certainly not got any better. Georgette had segregated the four affected hamsters, and placed them in the room where Holmes had recovered. There was no discernible problem with the remainder but then she'd had to use the maze to see that Esther and Jonas were showing symptoms. What had Holmes meant by his elliptical comment about time not space? She had been pondering that in the car when Harry had called.

'Just checking my daughter hasn't had her throat slashed by some psycho killer.'

She apologized for not having called him.

'I heard about the Zebra Lounge,' he said. Then added, 'Seems your friend Percy was off the mark with his suspects.'

That was unfair of course.

'I think he helped Benson,' she said tactfully. 'What are you up to?'

'The Rebecca Chaney case. Turned out Brooklyn were already well down the track on a homicide that led to Queens. Everybody decided it was better to stick with what they had, than change horses. Carter and Gomez asked me to help.'

'No arrest?'

'She'd had a few threats from the ex but run-of-the-mill stuff and he has an alibi. Gomez spoke to the hairdresser though. I gave her your feedback. Hairdresser said Rebecca had been excited, she had a date, no pictures of the guy but she was pretty sure the name was Paul. Paul this, Paul that, works as an accountant, or at least that's what he told her.'

So likely white-collar type, Georgette was thinking. Rebecca wasn't dumb, she'd know if the guy was talking himself up a profession or two.

'Middle-class, then, quiet,' she said.

'That's what they are thinking. I better go. They've got me doorknocking bars where they might have had a drink.'

'Right up your alley,' she'd joked.

And then here she was back with her sick hamsters. Why didn't Holmes just come out and say what he thought? Why leave a clue like everything had to be a puzzle?

Time not space.

She'd been thinking that if it were bacteria spread through the air-conditioning, the other hamsters would all be sick by now. And in much worse shape. This was slow and seemed to affect cognition first. And then she looked up at the space where the four cages had been that she had since removed. Cages one through four. In a sequence.

Time.

Zoe was number one because she was the first hamster she had revived. Vernon number two. And now she understood in a blink what Holmes had meant and even why he had not come right out and said something. The hamsters were falling sick in the order that they had been revived. It wasn't so much an exterior illness that had made them sick but something about her process, a problem that hid itself for a period of time and then presented in weaker cognition and general sluggishness. Perhaps she had not defeated death, only stalled it.

And if her hamsters were dying, the same fate would befall Holmes. Sooner rather than later.

20

HOLMES

The thing most missing of his old world was the smell. The sweet stench of horse manure rising in the heat of the day, the constant drifting smoke from small fires, backyard braziers, potteries and foundries, all varieties and flavors of smoke: eel-tinged smoke marching from the river, mercury-laden heavy vapors that had rolled beneath lopsided gates of weathered wood, gossamer wafts that had squeezed their way up through ill-fitted tin-rooves of tanneries, the almost-living laneway bricks impregnated with centuries of odor of blood and flesh from halved steers, strung game birds, headless pigs, barrows of barnacled mussels and oysters and a legion of dead fish. And at night the great rolling fog that lifted like a devil's sulphurous tail from the oily sheets of the Thames and conjoined with piped ash dancing up from a half-million sooty chimneys to drift hither and thither an ugly lullaby over slate rooves, beneath which pots of carrots and potatoes and peas bubbled and burped in their own familiar domestic pong of tobacco smoke. The same smells repeated room to room, street to street, day after day, unless you rode a trail of coal and steam to a place beyond the great city, a hillock or stream where flowers grew and the smell of them was so sweet, so beautiful, so … heavenly, that the poet in you really could deduce God in the shape of a petal.

There seemed almost no smell in this new world. Yes, there was the exhaust of cars, the aroma of bright food and coffee … but not much beyond that. As if the brain's olfactory centre had atrophied for lack of use. In the supermarket one could buy strawberries the size of a badger but they didn't smell like a berry, just like everything else. A mushroom even.

He did not miss the stench of open sewage, not one bit – that, he had to say, was a big positive. Yet strangely perhaps, he did miss the occasional tang of horse shit; not stepping in it, mind, that was another positive. Watson, the old Watson, would have been pleased. No man in the history of the world could ever find his shoe in horse shit like his old comrade.

Perhaps as a consequence of the lack of foulness in the air, one did not notice women as quickly as one used to. Their smell would announce them, elevate them long before they entered a room. Perfumes now were no doubt at the same chemical strength as their forebears but they had nothing to rail against, as if a white handkerchief was tossed into the air against a white cloud rendering it invisible. Overall, modern people did not exude smell. They did not seem to sweat. Their unstained fingers did not reek of their telltale industry. Everybody, as far as smells went, had more or less morphed into the same ghost.

Except for Georgette.

He smelled her everywhere in the apartment, the soap she had used to wash her long neck. Her shampoo. Her skin.

Never before had he spent this much time in such close quarters with a woman. Always he had made sure he was strapped in a harness as if, stretching and peering in towards the ocean of womanly mystery – so dark, so alluring, so intoxicatingly inviting – he might be too bewitched to notice the angle of his incline had reached a hazardous level and, falling, plunge beneath the surface to join the legion of dead-sailors who had succumbed to sirens' calls. There had been times, of course, when he had dropped so low his lips had tasted the brine of the sea but the harness had held. Until now.

It was not simply that she was of the highest intelligence, it was the very nature of that intelligence: the order, the scientific discipline that he found so compelling. Beautiful? Absolutely. The other night when she had emerged, her hair wet, her form so ... pristine, as if God's finger had that moment created her from the elements, how compelled he had been to stare at her. And then armed with the certain knowledge that beneath her bathrobe, her bare bosom and her beating heart were so tantalizingly close like an ear to a whisper, as if he were the husband and she his wife; well, he was embarrassed and full of guilt at the thoughts he had, which were ... primal. And here was the truth that made Georgette so unique, so dangerous to his ordered way of life: her physical attributes were inconsequential farthings to the real gold – her loyalty, no less than that of her progenitor, her compassion even for her hamsters, her humor. For him to lose his bearings it would likely have been enough for her simply to be an attractive young woman with whom of necessity he had come to share an intimate domestic arrangement. But Georgette was much, much, more, there was nobody he had ever encountered, even his dear friend John, who had her qualities.

He had no prior experience of love. Certain women had impressed him, made him want to possess them but never had he felt the urge to stay with them, with the yearning expressed in the lyric of one of those popular songs, 'forever and ever'. To lie on a grassy bank, cheek to cheek, hands entwined with a paramour while birds twittered overhead, to row her up a glistening river, the sun scorching his back while she faced him under a parasol and even the fish below the surface seemed driven to leap up and out to catch a glimpse of his princess. These desires had never been found in the wardrobe of Sherlock Holmes. And yet here they were as bright as a red muffler that his hand reached for no matter the weather. It was ludicrous, adolescent, but there. All of these things, and more, he desired to share with Georgette.

That night when he held her, showing her how to defend herself, well, he had never experienced that. He should have said something to Georgette right then, declared himself as a candidate for her affections. He squirmed. Even the way he *thought* of that sounded archaic and manifestly stupid. How was he ever going to express himself in a way that would not simply confirm the enormity of the gap between them? He was an accident, a blip in the continuum of time. And yet, he was real. His blood spilled like any man born a hundred years after him. His heart beat as theirs, his brain, while perhaps not as sharp as it once had been, was superior to most.

It was his courage that had been lacking because if she did not share his feelings – and let us be honest, why would she? – then what option did she have but to send him on his way?

This would happen inevitably when love bloomed between her and some other man so, what had he to lose except the one thing about which he had never cared a jot: his dignity. But he had said nothing. All in all now a good thing, because there was nothing he could guarantee her except early widowhood.

Georgette was a beacon that could light a world, not just a square of it, not just a corner, and when he was with her, he did not feel like a freak, an anthropological accident, he did not sense the darkness all around him as he had always done from his brow to his bones.

He felt alive.

Here was the irony. He was almost certainly dying. Yes, yes, of course, we are all dying and at any moment we could be run over by a night cart – well, perhaps in this day and age, a large car. That wasn't his particular curse, rather the process that had breathed life into him, that had brought this angel to him, had at the same time signed his death warrant. Wild and ridiculous thoughts that had roamed his mind: a future with Georgette, marriage ... children, imagine the love and tenderness she would possess for their offspring? Ridiculous schoolboy, headlong-rush sentiments that had promptly hit a stone wall.

The truth was, however, he could not chide himself, for he would do it all again and gladly accept what fate had in store. It was a small price to pay for that which had already been ladled out. To crave more was human but still he thanked the Almighty, the stars, science and his old friend John, for what he had been given. Even if it were to end now, this instant.

What was more difficult to accept with equanimity was the blunting of his reasoning powers. Up until yesterday he had assumed that may have been simply because he had lain idle for one hundred and thirty years. He had hoped it would come back in time but that rather scanty analysis was perhaps absolute proof of a permanent loss of mental capacity. More likely it was the same malaise as was affecting the hamsters. Where he was absolutely critical of himself was that he had wilfully pursued his profession while in proximity to Georgette, had used her and exposed her to danger. He would not have blamed Harry had he pulled out a birch and whipped him.

What on earth had possessed him? What could he have been thinking? Well, he knew the answer to that. He was thinking he was going to catch Noah and show the modern world the greatest detective mind of all time. He was Ozymandias, king of kings, a vain, foolish man who had endangered the world's most precious and unique creation: Georgette. Had he achieved his goal, captured Noah, he might have been able to, with a contrite heart, learn from his mistake for the future. A future that might include somebody beyond himself.

But he had failed and now in the mirror there was his unworthiness, mocking him.

And yet ...

He could not deny his nature. Until that last stitch was sewn, he must remain in the same old suit that had served him so well. Sherlock Holmes, professional detective. Professional. And more. His very core that demanded he answer every mystery, and this one was surely easier, far easier than many in his past. The murders had to be related to the reappearance of the book. Yet it seemed none of his suspects could themselves be the killer.

What he needed was stimulus. Or a stimulant.

He eyed the white powder in the little plastic bag that he had removed from the drug dealer after meeting with Valerian. It had been a necessary omission in his conversations with Georgette. There was nothing to it really. A mere thirty minutes observation told you who was selling cocaine and what firearms they were carrying. All he needed was a cane and a slight limp. After securing cash via the shell game, the cane he rented for the sum of five dollars from an elderly fellow feeding pigeons. The drug dealer, a revolver in his waistband and a derringer in his sock, was only too happy to lead him to the deserted laneway and, as Holmes predicted, propose a trade: Holmes' money in return for not being shot. The cane broke the fellow's wrist before he could blink. The follow-up blow to the temple stunned him and Holmes calmly removed the cocaine and the firearms. He drew the line at taking the fellow's drug-money. His moral logic told him that as he had been threatened he was entirely within his rights to remove the guns, and the cocaine had been forfeited by the seller's actions, but the other money was not his business. Frankly, he thought that any society that banned cocaine deserved to be exploited by criminals but he was prepared to follow the adage that 'When in Rome ...' He had returned the cane and found his way back.

And now for two days the cocaine had sat there, gesturing to him. At first, he had resisted out of deference to Georgette. No, he told himself, it was wrong. She did not approve, she was his host. Then he began to wonder if he could do without it, for to that point, things were going well. He appeared to have narrowed Noah to one of four possibilities.

That seemed an awful long time ago now. He remembered from his earlier lifetime the thrill of the drug, the way it would open his mind to a thousand combinations of possibilities that he could view and discard in a shard of a second. From what he had read, Conan Doyle had made him seem like an opium smoker, all languid and reflective, but then Watson had rarely been present when he had indulged, so, devoid of first-hand accounts, Conan Doyle had likely called upon his experience of various associates from his club who enjoyed to lay with the pipe.

He weighed the bag in his fingers. It would help, he knew it must. It was a double-edged sword, both blessing and curse, but nothing liberated clues locked inside his skull like that white sand. He picked it up and flicked it, watched remnants drop from the sides.

He placed it back down. Not yet. Not until every pick had been tried on that lock.

Was one of the persons of interest lying? Had they told somebody? Morris, as the police surmised, or Scheer bragging to a fellow psychologist, or Edwards seeking a sale, or had Melissa Harper told more than one person as she so desperately sought a friend?

He lay down and methodically began to replay every scene of the case. He was looking for that splinter that caught, that tiny fact out of alignment.

He'd only just started when his phone rang. It had to be her. She had solved his riddle about time and space. He was surprised it had taken her that long. He switched it off.

Normally, Simone did not get nervous but today she was. This could be it, the big break all performers pray for. Mr Keely had seen her Janet and raved. She had waited a day, so as not to look too desperate, before having her agent call him, and Keely had said sure, he would be happy to see Simone, he had one or two things in mind already. He wasn't like some mammoth casting agent, she knew that, but Vonny said he'd found work for a couple of her clients previously and didn't just do ads but also some TV here and there. The office was nothing special, third floor on West 40th surrounded by offices with cheap fashion accessories. And there was no receptionist, although there was a desk, so maybe he had somebody part-time. She was sitting in a plastic scoop chair and she was the only one in the waiting area. The walls were decorated with impressive photos of live film shoots and one or two billboards shrunken to fit the frame. Keely had poked his head out to say he'd be with her shortly. The magazines didn't take her fancy, they were tattered and four years old: power boats, fishing, one or two advertising ones. But she was not going to be negative. It was a start, one or two rungs higher than the bottom. Her phone rang: Georgette. Not the best timing but it would soak up a minute or two.

'What's up?' she said.

'It's horrible ...'

Was Georgette crying?

'... he's dying.'

Simone's heart clamped. 'Dad's dying? What's the matter ...'

'Not Dad, Holmes. There's something wrong with my process. My hamsters are getting sick, starting with the oldest, and now there's three more and Zoe my first one is almost gone and if I can't figure out what it is, Holmes is going to die.'

Simone thought she'd followed. 'They're hamsters, not humans. Maybe he'll be good.'

'I don't think so. It might even advance more quickly.'

Poor Sherlock. Poor Georgette.

'Does he know?'

'Of course. He's Sherlock Holmes. I tried to call him just then and he wouldn't answer. I'm at the lab.'

The door opened and a young woman Simone's age came out and gave her that comradely smile that said, hope you go okay but don't get my part. Keely was standing there expectantly.

'Look, Georgi, I have something on ...'

'Pilates with the drummer?'

There was a lot of snap in Georgette's tone.

'No actually. A casting. I'll call you when I'm done. Promise.'

She ended the call, feeling guilty. Keely stood waiting with the door open.

'Everything okay?' he asked.

'My sister,' she said.

'Family,' said Keely knowingly and showed her in. Simone tried to focus. This was important but then so was her sister.

'Nice photos,' she said, striving for a friendly tone and trying to banish the recent worrying news from her head.

'One thing I've learned in this game, the photographer is your lifeline.'

Her headshot had been done by girl who did her band posters. At the time she'd thought it was sensational, and maybe it was good for rock-and-roll but it was time for a change. She took a deep breath. She was ready for fame to come and grab her.

There was no point wallowing, Georgette decided, she just had to get on with it, nobody else could help her. She was angry with herself for getting caught up in the case. Noah wasn't any of her damn business, this was. Had she been devoting all her attention to it, she may well have noticed the problems earlier. Zoe was at death's door and Vernon was where Zoe had been twenty-four hours earlier. Their decline was following a predictable pattern. She dried her tears on her sleeve, and took blood samples from all her hamsters. One saving grace was there was a gap between her first six revivals and numbers seven through ten, so maybe no symptoms would show in those others. The facility had its own lab specialising in bloodworks of the research animals. Mark, the nerdy guy who was point-man, would need a personal touch.

She took the elevator to the fourth floor and was in luck. Mark was sitting back playing whatever the latest geek computer game was.

'Need a big favor.'

'No fucking way, Watson.'

'Yes, way.'

'You getting me a date with that hot sister of yours?' He raised his eyebrows. When had he seen Simone? Oh that's right, the party last Easter. Simone her plus one, instead of Vance not long after that debacle.

'How about a mint-condition Alf still in its plastic packaging?'

That got him sitting up. 'Alf the alien?'

'Yep, with the snout.'

'You have it on you?'

It was still back at Harry's. Simone had given it to her years ago in lieu of a real birthday gift. Something she'd grabbed from a boyfriend as payback after a bad bust-up. Georgette hated it.

'You'll have to take my word for it.'

He pursed his lips, nodded.

'Today,' she said.

'You're pushing.' But he was bluffing.

'It's officially vintage now. You'll owe me and then some.'

He took the samples off her. 'What am I looking for?'

'Everything.'

As she was heading back towards her lab, Simone called her phone.

'Sorry about before but I had a really important meeting with that casting agent.'

Georgette figured for once she wasn't going liberal with the truth.

Simone said, 'You're smart. I'm sure you'll figure out a solution before it hits Sherlock.'

What Georgette had been thinking was that if they went public, Holmes would have every expert in the world trying to help him. She kept this to herself, asked how Simone had gone.

'Good, I think. He says he has this hush-hush feature he can't give details of yet but it's a Hollywood A-lister's vanity project and they want unknowns, and well, you can't get more unknown than me.'

'Are you driving?' Georgette could make out the telltale crunch of gears and angry horns.

'Yeah. On my way to my lesson with Ambrose.'

'He teaches you, right?'

'Ha ha. I gotta go. I will call you, okay. Give Sherlock a big kiss from me.' Then instead of ending the call, there was a gasp. 'Oh my God!'

'What?' she was worried Simone had hit somebody.

'You've fallen for him. Don't deny it. I can tell. You didn't even cry for Vance.'

Actually she had. Worthless buckets.

'Vance wasn't dying.'

'No, then you'd have been laughing, we all would have. You're invested, admit it.'

What the heck. 'Yes, I'm invested.'

'Knew it.' Georgette heard Simone greet Ambrose. Then she came back on line.

'I'm here for you, okay?'

After Georgette ended the call and stepped back into the lab, she began crying all over again.

Hours passed. Holmes drifted away and back, a shipwrecked man in a vast ocean, slowly, very slowly. Words were strained through an ever-smaller diameter netting, muck cast aside. He considered inflections, physical tells. The cocaine called to him, his own personal siren.

Not yet.

More absences swirled through him like the spirits of the long dead: the jingle of spurs, the creaking of hand-carts, the clang of iron hammered on anvil, the smell of newspaper, mown grass, a leather cricket ball, varnish and boot polish, and a train conductor's swooping cry like a gull as the moment of departure fell due, and images of shop signage, the lettering in faux gold borders, symbols for pennies and pounds, half-pennies. And postcards, and corsets and the sight of masts and rigging in harbors and at the extremity of the horizon while on a coastal stroll to the rustle and swish of a woman's best dress.

Banish it. Now. He could not afford the luxury of nostalgia. He must find Noah.

Now he was wading through a swamp. Over and over, the same faces loomed out of the mist: Morgan Edwards, he had purchased the books and immediately snagged Avery Scheer. Did this make Scheer a sociopath? Not necessarily. He himself might have done the same had he seen the book on offer. And Scheer, unless he was lying, did not even speak Italian. Edwards did.

Had Edwards been a bomb waiting for the fuse to be lit? The book was the match? And there he was, voila, at the theatre. But he can't have done it. None of them could. They all had alibis. Somebody then that one of them had inadvertently shown the book or excerpt to, or somebody who had stumbled across it visiting Scheer. Likely by now whichever one of them it was knew and they were covering for ... a lover, a son, daughter ... patient.

Avery Scheer claimed he suddenly remembered he needed to make a call to a patient but had forgotten his phone. Could he have recalled such a phone number without assistance? How often had he called it before? That was something needed to be reviewed with Benson. Holmes himself would have remembered such a number, but was Scheer his equal in this? Had the police checked whether Scheer had tried that number again when he had returned home? Unlikely, because they had found Leonard Chester, the man with whom Scheer had wanted to speak, and having confirmed Scheer was indeed his counsellor and that Chester was alibied, eliminated Chester as a suspect.

No, that was not quite right was it? There was something they had missed.

Holmes sat up and seized the cocaine.

Once more Georgette had put the hamsters through their paces. Thankfully, today no more were showing symptoms. Zoe was lying down panting. A matter of hours. Better she euthanize her now, thought Georgette. An autopsy would be the best and quickest way of isolating the exact problem area. She did not want to do it, these animals were like pets. And Zoe had been the first. The phone rang. It was Holmes. Her brain was scrambled.

'How are you?'

'Good, Watson. Don't trouble yourself on my account. There is some time yet before the coffin-maker will need his tape.'

'I've been thinking –'

'I would expect nothing less. I want you to spend this evening with your father. You should be safe there.'

'Why?'

'I am leaving shortly.' Sounds in the background suggested an echoey station. 'For Boston. It may be a wild goose chase but then again, if we don't look, we shall never know if the nest was empty.'

With that, he asked her once more to be careful and then ended the call, leaving her with nothing but the weight of a silent phone in her hand.

21

Harry was more than pleased to see Georgette sitting across the table from him.

'Pretty good salad, huh? Olives, onion, tomato. My opinion, you gotta have onion.'

'Me too.'

'We should do this more often.'

'Yes, we should. You want to do Thanksgiving here?'

Harry always celebrated Thanksgiving with the girls and nearly always here. He considered himself as good at roasting a turkey as grilling steak. It was that or eat out. He couldn't trust either of his girls with it.

'Sure. I got the room. I suppose you want to invite Percy?' It was a gentle probe.

'Of course.'

She didn't elaborate, so fine, if that's the way she wanted to play it ... Harry dropped further inquiry.

'I haven't seen Simone's place in like a year.' He was thinking last time he'd visited, it reminded him of the Nancy Spungen murder scene. 'She tell you about her meeting?'

'Yes. She's optimistic.'

'She's nothing if not that. So where has Percy gone?' At first, he'd been hoping there might be some romance there but that had vanished when he learned how irresponsible Turner had been.

'New England. Something academic.'

'I know you're going to defend him but he shouldn't have got you involved.'

'Dad ...'

'You're my daughter and I don't want to wake up terrified every day that you may never return.'

'Join the club.'

He hadn't forgotten what she'd said back there at Astoria Park, about the girls worrying about him, had been chewing on it since.

'You and Simone were worried?'

'What do you think? We'd lost Mom. You were our whole world. Somewhere at the back of my mind every day I was thinking "Dad's out there running down low-lifes who would shoot their grandmother for five bucks." There wasn't a day it didn't cross my mind that by the evening we could be orphans.'

It hit him hard in the gut that he had never considered this. All he had ever thought about was that he needed to work as hard as he could to provide for the girls.

'I'm sorry, baby. I never realized.'

She reached across and put her hand on his arm. 'It's okay.'

He felt humbled, like he was the kid now. 'You like him?' he asked.

'He's a friend.'

'Just a friend?'

'Stop that.'

Harry wasn't convinced his eldest daughter's instinct with men was high but he heard Helen's voice in his ear: 'Stop being a cop, enjoy your daughter's company.'

They used to play cards together when she was about twelve. He wondered if she'd play a hand or two but didn't want to risk rejection if he asked her outright.

'Mirsch's winning run came to an abrupt end in the Catskills,' he chuckled.

'All good things ...'

How true. He had a flash image of Helen sitting opposite where Georgette was now, the two little girls, what – six and four? – either side. Georgette broke the spell.

'I'm guessing you mentioned Mirsch because you want to see if I can still whip you at poker.'

'You never whipped me.'

'Whipped you good. You get the deck, I'll clean up. How's the Rebecca Chaney investigation progressing?'

'I don't think they have much. Gomez was hot for a while on the super at the apartment building but that ran out of steam, and the ex was alibied.'

'Wasn't she meeting somebody though? Surely somebody saw them together some time.'

'Not many. Witnesses! Totally unreliable: age anything from twenty to forty. And no cameras. I'm thinking he was being careful, maybe he had it planned all along but I'm not the Homicide Squad.' He held up the cards. 'Gin rummy or poker?'

It was like she'd never left home. Never gone to college. Never had a boyfriend or too many vodkas. The gentle slap of the cards was as timeless as a Christmas carol. She was giving as good as she'd got, one game each. Third in play. She'd speak to Simone about her staying here a night or two. The company was good for him. Most men widowed early in their lives married not long after, or at least that's what it seemed like to her. Not her father. He'd had girlfriends, a couple for quite a long time but he'd more or less lived alone here.

'How come you've never remarried?'

He studied his cards, shrugged. 'I thought about it a couple of times. If I'd have met a woman where I wasn't comparing her with your mother, you know, if I had reached that stage, I would have been open to it. But I never did. Amelia, you remember her? She was very nice, and we hit it off but I couldn't give her what she wanted. She found a guy, nice guy. She's very happy. It was the right move. And then ... I don't know, it just gets away from you.'

'How do you mean?'

He chewed, thought some more. 'You reach an age you don't want a better future, you just don't want to lose the good bits of what you've got.'

The last few days had been growing successively colder. Good. The little lake was near frozen now and everything was in readiness. He'd gone onto his computer and checked a backroads route for the Catskills. No stone to be left unturned, everything in its place. They thought they were so smart. How many bodies did they have working the Noah case now? And how gut-wrenching when he struck. They all wanted the high-profile glory but they couldn't save the life of one poor girl, could they, Rebecca? He'd given them more than enough to go on with, just in case he might be wrong in believing he was God's chosen instrument of justice. If that were the case, if they honestly could apply themselves, they might stop him but he didn't think so. Que sera.

She had tried Holmes but he hadn't answered and she couldn't say she was all that surprised. He would contact her when he was ready. Thoughts pecked her – had he remembered to take a charger? Yes, surely he would. How did he have the money for a train fare and accommodation? Was he thinking of sleeping at the Y? It was too cold to be outdoors for any length of time and his health was likely compromised. That afternoon she had taken Zoe's limp body to her friend Charmain who performed autopsies on the lab animals. The autopsy demands were not as high as for bloodworks and Charmain assured her she would get onto the autopsy that evening or first thing tomorrow. She had seen how upset Georgette had been.

'She was my first success but I am worried about losing them all,' she had explained and detailed the apparent cognitive deterioration. Charmain had reassured her she would do her best to pinpoint a problem. Mark had called not long after Georgette had left the building. He had warned her that he would not yet have the results for specific virus markers.

'But what I can tell you is that they are all low in red blood cells; subjects one and two critically so.' That was Zoe and Vernon. She'd thanked him.

'Don't forget Alf.'

No, she wouldn't forget Alf, in fact she was looking at him right this minute. I need to get Holmes' blood checked, she was thinking. If it's something like leukaemia then that is bad but there are treatments that can be implemented. At any rate, he may need some kind of transfusion.

There was something confronting about being in your old bedroom. For more than half your life this had been the room in which you'd laid your head on the pillow and dreamed: of being famous, or better looking, or kissing some non-entity like Dan Frelling in junior high. He was the reserve for the debating team. They only kept him on it because she insisted. And, ignorant his debating life was on thin ice, Dan then had the hide to demand game time. Ha. He had blown it when he'd hooked up with Maya Sheddick, so with that she withdrew her support and he was never seen near an affirmative premise again.

She was pretty sure this was a different bed. Maybe Simone's old one. It was touching when she walked into the room and saw her father had made the bed up himself. The sheets smelled clean but at least one of the blankets was musty. It was too cold to pull it off though – she was frugal with heating but, compared to miserly Harry, extravagant. She'd forgotten that – so she stayed bunched and huddled.

The teen posters were long gone, the walls bare but not repainted.

Towards the end, when her mom was really bad, Georgette would lie in here awake, in tears, and some nights she could hear a wail and then her father comforting or hushing her mom.

Georgette had her first period here. God, that had been terrifying even though she had read up on it and Mom was still alive to help. There had been a few years early on where Simone had shared the room with her. That naturally ended badly: an image of an angry young self chasing her sister around a softball diamond while wielding a bat came to her. Simone had borrowed her favorite blouse and wrecked it.

Across the other side of the room was the simple bookshelf where all her Harry Potters had stood, obediently awaiting the call for yet another read even though they were tired and worn and had hot chocolate spilled on them from when Simone had purloined them yet never finished reading them. She didn't recall wanting to be a scientist back then although it was a bit of a fog. She wanted a pony badly, she remembered that much.

Her phone pinged. It was sitting on top of a cardboard box of her dad's old vinyl records. Holmes had sent a text.

Arrived Boston. Are you safe with your father?

She typed, *Yes at Dad's. Cold. Lots of memories.*

Ping.

Just like me, Watson.

Not for the first time she had an inkling of what Holmes' life must be like here. Everybody, everything he had known was a ghost, a footnote of history. There was just him.

Where are you staying? she typed.

Ping.

Sunrise House.

That distressed her. She could have paid for some decent accommodation for him. She was going to type something about the blood test but held off. He doesn't want to hear that now, she thought.

Instead she typed, *Are you sorry I brought you back?*

She waited in the dark, bare room. A long time. My God, how many years was this my world?

Ping.

I have a purpose, and you, Watson. Sleep well.

Perhaps it was ridiculous but those words seemed to wrap themselves around her and warm her. There was no further communication.

And then sleep, smelling faintly of aromatic tobacco, stroked her forehead, and her eyes closed to the imagined rattle of carriages and the bellows of fishmongers.

Holmes nursed the phone in his long palm the way a schoolboy nurses a dove. Absurd as it was, he missed her. Georgette was as big a part of his life as John had ever been. Would it could be more but with a death-sentence hanging over his head such ideas had to be banished. And this was a good place to banish them, a pitiful receptacle for life's defeated. The dormitory was six-berth, three double bunks: four of the other beds were occupied. He was on a top bunk above a snoring, bewhiskered old seaman whom he had befriended on the street corner up from Sunrise House, not long after arriving. Sunrise House itself looked like it might once have been a guest house. It was three stories, gabled, wooden, with a slate roof. What had once been wide verandas had been enclosed more than sixty years ago. His guess was it could house around twenty. His decision to wear the second-hand clothes and to leave his suit hanging in the wardrobe in Manhattan had been the correct one. The staff at Sunrise House, a female administrator and a young male health-worker, had been in two minds about him when he presented himself but his correct use of English appeared to convince them that though his brain was addled – just the right touch he congratulated himself – he posed no threat. Fortunately, they did not realize that the walking stick he'd found at Penn Station was, in his hands, a formidable weapon. The revolver he had left hidden in New York, the derringer was strapped to his ankle and covered by baggy trousers. The seaman, Arty, had told him that most of the rooms at Sunrise House were 'vouched'. This seemed to mean that some organization or medico had signed a form which guaranteed a period of stay. There was, however, Arty told him for the price of a cigarette, a short-stay dormitory where those down on their luck might stay for a night. And then for another cigarette, Arty had shown him to the front desk and made up a yarn about Holmes being a young fellow down on his luck after a motor vehicle accident. By then it had been near seven o'clock and the air outside was cold and pressed down like a giant's fist. Holmes had been just in time for a meal, something called baked beans, which he quite enjoyed. He had already identified the telephone, a single wall-mounted phone in the second-floor hallway. Over this meal in a large common room, on hard chairs with a mumbling television mounted high on the wall near the servery, Holmes had discretely enquired about the police coming around to ask about a phone call. This caused a bit of a hubbub among his group of six new chums, men ranging in age from about thirty to seventy-five. Clearly it had been a moment of intense excitement in this otherwise stultifying world of ill-matched cutlery and linoleum flooring that gave off a smell of impregnated disinfectant. Two uniformed police had come in looking for a man named Lenny who often stayed there, but he wasn't in.

Lenny, Leonard Chester, thought Holmes, keeping this knowledge to himself.

'Something about a phone call,' said a young fellow, Jordan, who wore a tee-shirt under a V-neck sweater that looked like it had been hit with a shotgun blast. Holmes sensed opiate addiction at some time in his past, and a constant struggle to keep it there.

'What was the big deal about this phone call?' asked Holmes.

They all shook their heads.

'He wasn't even here,' said Jordan, and some of the group seemed to know this and nod while others stared blankly as if wondering if there would be any more beans.

'So who answered the phone?' asked Holmes.

As one, at least three of them said, 'Barron.'

'He acts like it's his job', said Arty. 'Phone rings, he jumps on it.'

'Is Barron here now?'

No. Barron, he was assured, would only come in five minutes before the doors were bolted at 10.05.

'He likes to drink at The Duchess,' said Arty, who had earlier explained that booze was not allowed at Sunrise House, although you were allowed to drink off premises so long as you didn't turn up dead drunk. Holmes had joined old Arty and three strangers in the single-night dormitory and claimed the top bunk in the big, cold room. A stack of worn but clean blankets was piled on a chair near the doorway. Holmes had taken one and lay under its coarse skin the way a million innocent maidens must have lain at night under the body of their husbands: farmers, miners, gangers and dockers with calloused hands and chins of rough whiskers, and the smell of coal, or earth or salt seas emanating from their heavy, crude bodies. Almost none of these men meant harm to their wives, the opposite, they were embarrassed at their roughness. Holmes was pleased he was from an earlier time where femininity was allowed, perhaps even encouraged, to be the greatest mystery a man could encounter. It confused him that the thinking of this era equated femininity with weakness, where the difference between sexes was rubbed down and painted over, where the heroes of those ubiquitous screens seemed to be women who could shoot and fight and curse. If a man was not constantly reminded of his physical dominance, was not inculcated from his first angry shake of the rattle in his sister's face, of the damage he could do and the restraint he must show, how on earth were women to be kept safe, how was the inner brute that dwelled within a man's bosom to be tamed? From what he had seen, there appeared to be a belief that slogans and campaigns could somehow achieve what had formerly been a continual process of education that a boy was given from the time of his first tooth: stand when a woman enters the room, throw your coat over a puddle or ditch; and never, ever, whatever the provocation, raise one's hand to a woman. True, women now could be prime ministers, lawyers, soldiers, and well they should be. It had always irked him that fifty percent of the population had a lid placed upon their opportunities, but remove from men the idea that women were divine – more noble, more caring, more delicate ... more *special* than men – and you risked the catastrophic consequence of the chained brute breaking free.

There appeared to be so many murders of women now, that the public only seemed to stir at the most outrageous, like those of Noah. And the likes of Noah, in any era, would remain immune to any moral education. He chided himself for not having treated the murder of Rebecca Chaney with the same application he had reserved for Noah's victims. Perhaps he would be able to make amends.

Perhaps.

Or maybe he was like a champion pugilist who tried to resurrect a glorious career. You are an anachronism, Holmes. He heard the words in the voice of John Watson, his dear friend who had preserved him in the belief that he could made a difference. Thus far the evidence had shown that confidence misplaced. Perhaps this is where you belong, he thought. On a thin mattress under a coarse blanket surrounded by a chorus of coughs and splutters and men who must have had dreams of their own, families no doubt, lost to alcohol or drugs or Fate's ill wind. What had they done to wind up here, playing out their days among the props at the back of a dusty stage with the warm houselights and the well-dressed audience all pointing in another direction? Every one of them had once walked with a swing in their step, money in their pocket, love for a mother or a girl in their heart. They had waded through streams casting for fish, lain on their belly in hot desert sand while cannon fire exploded around them, rode the bus with the tiredness of hours standing behind a shop counter throbbing in their calves, run behind bicycles trying vainly to catch them, rolled stiff paper into a makeshift horn to put to their lips and blow, or to one eye like a telescope, forked a last morsel of bacon, swilled tea, applauded a sportsman who had cut across the tennis court like a cat, sat on the stern of a small boat staring at the infinite heavens, danced joyfully with a woman to music that even now stirred their toes with the memory, swung a heavy ax to dissect a fallen tree, jumped aboard a wagon for a free ride, tumbled down a grassy slope, sung a Christmas carol with snow falling outside the window, missed a stop because they were engrossed in a newspaper, held a baby in their big hands as if they alone were responsible for the wellbeing of the whole world, knelt in supplication for forgiveness or a favor or a proposal, pushed an umbrella against the falling stream of cold rain, cried over the death of a pet.

They had all not just tasted life, but been life, as life had been them, the boundaries of skin and bone and self-reflection lost in a oneness with the humanity of the moment, nature and man, man and nature. He had felt that, of course, but now something more, something different, stratospheric, the intimacy of a man and woman, indivisible, his breath against her neck, his hand across her beating heart, the hook and eye becoming something new, a clasp, an entity, a wish, a hope, a steam vapor. Perhaps that was what Noah felt in that moment when he took the life of his victims, a majesty, a vastness beyond the worldly. The opposite side of the same coin, the transcendental and the abysmal, good and evil, Cain and Abel.

When he had held Georgette, what he experienced must have been something like what the first person to have encountered Victoria Falls had felt, not Livingstone but the tribal hunter or daring girl who, drawn towards the roar had pushed aside the frond, and felt not just that they were seeing something divine but they were fused with it, that they had become the moment itself. And so, for once in his life, he allowed himself to imagine what might be. And these men with him in this room tonight, and those that had preceded them and would follow them, he had no doubt, had experienced such moments in their lives too, yet here they were, rusted hooks on rotting piers.

Without Georgette, this was where he must inevitably arrive, the hold of doomed men for whom the world no longer had a use. And there was no possibility of Georgette. There could not be. He was dying. He felt it, not much physically, not yet, but mentally, oh yes. It was wrong for him to even contemplate a future with her. But he could attain justice one more ...

He heard the big door close, muffled voices, the sound of a heavy bar dropped into place and then footsteps. He checked his watch: 10.03. He did not know exactly where Barron's room was, and he did not need to. He held his phone and dialled the number of Sunrise House.

The phone in the hall rang. Barron Langdon walked towards it and answered it, thinking that at least he'd not had to get up out of bed. There was no point leaving the phone for anybody else, they all expected him to answer it.

'Hello?'

'Barron?'

He turned at the voice behind him and saw a tall slim man standing there studying him carefully.

She was worried, couldn't help it. It was after seven now, an hour since she'd texted Holmes without reply. She'd tried calling but there had been no answer. She was aware of Harry, making pancakes, looking over at her.

'I'm sure he's fine. Probably forgot to charge his phone.'

She had drilled that into Holmes. Surely, he hadn't forgotten? What if he had gone off chasing Noah on his own? Or what if he had forgotten because his cognitive function was diminished? That in turn made her think of her hamsters and the autopsy. She needed that, as soon as. The phone rang. Holmes.

'Where are you?' the words were out of her mouth before she even had it to her ear.

'Returning on the train. My phone had no charge.'

'I told you to charge it!'

Harry was nodding sagely to himself as he dished pancakes.

'Sunrise House had nowhere to do that. I shall see you back at the apart–'

The call ended. No charge. Idiot.

How damnably infuriating, thought Holmes. He had wanted to get a message to Benson but now that must wait. Oh well, there was much to occupy his brain and there was something about rail travel inherently conducive to pondering the inconsistencies of a case. In his day, it had been the rocking motion of the carriage on its steel tracks but there was minimal rocking in these carriages. When he had left for Boston yesterday, he had carried with him not even a hunch, simply a notion that a stay had not been properly tied. His mind slid back to last evening as he found Barron and asked if they might discuss the matter of the police visit.

'We might,' he said, 'but the police never spoke with me. What's it to you anyway?'

Barron was late-fifties, estimated Holmes. At least five of his teeth were still housed in his mouth. Holmes offered the cigarette packet.

'I am a curious man,' said Holmes.

Barron looked at Holmes, looked back at the proffered packet.

'The whole packet?' he asked, not willing to believe such bounty might truly be his. Holmes flipped it to him. Barron looked about suspiciously.

'Best we go private,' he suggested and Holmes followed him to a swing door that led into the shared bathroom. It was several degrees cooler in here on account of the tile floor, the large space and lack of any heating. A shower head dripped somewhere. A fug of soapy drains, disinfectant and stale urine welcomed them.

'I wasn't here when the cops turned up,' explained Barron.

'But it was you who answered the phone?'

It was. The toff on the other end – not his vernacular but Holmes' – had asked not for Leonard Chester, or Lenny, or Chester, but for Mat.

'Who is Mat?'

Mat was a young fellow it seemed who stayed infrequently at Sunrise House and never for longer than one night. He kept to himself. Barron was not sure what Mat's poison was but nobody, according to Barron, stayed at Sunrise House by choice.

'They're not all junkies or booze hounds,' he said, somehow distancing himself a step from his cohabitants, 'only ninety percent.' Sometimes it was just people with no money, 'urban poets, rappers, them kind', or men who had been kicked out by their women and needed a bed. According to Barron about half who fitted these categories had 'issues'.

'Such as?'

In the universal gesture to denote lunacy, Barron wound his finger around the space in front of his ear.

'Was Mat that way?'

'Don't know, like I say, never spoke to him really. But he had that look.'

'The look of a mental patient?'

'The look of Davy Travers.'

'And who is Davy Travers?'

'Used to stay here. Grabbed the breadknife one day in the kitchen and stabbed two guys who he said were Gestapo.'

First thing that morning, Holmes, at his most presentable, had spoken to the female supervisor of the house about Mat on the pretext that a friend might be able to offer him a job. She could not help with Mat's surname either.

'We don't pry into any of you', she said. 'I can pass a message on if he comes back here.'

'When was the last time he was here?' asked Holmes.

'At least three weeks', she replied, peering at him now, suspicions aroused. Barron had estimated three to four weeks since Mat had been there.

Over breakfast Holmes enquired of the other Sunrise House clients if any knew Mat. A few said they did, but like Barron, none of them had so much as a surname for him, nor any idea of his occupation, if indeed he did have one.

Now as the train powered on, Holmes evaluated. He had uncovered no solid evidence to suggest Mat might be Noah. Barron was credible, Holmes did not believe him a liar, yet it was possible he was mistaken. He was after all, a regular at Sunrise House and as Barron himself had admitted, nobody stayed there unless they had some issue. Even if Barron weren't mistaken, there might be a number of valid reasons why Scheer had made a covert call to Mat. He could be Scheer's homosexual lover or drug supplier. But equally, he could be some mentally unstable patient who had somehow become exposed to *Crimini d'Italia* and began imitating the murders therein.

Harry had lost none of his touch with pancakes but all Georgette could think about now was Holmes. And the hamsters. And Holmes. She could have gone straight to the lab but the apartment had all she needed and was more comfortable. She nixed Harry's offer to get time off work to mind her.

'None of those people I met with Holmes can be the killer, and Benson has a team on them anyway.'

Reluctantly Harry came around but he had insisted on driving her and now he demanded he accompany her inside. She waited while he checked around, just as Holmes had done.

'All clear', he announced. 'You go to your lab, you have the driver meet you right out front.'

She assured him she would. He hugged her.

'And make sure your sister is on for Thanksgiving.'

When he left, she savored that previous night she'd spent with her father. I wonder if it will just be him and me growing old, she thought with a touch of self-pity. There was a knock on the door. He must have come back for something. She opened the door. Avery Scheer barged in and slammed it shut.

'You played me, Georgette.'

'Get out of here right now.' Like the feet of a falling mountaineer, her brain sought solid ground.

'Or what? You'll call your police pals? I wouldn't be counting on any help from them.'

She tried to back towards the kitchen and potential weapons but Scheer moved as she did, shutting her down.

'It's alright,' he said. 'I understand. In fact, I admire you, even though it does wound my pride. I need you to help me.'

She made a dash. He seized her arm.

'No, please!' he cried.

She'd practiced the scenario in this very room. Rather than pull away she went with the momentum and drove herself forward, slamming her foot into the side of his knee, felt him buckle, pivoted and threw him over her hip. He landed with a crash. She grabbed her phone from the table, ran to the bathroom, locked it.

22

Holmes was still on the platform, having barely left the compartment, when he sensed movement behind him. He swung around to defend himself and was confronted by a uniformed policeman.

'Percy Turner?'

'Yes?'

'Wait here, sir.'

The policeman made a call on his radio.

Oh my God, thought Holmes. It's Georgette, something has happened to –

A familiar face speared through the crowd. Holmes recognized Feeney, Harry Watson's partner.

'You need to come with me,' he said.

A savage fear ripped at Holmes' heart.

The body lay on the carpet in a pool of sticky blood. Avery Scheer's head had been caved in by the marble bust of Freud which had been dropped on the floor nearby, scalp and hair still attached to the base. Five techs were working the room, checking the walls, the carpet. Georgette stood with Benson at the doorway. Less than an hour earlier she had been shaking, terrified in her bathroom as she dialled Harry and yelled that a deranged Avery Scheer was loose in her living room. Within minutes, her father was holding her in his arms but her heart was still a locomotive. Of Scheer there had been no sign. Harry had called Benson. Teams had been sent to Scheer's house and office. Being a Sunday there had been a slight delay in getting a key for the office but when they opened it they found Scheer sprawled dead on the floor. The blood was still fresh.

'Scheer must have come back here straight away,' said Benson, who explained that he had chewed out the two men he'd had on Scheer. 'But to be fair they were in a difficult situation. There was a shooting two blocks from where they were watching his house and they felt they had to respond. If I'd have had more eyes on him, he wouldn't have slipped away.'

'Any cameras?'

'We'll check. This door was locked. The killer went out the window.'

'You think Scheer let him in?'

'Looks that way.'

'Watson!' The cry turned her head to the end of the corridor. Holmes was striding towards her, Harry at his side. She felt an urge to rush to him but withstood it. Not only would that have been severely embarrassing under any circumstances, she reminded herself that what he felt was entirely different.

Holmes wanted to wrap her in his arms but knew that was risible. His eyes traced every inch of her body. Thank God she seemed unharmed. He'd been hollow with worry until Feeney assured him that Georgette was fine. Harry had been waiting at the reception area here for him and had filled out the events.

'You are uninjured?' he asked, and felt this completely inadequate.

'Thanks to your training.' Georgette told him about her self-defense.

'Your father said there was no weapon?'

'That I saw.' She described in exact detail what had happened. Then Benson told him what they knew thus far of the turn of events.

'All persons of interest were being watched when this happened,' he said. 'Scheer got a call at his house at two-oh-six this morning. The call came from a cell belonging to a young woman who at the time was clubbing in Chelsea. She thought she'd lost her phone but it turned up on the bar.'

'Somebody took her phone out of her bag and called Scheer,' deduced Holmes.

'That's what we think. The club has CCTV. We might get lucky but I doubt it. We don't know what was said on the call because we have no warrant to tap the phones of anybody other than the Bed-Stuy drug dealer used by Morris. We're still chasing a link between Morris and Ricky Coleman. Whoever made that call, it wasn't any of our persons of interest, including Coleman, because they were all under surveillance and none of them were anywhere near Chelsea. For now, it looks like

Scheer was Noah and had some accomplice, or he was involved with Noah and something went wrong.'

Harry speculated they would get evidence from this scene.

'Looks like it,' agreed Lipinski, who had been in conference with the techs. 'Prints, likely DNA.'

Holmes craned for a look at the murder scene.

'Is there any possibility that I could –'

'No,' said Benson. Holmes had expected as much.

He said, 'You might want to locate a fellow named "Mat", surname unknown.'

They had found a staffroom down the corridor. Harry nursed a coffee, Lipinski rifled biscuits. Neither Benson or Lipinski looked like they had slept in days. Holmes had told them what he had learned in Boston.

'I apologize but I was not investigating as such, just tidying up a potential loose end and saw no reason to waste your time.' Holmes stirred his tea slowly.

Georgette waited for the explosion but Benson remained calm. Without further engaging Holmes, Benson dialled Boston Homicide and asked them to get two crack detectives onto learning Mat's identity.

'We need you to get down to Sunrise House and sort this out now. Find a guy named ...' he looked to Holmes for a reminder.

'Barron.'

'Barron. Thank you.' He ended the call and said to Holmes. 'It was a good pick-up. I'll give you the benefit of the doubt you that were going to tell me all about this when your phone cut out.'

'Since we're in this spirit of cooperation, perhaps we could check Scheer's phone records for the day we first visited here?'

Georgette saw Harry's eyes narrow. That was still a sore point.

'Wednesday November eighteen,' she said.

Holmes said, 'It would be interesting to see if Scheer tried to call Sunrise House immediately after our visit. If he had foreknowledge of the crime and Mat is some confederate ...'

'Yeah, we get it,' said Benson as Lipinski trolled through her phone.

Through a mouthful of biscuit, she said, 'Looks like he called at two forty-eight p.m.'

Georgette said, 'That would be about forty minutes after we left.'

Holmes said, 'Melissa Harper had a meeting with Scheer, so perhaps he needed to wait until that meeting was over. Then he called Sunrise House at the earliest opportunity.'

The call had been less than a minute, noted Lipinski.

'Perhaps an inquiry as to whether Mat was there, answered in the negative.' Nobody disputed Holmes on that.

'There was another call three hours later,' Lipinski reached for another biscuit.

'Trying to reach the elusive Mat again.' Holmes used a tone that intimated he was speculating.

'Or he could have been reminding Leonard Chester or another patient to take his medication,' said Benson, and Holmes nodded graciously. That second call had also been short.

'Unfortunately my friend Barron will not be able to assist us on any of these calls. He told me at the time he had taken up the offer of two weeks at St Joseph's, where, to quote "the food is to die for". He had only just returned from this sabbatical and resumed his phone answering duties when he took Scheer's call from the bodega. It is possible Scheer did not actually mean to assault you, Watson.'

She felt like slapping Holmes.

'He grabbed me!'

'True but he did not threaten you with a weapon.'

'He was pissed at me for duping him.'

'Also true but did that warrant a trip to your apartment? You recall your conversation with Scheer over lunch at which he avowed that you and he were both the target of authorities threatened by your work?'

Georgette did, and saw where Holmes was heading. 'You think Mat is a patient of Scheer's who Scheer was trying to protect?'

'That would make sense. He might have thought you could make representation to the police, arrange some kind of way for Mat to be apprehended without being killed. Against that, how would Mat be able to follow the method of the Picture Book Killer unless Scheer had told him about it? Surely a professional like Scheer would not divulge such information to somebody unstable. And yet the fact Scheer called Sunrise House immediately after we had first visited him, and then made a call from a corner-store phone after being questioned by police, suggests there was some link.'

Harry said he might have just been careless. 'Maybe Scheer left the book around and this Mat found it.'

'Then why not admit that?' queried Holmes. 'One could hardly blame him for leaving a book lying about.'

Georgette sensed the two homicide detectives had been listening with interest. Now Lipinski said, 'Shall we tell them?'

Benson said, 'An analysis of Scheer's computer shows he was looking for a copy of *Crimini d'Italia* as far back as April. Well, certainly searching for books by Pasquale Ometti. He was even checking out European sellers of rare books.'

Months before it turned up on Edwards' site, thought Georgette.

'So, he already knew about the book,' said Holmes stroking his chin. 'That is interesting.'

'Maybe Scheer was like some puppet-master,' said Harry. 'You know, using some vulnerable kid to do his dirty work.'

He was arrogant enough, thought Georgette.

Holmes said, 'It seems unusual for somebody to derive pleasure from bloody killings like this by proxy. I can't imagine Jack the Ripper brainwashing some underling. The pleasure is the participation.'

Benson seemed to agree. 'If Scheer was setting this up, you think he'd want the trophies for himself but there is no sign of anything like that here, no cubes of flesh from the victims, no gadget to excise the tissue. And when we tossed his house, same deal.'

Holmes said, 'If the killer was indeed a puppet and this murder is a sign of his rebellion, the killings may stop. If not however ...'

'He will escalate.' It was Lipinski who spoke. None of them disagreed.

Kate had been in New York two weeks and the money she'd brought with her was nearly drained, even though she'd picked up a few hours daily work handing out pamphlets for a pancake place. Trouble was she was still spending faster than she was earning. She needed to go out each night to shorten the next day and therefore spend less money, but even sitting on a cocktail for hours she hadn't been able to make the money stretch far enough. And if you were having a good time, you couldn't just fold up. Megan had scored a job waitressing but then Megan had more going for her. Being blonde for a start, and bouncy, dimples when she smiled. Kate's hair was boring brown and, let's face it, her thighs were large and ugly. The Mexican kid they'd met at the skate park said he was earning good bucks at a call centre. And he didn't speak nearly as good as she did. Call centre it might have to be. She checked her watch. The dude had said he'd be here at ten, in the little playground in Riverside Park near West 76th, and it was already nearly twenty after. And too cold to hang around. Kate was annoyed. She could have slept in, saved money. Kate stamped her feet. She'd invested in good boots, that was one thing. The jacket and scarf were cheap but efficient, but it was way colder than what she was used to. They'd met last night in the Heights near the skate park: Megan, the Mexican kid, the Mex's pal, just turned a corner and there the dude was, bandanna like a cowboy robber, spray can in each fist. He was good, real good, the elephant he'd done was huge, standing on two legs.

'He's dope,' Kate had said, pointing at the image which was lit by the only remaining working streetlight. She wasn't wanting to come on to him or anything, just it was how she felt.

'It's a she,' he'd said and she could see his eyes were really studying her above that mask. And so when he'd said he could show her some stuff tomorrow, she'd said sure. But now she was wondering if he'd been having a joke at her expense because here at the playground was this little elephant statue and kids were climbing around it. She was just about to go when there he was, ambling towards her, no bandanna this time but she recognized him anyway.

'Thought you weren't going to show up. You should have given a phone number.'

'I don't have a phone.'

'I'd give you mine but I don't even know your name.'

'Noah,' he said.

No cocaine but he had his pipe, that was something. Think. He had worked his way to the park near the lab where he had rendezvoused with Georgette that first time after believing he'd been kidnapped by Moriarty. How long ago it seemed now. While he was out here, Georgette was in the lab trying to find a way to reverse whatever was happening to the hamsters, and by extension what would happen to him. He could not afford to dwell upon that. He would not.

His task was solely to prevent another murder. So, think, Holmes. For the umpteenth time he calculated the state of play. Very well, rule out Morris as Noah: the Morris–Coleman drug connection, well, vaguely possible but it relied on Coleman being dumb enough to leave a fingerprint while being smart enough to conceal his DNA. Every investigation threw up time-wasting leads. Holmes made the decision that was all Walter Morris and his narcotics friends were.

Which returned him to Scheer. Scheer had been looking for the book as far back as April and now Scheer was dead. Here is the conundrum: Scheer learned about *Crimini d'Italia* by sometime around April and had sought the book without success. There were no mentions of it on the

Internet, however, and his search had proven futile. Until July when he had been directed to Edwards' listing. And now something else pricked Holmes. Edwards had said he'd not even time to do his usual precis of the book, and at the time Scheer's inquiry had come through, had only loaded the cover. Scheer hadn't just got lucky, he already knew about that book. How?

Scheer had held his seminar and then Noah had begun his work in October. Who would Scheer tell about the book? Another professional, a psychologist or perhaps a writer, somebody he thought could turn the tale into an interesting read, like Watson with his chum Conan Doyle? Yes, that was possible. But how did he even know about it back in February? That was the nub of the matter and it was eluding him.

Try another angle. He looked up into the grey sky, like a giant tombstone, he thought, pressing down. What do we know of Noah? What have his victims told us? Like a starving dog, his mind sniffed every inch of the case looking for a morsel.

'It was weird. All the organs were free of cancer and infection but atrophied.' Charmain had grown up in Sri Lanka. She had gorgeous green eyes and frizzy, dark hair. She looked about twenty-one but was in her mid-thirties with two children. She was very, very good at her job. She pointed at the screen on her desk and Georgette could clearly see what she meant about Zoe's brain. The worst imaginable outcome was becoming a reality.

'How old was she?' Charmain was selecting autopsy images of Zoe on her computer. Georgette tried to stop her head spinning.

'Not yet two.'

'Really? She looked ... old. I would have thought three at least.'

Georgette felt the shadow of doom hovering, chilling her.

'And look here.' Charmain zoomed in on the image. 'This is a cross-section of the brain. This is not dissimilar to what you find in Alzheimer's sufferers although I can't see any actual lesions.'

'Is there anything I might be able to use to reverse this?'

Charmain dropped her pencil on the desk and leaned back. 'It's not my field at all but let's face it, if there was a cure for Alzheimer's we'd know about it. But then, like I said, I don't see lesions.'

'I'm trying transfusions. The red cell count was very low.'

Charmain nodded, said, 'Diet?'

'Needle in a haystack but I've split the remainder into three groups and I'm trying different dietary combos.'

'If I think of anything ...'

Her cue to leave. She thanked Charmain.

'I'll probably be back soon.' Vernon would not be much longer for this world.

'A comparison will help.'

Georgette had just reached the lab when her phone rang. It was Holmes, excited.

'He has something to do with art.'

A few minutes later, Holmes sat in front of Georgette's lab computer on a Skype link with Benson who was at the command centre locked in a soundscape of constantly ringing phones. Holmes had directed Benson to the open the crime scene photos of Carmen Cavanagh's living room.

'Look at those paintings on the wall.'

'Every ritzy apartment has expensive art,' countered Benson.

'Call up the photographs of the Zebra Club.'

Benson did. The first thing that struck Georgette now was the expansive murals.

'Wouldn't you say art was a feature of this room?'

'True but again, every second club –'

'Lucy Bassey worked at the museum as a restorer. You recall I smelled turpentine on her. I assumed that was to do with her work but what if that was from Noah?'

Benson was nodding. Holmes was seized by a fierce drive now.

'Today I was not close enough to smell Scheer's body but the attack seemed less premeditated. If he is an artist perhaps there is more turpentine, transferred to Scheer's body or the room.'

'Checking it now.' Benson gestured to somebody, possibly Lipinski off-screen.

'Gina Scaroldi's apartment was plain as,' said Benson, not as if he were pointscoring but pondering.

Holmes asked if they had identified Mat yet.

'No. They're trying but nobody has a surname on him let alone a photo. He lived on the street, crashed at halfway houses. The art angle might ...'

Benson looked off-screen again. Georgette heard Lipinski's voice but couldn't make out what she was saying. Benson got up, leaving the screen focused on his chair. She thought she heard him curse. Then his face reappeared.

'We've had a request out for any violent assaults, abductions or murders in the five boroughs. Greta says a report came in of a young woman, missing. Her friend says this morning she was going to meet up with a guy she met last night and then come to the café where the friend works for lunch. She never showed up, didn't call and is not answering her phone.'

'Maybe they're taking in a movie or ... other stuff,' said Georgette.

'What we figured. Except the friend's report says this guy she was meeting is a street artist.'

23

'Do you think she might still be alive?' asked Georgette.

'If she is, it will not be because of any action on my account.'

Holmes was even gloomier than the sky. They were standing in the crisp air looking up at the large painting of an elephant that adorned the wall of a building close to the Highbridge skate park. Crime-scene tape surrounded the area and techs were beavering away. Benson and Lipinski had already interviewed the friends of the missing girl, Kate Odenhall, but they hadn't got a particularly good description of the artist. He had been wearing a bandanna across the lower part of his face and it had been dark. Apparently after a short conversation he'd agreed to meet up with Kate, who had the morning off somewhere in Riverside Park. Regrettably, Kate's friend did not know the exact meeting place.

Georgette was terrified for the girl. Her friend said the two of them looked out for each other and would call if they couldn't make a meeting. Benson had checked hospitals and lockups just in case but there was no sign of Kate. He was trying to get a lock on her phone.

Holmes, as if he had considered his previous response and declared it mean-spirited, now added, 'The fact that her body has not been found is encouraging. He is freed from his script now. The Picture Killer murdered on the spot leaving a picture. Noah – Mat – faithfully followed that, but not now. Now he can write his own history.'

You are a shadow of your former self, Holmes, he told himself, but you must still try. If you were brought back into this world for any reason it must have been to make a difference. Think. He returned to the same stumbling block. How had Scheer known to look for the book? Who had told him about *Crimini d'Italia*?

He pulled himself up. The first tug at his sleeve. And all of a sudden his frozen mind was moving again –

'Holmes?'

He held a finger up to quiet Watson, moved off, mustn't lose this thread. Scheer hadn't been searching for *Crimini d'Italia*. No, he had been searching for Pasquale Ometti! Of course, it had to be ... it was the only thing that made sense. He was about to yell for Georgette to call Benson but remembered she had already put the number in his phone.

He dialled now.

Benson answered immediately. 'Yes?'

'I think Mat may be related to Pasquale Ometti. Then he would know the story without needing the book. It would have been handed down.' He met Georgette's excited gaze and thought: just like you and John Watson. The past determines the present. 'I think it wasn't Mat told Scheer about this story but the other way around. Look for any Ometti in Boston or New York. Check Immigration –'

'I got it, Percy.'

He rang off. Holmes saw Georgette had overheard and understood.

'With a name they can hunt him down.'

And she squeezed his arm, such a small but effusive gesture that for John, for all his loyalty, would been too reserved.

Time, though. The hour glass had long been upturned.

Kate woke to a throbbing head. It must have been the cold. She was freezing and stiff. She went to rub her forehead but couldn't move her arms that far. Her wrists ...

She blinked awake. Shit. She screamed but realized her mouth was taped. And her jeans had been taken off so she was only in her underwear and top. The panic shot through her. Her wrists were bound with plastic ties and then looped to an unlit metal potbelly. She was on the floor. She tugged hard as she could, succeeding only in hurting her wrists. The room smelled damp, and of river. Maybe a basement. There was furniture around, simple stuff, like a living room. No light. Blinds. Where the fuck was she? Coming back now. That asshole, Noah. After they met, they walked in the park. He told her he'd scored some amazing pills. She'd swallowed three. Then felt tired. She remembered trying to walk. Then nothing until now. Had he raped her? She didn't feel anything but maybe she wouldn't with those knockout drops. Fuck, fuck, fuck. No shoes, he'd taken those too. It was so dark and cold here. Megan would check in, wouldn't she? She'd call the cops. But wasn't it like forty-eight hours before they'd do anything? She was lying in the middle of the floor and stretching as far as she could and sweeping her legs, she couldn't reach anything except some low cupboard, the kind like some kids' beds have so you can put a mattress on top and toys below. Were there rats? she wondered. Please God, no rats. Thankfully he'd not bound her feet. Using her toes she was able, at full stretch to slide open the cupboard, and get her feet in there. Nothing hard. But something, something material ... a blanket maybe? Slowly she extracted it. Yes, a blanket. Eventually she got it far enough, she could get her legs under it one at a time. Warmer. But she was terrified of what was going to happen when he came back.

They were heading downtown using the subway. Holmes had finally agreed to return to the apartment. He swayed with the motion of the car but his mind was fixed on the same thread.

'If Mat is from the distaff side, his surname may not be Ometti.'

Georgette wasn't even thinking when she said, 'You know if he comes from Boston, he could have an Irish name. Lot of Italians and Irish married, the Catholic thing.'

Holmes looked like she'd swung a brick into his forehead. Then he shouted, 'That's it, Watson. It's been staring us in the face.' A couple of commuters did no more than raise dull eyes. 'You are pre-eminently smart. We must decamp immediately.'

They broke the surface at one hundred and twenty-fifth street, Holmes' long legs pumping as his fingers worked his phone.

'Benson,' he explained.

She could almost see the workings of his brain as he waited. Benson must have picked up, for Holmes barged in without preamble.

'His name may be Mathew Mahoney.' Benson must have asked why Holmes thought that, because Holmes said, 'The painting in the office, *Cain and Abel*, it is by M. Mahoney. Scheer told us he'd purchased it at a flea market in Boston. It may well have been when he first connected with Mathew.' Holmes turned to her and said, 'He is checking.'

Georgette marvelled at how quickly Holmes had taken to some of the vernacular and how the phone was now like a sixth finger. She saw something else had occurred to him now – as if the school bell in his brain had sounded and the thoughts, like cooped-up children, were running wild.

'And that may explain the lack of art with Gina Scar–' He cut himself off. She heard him say 'Yes,' three or four times, then he turned to her, nodding with animation. From this, she deemed that Holmes' supposition had been confirmed. 'Something else,' Holmes added for Benson. 'I think we can assume that Mathew had some prior contact with Carmen Cavanagh, possibly an art exhibition, and also with Lucy Bassey, similar, or perhaps they even worked on something together, and he may well have been involved in the artwork at the Zebra Lounge. But there was no obvious connection with Gina Scaroldi and that may be because she was first in the sequence. Perhaps he happened upon her because he was staying on Roosevelt Island or nearby. Look for an artist community or some such ...'

'Collective,' suggested Georgette, now aware where he was heading.

'Did you manage to trace Kate's phone?' asked Holmes of Benson. He looked over at Georgette and nodded as Benson peeled off answers.

'We shall see you there.' He ended the call.

'Roosevelt Island?' she guessed.

He nodded. 'Perhaps something will catch my eye. Kate spent a deal of time at a playground in Riverside Park then her phone was switched off. Police are canvassing the playground now.'

It was after five now. Street lights gleamed like the eyes of a miner, face covered in coal dust.

She dialled. 'Dad? Want to pick us up? Percy's onto something.'

'Wish I could but I'm in Brooklyn following up a lead on the Rebecca Chaney case, a boater who may have seen something. You be careful. Stay away from any action, understand?'

She assured him she would, ended the call and scanned for a cab. Then she thought of a better alternative.

Twelve minutes later, Simone's Silverado screeched to a halt. Holmes jumped in front.

'Good thing I was nearby,' she said as she accelerated off. The adrenalin had blunted night's fang but once in the car Georgette realized how cold she had been out in the open.

'You know where on Roosevelt?' asked Simone.

'No. Look for murals.' Holmes chin was set, his body tense.

Georgette's phone buzzed. It was Benson and he sounded desperate.

'You with Percy?'

'Yes. I'll put you on speaker.'

Benson's voice fought above the rattle of the car. 'Just got a report from Fortieth Avenue in Queens of what might have been a young woman being dragged into a red van.'

Roosevelt Island was just across from there.

Georgette said, 'You think it's Kate?'

'Could be unrelated, but it could be another Noah victim. He might be cutting loose now. Greta's heading there, I've just arrived on Roosevelt, an artist collective about ten minutes' walk from the running track where we found Gina. Gotta go. Don't get too close.'

'Got it,' said Simone and edged the speed higher.

'Wait!' Holmes shouted. 'Pull over.'

Georgette was confused by this sudden demand. Simone speared for the curb and braked hard. Holmes turned to Georgette.

'If this latest abduction is a fresh victim – and, who knows, there might be more – what does it suggest?'

She felt dim.

'He's starting a harem?' said Simone.

That gave Georgette the spark she needed to catch up with Holmes: Noah would do what his namesake did.

'He's filling his ark,' she said.

Holmes looked downcast. 'Exactly, Watson. I do not believe we shall find him on Roosevelt Island. I think he's on the water. And that I am afraid is beyond our capabilities.'

'He could be using a houseboat,' said Simone. 'That looks like an ark, right?'

Holmes visibly brightened. 'Not only looks like one, it is as close to an ark as one might find. Are there houseboats in this city?'

'Far Rockaway,' said Georgette, remembering Harry taking them there once for a trip on Mirsch's boat.

'West Seventy-nine,' said Simone with confidence. 'I went to this amazing party there once.'

Holmes asked if there were any others but neither Georgette nor her sister was aware of any.

'West Seventy-ninth,' declared Holmes. 'He could have walked her there from the playground. It is closer, so may be our only chance to affect the outcome. Benson can get police to Far Rockaway.'

'Less than ten minutes,' said Simone as she threw on an indicator and slammed her foot on the accelerator.

Georgette called Benson.

The sound of heavy feet approaching filled Kate with new terror. She had heard the hooters of tug boats and was sure now she was right by the water. It was possible, she realized, that she could even be on some kind of boat, she had thought she felt the slightest of movements every now and again but then her head was still woozy after the drugs. She tried to scream but could not. Then she'd heard a door open somewhere and that heavy, slow tread. Her stomach squeezed itself in, she heard herself whimper, couldn't stop it. In the gloom, a tongue of light swam towards her, and behind it a gargantuan shape. When the shape drew closer, she realized it was her captor, advancing by the beam of a small flashlight with a sack of something slung over his shoulders ... no, not a sack. He knelt before her, and carefully lowered a woman's body to the floor. She could be alive, realized Kate. Her clothing was intact and she could see no injury, though it was too dark to see blood anyway.

'Alligator,' he said.

The terror was like a knot that had worked its way up to Kate's throat where it threatened to lodge and choke her. She pleaded with her eyes, *untie me*, but he was blind to her request. She forced herself to calm, breathed steadily through her nose.

A backpack he'd had slung across his shoulders like a satchel, he let slide off and hit the floor. Placing the flashlight in his mouth he unzipped the backpack and extricated something light colored and plastic.

Oh my God! Terror seized her as she recognized what it was, one of those crime suits like Dexter on TV wore. She was trembling uncontrollably. She wet herself, couldn't stop it. He slid the suit over his clothes. She was whimpering louder now.

'Don't be scared. You have been selected. You are special.'

He placed surgical gloves on his hands, snug. Then he reached into the backpack and brought out a cruel scythe, the sort you saw in those old books, sharp and curved for cutting an animal's throat. He placed it carefully down on plastic and then he pulled out some other contraption.

Kate fainted.

Simone swung onto the service road that fed into the underground parking lot used by the boaters.

'Look for a red van,' commanded Holmes but the colors were masked until the headlights slashed each successive chunk of gloom.

'There!' shouted Georgette, spying a high red van. But who knew if it was the right one?

Benson was sending a squad car but it might be ten minutes yet.

'Wait here.' Holmes bolted before the car had come to a halt. The only weapon he carried was the walking stick.

'Wait for backup,' Georgette shouted in the loudest hoarse whisper she could muster but Holmes wasn't listening.

He tried the back of the van, locked. Pressed his ear to it but could detect no sound. He quietly walked around and, using his phone as a torch, peered inside the front cabin. He noticed an oil-slick by the driver door, possibly from another vehicle that had been parked beside it. He moved swiftly back to the car.

'I'm going to take a look.' He nodded to the exit that opened onto the broad pavement that ran by the series of piers.

'Pier C or D,' said Simone.

Holmes stepped out onto the low concrete apron and surveyed the scene. Lights twinkled from other side of the Hudson. Narrow but tall iron gates stood between the path and the start of each pier. The rest of the fence was low but there was no support on the other side and if you climbed over you'd be pitched straight into the water. The shape of houseboats could be made out about a hundred yards to the south, thin jetties running out to them like skeleton arms.

'You need to wait!' Georgette had followed. She did not want to lose him.

'Don't worry, Watson. I can handle myself.'

'Oh, I'm sure that is what you said to John at the Reichenbach Falls.'

'Something similar. Watson ...' he paused, '... thank you for everything.'

And then he raced towards the gate whose pier led to a handful of moored houseboats. Probably most had left for warmer destinations. Georgette was torn. She bit her lip.

She went to follow but Simone held her back.

'You might be a liability.'

And Georgette knew that was true.

The gate was a tall iron grille, locked. No more than twelve feet but at the top, spikes pointed out towards him. He poked his stick through the bars and it clattered on the other side. Then he took four paces back and ran at the gate. He leapt as high as he could, held on. It was an easy climb with such handholds, far easier than the Matterhorn, tough on the fingers but that was all. He reached the top in seconds, negotiated the overhang thanks to his study of Chinese acrobatics, cursed as his jacket ripped, then dropped to the other side landing more heavily than he would have liked.

You are certainly not what you were, he thought. Up to your feet, old son, go!

He retrieved his stick and in long, near-silent strides made for the houseboats. He counted seven. Mahoney could be on any of them.

No, wrong, Holmes. He won't be on anything lit. He needs darkness. He has either killed the owner or found some abandoned boat. There, the last boat on the north side of the second pier. Total darkness.

As soon as Holmes reached the pier, he cut his pace and edged slowly and quietly along the wooden slats. Most other boats were well lit, people could be seen inside some, too cold to be out on deck. But the last boat here was dark as a tomb. Holmes reached the bow and listened. He could hear nothing. The boat looked like an ark. It was a high top-heavy wooden structure, a barn moored on the Hudson River. He contemplated using the gangway. Tempting, but if Mahoney was listening out, foolish. Instead, he took a running jump and landed cat-like on the deck. He paused a moment in case he had given himself away. No sound. The windows around the boat were all covered in blinds and drapes but a narrow slit where a blind did not quite cover revealed a flash of light. He edged forward towards the door. Faintly visible in the moonlight was an oily shoe mark. A sound came from inside, just a dull thud, nothing more. He tested the door. Locked.

He slipped his hands in his pockets, brought out two small picks. In the distance, sirens. Should he wait? Another thump from inside, louder. No time. Deftly he picked the lock. The revolver would have been useful but then, in such a confined space with potentially multiple hostages, likely unusable. It was dark inside and Holmes was forced to allow his eyes to grow accustomed. He edged toward a low babbling.

'... will thank me, believe me. The others will perish, body and soul but our line will live on. The Jews sprinkled blood on their doors and the sign saved them, this sign marks you as safe for eternity.'

Holmes wanted to move faster but did not dare. He had no idea even which way Mahoney might be facing. He heard something mechanical, a spring, wires or some such, followed by thrashing and a muffled squeal as if a dog had been kicked. The punch. The mark of the ark. His rational brain tempered his revulsion at the cruelty by the logical consideration. At least one captive must be alive.

Just in time he noticed a narrow step to the next level. He eased down it, his walking stick at present arms. An electric torch lying on the floor lit all he needed to take in the scene. Mahoney holding a slim metal gadget in his hand, a young woman bound and gagged, another body on the floor. Mahoney was about twelve feet from him and Holmes would have been able to intervene had not the sound of the sirens racing into the car park snapped Mahoney's head up.

'Who are you?' Mahoney cried, a cruel scythe materialising at the throat of the young woman whose terror made her eyes enormous and opalescent.

'I am the Lord's messenger, Mathew,' he said. 'It is time to desist.'

For an instant, Holmes thought his ruse had worked, but then Mahoney yelled, 'Liar!'

Mahoney pulled back the woman's hair to expose her throat for the fatal slash. Holmes hurled his stick like an assegai with all the force he could muster.

The rubberized tip smashed into Mahoney's forehead and he dropped like a stone.

24

In the bright light of the interview room, Mathew Mahoney was revealed as a slightly built young man in his twenties. His great-great-grandfather's Italian genes had long been swamped by Irish blood. Wispy ginger hair topped a gaunt, freckled face. A dark bruise was still visible in the centre of his forehead. The time and date of the interview were stamped across the tape. It taken place only a few hours after Mahoney's arrest, the night before last. How quickly time slips through our fingers, reflected Holmes, how suddenly our life can take an unexpected turn. The two young women had been saved, although Kate Odenhall had been sent straight to surgery with the deep wound Mahoney had inflicted with his punch. It had cut through outer layers of skin, then muscle, almost down to the bone. Cubes from the other victims had been found inside the refrigerator on the houseboat. Mahoney had the look of a stableboy, thought Holmes. Benson had slipped them the interview on a USB. The interview was well in, and the basics had been established. Holmes had the apartment to himself, he forced himself not to think about that, to concentrate instead on Mahoney. The camera was solely on him.

'I first met Professor Scheer about a year ago. He bought one of my paintings, *Cain and Abel*. We got talking. He was interested that I painted in the style of the old masters. I explained that it wasn't I who was painting. My hand was guided by an unseen spirit.'

Benson's voice came from off-screen.

'You mean while you were painting?'

'At first. Then more and more often. Until ... there was no me anymore. My voice, my eyes, his will.'

Holmes craned in. He imagined how this tale would have fascinated Scheer.

'Who are you talking about, Mathew?'

Mahoney looked about warily. 'Giuseppe Lorato.'

'Who is Giuseppe Lorato?'

'The son of a Roman cloth merchant. He was born in Ostia in eighteen sixty-four. He murdered women, leaving a picture cut from a story book on their body. The police were confused about his motivation but I knew.'

'What was his motivation?'

'To save them. To the police, to others, they were simply women, but Giuseppe understood their inner nature. Each was as unique as a beautiful animal that needed to be saved from the flood.'

'The flood?'

'Not a physical flood, rising water, but the inundation of sin and hopelessness that is our lot on earth.'

'How did you know about Lorato and his murders?'

'My great-great-grandfather was a kind of detective. He was Italian. He spent years searching for the killer. He wrote it all down, published a book.'

'*Crimini d'Italia.*'

'Yes. There were no English language copies. Very few Italian ones. My family apparently used to have one but ...' He trailed off.

'There is no mention of a Giuseppe Lorato in this book.'

'There wouldn't be. My great-great-grandfather never publicly named Lorato.'

'Why is that?'

'Because he killed him.'

That hit Holmes like the kick of a wild colt. Benson took his time.

'You know this how?'

'My grandfather told me when I was twelve years old. His father had told him. My great-great-grandfather had cornered Lorato, finally tracked him down by finding which picture book was being used and who might have a copy. Lorato did not deny the crime. He said he would never be convicted. Told my grandfather to his face, he was saving these women. Saving their souls before they were stained, just like Noah saved all the animals of the world. Then my great-great-grandfather pushed him off a roof.'

So that was it. Ometti had taken the law into his own hands. Holmes' wished Georgette were here. She had looked so beautiful when Benson had called to pick her up. Benson had agreed to keep Holmes' involvement out of the media but there was still the risk of a trial in which he would have to testify, although the confession had reduced that likelihood.

'When did you tell Professor Scheer this?'

'About the second time we met. He thought I was making it up. He wanted to help me.'

'How?'

There was a long pause.

'He thought he could talk Giuseppe out of my head.' A bitter laugh from Mahoney. 'A soul is immortal. It is not like a piece of furniture. Lorato is punishing my family by punishing me.'

Benson did not get distracted. 'Scheer told you he had located a copy of the book.'

'Yes. He found the book. He thought that would somehow help me understand that Giuseppe was not a spirit but just a voice in my head. But most of the time it was Guiesppe he was talking to. I am doomed to carry on his work.'

'To fill his ark?'

Mahoney was silent for a long moment. Then his face twisted as if in pain and he began to cry.

'What is the matter, Mat?'

He shook his head from side to side. 'I let Giuseppe down. I didn't finish the task.'

'Is that why you killed Professor Scheer?'

'He was going to make me stop. He told me he would have to turn me in.'

'Completely nuts,' said Benson, swigging from a longneck. 'He'll wind up in an institution for the rest of his days.'

They'd had a low-key night. A nice meal, beers, chatting over the case. She'd been nervous. Benson hadn't called it a date but that's what it was and they both knew it. They were on stools in a cool bar around Hell's Kitchen. It might have been Pearl Jam playing on the speakers, she wasn't sure. She'd never been big on rock music. Harry or Simone would have known. As she left, Holmes had said she looked 'bonny' but had barely glanced up at her. What had she expected anyway? The last two nights she'd lain in bed awake and heard him pacing outside. Part of her wanted that door to swing open and ...

She realized Benson had said something.

'What was that?' she was forced to ask.

'I asked if you wanted another. You were miles away.'

'I'm sorry.'

'I bore the pants off you.'

'No! No, it's ... I've forgotten how to relax. I was worrying about my hamsters.'

And that was true. Vernon was dead and the autopsy had shown identical physiological degeneration to Zoe. More hamsters were growing ill and the transfusions were having minimal effect on slowing their decline. She'd worked sixteen hours straight yesterday and another dozen today, reading, consulting. Holmes' life was on the line and she was sitting here drinking beers. Benson took her hand. It was always a bit scary when a guy touched you like that the first time. Like you were coming to a bridge and over the other side was a town, could be filled with flowers and magic or ... dragons. Not with Sherlock, mind you. Perhaps, despite his protestations, he blamed her for his predicament. He had every right.

'We could go back to my place, do a little slow dancing, or heck, we could play rap. I'm not fussy and I'm not far.'

She looked up into Benson's eyes. Did she dare make it across that bridge?

She wasn't coming back tonight. It was after two and still no sign of her. He'd once trapped an embezzler who, rather than face disgrace in court, had swallowed quicklime. The pain of his intestines dissolving must have been intense. Only now though, did Holmes appreciate something of how the fellow must have felt, for his own insides were a mess, actually throbbing. He'd never had this before, never.

When his old friend Watson had married and left him, he'd been hurt. No, he had never let on, and perhaps, he had not realized until some time after Watson had left their old rooms, just how much he relied on Watson's fellowship and humanity.

He had been lonely then. Sometimes the tick and tock of the grandfather clock had been like a lash.

And this was so much worse.

He thought of Georgette's father, Harry. He'd been alone for nearly twenty years. Being alone had never troubled Holmes in the slightest ... until John Watson, and then now. Loneliness is about the absence of love, he realized, and until you sense love, its possibility at least, then what was the fuss? Harry must have loved Georgette's mother very deeply. Thinking of Harry jarred something in him. What?

It had only been there for an instant, like walking barefoot over a rug when one feels a tiny sharp prick. It was in Holmes' DNA to be constantly, unceasingly, a detector of the jarring crime-scene fact. Therefore, he could deduce that whatever it was regarding Harry must be to do with the only case on which he had seen Harry working, the murder of the young woman dragged from the river. What had he seen without realising he had even been looking, heard without listening, touched though his hands were jammed in his pockets?

Something.

He would have to ask Georgette to check whether that case had been solved.

Georgette.

Perhaps he should head outside again for a pipe? That cocaine would have been damned –

The key turned in the lock.

He threw himself into the armchair and grabbed the first thing that came to hand, a magazine which he flipped open on an article about breast enhancement. With spectacular control, he forced himself to look over with casual interest. My Lord, she was handsome. Her dress seemed intact. He took his pulse down. He stood.

'How was your evening? Or should I say, morning.'

Why did he say that? What devil inside him would urge that snide remark. To punish her, show disapproval?

'It was fine, thank you.'

Formal. His quip had nipped her. That was wrong of him. What was happening here? Why did he feel the urge to challenge Benson to a bout?

'You watched the interview?' she asked, avoiding his gaze, clearly deliberately.

I must try and engage her, act less churlish, he told himself.

'Fascinating. The fellow believed he was inhabited by a ghost from the eighteen nineties. I know how he feels.'

He'd not meant it as a criticism but that must have been how she took it for she looked at him as if he'd poked her in the chest. She made for the bathroom and he sat there, listening to her brush her teeth.

It was only then that he realized every emotion he was experiencing was classic jealousy, a flaw he'd never thought would be one from which his character would suffer. He must do something to rectify the situation.

When she emerged from the bathroom, he said brightly, 'Would you care for some tea?'

'No thanks, I'm going to bed.'

She was heading for the bedroom. He had to find the courage to at least tell her how he felt, even if it came to nought. He stood.

'Watson ...'

She turned as if expecting another jab.

'I mean ... Georgette.' He had a feeling he might be blushing. She had stopped and was fully engaged. This was it. No stepping back.

'I have been ruminating deeply and I believe ... I am ...'

The words wouldn't come, the light in the room was flickering, any strength in his legs deserted him. Get the words out, come on, it is not that difficult. But his jaw was frozen. He saw alarm on her face and felt himself falling ...

... falling through the air, a sensation of complete liberty suppressing the fear of inevitable impact and death. The cold wind rifled through his clothing but he would not let go. Moriarty, howling now but from rage not fear, would disintegrate with him.

'Die, pestilence!' he shouted down at the villain whose face snarled up into his own.

'Madman!' screamed Moriarty.

No, logical to the end, thought Holmes, knowing he had found the only solution, the one premise the Prince of Evil would not consider, that Holmes would be prepared to end his own life to destroy Moriarty's. It had not been a difficult choice. Apart from his good friend Watson, he left behind nothing but melted tallow and empty beakers. Humanity and love had passed him by. The water's surface rushed towards him. He fought the instinct to tense up. Relax ... You are a leaf, a –

Bang.

Light.

A blurry indistinct shape hovered above him. He was conscious. His first thought was that it was a coachman, that he had fallen from a horse or cab onto a road. No, he told himself, you are dead. You plummeted from Reichenbach Falls. This is an afterlife.

But as the image focused he remembered that his afterlife was very real. It was the future and this was the one who had resurrected him.

Georgette. She pressed a cold flannel to his forehead.

'Where am I?'

He was embarrassed that his voice sounded croaky.

'Your bedroom. You collapsed.'

He reoriented like an actor who'd forgotten what play he was performing in that evening. Yes, that's right. She had been out with Benson.

'How long?'

'A good six or seven minutes.'

She rested her bare hand upon his forehead and it sent an electric charge through his body. He remembered his petulance, jealousy, unforgivable conduct.

'I shall be fine.'

Doubt creased her delicate brow. 'I'd feel better if we got you checked out.'

'I've simply overexerted myself. Please, I'm sure that in the morning I shall be hale.'

'I'm not a physician, Sherlock, I'm just a scientist. You might need more help than I can offer.'

'Watson, please.'

Her head dropped, chin pointing towards her décolletage. She looked him in the eyes.

'Okay, but I'm just over there, if you feel any pain just ... call out.'

'I shall. Goodnight, Georgette, and thank you for everything.'

She smiled. 'Until tonight you'd never called me by my first name.'

'Old habits are hard to break.'

She bent towards him so close he could count the strands of her eyebrows. She is going to kiss me, he thought, half-panicking, because the only precedent he had was a goodnight kiss from a governess while a string quartet played Mozart in a distant room and sabres rattled in their scabbards. But she did not kiss him, she stroked his forehead ever so gently.

'Please let me seek help. If scientists were to know –'

'Impossible. In the morrow I shall be spry. I promise.'

He felt her will melt.

'You're certain you're okay?'

'Truly.'

And he'd never meant anything as sincerely.

Georgette called in every favor she knew. Apart from making sure she had a clean tablecloth and napkins – not one of Harry's strong points – for tomorrow's Thanksgiving dinner, her day was a procession from hospital to hospital, showing the scans of the dead hamsters, their blood counts.

'How would you treat this kind of condition in a human?' she would ask. Her heart had been shredded last night when Sherlock had collapsed, and she'd not slept, burying tears in her pillow and resolving to get an early start. She gave no credence to his assertion that it was as a result of fatigue. Not of itself alone. So, after three hours in her lab checking the vital signs of the remaining hamsters, she had begun her rounds. Two hematologists, a neurologist and a geriatrics researcher. From this she gleaned that beta-amyloid protein was the main enemy in dementia.

'This seems to form the plaque, here,' had said the professor of neurology as she tapped the scans of Zoe and Vernon's brain. She had recommended the researcher, Paul Li. He sat in front of Georgette now. He looked eighteen but his wall was covered with a string of awards and degrees.

'We're trying to develop a vaccine that works. Our most recent vaccine was able to improve cognitive function in patients who were not presenting with symptoms; that is, our control group improved, but there was no improvement in the sufferers. However, we are tweaking that. We should have a new vaccine in about four months.'

Four months was far too long. She asked if there might be any chance of obtaining any of the older vaccine but was told that was impossible.

The hemotologist had said that the low red blood cell counts might indicate that gases she'd used had created some disturbance in the bone marrow and hence the red blood cell production. He'd be guessing some kind of over-hydration that could affect the kidney. There were drugs available that could help stimulate production, as might high altitude and diet.

Sherlock had consented at least to her taking a blood sample before she had left and by the time she was back at the lab the results were in. His red blood cell count was down, not yet to a critical level but well below normal.

And so here we were. Months of planning were nearing culmination, some strategies had been changed but the end game had remained the same. He was proud of what had been achieved ...

He pulled himself up. Not yet, nothing has been achieved yet. Don't go into the ring overconfident, wait your moment – then a right, followed by the left they don't see coming. Ponds and lakes had frozen up nicely. He took from his pocket the garotte, silent, effective. He would wear gloves. His DNA was not in the system but these days they could look for distant relatives, track backwards until they found a link. Which of course they would, but let's hope by then it would be far too late. Had he made any mistakes? What he had needed had been rented, false names, paid by transfer from the account that would not link back. Not until he was ready. He put the gloves on, they fit snug.

The thing about being Sherlock Holmes, reflected Holmes, is that I can never stop it, the analysis of everyday dross. I am like one of those diggers on the Australian goldfields, no matter how much money I have made, I have to keep fossicking. Even his collapse, perhaps a precursor of what he could expect in future before an inevitable slide into some kind of coma, was insufficient to extinguish this instinct. So, regardless that having Georgette comfort him had been the most exhilarating moment of his new life and perhaps even his former one, it was not long before his mind drifted over to its well-worn, natural path. After he had taken himself out in the freezing air for a pipe and wound his way aimlessly along the treacherous sidewalk under drifting snow, it had come to him what exactly that tiny sharp prick on his bare feet had been in relation to Harry Watson's case.

Why had the murderer moved the body?

That question had been raised but not satisfactorily answered. He looked in his phone and found Harry's number. His status with Harry was problematic. Although Georgette had remained in the car in the confrontation with Mahoney, she had still been at the scene. Oh well, in for a penny. He hit the button that dialled automatically.

When Harry saw Georgette was calling he was delighted. He'd only just finished up having a coffee with Simone, who was over the moon, things finally breaking for her. He needed to remind Georgette about bringing a clean tablecloth, although probably he didn't, she was too well organized.

'Hi, Treasure,' he said with enthusiasm. Until the coffee with Simone, he had been on his feet all day, chasing down dead-ends.

'Actually Harry, it is Percy.'

'Is Georgette okay?'

'So far as I know, she is at her lab. I wanted to speak with you.'

Simone had warned him that Georgette had feelings for the guy but didn't know where Percy stood. Harry had been on the verge of forgiving him until that take-down of Mahoney. Sure, it went alright, but it might not have.

'What is it?'

'Has the case of the body in the water been solved?'

'Not yet. They looked at the former husband but he was cleared. Why?'

'Something bothers me: Why move the body?'

It had bothered Harry too. Though not a homicide detective, that didn't stop him analysing the cases he worked on. It wasn't to violate the body in private that it had been moved. Likely the killer could have done that in the victim's apartment anyway but regardless, there had been no sexual interference, no bashing. The murder was ... clinical.

'I don't know,' Harry admitted.

'What were your impressions of the scene?'

For a moment Harry forgot his animosity. They were just two investigators, talking a case. 'It felt like a blind to throw us off, you know? The madman writes on the mirror and all that, I thought it's going to be the ex. You?'

Percy, he was pleased to hear, agreed.

'There was something ... controlled about the crime scene. I was thinking, would you like to meet back where you found the body?'

Harry checked his watch. He could keep working away. On the other hand, he was ahead of what he'd been tasked and the Brit was one hell of an investigative brain. Even though his old pal from the Yard, Dougal Gray, had never heard of him. Of course Harry had called him. He'd been retired for a couple of years now, said he would ask around.

'I'll meet you there,' said Harry.

It was already growing dark, headlights pushed against the gloom like lanterns amid ruins. Holmes hoped he would have enough money for the cab fare. He was tired of living like a pauper. He needed to pay his debts. But first ...

Why would you move the body?

Examine Feeney's speculation: Because it might be known that the killer, he or she, was visiting the apartment? Perhaps, but how did that really help?

The killer could simply say, 'I turned up and found her dead'. Then he did not risk being discovered while moving a corpse. But if the killer is a madman, moving the body seemed at odds with leaving a message scrawled on a mirror. Mathew Mahoney had not moved those he had killed. Nor Jack the Ripper.

Examine the next logical question: Why risk getting a body out of the apartment and into a vehicle only to dump the body in the river?

No, there was something off with this murder, which Holmes now admitted to himself he had taken far too lightly because of his Noah obsession. Moving the body could have been ritualistic, washing it in the river. But why all the way over near Astoria Park?

The cab hissed to a halt where Harry's car waited. Flaky snow was drifting. Holmes paid and stepped into the cold. Harry's passenger door opened. Holmes couldn't see him until he stopped and looked inside.

'Climb in,' said Harry, who was wearing a fake-fur hat with ear flaps and a heavy overcoat. 'You must be freezing.'

His suit jacket ruined at the pier rescue, Holmes was wearing only a rain slicker he'd found in the wardrobe. He had been lulled by a life indoors with continuous heating.

'I had given that not so much as a passing thought.' Which was the truth. He'd been too preoccupied to think about mere physical comfort. Now he did notice how cold it was. The two men faced off. Harry, reluctantly, it seemed to Holmes, congratulated him on the Noah case.

'I apologize for not keeping Georgette and Simone further from the scene. We had intended to ...'

Harry held up a hand. 'What's done is done. I don't want my daughters in danger and you seem to make a habit of putting them there.'

In other words, thought, Holmes, not done at all.

'Lives were at stake,' said Holmes and left it at that.

'Shoot,' Harry said.

Holmes recounted how on the cab ride across town he had been thinking through the case and agreed with Harry that it seemed staged. He then ran through the reasons.

'What I can't fathom though, is why you stage that kind of thing unless you are an obvious suspect: husband, neighbor ...'

'Me too. "Save Me", like "Please stop me before I kill again". Almost as if he's preparing his defense before he is caught.'

'Yes,' said Holmes, 'but why move the body? Why take that risk?'

'Perhaps to delay discovery.'

'But it didn't, did it? How did you find out about the body here?'

'Anonymous phone call. They tried to trace it, no luck. It looked like the body was dumped in the water. It was my job to follow up a lead on a powerboat stolen from Brooklyn that morning. I also got a lead on another boat in the vicinity at the time. That boat was moored in Far Rockaway. I interviewed the owner. The day the body turned up, the owner was showing some out-of-town guests around. He saw a boat near here and gave a description. The description fitted the boat stolen from Brooklyn. We later found that boat, burned out up the Jersey coast.'

It seemed an elaborate effort. You have to steal a boat to dump the body.

'I know what you're thinking,' said Harry. 'Why go to that much trouble? Plus, the body was stored for a day in a freezer. Maybe he was wondering what the hell to do. Maybe he thought he'd bury the body but the earth was too frozen.'

That's right, Georgette had said the body had been frozen.

'So he stored the body, stole a boat, dumped the body, burned the boat ...' Holmes running through the steps.

'Yeah, and on my first day back, thank you very much.'

Holmes stopped, a retriever that smelled duck. 'You had been on leave?'

'Couple of weeks, every year.'

Holmes sat back with all the tension in his shoulders and back suddenly gone.

'What is it?'

Holmes said, 'The only logical reason for the body to be dumped here was for you to be involved. This is about you, Harry.'

'Me?' Harry was clearly perplexed but Holmes was already sifting his memory.

'You mentioned this place being the exact same spot as twenty years earlier where you retrieved another body.'

'That's right. It was the accident I told you about. Two boats collided out there. One had been stolen, couple of teenagers. They weren't showing lights. I was down here in my squad car, just a routine check. I heard the crash. I called it in, jumped in and swam. Nearly drowned myself. Lucky it wasn't so cold as this year. I found a girl floating, grabbed her, swam her back. She survived. I went back out, found another girl in the wreckage, she was still breathing but by the time I got her back, she'd passed. The paramedics worked on her but they couldn't bring her back. Her mother was killed too. The father had taken the young brother to the movies. Imagine, stepping out and learning that.'

'So the girl whose life you saved ...'

'One of the teens who stole the boat. Her boyfriend walked away without a scratch but went down for manslaughter, Joseph Levich. Girl was fifteen, no priors, got a caution. Levich died of a drug overdose about six years ago.'

'The girl's name?'

'Becky Borello.'

It has to be, thought Holmes, and asked Harry if he had a copy of the crime scene photos from the Rebecca Chaney homicide in his phone.

'Where you going with this?' Harry called up the photos and passed the phone to Holmes.

'Could that be Becky Borello?'

Drained of life, the face of Rebecca Chaney stared up at Harry. It was twenty years on, he'd never even seen the girl's face when he'd swum her in from the accident. It was dark and it took all his strength to fight the current. Others had taken over and he'd headed out again, ultimately to retrieve a body. He'd likely never have made it back that second time without help. He had seen Becky Borello months later in the courtroom. The mind plays tricks. It could be her. Only fifteen, she would have no record unless she had reoffended. He took his phone back from Holmes and dialled Feeney.

'Yes, Harry.'

'Could you check on a Becky Borello, see if there was a name change ... to Rebecca Chaney.'

Georgette couldn't stop the tears this time. She was able to stem them but everything just seemed so hopeless. She imagined herself as a tiny figure standing in front of a huge sheer wall. How could she scale it? The only hope was to go public on Holmes. Every specialist in the world would be on it, but she knew what Holmes would say: how many other people might die as a consequence because these specialists were devoting their time to save him? But these things always produced positives, new breakthroughs ...

Her phone buzzed and she saw it was Simone and was flooded with gratitude.

'How's it going?' asked Simone, and Georgette couldn't help it, she started crying again.

'Hopeless. There's a vaccine that might help but I can't get it because the clinical trial has expired. There are suggestions of diets, or taking him to Tibet or ...'

'Settle down, Georgi.' Simone's voice was soothing, mature. Funny how the roles had changed. '... And turn right here. Sorry, I'm in the middle of Ambrose's lesson. How's Percy?'

'As far as I know he's alright.' She told Simone about the collapse, blabbed about going public but realized they couldn't discuss it freely with Ambrose in the car. 'I'm sorry. It's just nice to speak with someone.'

'... And shift down and then boom! Hit the pedal. Good. I can come over later? I've got this audition, super secret, out of the blue ... down Rockaway looking for Newport, good ...'

Georgette felt bad. Simone was heading to some important audition and here she was burdening her. Simone would be hurting too.

'I'll let you go.'

'Tomorrow, Dad's, Thanksgiving, right? You and Sherlock. I'll bring salads.'

'Yes of course. Break a leg.'

'I'll break two. Love you, sis.'

When Georgette ended the call, she felt empty and even more alone. Tempted as she was to call Holmes, she let it go. That wasn't going to help. She needed to find a solution here. If that giant wall didn't topple on her first.

Harry had started driving back towards the station house. The growing warmth of the car seemed at odds with the increasingly heavy snow. So much better than a hansom cab, thought Holmes, as Harry spoke again.

'Something else. That accident. It was Thanksgiving. Same time of the year.'

The radio crackled. By now Holmes recognized Feeney's voice.

'You were right. Rebecca Chaney was formerly Rebecca Borello. She kept the married name and used her full Christian name.'

Harry thanked him. Holmes met his gaze. And now his brain, so slow to grind into motion, was moving like a locomotive. Harry's phone was on the seat between them.

'May I?' he scooped it up but did not wait for a reply. He found the crime-scene photos again, knowing he had seen something earlier. There. He stopped at the photo of the mantelpiece. Placed upon it was the figurine of an ice skater. His skin was on fire.

He checked back again at the other photographs on a corkboard: pictures of three young women in front of Rebecca's mantelpiece. Expand.

No figureskater on the mantelpiece in those photos, everything else the same.

Every cell of his body was crawling terror.

'Rebecca Chaney's flat: on the mantelpiece is an ice skater. It is not in the other photos. The "Save Me" on the mirror, Harry, is written directly above it. It's not the murderer asking to be saved. He's taunting you. He's saying, "Save your daughter". His target is Georgette.'

Sapped as she was, Georgette wasn't stopping. She had been reading studies that had sought to increase the life span of hamsters through diet and was now in the process of dividing her hamsters into specific food groups. There was a knock on her door. Wearily she got up and opened it. It was Dwayne the security guard.

Her phone began to ring.

25

Simone was upset by the way Georgette had sounded on the phone. She'd let Georgette down before and she would have asked to reschedule except that the casting agent, Keely, had called and asked her if she could basically come straight away to do a script read for a producer who was only in town for a few hours. It had to be someone from Hollywood. Keely had asked if she was alone, and of course she lied because obviously the answer he wanted was 'yes', and every actor knows you always say 'Yes, I can ride a horse bareback, yes I can speak fluent Romanian', and then you bother about the consequences later. He told her the A-lister didn't want to be recognized so he'd had to find a rehearsal studio at short notice. He'd said he was trying to reschedule meetings and if he wasn't there, not to worry, just to go in.

'But you can't tell anyone. They impressed that on me. You are to come alone and not tell a soul.'

Simone hadn't dared say she was doing a driving lesson. Surely the casting meeting wouldn't take that long? She had to get Ambrose back, he was getting picked up from St Christopher's for Thanksgiving. The address was in a dumpy block in Brownsville, past body-repair shops and locked garage doors. Keely had told her there was a space around the back she could park. She told Ambrose to drive slowly over the narrow entrance lane. It was cracked and broken. Luckily she had on her shortest, sexiest skirt because earlier in the day she'd been to see the letting agent about how she had fallen behind in her rent, and a high hemline worked wonders. They came to a quiet stop. There was one other car in the small lot, an early model Taurus.

'What do you think?' she asked Ambrose, checking herself in the rear-view mirror.

'You look hot but, remember, you don't need to flaunt your body for this, Simone, you are a talented actor. If he suggests a private photo shoot, you walk.'

'Thank you, Ambrose. Wish me luck.'

'You don't need it. You're a star.'

She saw him looking around nervously, didn't blame him. The neighborhood sucked.

'Lock the car after me.'

Simone stepped out of the car. She wondered who might be behind the door. This was the most important day of her life.

They were speeding over a bridge crossing into East Harlem. Harry had activated the siren, Holmes gripped the phone so hard his knuckles popped. Each unanswered ring pumped more terror into his heart. How stupid, foolish, arrogant of him to –

'Percy?'

Her voice!

'Are you alright?'

'Yes. The security guard told me he'd been ordered to stay with me. What's going on?'

Holmes turned to Harry Watson, understood he was no less fearful.

'She is fine,' he told him. 'The guard is with her.' He saw Harry mouth thank God and then pick up his own phone and dial.

'Tell me,' Georgette said.

Holmes told her then. They thought somebody was out for revenge on Harry by targeting her. Squad cars would be there any minute.

'Who?'

'Possibly the man who lost his wife and daughter in the boating accident, where your father rescued a young woman.'

'William Burgess,' Holmes heard Harry shout into his own phone. 'He'd be about my age. Lived in Queens. Near Jamaica Bay. Call Gomez, tell her this is the likely killer of Rebecca Chaney. Call me back. We're heading to the Upper West Side.'

Georgette told Holmes that police had just arrived.

'We shall be there presently,' he said and ended the call because he would have felt foolish hanging on, even though it was what he desired. He told Harry the police were there now.

'I owe you,' Harry said.

'You owe me nothing.'

'Well, I could have been more understanding. Her mother was stubborn too.'

Harry's phone buzzed. He answered, driving with one hand. 'What have you got? – Where's he been the last three years? ... Okay send it through. And can you copy it to Georgette? Maybe she's seen him hanging around.' He stopped the siren, told Holmes, 'Feeney has the most recent license photo on William Burgess.'

Holmes spoke thoughts his brain had long processed. 'He must have kept Rebecca's body frozen so he could deliver it when you were back at work.'

A few minutes later Harry's phone pinged. He glanced at the photo. 'I doubt I would have recognized him without knowing who he is.' He handed the phone to Holmes. 'Three years ago. Seen him hanging around?'

A man close to Harry's age, a wide face. There was nothing distinctive about him.

'What is his occupation?'

'At the time he had a video business, weddings, that kind of thing. Those businesses died when everybody got a camera in their phone.'

When Dwayne had appeared in her lab, Georgette's first horrified thought was that Holmes had had some kind of relapse. After Avery Scheer and Morgan Edwards, the news that she could have a killer targeting her was less alarming than it would have been a month earlier. She was toughening up. Plus, she had an armed security guard. A text came through from Feeney with a note that said this was the most recent photo of William Burgess.

She stared at it. Was she imagining that he looked familiar? No. She had seen him. Where? Not looking exactly like that. Her phone buzzed. Sherlock.

'We are about seven minutes away. Do you recognize him?'

'I think so but he might look different now. A beard maybe. Where the hell have I seen him?'

'Was it recently?'

'I'm fairly sure.' But where had she been? A couple of restaurants with Holmes. Otherwise stuck in the lab ... Edwards jumped into her memory like a home invader. It wasn't Edwards though but it was something about that night ...

Holy shit!

'It's the casting agent who came to see Simone. And right now she's on her way to some script reading.'

I have given Harry Watson more than a fair chance, he thought. A lot more than was ever given him. He had been obeying the rules, minding his own business when fate had broadsided him. Not his fault or that of his beautiful Stephanie or their little princess, Lee. Yet they had paid the full penalty. And he had not been spared: the instant terrible pain and loneliness that burned your gut from morning till night, then those lost years; the drinking, the collapse of his business, the estrangement of his son. How many times had he contemplated suicide? But something had held him back. Not fear, for he had nothing to lose. No, it was the stupid conceit that behind all this, hidden from him, might be a plan, a role for him. Bit by bit he had scraped himself back together. Sobriety, a new job, new name – that, a necessity because of the money he had owed in Cleveland. But still that emptiness plagued him. Until a year ago when he had seen the news story about the brilliant young female scientist who had survived after drowning. Of course, any story about drowning perked up his interest. If a parent could be spared what he had suffered, that was to be celebrated. And here was this young scientist saying that she believed people might be able to be revived days after being believed dead. The sort of situation where Lee had lost her life.

And then he read the story, noticed the name. Her father was a cop.

Him.

And angry as he was, he knew then that here was his purpose, to deal with those who had escaped their deserved punishment. Harry Watson had saved the life of the stupid, murdering young bitch who had killed his wife, and in the time it had taken to do that, Harry Watson had also forfeited the life of Lee. She could have been as successful as Georgette Watson. Her sweet nature would have been suited to any number of caring professions, doctor, nurse, teacher.

In the end however, he had been presented with his chance. Fate owed him that much. It had snatched from him his whole world, those he loved more than life, murdered by a couple of kids whose only thought had been to get high. They had created chaos, death, misery, and their punishment had been nothing: a 'try better next time'.

Fuck that. Harry Watson'd had twenty years more to spend with his daughters than he got to spend with Lee and Stephanie. Twenty years of gnawing pain, guilt, loneliness. No, Watson wasn't as directly responsible as that murdering bastard or his bimbo girlfriend but Watson could have saved Lee. *The autopsy indicated it was a matter of minutes. If that had been Watson's own daughter, it would have been a different story. Watson would have moved heaven and earth, or died trying. Well, Lee would get justice, Watson was going to become acquainted firsthand with a father's pain, no miracle this time.*

You'll be able to taste the loneliness, Harry, the dark nights when you can't sleep so you get up and try and watch television but that doesn't work so you head outside and walk, anywhere, and all you can hear are their screams, and all you can see is the fear in their eyes. Over and over, each new night another brick, sealing you in to your own endless hell. You drink, and that works for a while. And then it's a scourge, drinking is all you do and you're no good to anyone. And you lose everything.

Until fate drags you back, sits you down and says, 'Is that all you've got you pathetic coward?' And you see light, sense there is hope. But you have to be the one, nobody else can end the hell. There had been false starts, doubts. And then after he had built real momentum, setbacks. First Georgette Watson went overseas. Then the Englishman turned up to complicate matters.

But it was all for the better, actually. It had given him time to plan properly for the Borello bimbo, and there was something more enjoyable about stretching out the climax of his work. Quite fortunate, the whole casting agent thing. He'd only started that six years ago because it was a job that gave him plenty of time to drink, had low overheads, and his social interaction was limited to words on a computer screen, or the odd meeting and audition. It only occurred to him around a month ago that he could use that with the other daughter. Good God, another actress, just what the world needed.

There was a real chance he wouldn't get away with it, he knew that. He'd hired this dump using a false name, paid cash, called her and said he needed to see her immediately, told her to come alone, not to tell anybody because there was a total embargo on the script – all things that would hinder detection. But actors talked, incessantly. She might have told somebody: her father, the sister. If so they would run a check and no doubt eventually they would discover the agent was the same man who had lost his daughter because of Harry Watson's failure. Then they'd come looking for him. Maybe they'd find him, but if they did, it would have been worth it. And perhaps they wouldn't. Perhaps she had told nobody, and then their leads would turn to dust and his precautionary absence may become a short vacation, no more.

As Simone reached the door, her phone began ringing in her shoulder bag. Likely it was Georgette. She did not want to let her down but she had to be strong. She checked the phone – yep, Georgette. She silenced it, let it run to voicemail. She cleared her head the way they had taught her in drama class. Leave yourself behind, that was the mantra. Whatever words you find in front of you must become yours, strip away the you who you woke up as.

It was freezing in this room. It was nothing more than a big empty space that still smelled of whatever heavy-metal band had used it for rehearsal last. The single-bar radiator was feeble and he needed every thread of his overcoat to keep the chill at bay. There was a knock on the door. Right on time.

He felt in the pocket of his coat, reassured himself the cord was there. He opened the door. And there she stood, quite a pretty thing, really.

'Simone, come in to my ice block. It's freezing in here. I apologize. I never would have booked this if I had known.'

'Never been to a warm rehearsal room yet,' she laughed.

He closed the door, heard the lock click.

'You came alone?'

'Yes.'

'And you have told nobody?'

'No.'

'Good. They rang to say they were running slightly late so it's a good thing I was able to make it after all. It is a very secret project.'

'Can I ask who?'

'That would spoil the surprise.' He indicated a metal fold-out chair. 'Just sit hit here and take a read.'

He'd left out a script on the chair for her. It was a shocker some waitress had insisted he read while he was trying to have a quiet coffee.

'Which part?'

'We'll get to that. Just take in the general vibe.'

Of course, they wouldn't actually get to reading for any part. She'd be dead before she had finished the first page. He walked around behind her. His hand reached in and began to pull out the wooden handle of the garotte. It fit nicely between his ring and index fingers. He felt charged.

Georgette was falling to pieces. She'd tried Simone's phone, got only voicemail, screamed a message for her to head for a police station. Tried again. Same deal.

'What's Ambrose last name?' Harry's voice yelling now at her through the speaker.

'I don't know. She never mentioned –'

She heard Harry roaring at somebody to try St Christopher's, find a number on a kid, Ambrose, who directed the play.

Holmes came on, tense but calming.

'All patrols have been notified to keep watch for her vehicle. Did she reveal a destination?'

'No. Ambrose was driving ... wait! Rockaway and ...' What was it, what was it? Newton? No. 'Newport!'

Harry started barking into his radio, 'Concentrate the search in Brooklyn, Brownsville, anywhere on or near Newport.'

'You're doing well, Watson. You don't happen to have a copy of the theatre program with you? That might help with Ambrose's name.'

She cast about desperately. There was one in her apartment, she thought, not here. Her mind was churning.

'What about Valerian? You could try him.'

'I did already. He is at a different school and only knows Ambrose by his first name.'

I must have read that program twenty times, she thought. Ambrose what? She tried to picture it, conjured Ambrose's face ... Flash!

Ambrose had sent her that photo!

'Call you back,' she yelled. Her fingers danced, found the text Ambrose had sent. She called the number. It rang, a long burr.

26

The girl was reading, engrossed in the awful script. She wasn't even looking at him. He raised his arms, formed a perfect loop.

There was a knock on the door.

Fuck. He just had time to drop the garotte back in his pocket as she swung around.

'It must be them,' she said, trying to keep the excitement from her voice.

Calm, stay calm. So far you have not even committed a crime here. But they must not see your face. He waited. Perhaps whoever it was would go away. Another thump. Damn. He walked to the door. It was thick to keep in sound. He opened it a crack, presented no more than one eye, keeping his body behind the door.

A teenage boy stood there, alone.

'Get lost,' he hissed at the boy.

'The chick needs to move her car.'

'What?'

The boy sighed like he had important stuff to attend to. 'The chick asked me to mind her car. Looks like they are getting ready to tow it.'

Simone was confused. It sounded like Ambrose but she hadn't asked him to mind the car. What was it? Had something happened to Sherlock maybe? Something terrible? She looked over at Keely, who was clearly pissed but trying to not show it. At least Ambrose had thought on his feet and wasn't giving too much away. Keely would think it highly unprofessional of her to have brought him along. Keely arched a brow at her. Ambrose's voice came though.

'Look, doesn't matter to me if they tow it, but I want my ten spot.'

'I'm sorry about this,' she said and dived into her purse and headed over. What the hell was up?

She noticed that Keely remained behind the door. Her eyes met Ambrose's. What was he trying to tell her?

'Lady, I'm sorry, I done my best but they got a truck and all. I told them you'd only be a minute. You need to move your car.'

None of which made sense because, as Ambrose well knew, her car was already in the lot out back. Obviously he wanted to speak to her in private but surely it could wait?

'I can't do that right now.'

She looked at Keely who nodded approval of her hard line.

'They're going to tow it. You're crazy. What's so important you can't move your car?'

She turned hopefully to the agent.

'Perhaps I might...?'

Keely said gruffly, 'Move it into the back like I told you. Then you, scram,' he pointed at Ambrose.

She stepped out and whispered, 'What's going on?'

But Ambrose didn't answer, just dragged her away from her car and towards the street. As they reached the end of the short alley entrance to the lot, strong arms seized her and pulled her against the wall. Cops, a male and female uniform. Four more moved quickly up the alley to the building. She looked fearfully at Ambrose who held up his hand to stop her speaking. She heard somebody thumping on the door again and then shouts like at the start of a Shakespeare play.

'On your knees. Hands on head. Now!'

This is real fucking drama, she thought, looking up to see a whole line of squad cars arriving.

Holmes peered through the viewing mirror. It was his first real look at Burgess. By the time he and Harry had arrived at the intended murder scene, Burgess had already been surrounded by police dressed ninja-style. He looks a lot like my baker, Chipworth, thought Holmes. Chipworth took too much rum and it showed in the area between his eyebrows and nose. Burgess was, or had been, a heavy drinker. Saving Simone had been touch and go. In all honesty, he had thought they might already be too late. When Georgette had called them back to say she had Ambrose on the line and that Simone had already been inside the building at least five minutes he had grasped that there was no time to wait for police, that

Simone's life rested at that moment squarely on the narrow shoulders of the schoolboy. But Burgess, if he had not already killed Simone, would likely do so immediately he knew the game was up. After all, that was the singular aim of his whole grand plan. Escape would be but an afterthought to the fellow who was bent on revenge. It was Ambrose who had come up with the idea of pretending to be paid to watch Simone's car but they dare not risk the boy's life as well. He was told to stay out of reach and to delay as long as he could. That he had done magnificently. Harry, recovered now, stood next to Holmes. His reunion with Simone had been very emotional. Holmes felt a pang that he himself would likely never experience that with a child of his own. The voice of Carter, the male detective, sounded clearly through speakerphones above his head.

'So how did you meet Rebecca Chaney?' asked Carter.

'I first met her as Becky Borello after the drugged-up little slut killed my wife and daughter.'

'You've been following her all this time?'

'No. I had an awakening, I suppose you would call it. About a year ago I understood that it was my task to restore the moral balance of the world. Nobody else was going to. I'd been all this time punishing myself and my loved ones, instead of those who deserved to be punished. I went to her old neighborhood. Her parents are still alive. It wasn't hard to learn she had changed her name and then I tracked her down via Facebook. Staged a meeting in a bar at happy hour.'

'No offense, but you're telling me she went for you? You sure you didn't just grab her?' Gomez this time, the female detective. Holmes could see they were using her to goad him.

Harry whispered, 'She's making it airtight, making sure his confession matches the science and more important that she is in no way leading him.'

Burgess sat back, relaxed. 'Being a casting agent has its value. Everybody wants to be a star. Believe me it wasn't hard.'

'Smug,' said Holmes.

'Huh?'

'The word one would use to describe him.'

'Yeah.' Harry nodded. 'Smug. Like he's holding some ace.'

Carter said, 'How long have you been tracking Simone Watson?'

'Long enough.'

'What were your plans for her?' It was a routine question but for the first time Burgess balked.

'Strangle her,' he said.

'And dump her in the river like Rebecca?'

'What's it matter now?' Still sitting back like the cat swallowed the cream.

Harry said, 'I expected Burgess to clam up, demand a lawyer but the guy is revelling in it, like he's a winner.'

Carter said, 'You think it was okay to strangle Rebecca Chaney because when she was fifteen she went on a joyride that turned into tragedy?'

'Becky Borello, you mean? It's not a matter of being okay. It's a question of what is just.'

'So you admit you killed her?' Gomez.

'Yes.' Not the slightest hesitation.

'And wanting to kill Simone Watson, who has never done anything to you, that was just too?'

'Yes, perhaps not to her, but if you look at the bigger picture. Our warplanes bomb targets where innocent people will very likely be killed. But it is calculated by somebody to be morally acceptable because it achieves a higher goal. Collateral damage, I believe is the term.'

'But when you target that civilian just to punish somebody...'

'Evil begets evil.'

'You think Lieutenant Watson is evil?'

'I think he was criminally negligent. And still is. "Save Me". He should have realized then if he'd been any good. But I guess that's why he's not in here now.'

Holmes looked at Harry, who shook his head and through gritted teeth said, 'I'd love five minutes alone with him.'

'You sure you're okay? I could come over to the station?' Georgette had never been so grateful to be able to talk to her sister. She had been trying to keep her mind on the lab work but it was proving impossible.

'I'm fine, truly. You guys saved my ass. Ambrose was Oscar material.'

Georgette asked what was happening and Simone explained that Burgess was being interviewed and that Harry and Percy were watching on.

'You're in love with him.'

It was a statement Georgette felt unable to contradict. 'Unless I find something, I've as good as signed his death warrant.'

'Don't give up.'

But Georgette had just finished looking at the latest results. All bar four of her hamsters were showing some signs of impairment.

Simone must have picked up on her silence. 'You want me to come over?'

'No, I need to keep ploughing on. But keep an eye on Sherlock. I think the process has started. He's trying to act like nothing's happening ...'

'Why not tell the world who he is? You would have every brain in the world helping.'

'He doesn't want that.'

'Sometimes we have to not get what we want.'

'There's one option I've been thinking, if I can't crack this.'

'What's that?'

Three weeks ago she would never have trusted Simone but that was three weeks ago. 'I could refreeze him.'

Just like John Watson had done, she thought.

Holmes watched Burgess through the glass and sensed the ghost of something he'd seen before. He threw memories out of his suitcase, willy-nilly, like a bride searching for a misplaced engagement ring, pinned it down: Henry Irving, the master actor. Holmes and John Watson had seen him numerous times. There was a theatricality about Burgess though he disguised it deftly. Burgess was, Holmes reminded himself, at home in the theatre but it wasn't just that. Smug. Too smug. Holmes turned down the volume on the microphone feed.

'Something is not quite right.'

Harry nodded. 'I was thinking the same thing.'

'We're missing something,' Holmes said.

Harry said, 'Like he's playing with us.'

Holmes' brain was a toboggan down an icy slope. The Rebecca Chaney crime scene loomed.

Think. Something is not right. In your brain at the time you realized it, but you were distracted and your brain is not what it was. The crime scene. Rebecca's apartment. Why is that stabbing you?

'Did they find an extra baking dish at Burgess's apartment?' asked Holmes.

'The techs will be there for hours.' Harry dialled. 'Of course, he may have several.'

Somebody came on the phone and Harry asked about the missing baking dish. Holmes felt he was pushing through a heavy snowdrift.

'Are you sure?' he heard Harry ask. Then Harry ended the call. 'No baking dish at all. Only a microwave. He could have ditched it. No freezer where he must have kept Rebecca but it looks like he has a lock-up in

Brooklyn not far from where he lured Simone. Likely where he stored the body.'

Holmes did not bother with photos this time, he simply transported himself back to that crime scene. The mirror, 'Save Me'. Just above his eye line.

An idea exploded in his head. 'Get them to make him stand,' he commanded.

Harry didn't question him, he disappeared out of the room. Holmes watched as there was a knock on the door and Gomez got up.

Gomez returned as Harry re-entered the interview room.

'What is it?' asked Harry. Holmes just pointed at the interview room.

'Could you please stand, Mr Burgess,' asked Gomez.

Burgess, still the ringmaster, stood, opening out his arms as if to say 'search me'.

Holmes stamped his foot. 'Don't you see? If he had written that message, he would have written it lower down. People write just above their eyeline. He's not tall enough.' And even as he said it, that toboggan was twisting and turning. Burgess had an accomplice! The truth crashed through. 'You said he had a son.'

Harry was already moving fast to the door, Holmes in tow.

'Listen everybody,' Harry shouted, as he hit the main room. 'We need to find Burgess's son. Who was on relatives?'

A diminutive brunette put up her hand. 'Burgess has a sister in Houston. I spoke with her. She said the son, Ryan, hasn't been seen since college. He went to Europe six years ago to study art. Photography, I think she said. He became estranged from his father because of Burgess's alcoholism.'

But Burgess may have reformed.

'He's ...' she checked her notes, '... thirty-two.'

'See if he has returned to the country. Maybe he's changed names.'

'I got a press photo of the funeral,' yelled a young man, 'but you can't see the kid's face.'

A photo leapt up onto the main screen. Shot from behind it showed a man, presumably Burgess, leading a boy about ten. Gomez had been right. Rebecca Chaney would not have been attracted to the middle-aged Burgess, but this boy was now the right age. Panic rarely presented itself to Holmes but it did now. Pulling out his phone he said to Harry, 'Get a squad car to Georgette's lab.'

'I'll call the security guard.'

Holmes cautioned. 'Burgess has prepared for this. Until we know who the son is, I wouldn't do that.'

Columbus was still perky and that cheered Georgette as she precisely bisected the vitamin tablet with her miniature pocket knife. The doses had to be exact or she would have no idea what might be working. She crushed the tablet into the food bowl, picked Columbus up gently and placed him in his cage, the last of them, fed and exercised. She had only come up with the refreezing option early that morning. If she could buy time ...

There was a knock on the locked lab door. Had Holmes decided to come here after all?

'Dwayne?' she asked.

'Kelvin. Your dad wants you at the station. I was the nearest.'

She opened the door, grabbed her things. 'What's going on?'

'Didn't say, just whoever was near to get you and bring you to the station.'

She turned and switched off the lights. Felt a terrible jolt, saw blue and white spirits dancing, collapsed helpless.

Holmes' call went to voicemail. He fought to remain composed.

'She's not answering.'

Simone was stricken. 'Georgette? What's happening?'

Harry was back on his phone. 'Where's that squad car?' He listened, turned to Holmes. 'One minute away.'

The nightmare day was on an endless loop.

'Where did the son go to school?' yelled Harry. 'Get a class photo.'

Simone still in the dark, asked again with rising panic, 'Is Georgette okay?'

Holmes seized Simone.

'Can you drive me?'

'Of course.'

Harry waved them on. 'Go.'

Holmes was at the door when it hit him. He turned back to Harry.

'How did Burgess know you were at the crime scene?'

Harry blinked, tried to process. Holmes helped.

'In the interview room, Burgess said you should have recognized "Save Me". But you're not the case detective. There was no way of knowing earlier that you would be there.'

'The super?' said Harry in a fog. 'I interviewed him, remember.'

'Or ... ' said Holmes speculating aloud. '... Burgess could have infiltrated a technician. He has had more than a year to plan this.'

Simone thought back to Burgess's office. Well-shot photos on the wall. 'Or a photographer.'

'Where is Kelvin?' asked Holmes, looking around but before anybody could answer, the dark-haired woman yelled out.

'We have officers at the lab. The security guard is unconscious, no sign of Georgette.'

Simone swore and gripped the wheel, hunched, the car spearing through tumbling snow, sparse night streets. Holmes was furious with himself. How could he have ignored that the ice-skater figurine spoke more of Georgette than her sister? That had been the plan all along, hadn't it. To steal both Harry's daughters from under his nose. Perhaps there would be something at the scene of the abduction he could spy that would lead them to Georgette in time. His phone rang. Harry.

'News?'

'It's Feeney. They've let Harry go in with Burgess. I'll be monitoring this phone if you think of anything.'

'Kelvin's car –'

'Statewide alert. FBI are being informed. Benson and Lipinski are heading to Kelvin's apartment.'

Holmes was cold from the terror in his veins.

'He's going to kill her,' said Simone.

Yes, thought Holmes, he would, in some symbolic, terrible way.

'Is it possible that I could overhear the interview?' asked Holmes into the phone.

'Sure. I'm going to the observation room. Stay on the line.'

'Where is she, Burgess?'

Harry wanted to seize him and smash his head into the wall. Carter watched Harry like a hawk. Burgess glowed with triumph.

Harry said, 'You want them both to die, is that it? Your son, my daughter. You hate the world that much?'

'Thanks to you, my son lost the sister he loved. And I lost him, for years. This brought us together. We're both comfortable with our choices.'

'Where is he taking her? You want revenge on me, fine. I'll give you my gun. You can do it. You can pull the trigger.'

Burgess smirked. 'Too easy. Life's hard, Harry. No miracle this time.'

'Where!'

'Somewhere in the globe, Harry.'

Harry's heart was bursting. 'Don't do this. The worst he's facing is an accessory charge on Rebecca. Save your son, Burgess.'

'Save your daughter, Harry. That's it. No more talkies.'

Harry tried to engage him but Burgess simply sat there with arms folded and a smile on his face. Carter gently edged Harry up and towards the door. Harry stopped.

'I'm sorry, I let you down. But I couldn't do any different. If I'd have seen Lee first and not Becky, I would have swum her in. Please.'

Burgess simply scratched his nose and sat back, silent.

Holmes heard it all, played the scene out in his mind.

With a heavy heart Feeney said, 'That's it. I'm going back out. Wait a second –'

Holmes stopped breathing, waited at least thirty seconds. Feeney came back on, excitement in his voice.

'The guard has regained consciousness but has no idea what happened. The techs found something though on Burgess's work computer: it looks like he planned a car route to the Catskills.'

Harry must have seized the phone, for his voice suddenly burst from the speaker.

'Kelvin is confirmed as Ryan Burgess. We found a school photo. He's taking her back to where she drowned, going to finish the job, that's his sick plan. We're getting roadblocks in place and hopefully a chopper. Tell Simone I love ...'

The phone cut out. Holmes' battery again. Damn.

'Can I have your phone, Simone?'

'The police took it. Evidence.'

Georgette woke in cold darkness, gagged, feet bound, hands tied behind her back with a thin rope, motion. A moment for her eyes to adjust. Metal, a glow of red, smell of gasoline. She was in a car trunk. The bastard had tasered her.

'If your father had done his job, I wouldn't have to do this. I owe my sister.'

That's all he had said. Then he had pushed a cloth into her face. Some sedative. She didn't recall how she'd been put in the car, wasn't sure when, had no clue how long but knew she had to try to free herself. She felt around as best she could with her hands behind her. Her fingers weren't numb. Good, probably hadn't been under all that long, just long enough to get her into the car. She had to escape. Was she still in her lab coat? Yes. The last thing she had done before that knock on the door was put Columbus in his cage. That meant using both hands ... please let it be there. She bent her arms around as far as she could to the right, her shoulder blade ached. Carefully she dangled her fingers into the right pocket, felt metal, her mini pocket-knife. Don't drop it, careful. She had it, used the fingers of her left hand to prise it open. Even though her hands were tied she was able to saw the rope. The tiny blade was sharp. She felt the strands thinning. She slipped, cut her wrist but ... snap! She was free. The car stopped.

'About three minutes to the lab,' said Simone, who hadn't eased the speed.

Could he possibly find anything of import there? He had to try, hope the police would cut Kelvin off. Dark possibilities swarmed his brain. Might she already be dead? Yes, but more likely Kelvin ... Ryan Burgess, would want to drag her kicking and screaming across the ice, drop her down a hole, stand there listening to her pleas. Holmes felt empty inside, desolate. He may as well have been a soul being ferried down the Styx, his life already ended. Traffic ahead was thin but slow.

Without Georgette, life is worthless. That was all Holmes could think.

'Move it!' yelled Simone and swung hard to pass a slow truck that had strayed into her lane. As before, the snow globe shot along the dash and Holmes caught it.

'I meant to glue that. Georgette told me. I never listened to her.' Simone was on the verge of tears.

Holmes looked down at the globe in his hands.

'Jesus, look at these morons, are they camping?' Simone hit the horn, swerved again.

He wasn't listening. He was thinking, this was found in Georgette's apartment. Burgess or Kelvin could have put it there. It would have been easy to take her keys while she was in the squad room, make an impression.

What was it Burgess had said in the interview room: 'She could be anywhere in the globe.' Not 'on', in.

The importance of keeping one's composure in times of crisis had been drilled into Holmes by his father, brother, uncles, prefects, ministers, mother and a platoon of teachers who could wield a switch with the effortless ease of a fly-fisherman. Keeping one's composure, an

Englishman learned early on, was what made England great. Drake had played bowls as the Spanish Armada had approached, W.G. Grace had stared down the thunderbolts of the colonials' fastest bowlers. For the first time in his life, Holmes discarded all those lessons, the way a man who finds himself on fire rips a blazing robe from his body, preferring nakedness and life to propriety and death.

Holmes yelled, 'Central Park, NOW!'

Simone yanked the wheel and cut across three lanes. Burgess had left a trail on his computer to the Catskills as a last sick amusement. Holmes was certain.

'Bow Bridge, where exactly is it?'

'Five blocks south of the entrance, spanning the lake.' Simone had the pedal flat down.

Georgette was trying to free her legs when she heard the key. No time.

The trunk flew up, she squeezed her eyes, feigned sleep. She smelled him close.

Now.

She opened her eyes and swung the small knife as hard she could at Kelvin's neck, felt it bite.

'Fuck!' he cried. Outside it wasn't much lighter than in the trunk but she pushed herself out over the trunk into snow, the knife dropped.

She tried to get to her feet, hop, pulled down her gag, began to shout for help but only got out the beginning of a grunt before she was tackled from behind and landed hard, all the wind knocked from her lungs.

'No, you don't,' he muttered.

She remembered Holmes' training, swung her right arm back, managed to connect with some part of his head, wriggled free, but then he was on her again. She groped for a stick, that's all she needed ...

Something hard struck her head. The night sky was blacked out by a shadow falling ....

He was falling towards the waters of Reichenbach Falls, the memory triggered by the relentless speed of the car through the gloom. Each second seemed ten minutes. Each minute an hour. Holmes could barely see through the windscreen, white snow tumbling. Simone ran red lights.

'We need the gates on West seventy-seventh,' shouted Simone. 'Nearly there.'

But she took the corner too quickly and this time the tyres did not grip on the icy road but slid. Neither he nor Simone screamed. Life had them in its palm.

A long moment of silence was terminated by a shuddering crunch. The car bucked like a mule. Holmes felt his body strain against the belt. The car settled against a fire hydrant.

'Miscue,' said Simone.

'Are you injured?'

'No.'

She tried the ignition, it clicked uselessly.

Holmes slipped his belt, shoved out into the street and ran, his feet slipping and sliding.

Could he save her? Did Kelvin have too much of a start? He spied salvation ahead.

Goodness knows what it was doing out in this weather but there was one carriage by the gates, the horse waiting obediently while the coachman fiddled with something at the back. Holmes charged forward and leapt up into the carriage.

'Hey, buddy, I'm not working...' the coachman got no further as Holmes seized the reins and yelled the universal 'yee haw'.

The horse responded, dashing into the park on its well-worn route. Holmes' knowledge of the park was rudimentary but he knew which way was south.

It had been more than one hundred years since he had driven a carriage but it is a skill that one simply does not forget. Cold tears of snow flicked down. The park was deserted here, someone's frozen nightmare, bare dark branches spearing up like beggars' hands beseeching mercy from the night sky, the horse charging as he urged it on. He guessed the direction of the bridge, yanked right, sending the carriage off the main path and down a walking track, the carriage bucking on the rougher ground. He was standing now, caught a glimpse of the lake shimmering, chunky and white and there to the left, the bridge. He cut that way, closing on the bridge itself. A scream rose above the sound of the bouncing carriage – a brief silhouette showed by the water's edge.

'Georgette!' he yelled at the top of his lungs and even with the turmoil of his brain, he was able to isolate a thought – this must have been akin to how Watson felt watching me tumble to my doom. By now the distance was down to one hundred yards. He could make out a figure near the bridge. Holmes slowed the horse as best he could, leapt from the carriage, rolled to break the fall, and ran towards a rescue ladder stationed handily.

'Nothing can save her now.' Ryan Burgess stepped out to block his path and raised a weapon of some kind, not a pistol though it looked like one. Pulled a trigger.

It was as if a rugby scrum had crushed Holmes from every side. Holmes dropped to his knees, conscious, but feeling like he was a stranger in the body of a ghost.

'Fate should have claimed her the first time,' said the young man.

Holmes felt his brain reassembling. Some kind of electric shock.

'I have been around a very long time, Ryan,' said Holmes, feeling his strength returning, 'and I can assure you, fate's influence is exaggerated.' He could not stand yet but he could flex his palm. 'Fate has no trick that cannot be overcome by planning and resilience.'

'I couldn't agree more.'

Ryan Burgess raised the weapon again but his hand was not as quick as Holmes', which emerged from his pocket holding the palm-sized derringer.

Holmes aimed and fired. One shot to the chest.

Burgess dropped. Holmes did not wait to see if the shot was fatal. He got to his feet, managed to pull free the recsue ladder, tried to run to the water's edge but collapsed again. His upper body had strength though. He dug his elbows into the earth and dragged himself forward, scanning the lake in the dim light.

There! A disturbance, little ripples.

He slid in. The shock was instant. It was not deep. His legs were infirm, melting like wax, but he struggled up, the ladder lost from his grasp. He waded as best he could to where he'd seen broken water ... but now there was nothing.

He scanned three-sixty degrees. Panic rising, he swam deeper, swept his arms around ... he was tiring quickly himself ...

His fingertips brushed hair. Follow. Georgette! He scooped her up under the armpits and began swimming her back until his feet found purchase. He hauled her backwards to the shore cursing his own weakened limbs. Please God, let her be alive. His strength was deserting his body, he could barely make another step. But he had to. Had to save her. Had to tell her ...

27

Her eyes flicked open and she coughed and spluttered. Only then she became aware she was lying on her back on top of ... what?

'You're not dead are you, Watson?'

She turned over so now her face was above his. Holmes looked weak and pale. Or maybe that was just the snow that littered his face. Panic hit her.

'Kelvin.' She stood, unsteady, ready to run.

'Ryan Burgess, the son. I shot him, hopefully dead, because I literally couldn't stand to save myself.'

And now she could see the prone figure of Kelvin on the ground. She helped Holmes to his feet but she did not remove her arms from him, and not just because he might otherwise fall.

'You saved my life,' she said.

'Not necessarily true but the converse definitely is: I would be dead but for you.'

She went to speak but he started in.

'Last night I felt a malaise, which I had never experienced before. Jealousy,' he said. 'There, I have admitted it. I was jealous.'

She was so stunned her thoughts ran aground. 'Of me?'

'Of Benson, because he was with you. Oh dear, this is damnably awkward but I fear another opportunity may never present itself. From the way I feel when you are around me, and worse, when you are not, from the fact that just the faintest whiff of the perfume you wear explodes my being into a million colorful atoms, I deduce I must be in love with you.'

Did he just say ...?

'Is this an experiment, Sherlock? Because if it is, it's not really funny.'

'It is an experiment for me. This is ground upon which I have never trodden but I assure you my sincerity is absolute. Of course, it is probably far too much to hope and definitely too much to expect, a reciprocity.'

She began crying.

'Oh dear, I see I overstepped the mark.'

She could only shake her head. Finally, she managed to find words. 'I feel the same way.' She saw his eyes light up. 'But I've failed you.'

He looked at her with great tenderness. 'You have not failed me, Watson. You have freed me.'

Then he collapsed, pulling her down with him.

'Is there any improvement?'

Simone brought her over a warm tea; perhaps Holmes' finest achievement – he had managed to teach Simone how to dunk a teabag. Georgette looked down at him now, stretched out on the sofa, sleeping.

'No. His concentration is really short and he becomes disoriented quickly. He drifts in and out of the past.'

It was five days since the events of Central Park. Within a minute or two of Holmes collapsing, Simone had arrived, moments ahead of police. They had just enough time to concoct a story. Holmes had been admitted to hospital. Georgette lied that he had fallen from the carriage while trying to rescue her. He had spent one night in hospital, his symptoms mirroring concussion enough for the story to fly. He had regained consciousness in the ambulance and been well enough to discharge himself from hospital after a ten-hour stay but his mental condition had deteriorated steadily and he had not been out of the apartment since.

'They're not going to charge me,' announced Simone as she stroked Holmes' forehead.

'Nor should they,' said Georgette.

To remove Holmes as far as possible from the story, Simone had volunteered to say that she was the one who had shot Burgess with his own weapon that he had dropped when Georgette had tried to free herself.

And so, driven by a desire for revenge, William Burgess had squandered the life of his remaining child.

Simone said, 'Dad interviewed Burgess again. He was the one who drove it, followed you, broke in here, and left the globe. It was Ryan who met up with Rebecca Chaney. His father killed her and then they both removed and stored the body. That's when Ryan wrote on the mantlepiece mirror. Ryan dumped the body and his father called it in. Burgess is still blaming Dad, still thinks it's all his fault his life fell apart.'

From what they could glean from remaining family and friends, Ryan had struggled after the death of his mother and sister and, when his father had descended into alcoholism, Ryan had left the country and drifted aimlessly around Europe. It seemed that the older Burgess had located his son and brought him back home. When Ryan found his father sober, functioning and driven, he had joined his dark enterprise. 'Like a cult,' the police psych had said.

'Is there anything you can try?' asked Simone, giving the recumbent Holmes a kiss on the cheek.

'I'm going to freeze him. I don't see any alternative. I'll keep looking for something that reverses the process.'

'The blood transfusions don't help?'

'They help the physical side of things but not this disorientation.'

'So it's like Alzheimer's?'

'Not exactly. The symptoms are similar but there is no physical scarring in the brain, no lesions. My neurologist friend says it is more like a battery running down; if it could get a recharge, it would be fine.'

But what was going to be the source of that recharge? That was the big problem. Looking at the brains of the hamsters, the neurologist had said they resembled those of people who had spent most of their lives malnourished. The physical weakness Holmes was experiencing was more a question of the brain transmitting to the muscles. The neurologist likened it to the effects of concussion, which Georgette had kind of intuited anyway. It might have suggested a way forwards; however, despite transfusions, massive doses of vitamins and protein supplements, both Amelia and Benji were now also showing signs of disorientation and physical weakness. Of all the hamsters, only Columbus powered on, but then, he was the most recent to be revived, so that was likely why.

Mirabella had called, but Georgette had not returned the call. Benson had also been in touch. Rather than avoid him she told him straight that she just didn't think she could be more than a friend.

'Percy, hey?'

She admitted she had discovered she had strong feelings for him.

'He's a lucky guy,' Benson had said. Looking at Holmes now, he seemed anything but lucky. As for Benson, he had wasted no time calling Simone to line up a date.

'You sure you don't mind?' asked Simone now as she stepped back from Holmes.

'Of course not. I like Benson. And he might be good for you.'

'When are you going to refreeze him?' asked Simone.

'Unless things change, this time tomorrow.'

It was later in the afternoon and she was in the kitchen making some pea and ham soup for Holmes, more as a treat than for any medicinal benefit, when she heard him call out with the kind of vigor of old.

'Watson, I believe I have it.'

It was exciting to hear him so boisterous. Maybe the regime of protein shakes and heavy vitamin dosage was working. He strode into the kitchen and stopped.

'Oh, I am sorry, I thought you were my friend Watson.'

An icepick through the heart might have been easier to deal with. His face showed absolutely no recognition.

'Sherlock Holmes,' he said, bowing from the waist.

'Georgette.'

'Smells very nice, what you are cooking. One of the only meals I can actually make, pea and ham soup or boiled egg.'

'Would you like some?'

'If it is no trouble.'

'No trouble. You can eat and wait for your friend. It is very cold out.'

He stopped then and looked around confused. 'I seem to be disoriented.'

'You may have forgotten. You are in New York.'

He shook his head, disturbed now, taking in the electric lights.

'Perhaps you should lie down?'

He played with the light switch. 'I seem to know how to operate these but have no memory of when I learned it.'

Her heart was breaking. 'I believe Doctor Watson mentioned you had received a heavy blow to the head.'

'He did?'

'Yes. He said it might affect your memory for a time. Perhaps some soup will make you feel better?'

She sat him down at the table and fed him the soup, watched his every mouthful. Before he had finished, he said, 'You must forgive me, Georgette, but I feel immensely tired.'

'Of course. Why don't you rest yourself on the sofa?'

He took himself back into the living room and lay down.

She could wait no longer. She was going to have to return him to the state in which she had found him.

Georgette had checked and rechecked the equipment. Everything was working. Amelia and Benji had already been placed into limbo without any issues but Columbus was still going strong. So far, she had managed to push away thoughts of what she must do after Holmes was in limbo but the charade could not continue. His body would need to be stored somewhere, identification papers would have to be produced. At least Holmes would be spared dealing with his celebrity. After his rest following the most recent lapse, he had awoken fully cognizant, except for having no memory that three hours earlier he had not even recognized her. But he had deduced from her reactions what had occurred.

'I reverted, did I not?'

'Yes.' He had nodded solemnly then and said, 'Then we must not delay. When I go back into that frozen limbo I wish the last thing I see to be your face.'

And now there was no reason to stall. Simone had just arrived. Holmes was sitting quietly in the room where three months ago he had been resurrected.

'It's time,' said Georgette.

Holmes stood. Simone hugged him, started crying.

'Just imagine it's a long movie shoot on the South Pole,' she blubbered.

'I shall.'

'And don't forget me.'

'Highly unlikely, Simone. Thank you for everything.'

Simone discretely moved away and then it was just him, standing in front of her.

'It has been quite an adventure, Watson.'

She knew she was biting her lip, trying to not dissolve into a formless mess.

'I'm going to miss you so much.'

'And I you,' he said, gently brushing the hair back from her forehead but there was no strength in his hand now.

She seized his face and said, 'I will do everything I can to bring you back.'

And she kissed him as hard as she could, until she had no more air in her lungs.

Holmes gently prised their bodies apart. His smile was wan but it was the same droll Holmes.

'I shan't be going anywhere.'

And then he climbed into the capsule which was just like you saw for astronauts on those deep space movies, and he lay down face up.

She leaned over him, trying to memorize every tiny line of his face.

'In all my years before, I never experienced such pleasure as my time with you, Georgette. Thanks to you I was not so much reborn, as born.'

Her tears were falling now, splashing his cheek and through them she could see moisture in his eyes.

'I won't ever leave you,' she said. And then, summoning all her will, she punched the red button that slid the capsule lid closed, the signal for the gases to begin pumping.

She pressed her face close to the perspex.

He smiled up at her. And then the swirling white vapor covered him and the lid began to steam over thicker and thicker until she could just barely see a tiny sparkle of his eye … and then nothing.

She forced the tears to stop and checked the gauges. Everything was working. Simone for once said nothing, letting her have this space as the monitors showed Holmes' brain activity slowing, slowing … one beep … two …

Gone.

After about fifteen minutes of rechecking every hose and seal and gauge, she announced, 'That's it. He's in limbo.'

Simone opened her handbag and pulled out a bottle of tequila. 'You need one of these.'

'No,' said Georgette, grabbing two small beakers. 'I need more than one.'

The alcohol dulled the pain and she could no longer see Holmes' body but she could conjure his voice as if he were next to her. Simone poured them both another drink.

'You and Benson could work,' Georgette said now, thinking about it in a kind of alcohol-riddled way.

'Maybe. I'm used to cops. And he's into speed metal.'

They clinked beakers, sipped.

'Do you think there was any purpose in all this?'

Simone was aware her sister was gesturing loosely with a beaker of tequila.

'Sure. It brought us closer together, it gave Holmes life, and you love. Or maybe the other way around. You love and him life. Although this lab still reeks of ...' by the looks of it she was carefully selecting the right word, '... lab.'

The alcohol worked. They both laughed.

Simone continued. 'It's too clinical and drab and ...' she peered around. 'Where's my plant?'

'Your own fault. You left open the cage. Columbus ate it.'

'I'll get you another. Geraniums, something he won't like.'

Georgette pulled herself up, instantly sober. Columbus ate it.

Columbus ATE it.

Columbus ate the fucking plant!

'Oh my God,' she said dropping the beaker which, being designed not to shatter, merely bounced. She turned back to the capsule, her mind running through options the way a dog who has been cooped up in a car crashes through a field.

'Where did you get that plant? I want every single one of those freakers you can get your hands on.'

NEW YORK 2021

You hit the water from that height, it should be like hitting the ground after leaping from St Paul's, but it must be something to do with the waterfall itself, breaking the surface tension because there is only black, then a few sparks in your head.

And then you remember nothing.

Or maybe you remember nothing anyway and this is just a trick of the brain, an invention as to what happened to you. Or maybe you are dead. Suddenly it feels very, very cold and looking up, you see you are in a heavy, heavy fog.

What am I doing, you think? Am I lying in a canoe or the bottom of a boat looking up at the misty sky? Are these the clouds that surround eternity, the afterlife?

No.

Memories, newer ones, crowd like seagulls, tentatively on a gunwale. A mighty city, the future: New York.

The mist is clearing.

It is not a canoe, is it? It is a capsule. You were dying after being resurrected.

Something is happening above you now, movement.

Life.

The mist is retreating rapidly, your lungs filling with air. A face slowly materializes.

Her face.

She is looking down upon you, smiling, and there has never been a more wondrous sight than this, than you ...

My dear Watson.

AUTHOR NOTE

On my twelfth birthday I was given a collection of Sherlock Holmes stories. While I was very grateful – I was an avid reader of Biggles and other books at the time – I did not realize how profound an influence on me this book would have. No doubt the new six-stitcher I also got, or the cricket pads or Bobby Charlton Casdon Football game (which I still own) seemed just a fraction more exciting. Yet here I am, more than half-a-century on, and Holmes and Watson are still dogging me through my subconscious.

In 2003, while my brain was burning through ideas for film and TV series, I had an inspiration that electrified me. What if Sherlock Holmes and Watson came back and Watson was a woman? This may have well come from me thinking about my own three-book crime series of the time where I had rock-and-roll detective Andrew 'The Lizard' Zirk in the Holmes role and his no-nonsense driver, Fleur, in the Watson role. I was excited by the possibilities of the restrained romance between them, and also of seeing Holmes in a contemporary setting. Whatever the exact stimulus, I immediately began developing the idea. At the time Conan Doyle's works were still in copyright and there was very little in the way of Holmes' material about.

My first version was a feature script titled *My Dear Watson*. Set in the present, female scientist Georgette Watson leads an expedition and finds the frozen body of her long-lost relative who has been buried by an avalanche on the North Pole. Remarkably it thaws out and voila, the 'body' is alive. It turns out it is Holmes not Watson, who turned back early on their voyage after a bout of sea-sickness. Holmes accompanies

Georgette to New York where she lives, and they investigate the death of one of her close friends.

Trying to get a high-concept idea like this off the ground in Australia is impossible, so I took it to Los Angeles on a trip in 2005 and tried to pitch it with some other film ideas of mine. When I heard nothing, I switched to a TV series idea and was making good progress when the Conan Doyle copyright cleared and the plethora of Sherlock Holmes movies started. I had reworked the concept to give Georgette Watson a connection to the NYPD. After getting caught up with other projects I finally decided to go all out with the TV series and had just got it ready to send out when a new TV series appeared out of the US featuring a female Watson. I have to say I was shattered. For seven years I had nursed this big new idea and now somebody else had done it – not only with a female Watson but based in New York!

I plunged into Holmesian melancholy for years off the back of this. Unfortunately, it is a fact of life for Australian writers that even if we come up with an idea a decade before the US, it will inevitably be ignored by local broadcasters and producers until the US has caught up. I am not the first Aussie writer to be gazumped after coming up with a hot original idea.

After I had finished my most recent novel, *River of Salt*, I thought, stuff it, my concept is still original because it features not simply a contemporary Holmes but the Victorian-era one in the present day. This time I decided I would not waste time trying to get it made as a screenplay but write it as a novel, which gives it the breadth to be more than just a crime story. It allows it to be a story of dislocation, of a man wondering where his place in the world is in 2020 – and that is not a question just for a 166 year old Holmes. It also opens up the possibility of exploring Watson more fully and looking at the relationship in a very different way. If you've made it to this part of the book, you likely enjoyed it but I thank you anyway for joining me on my adventure.

ACKNOWLEDGEMENTS

I am so very fortunate to have Georgia Richter as my editor and I thank her for always making the manuscript better. She needed to be something of a Sherlock Holmes herself to solve the riddle of this manuscript. Because I was dealing with a relatively unfamiliar setting in New York, I have called on a number of New Yorkers past and present, to scan the manuscript for dumb mistakes, so I thank them for their time and efforts: Jack Feldstein, Christie Moore, Christopher Adamchek, Ro Hume and Rachel Skinner-O'Neill. Rachel was my agent way back when I first began working on the movie script that became the novel. Thanks too to Manju Hallisey in Virginia for her careful eye. Thanks also to my current agent Wanda Bergin and to Jane Fraser at Fremantle Press and all those on the Fremantle team including Claire Miller and Jen Bowden. None of this would be possible without my wonderful wife Nicole. And thanks to my late grandmother, Maude, for giving me that first Sherlock Holmes book all those years ago and introducing me to the genius of Conan Doyle and those masterful characters he created.

ALSO BY DAVE WARNER

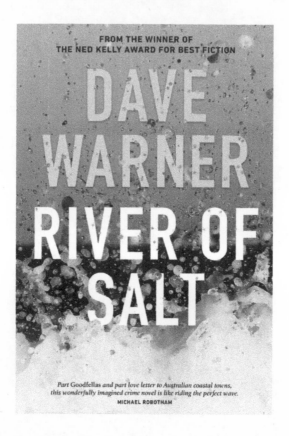

1961, Philadelphia. After having to give up his brother to save his own life, hitman Blake Saunders flees the Mob and seeks refuge on the other side of the world. Two years later he has been reborn in a tiny coastal Australian town. The ghosts of the past still haunt him, but otherwise Coral Shoals is paradise. Blake surfs, and plays guitar in his own bar, the Surf Shack. But then the body of a young woman is found at a local motel, and evidence links her to the Surf Shack. When Blake's friend is arrested, and the local sergeant doesn't want to know, it becomes clear to Blake – who knows a thing or two about murder – that the only way to protect his paradise is to find the killer.

"Australian crime writing at its apex." *Australian Book Review*

FROM FREMANTLEPRESS.COM.AU

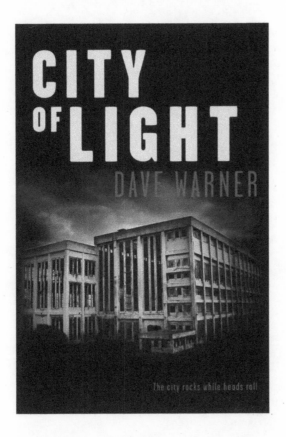
'Jesus Christ. I found one.' These words are blurted over the phone to Constable Snowy Lane, who is preoccupied with no more than a ham sandwich and getting a game with the East Fremantle league side on Saturday. They signal the beginning of a series of events that are to shake Perth to its foundations. It is 1979, and Perth is jumping with pub bands and overnight millionaires. 'Mr Gruesome' has just taken another victim. Snowy's life and career are to be forever changed by the grim deeds of a serial killer, and the dark bloom spreading across the City of Light.

'Lively, funny, with enough plot for three novels.' *Sun-Herald.*

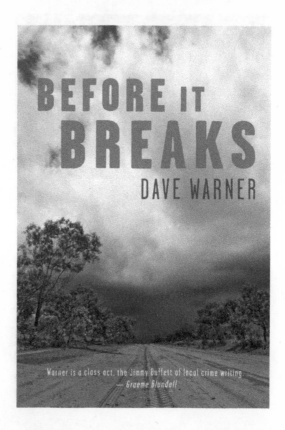

Detective Daniel Clement is back in Broome, licking his wounds from a busted marriage and struggling to be impressed by his new team of small-town cops. Here, in the oasis on the edge of the desert, life is as stagnant as Clement's latest career move. But when a body is discovered at a local fishing spot, it is clearly not the result of a crocodile attack. Somewhere in Broome is a hunter of a different kind. As more bodies are found, Clement races to solve a decades-old mystery before a monster cyclone hits.

'Laid-back and laconic, with sentences as snappy as a nutcracker.'
Books+Publishing

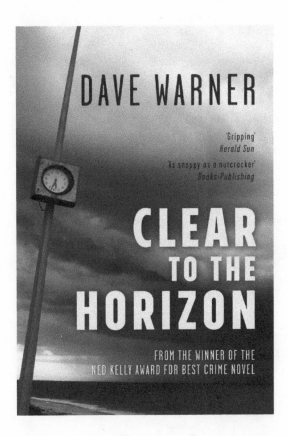

First published 2020 by
FREMANTLE PRESS

Fremantle Press Inc. trading as Fremantle Press
25 Quarry Street, Fremantle WA 6160
(PO Box 158, North Fremantle WA 6159)
www.fremantlepress.com.au

Cover photograph by istock; Arcangel, AA1903998
Cover design: Nada Backovic, www.nadabackovic.com
Printed by McPherson's Printing Group, Victoria, Australia

 A catalogue record for this
book is available from the
NATIONAL LIBRARY National Library of Australia
OF AUSTRALIA

ISBN 9781925816860 (paperback)
ISBN 9781925816877 (ebook)

 Department of
Local Government, Sport
and Cultural Industries
GOVERNMENT OF
WESTERN AUSTRALIA

Fremantle Press is supported by the State Government through the
Department of Local Government, Sport and Cultural Industries.

 **Australia
Council
for the Arts**
Australian Government

Publication of this title was assisted by the Commonwealth Government
through the Australia Council, its arts funding and advisory body.

 **MIX**
Paper from
responsible sources
FSC FSC® C001695
www.fsc.org